THE WOULD-BE WIFE

Lynn grew up as the daughter of a fisherman but longs to be free from the hardship and worry of life by the docks. When the handsome and ambitious Graham asks her to marry him, she ignores the warnings of family and friends and accepts. At first, life in Hull in the sixties is one long party, but soon the gloss begins to fade.

Four years later, with a young son to look after, she is trapped. She has no money of her own and has given up her job as a nurse. Lynn must fight to regain her independence – but will Graham let her walk away so easily?

THE WOULD-BE WIFE

THE WOULD-BE WIFE

by

Annie Wilkinson

Magna Large Print Books
Long Preston, North Yorkshire,
BD23 4ND, England.

British Library Cataloguing in Publication Data.

A catalogue record of this book is
available from the British Library

ISBN   978-0-7505-4610-2

First published in Great Britain by Simon & Schuster UK Ltd., 2017

Cover illustration © Roux Hamilton/Arcangel by arrangement with
Arcangel Images Ltd.

Published in Large Print 2018 by arrangement with
Simon & Schuster UK Ltd.

Magna Large Print is an imprint of Library Magna Books Ltd.

Printed and bound in Great Britain by
T.J. (International) Ltd., Cornwall, PL28 8RW

To The Fishermen's Wives

Chapter 1

Hull, 1967

At six o'clock on a May Saturday afternoon, twenty-five-year-old Lynn Bradbury was in the middle of setting the table when the dinky little white telephone her husband Graham had just had installed started ringing again.

Lynn answered it. 'Hello? Hello?'

All she heard was a click as the receiver went down at the other end.

Graham poked his head round the door. 'Who is it?'

'Nobody. They never spoke.'

'Probably a wrong number.'

'A lot of people seem to be getting the wrong number, then. That's the third time it's happened today.'

'Probably somebody wanting the people who lived here before us,' Graham said. 'Where's Simon?'

'I thought he was with you!' Lynn glanced swiftly round a dining room littered with toys, then hurried to the kitchen, where she found their four-year-old trying to measure flour into a mixing bowl, and succeeding in getting most of it on the tiled floor.

'I want to bake,' he said. 'I want to make gingerbread mans.'

11

'It's too late to make gingerbread mans. It's tea-time. What a mess you've made, Simon!'

He turned a pair of mischievous blue eyes on her and gave her a cheeky grin she couldn't help returning. The flour was soon swept up and he played with his toys while Lynn made her best efforts with the cooking. Since she'd started working in ante-natal out-patients and had the luxury of regular hours the evening meal was her favourite time of day, when they could all eat together and enjoy a chat before Simon went to bed.

The phone rang again later on, while she was lifting Simon out of the bath. 'Who is it?' she called downstairs.

'It's Kev. I borrowed his socket set. I'll nip round to their place a bit later on and take it back.'

'Go and have a pint, if you like. I don't mind, as long as you're not too late.'

She heard Graham's tread on the stair, and a second later he poked his head round the bathroom door. 'All right, I might, but if I'm going out I'll have to have a wash and a shave.'

'We'll be out of the bathroom in a minute,' Lynn said, busily drying Simon and dressing him in newly ironed pyjamas. He looked irresistible. She took hold of him and gave him a hug then carried him off to bed and sat reading him his bedtime story, with noises from Graham, splashing about in the bath and croaking the lyrics of some corny love-song. He was nothing of a singer, Lynn thought with an indulgent smile. Lucky he only ever tried it in the bathroom.

'Another story,' Simon demanded. While reading it she heard Graham run downstairs and out of the front door. He was gone without a word.

She closed the book and turned to Simon. 'Night night. Time all little boys were in the land of nod.'

He gave her a sleepy smile and threw a pair of chubby arms round her neck. 'A kiss and a cuddle,' he demanded.

He smelled divine and Lynn felt such a surge of love for him she could have kissed him to death. She was glad he would be brought up in a better area than the Hessle Road of her own childhood, with its skyline of ships' masts and smoke-oven chimneys where families lived on top of each other in warrens of tiny, close-packed terraced houses, the smallest and poorest with their front doors opening directly onto the street and their back doors opening onto a shared yard. The place was like an ant colony, always busy, never still, with ships constantly coming and going, and men landing or sailing. She had spent most of her childhood there, right in the hub of Hull's fishing industry, and although she had always been happy, she wanted something better for Simon than Hessle Road and the aroma of the smoke houses on fair days, and the stench from the fish-meal plant on wet ones, and sleep disturbed by the din of steel-studded clogs on cobbles in the middle of the night, as the bobbers poured down Subway Street and onto the docks to unload the fish for market.

No, there would be none of that for Simon, except maybe the scent of fish on rainy days. You couldn't avoid that, even on Marlborough

13

Avenue. But Simon would have a garden to play in, and room to breathe. There was a swing that would see plenty of action this summer and an old apple tree he could climb. Lynn could still hardly believe she was living in such a house, a home beyond her wildest dreams. Her father jokingly called it the family mansion – and it was in a perfect situation, with her best friend Janet living just round the corner in Richmond Avenue.

Her marriage to Graham hadn't turned out too badly, she thought, in spite of its impoverished start. She'd passed her nursing finals after Simon was born, while they were living in a cramped flat, and in just a few months she would be sitting her midwifery exams. Graham was doing well at the pharmaceutical company he was working for. Things were starting to look up, and with a mortgage and the help of a deposit from Lynn's father they'd moved into this wonderful house.

'Dead money, paying rent – besides, you get tax relief on a mortgage. You're never going to get tax relief on your rent, are you?' Graham had boasted to his old school friend Kev, who still happened to be renting.

Yes, she'd definitely picked a winner with Graham, and now he'd had a promotion it would be plain sailing. No more worries about money, and next weekend would be the first bank holiday she'd had off in years, thanks to her three months' placement in ante-natal outpatients. They could do something as a family on one of the days, and spend the rest of the time working on the house and garden.

The whiff of expensive aftershave that met her

on the landing smelled pleasantly masculine, but she soon found that Graham had left his less pleasant odours in the bathroom. The floor was strewn with his dirty underwear and a pair of disgustingly cheesy socks, lying like two skunks amid a liberal sprinkling of talcum powder. With a little snort of annoyance she picked them up and holding them at arm's length dropped them in the laundry basket, then tidied the shelf littered with his shaving tackle. He'd put himself to a hell of a lot of trouble just to go out for a pint with Kev, and when Lynn turned the tap on to clear the basin of his shavings she discovered he'd run all the hot water off as well. She flicked the immersion heater on, and while the water heated again she went downstairs to tidy up and lay the breakfast table for morning, cursing Graham's mother for bringing him up to be such an inconsiderate slob. There would be none of this when Simon got married. She'd make sure her son was properly house-trained.

Half an hour later she stripped, looking critically at herself in the long bathroom mirror while waiting for the bath to fill. A short crop of glossy dark hair, dark eyes and eyebrows, rosy cheeks and red lips, she looked a picture of rude health, altogether Graham's ideal of womanhood, he often told her – pallid, insipid blondes left him cold. But she was becoming too much a picture of health, she thought, grimacing at the sight of a belly that had a bit too much of the pot about it. That was the result of contentment – she'd look like a little Buddha if she wasn't careful, and over-weight women held no attraction for Graham.

15

Resolving to go on a diet, Lynn climbed into the deep, Victorian cast-iron bath and soaked for an hour, topping up the hot water a few times before getting out, tired and relaxed and with all her irritation soothed away. She would have a cup of cocoa and flick through a magazine for half an hour and then go to bed. Hard luck for Graham if she was asleep before he got in – he'd have to manage without getting his leg over, for once. It had been a long day, and she was too tired to wait up for him.

Chapter 2

'You knew what he was before you married him,' Lynn's mother insisted, the following Friday afternoon. 'Janet told you he had a reputation. "Be careful," she said – "he's had more girlfriends than most blokes have had hot dinners." I remember you telling me. He was noted for it. I tried to warn you then.'

That was Nina Carr's usual line, Lynn thought. *She'd always known; she could have told you* – except that it was hardly ever true. She looked at her mother through puffy, bloodshot eyes, taking in the new way she'd made up her face with blue eye shadow and black eyeliner flicked up at the eye-corners, just like Lynn applied hers, except her mother had used far too much mascara and the black didn't really suit her. With her blue eyes and blonde hair a paler shade would have looked better. And that new mini skirt! A mini skirt – at her age, pushing fifty! How some middle-aged women try to ape the young ones, she thought – and it never works. Desperately hanging on to youth, when they'd be better dressing their age and acting with a bit of decorum – acting like middle-aged *mothers,* in fact. She might have dropped a hint to save her mother the embarrassment of making herself look ridiculous, but now was not the time.

'I thought he'd changed,' she wailed, sounding pathetic even to herself. Pathetic and *stupid.* But Graham had given her good reason to think he'd changed. He'd sworn that she was the love of his life. She was the most beautiful girl he'd ever laid eyes on. It had been love at first sight. She was the one he'd been looking for all his life. None of his other girlfriends could hold a candle to her. He'd sown all his wild oats, he said. He was ready to settle down and she was The One, the one he'd chosen to be the mother of his children. The sweet nothings had been poured into her ear in an endless stream, and Graham had finally proved his good faith by getting her in the family way and then marrying her – much against his mother's wishes. Against her mother's wishes come to that, as Nina had made plain when Lynn had told her they were getting married.

'I'm not ready to let go of the last chick in my nest just yet!' she had said, and meant it.

'You've still got our Anthony,' Lynn had consoled her.

'I haven't. Our Anthony flew the nest when he went to sea. He's hardly ever here, and when he's

17

supposed to be at home he spends more time with his mates than he does with me. When you've gone, I'll be sitting in on my own all the time, except for a couple of days every three weeks, when your dad's ashore,' her mother had protested. 'What sort of a life is that?'

How times change! These days Nina Carr seemed to have washed her hands of motherhood altogether and was busy making a stab at being a teenager again. Lynn lit another cigarette, and inhaled deeply.

Nina shook her head. 'He picks his time, don't he? The week before Whit – the first bank holiday you've had off work since you started midwifery training. You should be going off somewhere, enjoying yourselves as a family, but he's buggered that up, hasn't he? And you want to stop smoking so much, it's bad for you.'

'You smoke.'

'Not as much as you. You've no sooner put one out than you're lighting another one up. Anybody'd think you were trying to kill yourself with cancer. And you've eaten nothing all week.'

Lynn had only just dried her eyes, but fresh tears swam up at the vision her mother's words conjured, of herself with cancer, wasting away on her deathbed, saying her final farewell to poor little Simon and leaving him an orphan with his mother dead and father absconded with some floozie he'd met on a course. The scene was so heart-rending she sucked frantically on her cigarette, desperately drawing nicotine and tar-filled smoke past that awful lump in her throat and deep into her lungs.

Nina softened her approach. 'Well, he's had a week of having to get his own meals, he should be ready to listen to reason by this time. Anyway, it might not be as bad as you think. You might be jumping to conclusions.'

'What?' Lynn choked. 'I pick the phone up, and as soon as I speak it goes down at the other end – not once but half a dozen times. And then he answers it, and an hour later he's off out – with his socks and underpants full of talcum powder and his face stinking of aftershave – and then he stops out all night? And then on Sunday I pick it up again, and *she's* got the brass neck to ask to speak to him? *My* husband! How much jumping did I have to do? Conclusions were smacking me in the face – apart from the fact that he more or less admitted it. He could hardly deny it when she's chased him all the way from Leeds and booked herself into the Royal Hotel just to be available to him. The *Royal!*'

Lynne's mother thoughtfully smoothed down her mini skirt, as if trying to cover a little more of the long expanse of thigh she was not yet used to revealing. 'Well,' she said, slowly, '*she's* chased *him* and she's in a hotel – but it doesn't mean she's caught him. He probably stopped at Kev's for the night. Anyway, it's too late for you to bale out now – you've got our Simon to think about. And Graham belongs to *you* – you've got the marriage lines to prove it. He's yours. You're not going to let her waltz off with your property, just like that, are you? Get round to that hotel and send her packing, if she's not already gone.'

Lynn had imagined she'd be welcomed with

19

open arms at home, but without coming straight out with it, her mother was making it clear that she'd rather not have her life littered up twenty-four hours a day with her daughter and grandchild. Lynn dabbed her eyes again. She managed to restrain her crying at work, because at work she had plenty to distract her – but at home, Graham's treachery was all she could think about. Five solid nights of gushing tears ought to have rusted up the waterworks, but they were flowing as well as ever.

'And you've just got your house; you've hardly been in it a month – and that lovely kitchen the last lot had put in. And that built-in double oven! You're not going to let her take all that off you, are you?' Nina demanded, blue eyes flashing as she worked herself up into a frenzy. 'I'd rip her bloody head off and shove it up her arse before I'd let her get away with that.'

Lynn laughed through her tears. 'You talk ridiculous, Mother.'

'What's ridiculous is sitting around here when you ought to be at home, fighting your corner. Get back there before it goes any further, and make him see where his duty lies. He's got a family to consider now. I'll come with you.'

After nearly a week with her mother, Lynn was beginning to think that returning to her adulterous husband might be the better option. He had tried to stop her leaving, but Lynn had refused to listen to his pleas and his excuses and had stormed off with Simon in too much of a hurry to pack enough clothes.

'Where is Simon?' Lynn started. 'He's gone

20

quiet, all of a sudden.'

'He's up to something.'

The two women looked at each other, then raced upstairs to find him playing with the stuff on Nanna's dressing table. He backed away from them with his face plastered with her new lipstick and reeking of Chanel No 5, trying to hide the new cut-glass perfume spray he'd pulled apart behind his back.

Nina was not amused. A glance at her mother's face, and Lynn's heart sank at the thought of living there permanently with a four-year-old who couldn't keep his fingers out of anything.

'All right,' she said, snatching the perfume bottle and pushing the rubber pipe back onto the gilded metal tube. 'I'll go round and see him, this minute. You're not coming, though. You'll have to keep Simon here. I don't want him upsetting, if there's a row.'

Chapter 3

There was a nip in the air when Lynn started the long walk from Boulevard, passing gardens bursting with May flowers unheeded, wrapped in a grey world of her own. On Marlborough Avenue her own front garden was overflowing with beautiful perennials planted by the green-fingered former occupants, but they made no impression on Lynn. She had her key ready in case Graham was out at his mother's or Kev's, or with the voice on the phone. The cast-iron gate gave its usual warning creak as she opened it and went in, and half a dozen steps took her across the small front garden to the heavy, green-painted front door. It was locked, just as she'd thought, so she let herself in – and almost jumped out of her skin when Kevin Walsh came bounding out of the sitting room with mouth open and eyes popping, falling over himself to get to her.

'What are you doing here, Lynn?' he almost shouted.

She stared at him in astonishment. 'I live here, Kev. Have you forgotten? Where's Graham?'

'Out,' Kev said, even louder than before.

Lynn walked towards the stairs, but Kev got there before her and blocked her way. In the same bellowing voice he said: 'I wouldn't go up there if I were you.'

Lynn heard a scuffling sound upstairs and glanced upwards, too late to see anything. She looked intently into Kev's eyes for a moment. 'Get out of my way, Kev.'

Kev didn't move, so Lynn pushed him aside and ran up the grand staircase with its lovely wooden spindles and mahogany banister rail, and into the bedroom she shared with Graham. There was neither sight nor sound of him. What there *was* was another woman's make-up and jewellery laid out on her dressing table, another woman's night-dress on the bed, and a suitcase full of another woman's clothes on the stool under the sash window. Lynn stood still for a moment, hardly able to believe her eyes, then quicker than thought she strode across the room and threw up the sash.

Out they all went, one after the other. First the contents of the suitcase then the nightdress, and then everything on the dressing table was swept off to go flying after the rest until garden, hedge and street beyond were festooned with items of seduction – skimpy knickers, sheer tights, lacy bras, mini skirts and low-cut tops, make-up, perfume and jewellery. That done, Lynn slammed the sash down and went back onto the landing. Kevin Walsh was still at the bottom of the stairs, still looking upwards with his sweaty hand still on the polished newel post.

'Where is he, then?' Lynn demanded.

'Out. He's gone out.'

'Huh!' Lynn checked Simon's bedroom and the spare room, and then tried the bathroom. It was locked. She hammered on the door and got no response.

'Open the door. I know you're in there!'

Still no response. She gave it a hefty kick, and after another couple of minutes of futile hammering and kicking she ran downstairs breathing fire, and left the house without another word.

Some school kids had left off playing and stared when she emerged. A couple of passers-by walking their dogs stopped to get an eyeful. Lynn barely saw them as she stormed out of the garden and pulled the creaking gate shut before marching past the underwear-bedecked hedge and over the littered pavement. She stopped suddenly, and walked back to something she'd seen lying amid various other items – a little gold watch with a pretty gold bracelet – the sort of thing a girl might be given for her twenty-first birthday. With narrowed eyes and a vindictive little smile Lynn carefully placed her boot-heel on the watch's dainty face and pressing on it with all her might she ground it slowly and deliberately into the pavement.

Chapter 4

In the short passage between Janet's front door and her dining room, Lynn spilled it all out. Janet listened without comment then went to the dark oak Welsh dresser that she and Dave hadn't quite finished paying for and extracted a bottle of brandy and a glass.

'You're in shock,' she said, pouring out a generous dose. 'Here, sit down and drink this.'

Sinking down onto one of the dark oak Windsor dining chairs Lynn took the glass and gulped, choking a little at the fiery feeling of brandy coursing down her throat. She had never liked the stuff, but drinking it made her feel a bit calmer. Janet replaced the bottle.

Good old Janet, the sort of rock-solid, two-feet-on-the-ground pal who never lets you down, Lynn thought. They'd been friends ever since the start of their nursing days. Janet was a bit taller than the average, with long light-brown hair that she wore taken up, the kind of girl you'd pass over in a crowd and only realise her sterling qualities when you really got to know her. All the girls in their set had been around the same age, but Janet

24

had always seemed older, more reliable, more capable and less excitable than the rest of them. Janet had soon become the leader of the pack, the one they all took their cue from – and Janet had been the first of them to be married.

Lynn recovered her breath and looked into her friend's calm hazel eyes. 'I'm shocked, but I'm not *in* shock,' she said. 'I'm hopping mad. I'm so furious I don't know where to put myself. I'd have liked to drag her out of that bathroom by her hair and chuck *her* out of the window, after all her bloody tarty clothes.'

Janet's face was expressionless. 'What about him?'

Lynn took another gulp of brandy and closed her eyes. 'I would never have believed it. I'd never have believed he'd do a thing like that. In our house. In our bed! Her nightie, next to his pyjamas – I'd never have believed him capable of it.' She opened her eyes and looked at Janet's face, so inscrutable it was obvious something was hidden behind the mask.

'What?' Lynn demanded

Janet's eyebrows twitched upwards for a second. 'Nothing. Just that something about leopards and their spots springs to mind.'

'Not you as well. You sound like my mother. I knew what Graham was before I married him, according to her. Well, I admit I knew he'd had a few women before I married him, but I didn't expect him to be having any after! I thought he'd changed. When he stood up in church and promised to forsake all others and keep only unto me, I actually believed him.' Lynn put her drink

25

down on the polished oak dining table and delved into her bag to find a pack of Embassy. 'God, I need a cigarette. Have you got a light?'

'Matches in the kitchen,' Janet said, discreetly sliding a coaster under the glass before going to fetch them. Lynn followed her.

Janet picked up a large box of cook's matches and struck one, holding it to Lynn's cigarette. 'What are you going to do?'

Lynn inhaled. 'My mother thinks I'm going back to him.'

'And what do you think?'

'I'm ringing the police! I'm getting that slut thrown out of my house.'

'There's the telephone. The number of the station will be in the book.'

Lynn rang and spoke to the desk sergeant, her eyes widening and eyebrows rising to meet her hairline as she listened to his answer.

'What did he say?' Janet asked, when she replaced the receiver.

'He said if she's there as my husband's guest there's nothing they can do about it!'

'His *guest*,' Janet repeated with a grimace. 'So that's what you call them these days. Guests.' She thought for a moment, and then gave a mirthless chuckle.

Lynn's face twisted into a wry smile. 'It takes the biscuit, don't it?'

'Not half. Most folk would have a different name for somebody like that. Well, what are you going to do?'

Lynn took another drag on her cigarette. 'Get a divorce,' she said, on the out-breath. 'What choice have I got, if he can move another woman into my bed after five days? He doesn't even care enough to try and hide it! There's no point going on with it, is there?'

'Don't seem like it,' Janet said. 'It'll mean going back to your mother's though, and it don't sound like she really wants you there.'

'Hard luck for her, then. I'm never going back to that house, once I've got all my stuff. And I'm never sleeping in that bed again, either.'

After a long pause, Janet volunteered: 'Brian Farley's good, of Farley and Brown. My cousin had him when she got her divorce.'

'I'd have liked his mother and father to have seen it – what I saw,' Lynn said, cheeks flushing and eyes darting fire. 'I'd like to fill them in on their Graham's antics. It's about time they saw their wonder boy in his true colours. It's about time they knew what a little shit he really is.' She took another gulp of brandy.

'They probably already know,' Janet said. 'Dave'll be home soon. He can drop you off at their place in the van if you like, and you can get Gordon to run you back home; let him get an eyeful. But she'll probably have scarpered by then.'

Lynn decided to take a chance on that. Dave drove her to Graham's parents, who kept a tiny fruit shop on Bricknall Avenue and thought themselves several cuts above the fisher-folk of Hessle Road. But now Lynn had something to show them that might just bring them down to earth.

'What are you doing here?' Graham greeted his parents, when Lynn led them into the living room.

His mother gave him an injured look. 'We've come to see you, Graham.'

'They've come to see what you're up to, is more like it, Graham,' Lynn said.

On the settee sat a girl in a yellow crocheted micro-mini and knee-high white boots, with her dark hair bobbed Mary Quant style. What struck Lynn most about her was the brilliant green eye-shadow covering her eyelids – not so much shadow, she thought, as traffic lights set to 'go'.

'Aren't you going to introduce us, Graham?' she demanded.

'This is Mandy,' Graham said.

Graham's mother gave Mandy a dubious smile. His father assumed a disapproving expression and gave her a brief nod.

'Hello, Mandy. I'm Lynn, Graham's lawful wedded wife. This is his mother, Connie, and his dad, Gordon. This is Mandy,' Lynn repeated, turning to Graham's mother. 'Mandy's living in my house, now, Connie. I'm out, with Simon, and she's in. She's sleeping in my bed, with my husband, and seeing she's still here, I reckon all her trollopy stuff is back on my dressing-table, as well.'

Graham faced her with a stunning composure. 'This has got nothing to do with them; I don't know why you brought them,' he said, and turning to his father added: 'You'd better go.'

'They're not going. They've every right to be here,' she said.

'They're going. None of this is anything to do with them.'

'It is something to do with us, Graham. We've

got a grandchild here,' Connie protested, her clear green eyes fixed on her son.

'They've every right to be here. My name's on that mortgage agreement as well as yours, and they're my guests, so they're staying,' Lynn insisted.

'No, you haven't got a grandchild here,' Graham answered his mother. 'Lynn took him to her mother's when she left me.'

'Left you!'

'Left you?'

Both Gordon and Connie turned to stare at Lynn.

'Last Sunday,' Lynn said, 'six days ago, when I found out about the green-eyed yellow idol there. I came back today like the dutiful wife I am, but he'd already moved her in. Quick work, that, wasn't it?'

The pink-lipsticked mouth below the brilliant green eye-lids opened. 'You broke my watch!' it accused.

'Well then, take it back to whoever gave it to you,' said Lynn. 'Explain how it came to get broken and tell them you want a new one. I'm sure they'll be happy to replace it, under the circumstances.'

'Her mum and dad gave her that!' Graham exclaimed.

'Hard luck for them, then. If they'd brought her up with better principles it'd still be in one piece.'

'You broke it, and you'll have to pay for it,' Graham insisted.

Lynn gaped at him, so taken aback it took her a moment to gather her wits. 'No, Graham, *I* won't have to pay for it,' she said at last. 'You're my husband, so you're responsible for my debts – by law. So *you* pay for it if you want to, and I'll be presenting you with a few bills of my own before very much longer. Put that in your pipe and smoke it. I'm going upstairs to get some of my things now, and then I'll be off.'

She took a last look around the living room, and felt a stab of anguish to see that not only had all Simon's toys been cleared out of sight, but his toy box was gone as well. There was not a single thing of his left in the room, nor, when she checked, was there anything of his in the dining room or the kitchen. Every trace of him had been removed. He might never have existed for all there was of him downstairs, or upstairs either – except for his bedroom. Everything belonging to him had been thrown in there, and the door firmly closed. In the master bedroom Mandy's suitcase stood open as before on the chair under the window, with all her things back in it, but none as yet arrayed on the dressing table.

As if in a trance, Lynn packed clothes for herself and Simon and went downstairs. The door to the living room was closed, and the company inside were talking to each other in murmurs inaudible to her. Feeling like an actress in some Brian Rix farce she left, without pausing to say goodbye.

She knew there was severe pain in the offing, like the time she'd had a wisdom tooth pulled with the dentist's knee almost on her chest as he dripped sweat onto her and nearly broke her jaw with his heaving and wrenching and twisting. The local anaesthetic had numbed her face and had given her a long respite before the agony started. Then it had arrived, with such excruciating intensity that painkillers had hardly touched it and she'd had to take two days off work. The heartache she had coming was going to be just as bad as that, and it would go on for longer. But for now, a total and merciful numbness engulfed the whole of her.

Dave was waiting in the van when she got out. He wound the window down.

'Made it up, have you?' he asked.

'No, and never likely to.'

'Hop in. I'll run you back to your mother's, if you like,' he said.

She got in the van, grateful for the kindness. He slipped into first gear and pulled away from the kerb. They travelled in silence until he said: 'There's something in the glove compartment might take your mind off your troubles.'

She opened the glove compartment, and pulled out a couple of girlie magazines.

'Not likely,' she said, putting them back. 'They're not really my cup of tea.'

'Oh well, never mind, eh? Still, there's no reason for a good-looking lass like you to go short, is there? So if you're ever feeling the pinch, just give me a ring. Ring me at work, and I'll pick you up, take you for a run to somewhere nice and quiet. Five one eight four three ... and I'll be with you in a jiffy.'

'Thanks a lot, Dave,' Lynn said, loading her voice and expression with such withering sarcasm he'd have had to be blind, deaf, and a moron to miss it. But she suspected he had.

31

Chapter 5

After an almost sleepless night, Lynn was up before the cold grey dawn, and leaving Simon and her mother in bed she went down to St Andrew's Dock. The scent of the Humber and the fish, the raucous crying of the white-winged seagulls as they skimmed over the waves and wheeled round the ships to perch on the rails and rigging, and the sight of the trawlers unloading or waiting to unload were all comforting reminders of a happy childhood. She'd hardly ever set foot on the dock after marrying Graham, but nothing had changed. There was the same constant movement in the same twenty acres of water space, the same shuttle service of twenty or thirty ships a day, in and out of the dock on every tide. The fishermen were still catching the fish, the bobbers unloading it, and arranging it in aluminium kits of ten stone, ready for sale. The quayside was swarming with men – fishermen, bobbers, barrow-boys, buyers and sellers, constantly jostling to and fro in a mile of covered market. The air was full of their cries and shouts and the rattle of boots on the cobbles. Set foot on St Andrew's Dock, and you were in a different world, she thought. When she'd married Graham and moved out of the area this world had ceased to exist for her, and she'd half imagined that it had ceased to exist at all. She was almost surprised to see it all still here, still going on as it

32

had in those far-off days when she used to stand at the lock pits and wait to be lifted onto her dad's ship as it eased through.

With cries of 'Cod! Cod!' 'Haddock!' 'Plaice!' a gang of bobbers was at work winching the last of the *Arctic Fox's* catch up in baskets from the hold and swinging them on ropes to the men waiting on the quayside – called 'bobbers', Lynn had been told, because they often had to 'bob' out of the way as baskets laden with roughly ten stone of fish came hurtling towards them. The bobbers tipped the fish into the kits and swung the empty baskets back on their ropes as if working to a rhythm, never missing a beat.

Lynn's father was walking towards her dressed in clean shore clothes after a good hot shower and change from greasy boiler suit and boots. Medium height, medium weight, good humoured and easygoing, he was the rock she had always been able to depend on.

'Well, this makes a change. It's not often anybody comes to meet me these days. I'd have thought you'd still be tucked up in bed with that husband of yours.' He gave her a quizzical smile and dropped his black oilskin sea bag to give her a bear hug. 'Did you miss your old dad that much then?'

She felt a pang of guilt at that, and for the first time she noticed the sprinkling of white hairs among the brown, and the lines around dark eyes that were as warm as ever. She took his arm and squeezed it.

''Course I missed you. I always did, didn't I? Did you have a good trip?'

'We caught plenty of fish, but I won't say we had a good trip until I know what the market's like.'

'Have you seen our Anthony?'

'He was in before us. Probably home by now.'

The kits containing the fish from the *Arctic Fox* and all the other trawlers would soon stretch for nearly a mile along the quayside, each labelled with the owner's name, ready for sale. The prices always started higher than anybody wanted to pay and gradually came down, Dutch auction style. Lynn and her father stopped for a while to watch.

'A hundred shillings,' the auctioneer cried, 'ninety-nine shillings, ninety-eight shillings, ninety...'

The buyers crowded round, watching him like hawks, torn between getting the fish at the lowest possible price and the risk of hanging on too long and losing the lot to a competitor.

'At!' someone shouted – the word that sealed the bargain.

Buyers and auctioneer raced on to the next lot without pausing for breath, while the buyer's labels were dropped into kits that were soon on the barrows, with the boys racing them away over the cobbles to the nearby fish processing plant, to be washed, filleted, trimmed, iced and boxed, and sent off on the lorries.

Her father smiled. 'Aye, it looks as if we've had a good trip,' he said. In reality it made little difference to him – as Chief Engineer he earned a good salary – but he was due a small share of the poundage – the profits of the trip. After the auc-

34

tion the salesmen would tot up the totals, and when the skipper arrived in the office at ten o'clock for his interview with the owners they would have the value of the trip, and the share of skipper and crew would have been calculated on it.

'I hope our Anthony's done as well,' Lynn said. Anthony was a bosun. Like the skipper and the mate, he was a shareman, his earnings geared more to the value of the catch. If the catch was poor, so was Anthony.

Chapter 6

'It's a dirty bird that fouls its own nest,' her father said, when Lynn had given him the latest news from Marlborough Avenue. The good humour was gone, and he pushed his empty mug towards Lynn's mother with a frown. 'Why didn't you tell me, Nina?'

Her mother filled the mug with more tea and pushed it back, undaunted and unapologetic. 'What would have been the point of spending ten bob on a telegram to tell you something you couldn't do anything about? What were you going to do, from hundreds of miles away? Not to mention the fact that we haven't got a code for "your daughter's husband's having it off with another woman", so I'd have been telling the sparks as well. It would have been all over the ship, from the skipper to the galley boy. Besides, I thought it was just a storm in a teacup. I thought it would all have blown over in a week, and she'd be going back to him.'

'Going back to him?' Lynn echoed. 'I won't be going back to him now, will I? *She* was showing no sign of going, and he evidently didn't want her to – and the police say if she's there as his guest they can't turn her out of the house. So what would I be going back to – three in a bed? And Simon in the middle of it?'

Her father jumped to his feet. 'I'll kill him. I'll break his neck with my bare hands,' he vowed, holding up hands that looked large enough and capable enough for the job.

'Shh!' With a warning look in her eyes Lynn jerked her head towards Simon, who was uncharacteristically quiet, with his eyes fixed on his grandad. 'He's taking it all in,' she murmured. 'Little pigs have got big ears, and they repeat everything as well. Anyway, where would it get us, except him fatherless and us visiting you in the slammer?'

Her father picked Simon up and sat down again with the child on his knee, holding him close. 'He'll never be fatherless while I'm alive. I'll be a father to him.'

'Not if you're behind bars, you won't.'

'I'll go round there and punch his lights out,' Lynn's brother threatened. 'His fancy woman won't want to be seen with him by the time I've finished.' A bit of a hothead, Anthony had just returned from his first trip as bosun, aboard the *Arctic Raven*.

'No, you won't,' Lynn warned. 'He's not worth doing time for. Mandy can have him. I'm going to the solicitor's as soon as this bank holiday's over, and that will be that.'

'As soon as it gets near eleven o'clock, you two go down the dock for the settling,' her mother said. 'Then you can take us to Hammonds and treat us to a three-course dinner and a new outfit apiece. You're coming out with us tonight, Lynn, we'll have you dressed to the nines. Let Graham Bradbury see what he's missing.'

'How's he going to see what he's missing, Mam? He doesn't drink in the same pubs as fishermen,' Lynn said.

'He won't if he knows what's good for him,' Anthony said. 'I'd love to catch him in Rayners with a few of our deckies there. He'd be out through the window, and we wouldn't bother opening it.'

Lynn tried to picture Graham in Rayners and failed. Rayners was notorious even on Hessle Road. Policemen went there in pairs. It was certainly not the sort of place to attract anybody like Graham.

'It's not very likely you'll catch him in Rayners, is it?' Lynn said. 'I doubt if he's ever been there in his life.'

'No, his mother never let him out to play with the rough lads, did she?' Anthony jeered. 'Anyway, I'm off to Brenda's. We'll probably be going to Hammonds, so we might bump into you. If not, we'll maybe see you on Hessle Road tonight. We're starting at the Halfway and working our way along to the Alexander.'

'You take Simon round to our Margaret's for a

37

bit, Lynn,' her father said. 'Me and your mam have got things to talk about. We'll call round for you after the settling.'

Anthony gave Lynn a sly smile and cast his eyes up to the ceiling. 'Aye, you take him to our Margaret's, and keep out of the way till you're called for, Lynn,' he said, and was out of the door.

'Cheeky little bugger!' Nina said as the door closed after him. '*A son is a son till he gets a wife, but a daughter's a daughter the rest of her life.* And there's never been a truer saying than that – except she's not even his wife. Lads! As soon as they start courting they don't want to know their parents.'

'Don't be daft, Nina. He came here first, didn't he?' their father said.

The probability of bumping into Graham on a pub crawl on Hessle Road was practically nil, but Lynn put on the trendy mini dress and the new shoes her father had bought for her and took a careful half hour over her hair and make-up, cheered on by her mother.

'That's right, lass, get your war paint on. Somebody who knows him might see you even if he doesn't, and run back with the tale. Let him know what he's missing.'

'I should think he already knows what he's missing, Mam. We've been married long enough,' Lynn said.

Nina handed Lynn her best perfume. 'It makes you irresistible to men. Spray at your own risk.'

Lynn sprayed generously. 'I should have a pack of 'em following me down the street now. If not, you can take it back and demand a refund.'

'Ready then?' her father grinned, looking smart in his best suit.

'I am.' Lynn slipped on the new burgundy-coloured three-quarter-length leather coat he'd paid fifteen pounds ten for only three hours earlier, and they set out for the 'Road.

In the Halfway Lynn's heart turned over when she spotted Graham among the crowd waiting to be served. He must have got rid of his painted doll and come here looking for her! She nudged her mother, with a nod in his direction and an apprehensive glance at her father, who was deter-minedly making his way towards the bar. 'It's too crowded in here,' she said. 'Can't we move on?'

'No point,' her mother said, obviously failing to see Graham. 'It'll be crowded everywhere.'

'No, look who's over there! Let's go, before my dad spots him.'

'Where? Where?'

'There!'

But when the man turned from the bar holding four pints of beer aloft his likeness to Graham dissolved.

'That's not Graham! It's nothing like him,' her mother said, 'but there's our Anthony at that table over there, with his new girlfriend. Come on, let's go and join them.'

Lynn dragged up a chair and sat next to Brenda, a round-faced, delicate-featured girl with a milk-and-roses complexion, pale blue eyes and a slight ginger tendency in her fairish, shoulder-length hair.

'I dig your frock, Lynn!' Brenda said. 'Psychedelic. A bit on the mini side, in't it?'

'Aye, well, I'm a dedicated follower of fashion, Brenda,' Lynn said.

'She's got good legs, that's why she's taken to minis. Best pair of legs in Hull, our Lynn!' Catching his girlfriend's expression Anthony quickly added, 'Barring yours, Brenda.'

A very masculine-looking young man in a smart grey suit appeared and set two beers and a port and lemon down on the table. Lynn glanced up into a broad healthy face under a crop of short brown hair.

'This is Alec, Alec McCauley. We had a good trip, didn't we, Alec? I'll soon have your job, though.'

Alec's wide smile revealed strong, straight teeth. 'Not until I've got the skipper's job! I want a glass sou'wester. When I'm on deck and the sea's drenching me and rolling me all over I look up and see the old man sitting up there on the bridge, nice and warm and dry, looking down at me, and I think: that's the best job. I'll have a dollop of that. Can I get you two ladies a drink?'

Lynn's mother returned his smile. 'No thanks, we've got one coming.'

'You're a long way from home, Alec, judging by your accent,' Lynn said, noting a lively interest in his steady blue eyes. Mariner's eyes, accustomed to scanning far horizons, she thought.

'I'm from Fleetwood,' he said, with a glance at the third finger of her left hand.

'He came with his dad. They've got digs on Bricknall Avenue with a retired trawler engineer and his wife – next door but one to your in-laws, Lynn.' Anthony grimaced, thumbing his nose in mockery of them.

'*Ex*-in laws – soon will be, anyway,' she corrected him, and in case Anthony hadn't told Brenda, she added, for her benefit: 'He's mucking about with another woman now.'

'Who? Gordon?' Brenda asked.

Lynn's eyebrows shot up. 'You know them, then?'

'A bit.'

'No, not Gordon – Graham,' Lynn said, and described her encounter with the unforgettable Mandy of the vivid green eyelids.

Alec spluttered, choking on his beer.

Lynn's father gave him a hefty slap on the back. 'That went down the wrong way!'

Alec coughed, his eyes watering.

'You all right, mate?' Anthony asked.

Alec nodded. 'I was talking to somebody like that not two hours ago,' he wheezed. 'She came round with a parcel. My landlady was out when the postman came, so he'd left it with them. I thought she was their daughter.'

Lynn's mouth fell open. 'Are you telling me they've got her *in the house?* She's staying there?'

'She was there to give me the parcel, anyhow – if it's the same lass. And if it's not, she's got a double.'

'I'll lay him out!' Anthony threatened.

Except for a 'Hah!' Lynn was speechless. Her mother-in-law had made so many sneering comments about a young neighbour who'd had a baby out of wedlock that Lynn could never for a minute have imagined her entertaining Mandy, not in her wildest dreams.

'That don't surprise *me*,' Brenda piped up. 'Graham's had plenty of coaching in how to be an adulterer from his dad.'

Lynn gaped at her. 'What do you mean?'

'Gordon! He was doing the dirty deed with his best friend's wife for years, as well as the barmaid at the Good Fellowship. Everybody knows that – except his wife, I suppose. He used to take Graham with him when he got older. Graham's seen him, chatting her up – the barmaid, I mean. He bragged about it to him. I know because my cousin went out with him for a while, and he told her. Oh, aye, Graham learned quite a lot off his old dad, by his own account.'

'Well, he never told me that, and I can't imagine Connie putting up with it,' Lynn challenged her.

'Nobody bothered to tell her, I suppose.' Brenda laughed, 'And she'd be too busy dusting her light fittings and polishing her floors to notice, my cousin reckoned. She's very house-proud, by all accounts.'

'Like father, like son, then,' said Anthony. 'You'll never have that trouble with me, lass.'

'I won't, will I – seeing you'll be at sea for three weeks at a stretch and only three days ashore. It don't leave you a lot of time for messing with other blokes' wives and chatting barmaids up, does it?'

Lynn's father came and put the drinks on the table, just in time to catch the tail end of the conversation. 'It don't leave you enough time to look after your own wife properly, never mind anybody

42

else's,' he said, with a wink at Nina. 'It's time I gave it up and came ashore. So who's chatting barmaids up?'

Lynn listened in total humiliation while Brenda told her father all about Gordon Bradbury and Graham.

Tom Carr listened to her with a deepening frown. 'Well, he's gone one better than his old dad, then, hasn't he?' He looked at Lynn with a warning light in his eyes. 'Tell him to sling his hook now and come home for good, while you've only got our Simon. If that's how he's carrying on you don't know what you might end up with.'

'What do you mean?'

'If a woman will jump into bed with a bloke she's hardly known five minutes, what's the odds it's not the first time? What's the odds she's not clean?'

Lynn gave a grimace of disgust, her head spinning with all this new and nasty information. 'I don't know,' she said. 'Anyway, I've already decided. I'm going for a divorce. Janet's put me on to a real good solicitor.' She glanced at her mother, who had said nothing so far. 'What do you think, Mam?'

'Well, if he's that bad, I suppose you'll have to,' Nina shrugged.

Lynn's father looked astounded. '*If* he's that bad?' he repeated. '*If?* He's shifted another woman into her bed! How bad do you want it, Nina?'

Nina turned to Lynn. 'All right, then,' she said, 'you'd better go and get the rest of your stuff tomorrow.'

'Hell, he's moved her into *your house!*' Brenda

43

exclaimed. 'He has gone one better than his old dad then. At least Gordon kept it outside.'

'Come on,' Anthony said, 'drink up and forget Graham Bradbury. We're supposed to be out to enjoy ourselves. We're supposed to be showing Alec how to get paralytic on a Hessle Road pub crawl.'

They drank up and headed for the next pub down that road, maybe two-and-a-half miles long from Dee Street to Osborne Street, and renowned for its abundance of fishing families and licensed premises.

'North to the Faroe Islands, south to the coast of
Spain
West with the whaling fleet and off to the Pole again
Over the world of water, seventeen seas I've strayed
Now to the north I'm sailing, back to the Trawling
Trade...'

The folk singer's fingers flew like lightning over his guitar strings as he accompanied his jaunty song. A few in the audience joined enthusiastically in the chorus:

'Come, ye bold seafaring men,
There's fortunes to be made
In the Trawling Trade
In the Trawling Trade!'

The place was packed to capacity, with no hope of getting a seat. Surrounded by people determined to enjoy themselves, Lynn felt marooned on her own little ice floe of misery, unable to think of anything but Graham and imagining she saw his face everywhere.

'We'll stay 'ere, shall we?' Anthony said, his speech a little slurred at this, their fifth port of call. 'I like a bit of entertainment, and this bloke's norra bad singer.'

'He's brill!' Brenda said, her feet tapping to the music.

*'Back to the midnight landings, back to the fish-dock
    smell,
Back to the frozen wind, as hard as the teeth of Hell.
Back to the strangest game that ever a man has
    played,
Follow the stormy rollers, back to the Trawling Trade!*

*Come, ye bold seafaring men,
There's fortunes to be made...*

'What do you think, then, Alec,' Lynn's father said. 'Do you reckon you'll make your fortune in the trawling trade?'

Alec raised an eyebrow and there was a gleam in his blue eyes. 'Tell me what other trade there is where you can get right to the top without years in college? I left school at fifteen with no qualifications, but I stand as good a chance as anybody else in trawling. If you've got enough gumption and a bit of good luck you can do all right – my dad's proved that.'

'Following in your father's footsteps,' Lynn's father grinned.

'I could do a lot worse. He's a skipper, and he's doing all right. Ten per cent of the catch, after

45

expenses. Not bad, is it? So what's to stop me doing the same?'

'Nothing, if your dad's paved the way for you,' Anthony said. 'The owners like skippers' sons.'

Alec shrugged, appearing not to resent the jibe. 'So, make the best of your advantages, is my motto.'

There was no slur in Alec's speech, Lynn noted, and his words seemed to be directed at her as much as at her father. Alec McCauley was going somewhere, at least according to Alec McCauley, and he evidently didn't intend to be long about it. So, his father was a skipper, and it was easy to believe that he would be one too; a successful one – maybe even a Don. He looked the type – broad shoulders, wide brow and steady eye, altogether built for command. While Alec's plans for his future washed over her Lynn sat half listening, wondering what Graham might be doing at that exact moment. Fishermen, she thought – after three weeks at sea you'd think they'd have had enough of the subject of ships and fishing grounds and what they could have done better than the skipper but the talk usually came back to that, one way or another, and she'd heard it all before.

'Where's your dad?' she asked. 'Didn't he want to come out?'

'He's still fishing, I expect. I haven't sailed with him since I was a nipper, learning the trade on pleasure trips in the summer holidays. You've got to cut loose sometime, and the sooner the better, I think. I'll get there on my own.'

Lynn saw her father's reaction to Alec – he

46

evidently respected him.

'Hell, aye. It's a bad idea to sail with relatives, and if your dad's a skipper, the rest of the crew would soon be crying favouritism,' he said.

She nodded vaguely, scanning the pub, engrossed in thoughts of Graham, but not too engrossed to realise that Alec was trying to impress her. That chap nearest to the singer – if that wasn't Graham it was his spitting image...

But when he got up to go to the bar she saw it wasn't Graham. Graham seemed to have had a double in every pub they'd been in, or she had Graham on the brain, more like.

Now Alec was looking at her, as if waiting for an answer. He'd obviously said something she hadn't quite caught.

'Pardon?' she said.

'I said if you're not doing anything tomorrow night, come dancing with us. I'm supposed to be going with Anthony and Brenda but I don't fancy it without a partner.'

'Well, there's our Simon...' Lynn said.

'Don't worry about our Simon. We'll look after Simon,' her father cut in. 'You go out and enjoy yourself.'

'Excuse *me!*' Nina challenged, looking her husband straight in the eye. 'What about me enjoying myself, after I've been on my own for three weeks? *We'll* be going out. *We'll* be going dancing ourselves, if we're not going to the theatre.'

Our Margaret probably wouldn't mind looking after Simon for the night, Lynn thought. Her sister seemed to have no objection to children and already had four boys of her own, although she was not yet thirty. Lynn had once attempted to share the knowledge about contraception she'd acquired in nurse training with her, but Margaret's only reaction to that had been to avert her grey-blue eyes, blush to the roots of her fair hair and change the subject, making it clear that her private life with Jim would be kept private. Lynn had been embarrassed then, and acutely aware of having trodden on forbidden territory. She'd never tried it again.

'Where are you going?' she asked Alec.

'Beverley Road, I think. Brenda knows.'

Beverley Road was one of the places Graham liked to go. He might even be taking Green Eyelids there. Lynn looked again at Alec, sizing him up as a rival to Graham. Not as good-looking maybe, but he was a full three inches taller, with a perfect physique and an air of assurance that commanded respect – all in all, a man that no woman would be ashamed to be seen with. A satisfying little scenario began playing in her mind, of Graham Bradbury looking on from the sidelines, mad with jealousy at the sight of his wife dancing in the arms of this imposing young stranger – and she knew for a fact that Graham would never have the guts to challenge the stronger man. Her mother was right, Lynn thought. Let Graham get an eyeful. Let him see what he's missing – and if he tried to talk to her, she'd cut him dead.

She came to life. 'If Margaret doesn't mind looking after our Simon, I'll come,' she promised. 'Definitely. You can count me in.'

Chapter 7

'I didn't really expect you to be in on a bank holiday weekend, Dave,' Lynn said on Sunday morning, determinedly behaving towards him as if the episode with the girlie magazine had never happened.

Dave looked intently at her for a moment and then stood aside to let her in. 'We never go anywhere on bank holiday weekends,' he said.

'Why not?'

'Because every bugger else is going, that's why not. Driving for miles in second gear, nose to tail behind a queue of cars waiting to get into Bridlington or somewhere, and having to get out of the van every two minutes to top the radiator up because the water's boiling is not my idea of fun. I'd rather stop at home and sit in the garden, and take my bucket and spade to the seaside when nobody else is going. Anyway, it looks as if it's going to piss it down with rain before long, like it generally does on bank holidays.'

Janet appeared in the hallway smiling indulgently at Dave, evidently quite happy with his determination to stay at home.

'He's a misery guts,' she said. 'You've had your hair done. Have you got a date?'

Lynn felt the colour rising to her cheeks. 'Well, if you call making up a foursome with one of our Anthony's shipmates a date, I have. Anyway I'm

49

glad you're in, because I'm going to the house to fill a couple of suitcases with the rest of my stuff, and I was hoping you'd come with me.'

'The house,' Janet repeated. 'Not "home" any more, then.'

Lynn's eyebrows twitched expressively upwards for a second, and the wry expression on her face gave Janet her answer.

'Do you fancy a cup of tea before we go?'

'I'd rather just get on with it.'

'All right, we'll be off, then.'

The rain had already started when they set out for the short walk from Richmond Avenue to Marlborough Avenue. Janet put up her umbrella.

'Sorry to drag you out in it, but I didn't want to go on my own in case *she's* still there,' Lynn said.

''S all right.'

'Seems like she's one of the family now. Somebody told me they'd seen her at his mother's the other day.'

Janet gave a disdainful little snort, and shook her head. 'Unbelievable. When Dave's cousin did a bunkoff none of his family would have anything to do with him, not even his mother and father. They stuck with his wife and kids.'

'Well, we're not talking about Dave's cousin's family, we're talking about mum and dad Brad – and it sounds like they're welcoming our Graham's latest with open arms,' Lynn said.

Janet gave another snort and shook her head. 'Shoved them in bed together, maybe,' she said.

The downpour started in earnest and Lynn shivered as they passed through the familiar creaking gate and walked up to the door. Her hand trembled slightly as she inserted the key in the Yale and turned it. They went through the hallway and into the living room with its lovely slate fireplace and then through to the dining room, with a few boxes still tidily stacked behind the door, as yet unpacked, months after the move. They wouldn't need unpacking now, Lynn thought. Not by her, anyway. The house was deathly quiet; no movement, no radio playing, no laughter, no child's chatter.

She shivered again. 'It's as cold as Christmas in here.'

Janet gave her a look of unadulterated pity. 'In more ways than one,' she said.

They walked through to the fitted kitchen, with its up-to-the-minute glossy units and the double oven built into the wall. Those ovens had been well used during the few weeks Lynn had lived in the house, and there'd usually been a sink full of pots either draining or waiting to be washed, and clothes either drying on the ceiling rack or in the basket waiting to be ironed, not to mention Simon's toys scattered about. Now there wasn't a thing out of place. The kitchen looked like a show room.

'It's a lot tidier than when I lived here,' she said.

'It can be, if you've got no bairns upsetting things every two minutes, and you never do any cooking or washing,' Janet said. 'His mother'll have taken his washing, and I've no doubt she's been in cleaning the place for him as well, probably telling Mandy what a rotten wife you were and how you never looked after her golden boy properly.'

Lynn felt the blood drain from her face. She felt sick.

'Sorry,' Janet said. 'Me and my big mouth. I ought to mind my own business.'

'It's all right. It's funny, but I feel sorry for him.'

'Sorry for who? Graham?'

Lynn nodded. 'Aye, I do.'

Janet looked stunned. 'What? Why the hell should you feel sorry for Graham?'

'Because one day he'll wake up and realise what he's destroyed and what he's lost – what we've all lost – and it'll be too late. He'll realise he can never put it right again or get back what he's thrown away – and he'll feel like I feel now. I think about him on that day, and I want to cry.'

'You're imagining he's like you!' Janet exclaimed. 'He's not! I've seen him in action before. He's a narcissistic little tosser who doesn't give a monkey's hang-down how much grief he causes other people, as long as everything's sweet for him. In fact, I'd go further. I'd go a lot further. I'd say he revels in it. He loves it! He gets off on it!'

'How, though?'

'Because it makes him feel so *important!*' Janet said, her face a picture of scorn. 'He's the star of his own show! He's the prize that women squabble over. He decides who the winner's going to be, and the loser can cut her wrists, for all he cares. In fact, it would only be another ego boost for him if she did. And then after a while he gets bored again – and it's time to spice his life up with another woman and another drama.'

Lynn was quiet for a moment, surprised at her normally undemonstrative friend. 'He's not as bad as that, but it's not just between women now. There's a child – his own son,' she said.

'Huh! That don't seem to bother him, does it? He *is* as bad as that, Lynn, and you'll see it before you've finished. His partner in crime gets the thrills second hand. They're a pair of tossers, him and Kev, a pair of complete wasters. If it weren't for Simon, I'd say you'll be a lot better off without him. In fact, I'd say you'll be better off without him anyway, because he'd be a rotten influence on him.'

'Well, I'll be without him before much longer, better off or not,' Lynn said.

'I just thank my lucky stars Dave's not that type,' Janet said.

'Come upstairs while I get my packing done, and then let's be off.'

'Get it all – get everything you want; you won't have to carry it. I'll go and fetch Dave. He'll run you back to your mother's in the van,' Janet said.

'Come with us, will you?' Lynn said.

There's something to be said for the heartache diet, she thought, while pulling on her pantee girdle that evening. It no longer cut her in two, and she could barely pinch an inch of fat around her waist. Buddha was on his own in the big belly stakes now. Her new slimmed-down figure was the silver lining inside the black cloud of her ruined marriage and her up-ended life – and the sight of her slender profile in the mirror gave her a definite boost. She went downstairs wearing a princess-line dress she hadn't been able to get into for months, and not one roll of fat to be seen.

Her parents were dressed up for an evening at the theatre. Alec had just arrived. A smile lit up his face when she walked into the room, and he gave her a nod of approval.

'You look as if you'd been poured into that frock,' he said.

'Take care of her,' her father warned.

'Don't worry,' Alec said, 'she'll be all right with me.'

'Give up, she's a grown woman. She can take care of herself,' Anthony jeered.

'You make a lovely couple,' Nina said, with a satisfied little smirk. The quick lift of her eyebrows and the knowing look she gave Lynn signified that she hoped Graham Bradbury would be around to see it.

Chapter 8

Alec was not much of a dancer, as could only be expected from a lad who'd been at sea since he was fifteen, Lynn thought – but he was good company. He did most of the talking, to begin with. He could spin a good yarn, and made her laugh with tales of his first days at sea, when he'd been so seasick he'd wanted to die, and had felt like bursting into tears when the skipper swore at him.

'Why on earth did you come to Hull?' she asked.

'I saw a deepwater trawler when we were fishing near St Kilda. I couldn't believe how big they are, and I decided I had to get on board one. So I came to Hull to do a few trips, see how I like it.'

'And do you like it?'

'I've only done one trip to Iceland, and it's bloody cold up there *now*. I'm wondering what it'll be like in winter,' he laughed, with a mock shiver.

'Not very pleasant, according to my dad. It'll certainly be too cold for you up at Bear Island, or the White Sea. Get to Iceland's North Cape in January and come back with frostbite – on your lips, your hands, and your feet.'

'Oh, sounds wonderful.'

'Greenland's even worse, according to my dad. He was in Godshaven, the capital city of Greenland; he says it's more like Godforsaken, one or two shops, no pictures, no pubs, no dance halls, no nothing – except glaciers, icebergs and plenty of snow. Apparently as soon as you tie up in Godshaven you're surrounded by girls, wanting you to get them pregnant.'

'What!' Alec laughed.

'Yeah, straight up. Because it's illegal for 'em to stay in Greenland if they're pregnant. It's the only way they can get themselves shipped off to Denmark. So you've got all that to look forward to, as well as everlasting darkness, gales, icebergs, black frost and ice that settles so thick on the ship and the rigging that you have to get on deck and crack it off just to stay afloat.'

Alec leaned back and looked at her, eyebrows raised and a smile of shocked amusement playing on his lips. 'Thanks for the encouragement!'

'Don't mention it. I was brought up in the

wrong place to have any illusions about deepwater fishing,' she said, warming to her theme. 'It's great for the trawler owners though, I'll grant you that. They never lose, whatever happens. They own the ships, they own the fish houses, the ice house, and even the fish meal factory. You have to buy all your gear from them, frocks, boots, mittens, knives, everything, and you can't get them anywhere else because they've got the monopoly, so they make you pay through the nose...'

Brenda and Anthony danced by. 'You make a lovely couple,' Brenda called.

'Thanks!' Lynn said, wishing that Graham were there to see it. She turned back to Alec. 'Where was I?'

'They make you pay through the nose.'

'Oh, yeah. If a fisherman has a bad trip, he ends up owing them money. If a ship goes down, the fishermen lose their lives and their widows and orphans go begging – and the owners get a nice insurance payout. They don't share it with the widows and orphans though, because when a ship sinks it's an act of God, and they're not responsible, by their reckoning. You're no better than their serfs.' She saw the look in his eyes, and thought: shut up, Lynn.

'We're not serfs,' he protested. 'Serfs have no choices.'

'Nor have the lads on Hessle Road, or very little,' she said. 'My mother nearly had a nervous breakdown when our Anthony went to sea, but there really aren't many other options for lads who don't get an apprenticeship somewhere. So the lads are bred to fishing, and the lasses are bred to being fisherman's wives – most of us.' She didn't go into her own determination to marry out of the fishing community and leave the life that was like Christmas for three days out of every three weeks – followed by the gut-churning feeling most of the women had when the taxis came to take their men back to their ships, not daring to wave them goodbye, not daring to look at the trawler as it left in case they never saw it again – and then three weeks of worry until they landed again. She didn't tell him she'd vowed to turn her back on all that and had deliberately chosen a man who risked nothing, who would be guaranteed to come home every night, who would probably live to be ninety, who got his thrills by breaking hearts rather than by braving seas. The only salt water Graham had ever braved were the tears of the women he'd used and cast aside.

'It doesn't seem to have put your dad off, anyway,' Alec said. 'It's not too cold and dangerous for him.'

'As long as the ship stays afloat it'll never be too cold for him, will it?' she said. 'It's nice and warm where he is. He generally picks a pile of sweat rags up at the Owners' Association Stores on his way to the boat.'

Alec nodded. 'Oh, aye – he's in the engine room. Maybe I should have become an engineer. But when my beard's frozen solid I can always cheer myself up with the thought of a tot of rum. That's one of the best things about deepwater trawlers – the bond!'

'Ah, yes, that lovely little duty-free shop, where

you get your fags and booze. They don't let you bring it ashore, though. That's always been a sore point with my dad and our Anthony.'

'It's a sore point with everybody,' he laughed. 'Joe Bloggs can nip across the channel to spend an hour or two in Boulogne, and bring his bottles of spirit back as well as two hundred fags. We do a five-day trip to the Arctic, maybe fifteen hundred miles, and the most we're allowed is two packs of fifty cigs. And the customs men are the first on board when we dock, rooting through all our stuff.'

'"Rummagers", we call them, but they were never the first on board here – we were,' Lynn laughed, her mood lightening at the memory. 'Many's the time we've smiled sweetly as we walked past them with a few packs of duty-free fags tucked in our big coats, or even in our knickers. They knew what was going on, but they never asked to search us. It was more a lip-service thing, their rummaging; they were quite sympathetic to the fishermen really, as long as they didn't overstep the mark.'

'Meet us next time we come home – I'll lift you on board and you can smuggle some for me,' Alec said, and gave her a wide smile.

'I would, but my mini's too short, my bell-bottoms are too tight, and I haven't got a big coat. I'd be sure to get caught. So how do you like Hull?' she asked.

'It looks all right from where I'm standing,' he said, gazing appreciatively at her. 'Full of good-looking women from what I've seen so far.'

Except that one of the women you've seen is

from Leeds, she almost said, her eyes searching the dance hall for Graham. The evening passed without any sight of him, and when the taxi carried the four of them to Boulevard at the end of it Lynn said a careless goodbye to Alec.

'I was going to hire a taxi for the day, maybe have a look round York tomorrow, Lynn,' he said, as she was getting out of the taxi. 'Do you fancy a day out? We could go and get a meal somewhere.'

Brenda jumped at the idea. 'We'll come with you!'

'I thought you wanted to go to Withernsea!' Anthony said.

'Well, I've changed my mind.'

'All right, we'll all go,' Anthony agreed, 'and split the taxi fare. What about it, Lynn?'

'I don't want to leave Simon.'

'Don't leave him, then! Bring him with us!' Alec said.

'Well, if you're sure you don't mind...'

Nobody seemed to mind, Alec least of all. What a smashing bloke he was, Lynn thought. Being out with him had gone a long way towards patching up her tattered self-esteem. Yet Graham had never been far from her thoughts all evening, and it sickened her to think that he would never see what a lovely couple she and Alec had made.

They set off in high spirits, passing through East Yorkshire villages that Alec had never seen, and that Lynn and Anthony barely remembered. Alec and Anthony kept them laughing with tales of their antics during their first days at sea and some of the characters they'd met on board, until Simon

59

demanded to be taken on a ship with them.

The taxi finally drove through the gate of York to reveal some of the beautiful half-timbered medieval buildings that Alec had wanted to see. Instead he got the driver to sweep straight past them all and down to the river, where they joined a queue to go on a pleasure trip. Simon raced up and down the riverside with Lynn chasing after him for fear he might fall in. Alec finally stopped him by swinging him up onto his shoulders.

'I'd have thought you two would have had enough of water,' Brenda said, when they finally found seats on board.

'Call this water? There's hardly enough to make a cup of tea,' Anthony said.

'No icebergs in it, either,' Alec said.

Brenda looked at Lynn, and voiced her very thoughts. 'I wonder where Lover-boy is today?'

'Probably taken his tart to the seaside, if she hasn't already gone back to Leeds,' Anthony guessed. 'Tell him to take a long walk on a short pier, Lynn.'

Lynn looked significantly towards Simon, and gave a slight shake of her head. The rest of the party took the hint, and fell silent.

They cruised peacefully along under an almost cloudless blue sky, with the sun shining on the water. The boatman gave them the history of various buildings they passed and pointed out the high water marks on the stone-reinforced river banks that bore testimony to the numerous times the city had been flooded. As they were returning to the wharf Alec was telling them a tale of having fallen into a tar barrel while skylarking with some other lads during his time in the net store in Fleetwood. Lynn was laughing, when she saw Graham and Green Eyelids in the queue waiting for the next cruise. Her eyes met Graham's and the laughter died in her throat. A second later she felt Brenda's elbow in her ribs.

'Over there,' Brenda said, nodding towards the lovely couple.

'I've already seen 'em.'

The sight of them together had knocked Lynn sideways, but to preserve her injured pride she recovered herself enough to make a good show of smiling and laughing up at Alec, happy to let him carry Simon off the boat and very pleased to let him help her off too. Graham's expression was a picture. It was obvious to Lynn that his shock on seeing her with another man was as great as hers on seeing him with Mandy. Good. She was glad that she had a strapping man like Alec to flaunt under his nose. Let him see he wasn't the only fish in the pond.

Anthony followed with Brenda and deliberately passed Graham within an inch or two of his face. 'Yes, you bastard – have a good look,' he said. 'They don't need you – they'll do all right without you, mate.'

Simon stopped, and took his father's hand. 'Daddy! Daddy!'

Graham stared straight ahead, his face like granite.

Simon looked up at him, bewildered. 'Daddy?' He gave his hand a shake. 'Daddy!'

No longer feeling quite so triumphant, Lynn took hold of Simon's other hand. 'Come on,

61

Simon. Come on, son,' she coaxed, sickened further at Graham's total lack of response to his own child.

With neither a word nor a gesture from his father to encourage him to stay, Simon allowed himself to be pulled away.

'Why didn't my Daddy come with us?' he demanded, as they walked off. 'Why didn't he hold my hand?'

'Because he's with somebody else,' Lynn said.

'Doesn't he like us any more?'

Anthony leaped up and thrust his fist into the air. 'I could punch daylight through him!' he burst out. 'I wish I'd chucked him in the bloody river.'

'Did you see the face on it?' Brenda said. 'Looked as if he was chewing a wasp. He must think he's the only one entitled to enjoy himself.'

'That *was* the same lass that brought my landlady's parcel round, but I wish we'd done what you wanted and gone to the seaside, Brenda. York was a really bad idea,' Alec said, glancing at Simon.

'It was a great idea before we bumped into Face-ache,' Brenda contradicted. 'Anyway, this is your last day ashore and we shan't see you for another three weeks, so we're not going to let that little prick ruin it for us, are we?'

That choice expression coming out of such an angelic face prompted shocked laughter from the other three, and Simon laughed at their laughter. It eased the tension, and Lynn warmed to Anthony's girlfriend.

Brenda grabbed Simon's free hand. 'Come on, Lynn, lets give him a swing,' she cried, and they ran along the path, lifting Simon off the ground

62

and carrying him along with them. Cries of 'Again!' and 'Again!' kept them at it until they got to the waiting taxi.

'You like walking on walls, don't you, Simon?' Anthony asked. 'I always did when I was a nipper. So we'll all walk on the wall round York, as far as we can go.'

'Then we could have a ride up to Scarborough. I like Scarborough,' Brenda said.

So after York city wall it was Scarborough for fish and chips and a look round the town – and then buckets and spades, sandcastles and tea. They arrived back in Hull long after Simon's bedtime.

'Get a babysitter, and come out for a drink with us, Lynn,' Alec said, but Lynn wouldn't be persuaded. She wanted to stay with Simon.

'I want to go home and see my dad,' Simon demanded, as they watched the taxi drive away.

'We can't.'

'Why not?'

'Because that woman who was standing in the queue with him lives there now. Come on, you've had a lovely day, and it's time you were in bed.'

Defeated, Simon reluctantly let himself be ushered upstairs and into the double bed they were sharing. He was still awake when she went downstairs, half an hour later.

She went into the kitchen and made herself a cup of tea, thinking how drastically his life had changed, and in only a couple of weeks. No hope of gardens with swings and apple trees now, and no father worthy of the name. He'd had more kindness shown him by a total stranger. Alec

McCauley and her brother must have spent a fortune on that day out. Lynn would have liked to pay her share, but had so little to spare she daren't even ask what the taxi fare was. She comforted herself with the thought that they wouldn't begrudge what they'd spent. On their two or three days ashore time was worth a lot more to them than money, and those two had certainly squeezed the most out of every minute.

They would be sailing on the morning tide. Fishermen! No sooner home than they're gone again, and pity the woman who falls in love with one. There were better ways to live. Being married to a trawlerman was no life for a woman. Like her mother said, not a proper married life at all.

Chapter 9

A couple of days later Lynn left Simon with her mother and dressed in suitably sober fashion, she took a bus into town to walk down Whitefriargate to Silver Street and the Land of Green Ginger, where the solicitors and legal people had their offices in Georgian buildings down cobbled streets. She looked on brass plate after brass plate until she found Mr Brian Farley and went in. After a long wait she was led by a young man who introduced himself as Mr Farley's articled clerk through two doors attached to the same doorway – an inner one and an outer one – into a small office.

'I've never seen that before,' she commented, indicating the doors. When closed they could only have been two or three inches apart.

'Oh, your secrets will be safe with us,' the clerk laughed, but left the doors open. They soon heard footsteps approach, which stopped outside.

The clerk glanced towards the doors with a wry expression. 'He'll be lighting a cig before he comes in. That's the usual procedure.'

'He should have lit it in here, and offered me one,' Lynn said, taking a packet of cigarettes out of her handbag. She wondered for a moment if Mr Farley lit his cigarettes outside the door just to avoid offering his clients one. So much the better, really, if the little she'd heard about solicitors and their charges was true. If she'd taken one of his, it might have appeared on the bill at three times the cost. The thought of that bill gave her a sinking feeling. Poor Dad, he'd paid a fortune for the wedding, and now she was going to have to ask him to shell out again, for the divorce.

The clerk left the room and a small, dark-haired, middle-aged, rotund figure of a man walked in with a cigarette between his lips. He closed both doors after him just as Lynn was lighting up. She raised her eyes from the flame as she inhaled and found herself looking into a pair of bright dark eyes with humour in them.

Mr Farley smiled, and extended his hand. 'A fellow sinner, I see.'

Lynn put her lighter back in her pocket and shook his hand, instantly feeling she had an ally. Under his sympathetic gaze, and prompted now and then by his murmurs of commiseration she was soon pouring out her story, and eventually had to blow her nose and dab away the tears that had begun to steal down her cheeks.

Mr Farley was all solemn sympathy. 'You could probably stay in the matrimonial home if you had a mind, and make him leave,' he told her.

She sat twisting her handkerchief for a moment or two, trying to remember what the monthly mortgage was. She hadn't a clue. 'Graham's always dealt with all the finances,' she said, finally, 'but I'm sure I'd never be able to afford it on my own.'

'What does Graham do for a living?'

'He works for a pharmaceutical company. He's just had a promotion.'

Mr Farley gave a smile of approval. 'Regular employment, and quite a good salary, I should think. Well, you'll have his contribution as well. He'll have to pay maintenance.'

Lynn realised with a sudden shock that relying on Graham to sort the money out was now a thing of the past. She would have to take all the responsibility for that on her own shoulders. She would have to take all the responsibility for everything, come to that. She sat up and took notice.

'How much, do you think?' she asked. The tears were gone.

Mr Farley smiled, as if at a private joke. 'How much does he earn?'

'I don't know! I never asked him. He paid the mortgage and the bills on his salary, and I did all the shopping on mine. We had a joint bank account, but he always saw to everything. I never had anything to do with it,' she said, horrified at her own lack of basic common sense. Her salary was still being paid into that joint account.

Mr Farley's smile broadened, and his eyes twinkled wickedly. 'People come in here and start weeping into their hankies, but the tears dry up as soon as we get down to brass tacks and start talking about the money,' he assured her. 'Who gets what, that's the crux of the matter.'

'But what if he won't tell us how much he gets?'

'He'll find he has no choice, Mrs Bradbury. Well, it seems to be an open and shut case, providing you haven't condoned his adultery.'

Lynn's eyebrows shot up. 'Certainly not.'

'And you have no extra-marital entanglements yourself. He could cross-petition, if so.'

For a moment Lynn was speechless with shock. 'If you mean am I committing adultery as well as him, I can tell you I'm not!'

He smiled. 'That simplifies things. We'll be very happy to act for you. Now about the co-respondent. Do we know the lady's name and address?'

'I wouldn't describe her as a lady. I only know she's called Mandy, and she's from Leeds.'

'Nothing else?'

Lynn shook her head.

'I'll send Jack round to the matrimonial home. He can get all the details, if they're still there.'

'Who's Jack?'

'Private detective. Your husband would be well advised to get a solicitor, if he hasn't already.'

Lynn had a sudden thought. 'I'd better give you his mother's address,' she said. 'He might find them there, if they're not at the *matrimonial home.*'

Mr Farley handed her a form. 'Fill that in and

post it. You'll get legal aid without any trouble, and the court will probably order your husband to pay the costs anyway. When you hear from them, make another appointment, and bring us your marriage certificate. You can't petition for divorce without it.'

'The matrimonial home,' Lynn echoed, as she stepped into the street. Now there was an impressive piece of solicitor jargon for the house she'd imagined she would be living in until her dying day.

Chapter 10

Careful not to wake Simon, Lynn crept into the bedroom that night and quietly got undressed, then with only the landing light to see by she began laying her uniform ready for the morning. On groping at the back of a drawer to find a pair of stockings, she pulled out the blue garter that Margaret had given her on her wedding day.

Something borrowed, something blue, something old and something new, she remembered, and what a stupid old superstition that was. She tossed the garter into the wastepaper bin.

It took an age to get to sleep. She awoke later and tossed and turned for an hour, unable to rest for thinking about that garter and her wedding day. Unwanted and unwelcome memories chased each other round her mind like hamsters on a wheel, and the more she tried to dispel them, the faster and more insistently they chased. In the end she switched on the bedside light and saw that it was past three o'clock. Sleep had deserted her, so she got out of bed and opened the wardrobe. Her wedding dress was still hanging in the furthest corner, protected by an old white sheet her mother had stitched together at the sides. She lifted it out, took off its covering, and laid it on the bed. The pearls and pearlised sequins on the bodice gleamed in the glow of the lamp, and the ivory silk of the skirt shimmered. Pearls for tears, her mother had warned, but Lynn had swept her objections aside. The dress was the loveliest thing she had ever seen; it had suited her perfectly and she'd meant to have it, regardless of silly superstition. Besides, the pearl superstition came from the notion that if you took something precious from the sea, the sea would take something precious from you – your man. But the sea would have had a struggle to get Graham; he never even went for a paddle. There was no chance of his ever being washed overboard, so 'pearls for tears' was irrelevant – or so she'd thought.

At the bottom of the wardrobe was a sea-green shoe-box, still containing her neat little satin wedding shoes with their Louis XIV heels. She lifted them out and inspected the decoration on the front. Pearls again.

Lynn sat on the bed and stroked the dress, held the silk against her cheek, remembering again Margaret chanting 'something old, something new, something borrowed and something blue' as she gave her the last-minute gift of the garter, and then their laughter as she struggled with her frothy underskirts to get it on. Her mother had lent her an old silver cross and chain to serve both as something borrowed and something old. Every superstition had been duly deferred to by a family rooted among the most superstitious people in the British Isles. Her mother and sister had seen to it that there was nothing other than the pearls to tempt fate, and Lynn had gone off to St John's Church beside her father in that flower-bedecked wedding car bursting with happiness and full of confidence in the future.

Poor Dad, the amount of money he'd lashed out on it all! A large tear rolled down her nose and landed on the beautiful ivory silk, followed by another. The dress was a work of art, and she felt it almost a crime to spoil it. She stood up and wiped her face with her fingers, then found a clean handkerchief and dabbed at the tears. Taking care not to drop any more on it she put it back in its cotton shroud and hung it in the wardrobe, then wrapped the little satin shoes in the yellowing tissue paper and put them back in the box with the few bits of faded confetti and lucky horseshoes. She retrieved the garter from the waste bin and laid it on top of the shoes, then replaced the lid and put them all in the wardrobe.

She shut the door on them. They were all relics of the past, and at Messrs Farley and Brown in Land of Green Ginger she had cut that past adrift from her future. She had no future now with Graham, and the gnawing emptiness inside her convinced her that without Graham she had no future at all, except for days without number filled with bleak, unending grief. She got into bed, her tears flowing on, copious and silent, not likely to disturb Simon.

Pearls for tears. She shivered. If only she hadn't insisted on having pearls.

At the end of the week Lynn was with Mr Farley when Jack himself walked in. 'I had to go round a couple of times, but I got them in, finally,' he said. 'He's admitted everything.'

A little smile lifted the corners of Mr Farley's mouth and made wrinkles around his bright brown eyes. 'Very good of him, I'm sure. Have you got all the details?'

'Yes.'

Mr Farley turned to Lynn. 'Well now, we can proceed with the petition – preferably as quickly as possible. With your legal aid it will only cost you thirty shillings. Better get the financial end of the business settled while he's still feeling guilty. That wears off very quickly, believe me – and when it does he'll put up a lot more resistance to a good maintenance settlement.'

'Well, if he's felt any guilt I've seen no sign of it, but whatever you think best,' Lynn said, with a smile as wry and fleeting as the solicitor's. She signed the papers he put before her and then went to catch the bus to Richmond Avenue. Half an hour later she was sitting in Janet's living room.

'We can proceed to a divorce,' she announced, 'and it'll only cost me thirty bob, with legal aid.'

'Thirty pieces of silver. Just the right price, for him,' Janet said.

Lynn nodded and leaned forward, making chopping movements at imaginary leg-irons.

71

'The shackles will soon be off, and I shan't have to ask my dad for a bean.'

Janet looked disgusted. 'Losing your home, though! Everything you've worked for. Having to go back to live with your mother!' she exclaimed.

'I know. I sometimes wonder whether this divorce will turn out to be the worst day's work I've ever done. Simon's still hankering after his dad, and so am I, truth be known.'

'Think again, then, if that's the way you feel.'

'Go back to him, you mean – after the way he's carried on? No chance.'

'But it's your house as well – your home! Everything you wanted for Simon: a garden with a swing, and even an apple tree. It's a lot to give up.'

'It's not the house, it's really not. I wouldn't go back to live in it, anyway.'

Janet said nothing, but Lynn caught an enquiring look in her hazel eyes.

'I mean it. I'd see her everywhere; I'd never be able to forget it. Apart from which, if he got away with it that easily it would be giving him the green light to carry on, wouldn't it? No. You had it right the first time, Janet. He's a tosser, and I've got too much pride to put up with what Connie put up with for years and years.'

'If she hadn't a clue what was going on, she didn't really put up with anything,' Janet said.

Chapter 11

June came, and the days were longer and brighter, but as grey as November for Lynn. Day after dreary day she left Simon with her mother and went to work, facing up to the new reality of her life. She was glad to go; there was plenty of distraction in a busy ante-natal out-patient department, and the work was rewarding. Most women having babies were happy to be having them, looking forward to welcoming a new life into the world, and something of that happy, optimistic attitude seemed to pervade the whole place. Day after day, Lynn threw herself into caring for the 'ladies in waiting', hoping that the married ones would never be confronted with faithless husbands and feeling a more acute sympathy for girls and women who were struggling alone, for whatever reason. It was cheerful on the whole, a good place to work, and she had good colleagues, Janet above all.

On her last afternoon in out-patients Lynn was assisting a qualified midwife in the routine tasks of the booking clinic. She was calling in one of the few remaining patients after a very busy afternoon when she spotted Graham sitting in the waiting room – the very last place on earth she would ever have expected to see him. Her heart almost stopped as she looked round for Mandy, imagining he'd brought her to book for delivery. Their eyes met and Graham stood up, as if he meant to come over to speak to her. Lynn hastily ushered her patient into the examination room and closed the door after them. She smiled brightly at the patient and then attended to all the routine tasks of height and weight measurements, blood pressure and urine testing with her mind in turmoil.

Mandy must be pregnant! She was probably in the toilet, producing a sample for testing at that very moment. Graham must have brought her to book for delivery – but how could he? They hadn't been together long enough for her even to suspect she was pregnant. No, but they'd met before, she remembered – while he was on that course in Leeds. It must have happened there. So, there would be another child for Graham – and a half-brother or half-sister for Simon, with Lynn nowhere in the picture – unless as the shadowy figure of the discarded former wife, painted into some dark, obscure corner. Lynn felt as though her stomach had been scooped out.

He was there when she went to call the last patient in, but there was still no Mandy to be seen. When the clinic was over and all the patients had gone, he was still in the waiting room. Lynn walked quickly towards the main part of the hospital, intending to avoid him.

He rushed to bar her way. 'Lynn, I've got to talk to you.'

She stopped, having no alternative.

'Mandy doesn't want to be named as co-respondent,' he said, looking directly into her eyes.

She stared up at him for a split second, and

then laughed in his face. 'Pity for her, then! What did she expect? She should have thought about that before she took the train to Hull and jumped into my bed – with my husband!'

A couple of the nurses who were clearing up after the clinic gave them strange looks. A scene in her place of work was the very last thing Lynn wanted. She made another attempt to sidestep Graham, trying to avoid it.

He obstructed her again. 'She doesn't want to be named because her husband won't like it.'

'Well, that just takes the biscuit! So, she's going back to hubby, is she? Whose idea was that, yours or hers?' Lynn demanded, taking care to keep her voice down.

Graham hesitated just half a second too long. Lynn gave a bitter laugh, and shook her head. 'Bad luck for him, anyway, if he's getting her back. What a prize!'

'Listen Lynn, there's no need...'

Lynn felt the rage rising inside her until she thought her head would explode. 'Mandy's the co-respondent, and I hope they'll publish it in all the papers. I hope they paste it on every billboard in Leeds. I hope everybody she knows sees it! She started this business, and I'm going to finish it. I'd tar and feather her if I could, and tie her up outside her own front door with a placard round her neck. Get out of my way, Graham.'

'There's no need to be spiteful.'

The other nurses were now openly staring, but goaded beyond endurance, Lynn was blind to them.

'Spiteful! You moron! What do you take me for,

a doormat? You both wipe your feet on me – and then you think I ought to put myself out to save *her* a bit of embarrassment? The woman who wrecked my home? *Simon's* home? No! She called the tune, and now it's time to pay the piper. There's one thing I'll say for her though – at least she was considerate enough to foul somebody else's nest, instead of her own. It's more than I can say for you. Her husband ought to think himself lucky!'

She saw the expression on Graham's face and another thought struck her. 'Unless ... of course! When you were in Leeds! That's where you went. Her house – to dirty his bed as well. I should have known.'

'Meet me later. I want to talk...'

'Go away, Graham!' Lynn pushed him out of the way and disappeared through the double doors leading to the wards, looking for a porter to have him forcibly ejected.

Little prick! Brenda had called him a little prick, and she'd hit the nail on the head.

Chapter 12

The *Arctic Fox* and the *Arctic Raven* were both due in on the same market tide, three weeks since they had last docked. Lynn's short-lived idyll on out-patients, working office hours with bank holidays off was over, and she was back on the post-natal wards. She was on a late shift so she got Simon up at dawn and they went down to St Andrew's Dock, to see them come in.

She took him to stand near the lock pits where some of the youngsters from Hessle Road were already waiting, where she herself used to stand as an excited, carefree child so many years ago. Sea-gulls were circling around the ship as usual, many of them sitting on the rails and making themselves thoroughly at home, as if they were part of the crew. The fisherman called them 'mollies', and most believed that they embodied the restless souls of drowned sailors. A gull flying before the mast was following the corpse as it drifted over the sea bed. Her mournful mood and the thought of all those drowned men lying unburied and alone in the cold, dark ocean brought sudden tears to her eyes, and a tightness to her throat.

The *Arctic Fox* squeezed slowly through the lock pits, and one of the deckhands began to lift the waiting children onto the ship. Lynn stepped to-wards him, holding Simon's hand – wanting him to see where his grandad was during his long absences, and to understand something of his way of life.

'He's the Chief's grandson,' she said, and Simon was lifted aboard after the rest. Lynn followed. While the rest of the children scampered all over the ship she took Simon down long, vertical ladders deep into the bowels of the trawler, feeling his terror as she helped him down, her nostrils full of the well-remembered smells of engine oil and fish. On the catwalk above the engine room she called to her father, but when he came to greet them in his oily boiler suit Simon

77

hung back, shy of him after three weeks' absence, especially in these fearsome surroundings. 'It's nothing to be frightened of,' Lynn encouraged him. 'I used to love coming onto the ship when your grandad came home.'

Simon was not convinced, but Grandad soon broke the ice, showing him some of the machinery until the docking tug towed the ship, stern first, to the berth on the market, port side to the quay. Then the skipper rang down 'finished with engines', and most of the crew jumped ashore and made for the taxis waiting at the back of the fish market.

While her father went to shower and change into his shore clothes Lynn took Simon back to the lock pits to catch the *Raven* coming through. Anthony was lifting another little clutch of Hessle Roaders aboard, and she and Simon followed them, to be shown the trawl nets, the mess deck, the galley, and the bunks, fore and aft – and then the bridge, where they found Alec with the skipper. The ship made fast alongside the quay, and they left it as the 'rummagers' stepped aboard.

Grandad walked in front with Simon on his shoulders and Anthony by his side. Lynn walked behind with Alec, towards the taxis and home. She felt the strength and roughness of his hand around hers, then looked up, and smiled at the gleam in his blue eyes.

'I can't understand your husband, letting you go,' he said. 'You're one of the best-looking women I've ever seen in my life. Is he blind?'

Lynn raised her eyebrows in feigned surprise.

'*One* of?' she queried.

His eyes twinkled as he laughed at his mistake. 'Oh, I got that wrong, didn't I? *The* best-looking woman I've ever seen, I meant to say. Come out with us tonight, and we'll carry on where we left off, down Hessle Road.'

Anthony heard, and turned round. 'Aye, five pubs down, and seventy to go,' he said.

'No kidding? Every other house on Hessle Road must be a pub, then,' Alec grinned.

'It's a long road, and he's counting all the pubs that are up the side streets as well. Dee Street's where the skippers and mates drink, and West Hull Liberal Club. That's where you belong,' Lynn said.

'I'll save that until Anthony's a mate, and I'm a skipper,' Alec said. 'So what about it, Lynn?'

'Sorry, no can do. I'm on a late shift.'

'What time do you finish?'

'Nine o'clock.'

'All right, we'll come for you in a taxi,' he promised. 'You'll get the last hour in, before closing time.'

'Do you realise how far the maternity hospital is? It's miles out on Hedon Road – next to Hull prison.'

'I'll come in a taxi for you,' he repeated.

'What a waste of money!'

'No it's not.'

'What, for an hour? 'Course it is.'

'I'm coming anyway. We'll go on to a club when the pubs shut.'

Let him come, then, Lynn thought. An hour out with Alec would make a welcome change. Her mother would take Simon round to Margaret's while she and Lynn's father went out, and Margaret would put him to bed with her own brood. She wouldn't mind. 'Well, if you're coming anyway, I'll take my glad rags and my war paint, and get ready as soon as I finish work,' she said.

The taxis were all gone for the moment. The day was clear and fine with a refreshing chill in the air, so rather than wait they walked all the way to the Boulevard to a hearty breakfast and an exchange of news and the making of plans which did not include Lynn. She would have to miss the excitement of shopping trips and three-course meals in town. She would be on the bus to work long before the men went to the office to settle.

The taxi was waiting for her right outside the hospital doors when she left work that evening, but further off in the car park she saw Graham's car waiting in the spot he used to occupy when he came to pick her up in the pre-Mandy days.

Graham had seen her, and was halfway out of the car. 'Lynn! Lynn!'

Her heart gave a painful little throb as she jumped into to the taxi beside Alec and closed the door. 'Let's move,' she said. 'We haven't got much time.'

The taxi drove off, leaving Graham standing looking after them, one leg on the concrete and the other still in his car.

The taxi stopped at the end of the drive, waiting to turn right along Hedon Road.

'I reckon that's your husband, just behind us,' Alec said, watching Graham's car through the wing mirror as it came to a halt at the back of them.

'Not for much longer,' Lynn said.

A gap in the traffic allowed the taxi to pull out, leaving Graham behind.

'He's doing his best to keep up with us. That lorry nearly took his front end off.'

'Well, how many Hessle Road pubs have you managed so far?' Lynn asked, signalling an end to conversation about Graham.

'One or two,' he grinned. 'We're meeting Anthony and Brenda at the Halfway.'

'Let's just call in and say hello, then go to West Hull Liberal Club. There'll be dancing there. I'd rather dance than just sit in pubs.'

'All right. If you can stand getting your toes trodden on, I'm game.'

'They survived the last encounter,' she said, and glancing into the driving mirror she was pleased to see that they had left Graham far behind.

'Have you ever been to Fleetwood, Lynn?' Alec asked, when he took her in his arms for the last waltz.

'No.'

'It's a nice place. I was thinking of going for a few days soon, to see my mother. Do you fancy coming with me?'

'Won't she be coming to Hull before long, to join your dad?'

'Why would she?' he asked, not breaking step. 'The bloke she's married to lives in Fleetwood.'

'Oh!' Lynn glanced upwards to meet his eyes. 'I've dropped a brick, then.'

'You couldn't be expected to know, seeing I never told you. But it's not the sort of thing you can come straight out with as soon as you meet somebody. You can hardly say: "by the way, my mother and father are divorced," as soon as you've finished shaking hands.'

'No, I don't suppose you can,' Lynn said. 'And I suppose our Simon will have a lifetime of explaining why we don't live with his dad, as well.'

'That's if you go through with it.'

She stopped dancing. 'Huh! I'm going through with it, all right!' she said, and hesitated for a moment before adding: 'But it must be embarrassing for a kid, having to explain.'

'Not embarrassing, exactly, just a bit awkward. People take it for granted that everybody has two parents who live together, and when they realise you've got a different name to your mother, you can see the cogs going round in their brains, wondering whether you're a little bastard.'

Lynn suddenly didn't feel like dancing any more. 'Simon doesn't even know what that word means.'

He put an arm round her, and led her from the floor. 'Neither did I, at first. I was seven when my parents split up ... but you soon find out.'

Lynn glanced quickly up at him, the cogwheels turning in her own brain as she wondered what sort of impact having divorced parents was going to have on Simon. If Alec's father was at sea he wouldn't have been able to look after him, so he must have lived with his mother and her new husband – unless he'd been farmed out with a grandmother. What must it have been like for him? She opened her mouth to ask, and quickly closed it again. That might be a touchy subject, best avoided altogether. So here she was, with a grown-up survivor of what Simon was to undergo. She consoled herself with the thought that Alec seemed none the worse for his parents' divorce. If Simon turned out as well, he wouldn't do too badly.

'Well?'

'Well what?'

'Aren't you going to ask why they're divorced?'

'No.'

'Will you come to Fleetwood with me, then? I've got a motorbike at my mother's; we could ride it back to Hull.'

'Thanks, but I leave Simon with my mother all day while I'm at work. I don't think she'd take kindly to the idea of me going off for days on end – she's too fond of gadding off herself. Besides, I don't want to leave him; I'm away from him enough. I don't want him to think his mother's abandoned him as well.'

'We'll take him with us.'

'Then you couldn't get your bike.'

'I'll get it another time. They won't mind keeping it for me.'

'Oh, better go and get your bike, Alec,' Lynn said. 'It's not only Simon. I can't take any leave yet. I've got my midwifery exams soon and I can't afford to fail. I want to be earning enough to get a house of my own.'

'You'll never get a mortgage – a woman on your own.'

83

'I know, but I should be able to afford the rent on something small.'

'Sounds as though it's going to be a struggle. Why not find a nice husband, and let him get the house for you?'

'I did, and look what happened.'

'He wasn't so nice, by the sound of it. I meant a nice new husband.'

She laughed. 'Are you volunteering?'

'Aye, why not?'

'You fishermen are too impulsive.'

'Fishermen have to make their minds up fast. We've no time to waste.'

'You're a bit too fast for me, Alec. And maybe I should get divorced from the old husband before thinking about a new one.'

Chapter 13

'How did you get on at work today?' her mother asked when Lynn got home after her shift the following afternoon.

'Good. I got two deliveries in, mothers and babies doing well. Where's Simon?'

'Out.'

'Out where? At Margaret's?'

'No, out with Graham.'

'Graham! What did you let him go with Graham for?'

'Because he wanted to go, for one thing. For another thing, Graham's his father, Lynn. I

84

didn't feel as if I had a right to stop him from taking his own son for an hour.'

'His own son didn't seem to matter to him while he was having fun and games with Mandy,' Lynn snapped.

'Well, Mandy's gone now,' her mother said, 'and he's got a right to see his son. Simon's got a right to see his father, come to that. And anyway, it's time Graham took some responsibility for him.'

'What time's he bringing him back?'

'He said he was taking him for an hour.'

'What time was that?'

'A couple of hours ago.'

Lynn picked up the telephone, and rang the house at Marlborough Avenue. There was no answer. She tried his parents on Bricknall Avenue, and spoke to her mother-in-law. Yes, Simon was there. Yes, she would put Graham on the line.

'We're having tea at my mother's. We'll be back home in a couple of hours,' he told her. 'You can pick Simon up from there.'

'You've got the car. If I come for him, I'll have to walk it. You can bring him back here, to the place you picked him up from.'

'No, you pick him up from home. I want to talk to you.'

Well, then! He'd failed at two attempts to collar her in the maternity hospital, and now it was evident he would stoop so low as to use Simon to bring her to heel. Lynn felt the heat rising to her cheeks. Alec was coming to take her out after tea, and her mother and father would be going out as well. For a fleeting moment she felt sorely tempted to tell Graham to keep Simon overnight

85

and give Margaret a rest for once, but instinct warned her against it.

'It's not *my* home, Graham,' she said. 'It hasn't been *my* home since you had Mandy in it, and it will never be *my* home again. Now put Simon on the phone. I want to speak to him.'

'He's out in the garden. My dad's pushing him on the swing, and he's loving it. I'll see you later, *in our home*,' Graham said firmly, and put the receiver down.

'What did he say?' her mother asked.

'He says,' Lynn fumed, 'that although he's got a car and he managed to pick Simon up from here, he's not bringing him back here. I've got to traipse up to Marlborough Avenue in a couple of hours, and either accept a lift back from him, or walk it home with Simon. Which means that Alec will probably be here before I'm back.'

'If you're thinking about Alec for your next husband, take a tip from me, before you make another mistake,' her mother said. 'Being married to a fisherman means hardly being married at all. It's hours and hours sat in on your own every night, wasting your youth.'

'I'm not thinking of anybody for my next husband. I'll manage without. And you had a day in town yesterday, and a good night out, and you'll be out enjoying yourself again tonight.'

'And after tonight, I'll be on my own again for weeks, not enjoying myself at all. Anyway, why don't you ring Graham, and tell him to keep Simon tonight, and bring him back tomorrow morning?'

'I don't want him to keep Simon all night,' Lynn

86

said. 'He's managed very well without Simon for over a month without even asking about him, so I hardly think that Graham's unconquerable love for his son's the reason he's taken him.'

'He probably wants to get back with you.'

'So he's using Simon to do it, do you mean?'

'You're your own worst enemy, sometimes, Lynn. By the way, there's a letter for you on the mantelpiece. It came yesterday after you'd gone to work, and then you went straight out before I could tell you.'

Lynn ripped the letter open, and quickly scanned it. It was a copy of her divorce petition, naming Mrs Mandy Jones as the co-respondent, and saying that since her husband had 'transferred his affections' to Mrs Jones, she, his wife, found it no longer tolerable to live with him. Well then, Graham must have had his copy yesterday as well, and maybe got an inkling about how much money 'transferring his affections' to Mandy Jones was going to cost him – which would certainly explain his second trip to see her at the hospital yesterday, and his sudden interest in Simon today. He was using him as bait for the sole purpose of getting her up to the house.

Alec arrived in a taxi just as she was setting out to walk to Marlborough Avenue. She briefly explained why she was going.

'We'll go in the taxi if you like,' he offered.

'*We* won't! Mr Farley warned me off boyfriends. I don't want to give Graham any room to accuse me of being as bad as him,' Lynn said, 'so I'm not having any boyfriends until I'm divorced. You're just a friend of Anthony's, Alec.'

'Take a friend's taxi, then, and get back as soon as you can,' he said.

'Thanks, friend.' She gave him a smile and a friendly peck on the cheek and went.

The taxi running the meter outside gave her a good excuse for grabbing Simon and leaving, cutting short any conversation with Graham.

Simon stopped at the gate. 'I didn't give my dad a kiss,' he protested, and ran back to Graham, standing in the doorway.

Graham lifted him up and squeezed him tightly, nuzzling into his neck. He put him down with tears in his eyes. 'I don't know why I did it,' he said. 'I felt nothing for her.'

Remembering the way Graham had cut him in York, Lynn took Simon's hand to usher him into the taxi. Graham followed them to the garden gate and Simon sat waving to him until he was out of sight.

Simon was very quiet and Lynn watched him, wondering at her child's capacity for forgiveness. Those tears in Graham's eyes had looked genuine enough to melt a heart of stone, and they'd certainly had an effect on Simon. Lynn's buoyant mood was gone. She tried in vain to dispel her feeling of misery and desolation, reminding herself that Graham deserved no better, but the feeling would not go.

Later, when Simon was safely at Margaret's she slapped on a bright and happy face and went out, determined not to cast a shadow on everyone else's enjoyment. She laughed and joked as if her life depended on it, but her gaiety was forced and her talk a little too fast and too feverish. Despite all her efforts she knew that Alec at least was not taken in. Something of her wretchedness had transferred itself to him.

Chapter 14

Their three-day millionaires were away on the morning tide, and Lynn knew her mother would clear none of their things away until the following day, nor would she do any washing, since washing clothes on sailing day meant you were washing your man to the bottom. Most agreed it was just superstition, but it was a rare wife who would defy it. Pegging three sheets on a washing line was un-lucky, too – another invitation to disaster at sea.

'There's plenty of time for housework before they land again,' her mother said, 'so why tempt Providence?'

'Why indeed?' Lynn agreed. She'd tempted Providence enough with the pearls.

'Ah, well, the fun's over for another three weeks,' her mother sighed.

But the fun seemed to be far from over for Nina. She was enjoying a much busier social life than she'd ever had before Lynn got married, always out at the pictures, or dancing, or to some 'do' or other with other wives of grown families. Lynn shuttled to and from work on the bus, and found herself alone most nights after Simon had gone to bed. She enjoyed having the house to herself for a few hours, and spent the time swotting for her exam, or watching television. Graham started calling two or three times a week to take Simon for tea at his mother's.

'I wish you'd tell me what your shifts are, then I could come when you're in and I wouldn't have to bother your mother,' he told her one day when she was home after an early shift.

'I don't know what my shifts are from one day to the next,' she said. 'They chop and change them at the drop of a hat.'

'I'm sure they don't.'

'I'm sure they do.'

'They never did when we were married, then. You knew what you'd be working for a full week.'

'Well, we're not married now, and things change.'

Graham corrected himself. 'I meant when we were living together, and we are married now. We're not divorced yet,' he reminded her, looking directly at Simon. 'And Simon doesn't want us to get divorced, do you, Simon?'

Although he didn't even know the meaning of the word 'divorce' Simon took his cue and gave her an emphatic 'No!' Lynn saw the drift of the discussion, and cut through it. 'It's no bother to my mother, Graham,' she said. 'She doesn't mind a bit. She's all in favour of you taking more responsibility for Simon. And you'd better get a move on, or your mother will be wondering where you both are.' She bent down to kiss Simon. 'Bye, son. Be a good lad.'

Simon seemed reluctant to move. He looked up at her with hope and pleading in his eyes. 'Come

90

with us, then we can go to the house with the swing in the garden, and you can push me.'

'I can't, Simon. I've got too much to do.'

Simon's whole body seemed to slump, but he puckered his lips and kissed her, before taking his father's hand.

Graham was evidently prepared to stand on the doorstep as long as Lynn would stand there with him, so she went in and closed the door, regretting her curtness only for Simon's sake.

He was back before bedtime in a distinctly truculent mood, and firmly stated his case. 'I want to go back to live in the house with the swing in the garden.'

'We can't,' Lynn said.

'Why not?'

'Because your daddy had another lady living there.'

'She's gone now, so we *can* go back,' he insisted, challenging her to explain the logic of staying away from the house with the swing in the garden because of a lady who was not there.

Some of the phrases in the divorce petition sprang into Lynn's mind: '...transferred his affections to Mrs Jones...' '...obliged to leave the marital home...' '...finds it no longer tolerable to live with him...'

All true. It was no longer tolerable to live with Graham, but it was hopeless trying to explain to a child of Simon's age, so Lynn made no attempt at it. And why hadn't she heard anything from the solicitors, she wondered? The petition was prepared, they had her affidavit attesting to the truth of it, they had her marriage lines. So what was the hold-up? She decided to ring them the following day. She wanted the whole thing over and done with as soon as possible.

Simon planted his feet apart and stared up at her, scowling like a little demon. 'She's gone now, so we *can* go back,' he repeated.

It was a balmy summer's evening and the *Arctic Raven* was due in around midnight, so Lynn went down to St Andrew's Dock with Brenda to meet Anthony and Alec off the ship. A party of young deckies who had just come ashore were walking towards the taxis at the back of the market, and a few of them stopped to ogle the girls as they passed.

One of the youngest gave Lynn the eye and called to her: 'How much are you, then, love?' He must have been all of fifteen years old.

'More than you can afford, you cheeky little twerp,' Lynn retorted. 'Come back when you're out of nappies.'

'Have you just come off the *Raven*?' Brenda asked him.

'Yeah.'

'You'll know her brother, then,' Brenda said.

'Who's her brother?' they heard one of the lads ask, after they'd gone by.

'The bosun, you daft bugger! The other one's his girlfriend.'

'He'll feed your guts to the mollies,' another said, and with hoots of laughter they made a dash for the taxis, and safety.

Lynn grinned and walked on, passing lads from

the *Raven* and other ships, some of whom recognised her and exchanged a word or two. Seven trawlers were already berthed on the wet side of the dock, with as many on the dry side waiting to sail. The dock was quiet, and would stay quiet until the bobbers turned up to start unloading.

Anthony was just off the ship, and Brenda ran to meet him. Lynn watched as he caught her and lifted her into a dizzying spin. The sight of them arm in arm under a bright full moon and a sky full of stars brought poignant memories of the heady days of her courtship with Graham.

Alec was not far behind them. He looked at Lynn and hesitated, and the way he looked sent a wave of excitement rippling deep inside her, telling her she'd lived the celibate life longer than was good for any grown woman. She wanted a man. He strode towards her to lift her off her feet and give her a suffocating hug and a kiss that left her weak.

'Did you get the flowers?' he demanded, nuzzling her ear.

'We've hardly got room for them all in the house!'

He released her, and set her back on her feet. 'Good.'

'I got the chocolates as well. You'll have to help us to eat them; I don't want to get fat. Did you have a good trip?'

'Terrible – we'll be lucky if we don't owe them money, when it's all reckoned up,' he grimaced. 'And on top of that I'll have to buy a new pair of boots. A catfish sank its teeth into one of 'em,

93

and went straight through – they've got teeth worse than any shark, and they don't let go. I've had one wet foot most of the trip, and I haven't been very pleased.'

'You shouldn't have thrown all that money away on flowers and chocolates, then!'

He pulled her close. 'It's not thrown away.'

She linked his arm. 'I'm off work tomorrow. If it's nice, we could get out for a long walk somewhere. That would be a bit easier on your wallet.'

'Preferably somewhere nice and secluded,' he said, with a grin. 'I used to roam for miles before I went to sea. Where shall we go?'

'Anywhere,' she said, calculating that since it would be Thursday Graham would be at work, and very unlikely to bump into them. 'We could get a bus out into the countryside, or go to Beverley and have a stroll on the Westwood. The pubs round Wednesday Market are open all day. I'll buy you a pint, if you're that hard up.'

'What if it rains?'

'We can sit in a pub or stay in the house, and play Monopoly or something.'

He stopped, his blue eyes gazing into hers. 'Or something would be nice, if we could get the house to ourselves.'

She dropped her gaze. 'Not yet awhile,' she murmured, and hurried him on to catch Brenda and Anthony.

A short taxi ride took them to Boulevard, where they saw that the lights were on. Lynn's mother was sitting up, waiting for them.

'Come in and have a drink,' Anthony said. 'She'll have some beer in.'

94

'Thanks, but it's too nice to sit inside. I'm taking Lynn for a stroll in the moonlight, and then I'll have to get back to the *Raven*.'

'What for?' Brenda demanded.

'Because it's the mate's job to oversee the landing of the catch,' Anthony told her, 'and give the dollarman a nice backhander.'

'I've got a fiver in my pocket,' Alec said.

'What's a dollarman, and why should he give him a fiver? Doesn't he get paid?' Brenda demanded.

'The dollarman's the foreman bobber; he sorts the fish out in the kits to make them ready for market and if he doesn't get his backhander, he's likely to make your fish look fit for nothing but fertiliser so it won't sell, and that won't do us much good when it comes to the settling,' Anthony said. 'There's many a first-class catch been sent to the fish meal factory, for lack of a five-pound note.'

'That's not right.'

'It's not, and it goes against the grain, but we have to work within the system we've got. The whole fishing industry runs on bribes and back-handers, and if you want a good price for your catch, you have to go along with it. Just think of it as an investment,' Alec said. 'Anyway, if you'll get out and go for your beer, I'll just have time to take Lynn for a stroll.'

'Oh, aye?' Brenda laughed. 'Where are you strolling her?'

'Hessle foreshore. I've heard that's a nice walk.'

'We'll come as well, then,' said Brenda. 'It'll be nice to get a breath of fresh air. Go in and dump your sea bag and tell your mother, Anthony.'

'Fresh air? I should think I've had enough fresh air, after three weeks at sea,' Anthony grumbled – but he carried out his orders.

A bright moon streaked the Humber's mud-brown waters with silver and a cool breeze whispered through the trees as Lynn strolled hand in hand with Alec along the shingle. There was not another soul in sight, except for Brenda and Anthony, lagging far behind them.

'This trip's been a complete washout,' Alec told her. 'The last couple weren't all that great, either. The skipper'll be lucky to get another ship. I wouldn't like to be in his shoes at ten o'clock tomorrow morning when he goes to see the gaffers. He'll probably end up having a long rest, or have to go back to being mate.'

'Well, they won't keep him on if he can't make a trip,' Lynn said, with the wisdom of one born and bred on "Road". 'They'll have no mercy on him if he keeps coming back without the money box.'

'I've got some sympathy for him; none of it was his fault, but he's had no luck at all. First we had to get a man taken off in Iceland because he'd broken his leg getting one of the trawl doors on deck, and then we were fishing over a wartime wreck that wasn't marked on the chart, and we lost all the gear. It took hours of hard work to get another set sorted out, and then we found out the ship was letting in water. It's just been a series of disasters.'

She shook her head. 'And you still want to be a skipper?'

'Aye, and the more bad luck some poor buggers have, the more openings there'll be for mates with skipper's tickets!' He laughed, his face brightening. 'It's a cruel world, i'n't it?'

'You'd be better off getting a job ashore, one where you get home every night, and you're not at the mercy of the gaffers.'

He stopped, and turned towards her, his eyes shining. 'Not me! Jobs ashore pay nothing for lads who left school at fifteen with no qualifications. Unless I win the pools, fishing's my only chance of making any money. And nobody could be as unlucky as our skipper – I know I couldn't. It's all a gamble, but I trust my luck ... and my instincts.'

'Let's hope your trust's not misplaced, then,' she said.

'It's not. Another six months as mate, and then I'm going for skipper. I'll fill the ship with fish, and get us a house in Kirkella.'

'Kirkella!' Lynn laughed, picturing that exclusive suburb to the west of Hull with its palatial houses set in acres of manicured garden that seemed to be the dream of many a Hessle Road fisher-lad. 'You'll need to make a fortune before you can look at a garden shed in Kirkella.'

You've as much chance of ending up at the bottom of the sea as in Kirkella, she thought – probably more. More fishermen went to the bottom than ever got to Kirkella, but no fisherman wanted to hear that, and saying it would seem like wishing it on him.

'I will, though,' he insisted. 'I'll do it, sooner or later.'

'You fishermen are all the same. You all think

97

you're going to be millionaires,' she scoffed, 'but for every fisherman who ends up with a house in Kirkella, there must be thousands who never get out of Hessle Road.'

'You're exaggerating.'

'Not a lot.'

'You'll see.' He gave her hand a squeeze and they walked on in silence for a while. 'A stroll by the river under the moon and stars... I'd have liked us to be strolling on our own,' he said, jerking his head in the direction of Anthony and Brenda, 'but we can't shake them off.'

'We could have shaken our Anthony off all right, but Brenda seems to have him well under the thumb. Anything she wants, it's: "all right, love" from him.'

Alec smiled. 'Best way to keep the peace, I reckon.'

They drew to a halt. 'I love to walk by the river, and there are some decent pubs round here as well,' Lynn said.

'Pity they're all shut. What about coming to Fleetwood, then, Lynn? It's lovely, this time of year. On a clear day you can see right out over Morecambe Bay to the fells in the Lake District, and if you turn landward, you can see right over to the Pennines. It's one of the bonniest spots in the British Isles.'

'How do you know? Have you been everywhere else in the British Isles?'

'No, I read it in a travel book when we were steaming back from the fishing grounds,' he grinned. 'Anyhow, I've looked up to Morecambe Bay from Fleetwood many a time, and it don't

98

look bad. I'll miss a trip, and go to see my mother if you'll come with me. She'll make you welcome.'

'What about your motorbike?'

'Sod the bike. I'd rather you came.'

'Oh, I don't know,' Lynn wavered. 'I'm not divorced yet, and there's Simon.'

'Bring him. I've told you, she'll give you both a right gradely Lancashire welcome.'

'What about your stepfather?'

'He'll make you welcome, as well. We could have a week there, maybe a fortnight.'

'Well, I don't know about a week – and a fortnight's out of the question. I might be able to do Saturday to Tuesday if I get a long weekend, but...' She hesitated for a moment, and then suddenly made her mind up. 'All right, I will. I'll come. I'll find out when I can have some leave, and I'll come – just to see if it's better than Cornwall. I've been there. It's magic.'

'It is, better than anywhere. It's there in black and white – in a book.'

'I'm holding you responsible if I use my days off, and it's not.'

They paused for a moment, and turned back, to see Brenda and Anthony in a passionate embrace, with the night sky and the silver-streaked waters of the Humber as a romantic backdrop.

'Aaah, look at that! I'n't it sweet?' Lynn mocked.

Alec laughed, and curling his tongue back with his fingers he sent an ear-splitting whistle in their direction. The lovers waved and as they walked towards them Alec held Lynn in a tight embrace and kissed her.

'How's your divorce going, Lynn?' Brenda laughed, as they drew near.

Lynn felt Alec's eyes rivetted on her. 'I don't know,' she said. 'I haven't heard anything since I got a copy of the petition. He must have got his at the same time, but I haven't heard anything yet.'

'You can get married a lot quicker than you can get divorced, by the look of it,' Brenda said, with an air of suppressed excitement and a surreptitious glance in Anthony's direction.

'Aye,' he said. 'That only takes three weeks. Shall we tell them?'

'I haven't told my mam, yet.'

'I haven't told mine, being as we've only just decided.'

'I can guess. You've asked her to marry you,' Lynn said.

'Well...' Brenda hesitated, and then burst out with it.

'We're putting the banns up tomorrow, and we're getting *married* after his next trip.'

'I'm making an honest woman of her.'

'I was an honest woman before!'

'Well in three weeks' time you'll be an honest married woman, then.'

'We could have had a double wedding if you'd got your divorce in time,' Brenda said.

Lynn shook her head. 'You'd have to wait a lot longer than the next trip,' she said. 'I don't know how long it's going to take to get the decree nisi, and you can't apply for the decree absolute until six weeks after that. I don't know how long it takes to come through after you've applied.'

'Oooh no! We can't wait that long, can we, Anthony?' Brenda laughed.

'No, we can't.'

'And have you thought about my dad? His ship doesn't get in until the day you sail, Anthony. If the timing's as bad after the next trip, he'll miss the wedding. So what's the rush?' Lynn teased, looking pointedly at Brenda's waistline.

'Don't worry, I shan't be going into labour halfway through the ceremony,' Brenda laughed. 'Not like that lass who just managed to say "I do" before she got rushed off in an ambulance! But we want to tie the knot as soon as we can, don't we, Anthony? Maybe your dad can miss a trip, make sure he's at home.'

'I doubt if he'll be able to do that. We'll just have to trust to luck, that's all,' said Anthony.

'Yeah, it'll be all right,' Brenda nodded. 'And it's not as if he's got to give anybody away, is it?'

'Well, no, but he might like to be at his only son's wedding,' Lynn protested, a little miffed at seeing her father's interests swept aside.

'I hope the *Arctic Fox* comes in with a better catch than the *Raven*. Silly buggers, calling a ship after a bird! They ought to know birds are unlucky,' said Anthony – changing the subject rather than oppose Brenda, Lynn thought.

'Tempting Providence, my mother would say,' she murmured.

Brenda laughed. 'That's just a daft superstition.'

'I know it is,' Lynn agreed, and had a flash of inspiration. Brenda was young, no nonsense, and not from Hessle Road. Here was a golden opportunity to unload that wedding dress on somebody who wasn't ruled by signs and omens.

'We're about the same size, you and me, Brenda,' she said. 'You can have my wedding dress if you want it. It cost my dad a fortune, and there isn't a mark on it. It's beautiful.'

Chapter 15

'Does it have to be in three weeks? And what about your dad? What if he doesn't land at the same time as you? Can't you give us a bit more time to get everything organised?' Nina demanded, early the following morning.

'We've already been to see the vicar and put the banns up, and my mother's got everything else in hand,' Brenda said. 'There won't be much for you to do.'

Nina pulled a wry face. 'Well, thank goodness it's a son getting married this time, so we don't have to do all the paying.'

'Talking of paying,' Lynn said, 'I can save you quite a bit, Brenda. Come upstairs.'

When she saw the dress, Brenda's expression alternated between admiration and dismay. 'It's gorgeous,' she said. 'It's the most beautiful dress I've ever seen, and I've been looking at wedding dresses in Hammonds ever since we started to get serious. It's the nicest one I've seen in my life, but so many *pearls!*'

'But you're not superstitious, Brenda! Try it on,' Lynn urged.

Brenda stripped to her underwear and Lynn helped her on with the dress and then pulled back the bedroom curtains. The folds of the skirt shimmered and the pearl-encrusted bodice gleamed in the sunlight. The silk rustled as Brenda twirled in front of the mirror with shining eyes, examining her reflection from every angle.

'It fits you all right,' Lynn said.

'Well, it's lovely,' Brenda kept repeating. 'Really gorgeous.'

'It really does something for you. It suits the colour of your hair. It looks better on you than it did on me.'

Brenda hesitated for a second, then shook her head. 'It really is gorgeous, but ooh, no. I couldn't have pearls. Not on my wedding day. And Anthony's already seen it, obviously, so that's unlucky, as well.'

'I thought you weren't superstitious. You're getting as bad as the fishermen.'

'I know, but I'm not so *un*-superstitious I want to wear so many pearls on my wedding day, when I think about the sort of things that sometimes happen at sea.'

'Ah, well,' Lynn sighed, helping her off with it.

With a last, lingering look at those glistening sequins and pearls and a 'Thanks anyway, Lynn,' Brenda bit her lip and withdrew.

Lynn left the dress on the bed and followed her downstairs, feeling curiously relieved. Her mother and Anthony looked at them expectantly.

'Did it fit?' Nina asked.

'Like a glove,' said Brenda.

'Do you like it?'

103

'Aye, I like it, and I'd have liked to save my dad a bit of money, but it's not for me,' Brenda said, with a slight shudder. 'And you didn't have much luck after wearing it, did you, Lynn?'

Lynn's mother spoke for her. 'No, she didn't.'

Anthony put his arm round Brenda and gave her a squeeze. 'Now who's superstitious?'

'Well, I'm getting into seafaring mode now, and it's no use tempting fate, is it?'

He gave her another squeeze, and a quick kiss. 'I'm glad,' he grinned. 'I'd rather buy you a new one.'

'With whose money?' Nina wanted to know.

'No, we'll do it right,' Brenda said. 'My dad'll buy it. I've tramped all over Hull, and I haven't seen one I really like, so I'm going to Leeds. I've heard they've got some beautiful wedding dresses in Schofields. Come with me, Lynn, and we can get Simon's pageboy outfit at the same time.'

Lynn's heart sank. She would have preferred to spend her day off in some obscure corner with Alec rather than ride the rails and tramp round shops, but this was a bride to be, and the girl who was going to be her sister-in-law at that.

'All right,' she said, with all the good grace she could muster.

'I'll go and get the money off him, then. Meet you in the station, for the next Leeds train,' Brenda grinned.

'Is she pregnant?' her mother asked, when they'd gone.

'Not as far as I know.'

'What's the rush, then?'

104

Lynn laughed. 'Head over heels in love, maybe. I dare say some people are, when they decide to get married.'

'Hmm,' her mother said, and after a pause asked, 'Why don't you have another go at your marriage, Lynn? Give it another chance? When I'm on my own with Simon, he talks about Graham non-stop; his daddy's got this, his daddy's got that. He wants to go and live with his daddy.'

'He never says that to me,' Lynn said. 'All he says is he wants to live in the house with the swing in the garden. So all right, I'll get him a swing for your garden, and that'll settle that.'

'And Graham's told me he's up for another promotion – he'll be earning good money,' Nina said, with the pound signs shining in her eyes. 'You could be made for life.'

'With a bloke who shifts another woman into my bed after I've been gone *two minutes*? And brazens it out when I confront him with it? That's not my idea of being made for life.'

'If you'd taken a bit more notice of him, he might never have strayed, but you're too wrapped up in that job of yours. Anyway, he's changed. He's learned his lesson. He'll never go off the rails again, after all this upsetment.'

So, Graham was working on her mother, as well as on Simon, Lynn thought. 'How do you know what he'll do?' she flared. 'What sort of crap has he been telling you, while I'm not here?'

Nina frowned. 'He's packed that Mandy up. He never wanted her in the first place; it was her that did all the running. He wants you back, is what he's been telling me, and you won't even give him the time of day. I feel sorry for him. I don't think anybody's ever regretted anything more than Graham regrets the Mandy episode. And I'll tell you this as well, while I'm at it. I don't like being snapped at like that in my own home.'

'I'm sorry.'

'Yeah, you should be. I've run my blood to water for you, more than the other two put together.'

'I'm sorry,' Lynn repeated.

'Two grown women in a house – it never works,' Nina muttered.

Lynn bit her comments back, and seethed inwardly. If only she'd passed her midwifery exams. If only she'd never started midwifery in the first place, but had gone for a decent job in general nursing, she might have been able to afford to rent a house of her own. Even then, she could only pay the rent by going to work and earning the money, and to do that she needed her mother's help. Whichever way she tried to work it out, it always came back to that. There was no escape. She felt a headache coming on and went to the kitchen cupboard to extract four tablets from the aspirin bottle. Since she had no option but to go to Leeds with Brenda, the last thing she needed was a banging headache.

'Simon, keep hold of my hand!' Lynn warned, before they got off the train. 'Leeds is a big place. If we lose you here, we might never find you again.'

She kept a tight grip on him and Brenda kept a tight grip on her bag as she steered them up the Headrow among the throng of shoppers, making a beeline for Schofields. The store was packed, with people milling around in all directions. They found the lift, and waited. The doors opened, and there stood a girl with luminous green eyelids, a dark, Mary Quant bob, and a man – presumably her own.

Mandy! Though taken aback, Lynn looked her straight in the eye and had just enough presence of mind to ask the question she'd rehearsed for weeks, the question she'd fantasised about asking if she ever crossed her path again.

'Have you got the time, by any chance, Mandy?'

The effect was as pleasing as Lynn had imagined in her most satisfying daydreams. Mandy was stunned, almost out for the count.

'I haven't got a watch!' she gasped.

'Oh, dear! Better get your old one mended, then...'

Mandy flushed and manoeuvred her escort away.

Triumphant, Lynn let go of Simon's hand, and took half a step after them, keeping her foot in the lift doors to stop them closing. '...or buy a new one while you're here!' she called after her. 'And don't forget to send Graham the bill.'

For a split second Lynn was torn between travelling up to Bridal in the lift with Brenda and Simon, and chasing after Mandy to ask for an introduction to her husband – only fair, she would argue, since Mandy knew hers so *very well*. Glancing down she saw the alarm on Simon's face and got in the lift. 'Who was that? Who's Graham?' she fancied she heard Mandy's escort ask before the doors closed.

'I thought we were going to lose you, Mum!' Simon protested.

Brenda was looking at her with some concern as they travelled upwards, as if she half expected her to burst into tears. Instead, Lynn gave her a beaming smile, elated at the result of her unexpected encounter with Mandy. Coming to Leeds hadn't been a waste of a day after all.

The dress Brenda chose was a sleek Empire line – a straight, long-sleeved affair in pure white satin, as different from Lynn's silk and pearls as possible, with cleaner lines, fewer embellishments, and a much lower price-tag. It was elegant, new, and looked well with the coronet of silk roses and the veil the assistant suggested. Since no alterations were necessary she wrapped it carefully in lavish amounts of tissue paper and handed it to Brenda in a carrier.

Simon tugged at Lynn's sleeve. 'Can we go home now?'

'Not yet; we've got to get a pageboy outfit for you.'

'I don't want a pageboy outfit. I want to go home. My dad's coming for me.'

After Brenda had rejected the second pageboy outfit he tried on, Simon grew rebellious, wriggling and pulling away from them, making it impossible to dress him, and acting generally like a little ruffian.

'When are we going home?' he demanded. 'I want to go home!'

Lynn gave up and handed the rejected outfits to the assistant.

'It's two o'clock already. I want a bite to eat and

108

a cup of tea. Then we'll go home,' she said, and promised Brenda: 'We'll get something for him in Hammonds.'

In the crowded café they managed to get a table just as some other people were leaving, and dumped their bags on the seats. Leaving Brenda and Simon to hold the table Lynn went to join the queue, but found her path blocked.

'Who are you, and who's Graham?' the man in front of her demanded.

Lynn saw Mandy sitting among her parcels at a nearby table. 'What's more to the point is, who are you?' she countered. 'Are you *that woman's* husband, or somebody else's she's just borrowing for a while?'

'I'm her husband!'

'Congratulations. Now, maybe you'll let me get past.'

Seeing that they were attracting some attention from the people at nearby tables he gave way, and Lynn continued towards the line of people waiting at the counter, glancing at Mandy on her way past. Rabbit in the headlights was an apt description for the look on her face. Lynn couldn't suppress a chuckle.

The husband stayed close behind her. 'You haven't answered my question,' he said.

She turned to face him, unable to wipe the smile off her face. 'I've given you enough clues, but if you can't figure it out for yourself let Mandy tell you. She knows.'

'She doesn't. She's never seen you in her life before.'

'All right,' Lynn shrugged, and joined the queue.

'You're a nutcase,' he said, and stared after her for a moment or two before returning to Mandy and her many parcels – glamour wear lavished on her by the doting idiot by her side, Lynn imagined. No wonder she didn't want to be named as co-respondent; she must have done her sums and decided she was better off with her blockhead of a husband.

Lynn made her choice of sandwiches and crisps, ignoring them both. By the time she'd waited for tea and orange juice and was taking everything back to her table, they were gone.

Brenda had heard some of the exchange. 'You should have told him straight,' she said, lifting plates of sandwiches off the tray. 'It would have served her right.'

'I did the best I could without a hammer and chisel,' Lynn shrugged, 'but he doesn't want to believe it, does he? So he won't. He called me a nutcase, and I'm calling him an idiot. No wonder she despises him.'

'How do you know she despises him?'

'Well, she went running after somebody else's husband, didn't she? Anyway, the code stopped me spelling it out for him.'

'What code?'

Lynn sat down. 'You know the one. The code that kept you and everybody else from telling Connie about Gordon and his best mate's wife and the barmaid at the Good Fellowship, and stopped all Graham's workmates and pals from telling me about Mandy. I thought I had a friend in Kevin Walsh's wife, but she left me in the dark as well.'

'Oh, *that* code,' Brenda said, through a mouthful of bread and ham salad. 'The tom cats' *omertà.*'

'That's it. Anyway, I couldn't say anything that might have started a fight in a posh shop like Schofields, could I?'

'I don't see why not,' Brenda said. Lynn liked her more than ever.

Chapter 16

'Where's Brenda?' Anthony asked when Lynn walked in with Simon.

'She went straight home. You didn't think she was going to bring her wedding dress here, do you?' Lynn answered, giving Alec a regretful smile as she sank into an armchair. 'You two passed your time in the pubs, I suppose.'

'Not all of it,' Alec protested. 'We went to the gents' outfitters to get sized up for morning suits.'

'Morning suits? With coat tails? And where are you going to wear them, after the wedding?'

'In Rayners ... why not?' Anthony laughed.

'We're not buying, only hiring, 'cause there isn't time to get 'em made to measure,' Alec said.

'It didn't take us five minutes. We didn't want to waste good drinking time.'

'I thought you had no money?'

'I've got a bit in the bank, 'cause I was never much of a drinker, before I met your brother. I used to save my money,' Alec said.

Lynn's eyes lit up and she gave him her most

caressing look. 'Ooh, a bloke with money in the bank!'

He laughed. 'Aye, I'm a good catch.'

'Has my dad been?' Simon demanded.

Anthony couldn't keep the look of disgust off his face. 'No, and he's not likely to, while I'm at home.'

Alec shook his head. 'Lay off, it's his dad.'

The phone rang, as if on cue. Anthony lifted the receiver and looked more than ever as if there were a bad smell somewhere. 'Well, speak of the devil. You'd better take it, Lynn.'

'Hello? Is that you, Lynn? My car's in for repair,' Graham said. 'There's no chance you can bring Simon to my mother's, is there?'

'No, sorry. I'm going out. I'll leave him at our Margaret's, and you can pick him up from there.'

'That's not very convenient. I don't know how the buses run.'

'Walk it, then.'

'That would take forever, and besides, it's a long way back for a four-year-old.'

'Not much further than me walking him to your mother's from here, is it? But you needn't bother taking him at all, if it's too much trouble. Take him next weekend, instead,' Lynn said. 'Leave him here while his uncle's home.'

'I don't want to stop here! I want my dad to come!' Simon howled.

'I don't want to leave him there. My mum and dad want to see him,' Graham protested.

'Lynn!' Alec said.

'Hold on,' said Lynn, and covered the mouthpiece.

'I'll have to go back to my digs to get ready to go out,' Alec said. 'I'll take Simon to his grandmother's in the taxi.'

Lynn nodded, and passed a slightly altered message to Graham. 'All right, we'll send him to your mother's in a taxi, then.'

'Fishermen throwing their money about again, I suppose,' Graham said.

Lynn's hackles rose. 'Well, they've earned it, haven't they?' she snapped. 'I *suppose* they can spend it how they want; and if it saves you the trouble of coming to fetch him you've got nothing to complain about.'

'Who's complaining? I'm not complaining.'

'Right, then,' Lynn said.

'Right, then,' Graham echoed, as she replaced the receiver. She lifted it again to add something she'd forgotten, then turned to Simon and gave him the message instead.

'Tell your dad to take you to Auntie Margaret's after tea, Simon. Tell him he can take you in a taxi if he's got no car.'

'I've often wondered what my life would have been like if I'd never met Graham,' Lynn said, in the pub that evening.

'It would be great. There'd have been no Graham in the way, and we could have had a double wedding with Brenda and Anthony,' Alec said.

'I'd probably never have met you at all. I had ideas about travelling the world on the cruise liners as a ship's nurse. That's what I really wanted to do, before Graham got in the way.

113

That's why I went into nurse training in the first place.'

'You'd have had the glamorous end of a life on the ocean wave, then,' Alec said. 'You'd have been mixing Alka-Seltzer for the idle rich, while we were hauling nets in, or sleeping in the fo'c's'le with a dozen other deckies.'

Anthony gave a wry smile. 'Oh, aye, I remember it well, the fo'c's'le. The first day I went to sea was on an old coal-burner. The bosun said: go and drop your seabag in the fo'c's'le. So I said: where's the fo'c's'le? Forrard, under the hatch, barmpot, he says. Then I couldn't find the hatch, so he had to come with me, and he wasn't best pleased. I only realised where it was when he shifted the ropes off it. So he yanked the lid up and I dropped my seabag down and it seemed to drop a mile. Get down there and find yourself a bunk, if you can manage that, he says, so I climbed down and there were two rows of bunks, three high on either side, and a metal pipe down the middle for the anchor chain. All the bottom bunks were taken so I had to climb up to one of the top ones.'

'Provide your own bedding, as well,' Brenda said, looking at Anthony.

'Be fair. They give us a straw mattress,' Alec said.

'Complete with vermin,' said Anthony.

'And you know why the bunks have got wooden sides when you get underway. You get thrown all over the place.'

'Your mammy never rocked you like a trawler does. It's worse than a fairground swing boat.'

'Ah, but when you're steaming home with a

good catch, and you get the lights on and the stove going, and you maybe have a game of cards, and all the old 'uns start spinning their yarns – it's magic. Really, sheer magic,' Alec said, a faraway look in his eyes.

'Aye, after you've slept for two solid days after ten days of fishing and gutting for eighteen hours a day. They tell some brilliant stories, though.'

'You must wish you were back in the fo'c's'le, then, instead of in your own nice private cabin,' Lynn said. 'You ought to ask to be put back to deckhand.'

'Oh, no!' Alec shook his head, jerked out of his nostalgia. 'You can never go back, you've got to go forward. But it was good ... some of it.'

'That's the thing about looking back,' Lynn said. 'You only remember the best bits. The rotten bits disappear down the memory hole.'

'Not with me, they don't,' Alec laughed. 'I soon made my mind up I wanted to be on the bridge, nice and warm under my glass sou'wester with the cook bringing me pots of tea every half an hour. Anyway, I'm glad you didn't go to sea.'

'I'm glad I didn't. I wouldn't have our Simon if I had, and I love him to bits.'

'Aye, he's a great little lad,' Alec nodded. 'Keen to see his dad, wasn't he? I used to be just the same.'

'Shame his dad's a waste of space, that's all,' Anthony said.

Conversation stopped when the landlady began a vigorous tinkling with a spoon inside a wineglass, calling for hush.

'Ladies and gentlemen, I give you...'

115

Lynn didn't catch the name. A local lad strummed a few chords on his guitar and opened with 'I'm so lonesome, I could cry...' She felt Alec's breath on her ear and heard a sly whisper: 'Your mother'll have gone out with her friends by now, won't she?'

She turned towards the most coaxing blue eyes that had ever met her gaze, and laughed. He meant to get her into bed, and the thrill she felt at the thought almost knocked her off guard. 'I wouldn't be surprised,' she said, 'but if you're thinking what I think you're thinking, we'd better not.'

'Why not? We're getting married as soon as you get your divorce.'

'Are we? I don't remember saying yes.'

'You didn't say no, so that must mean yes. Come on, Lynn – why not?'

She was sorely tempted, but she held back. 'Because I'm divorcing my husband on the grounds of adultery, Alec!'

'Come on, we won't see each other again for three weeks, after tomorrow. Why shouldn't we make the most of the time we've got?'

Lynn wavered.

'We might not get the chance again for months. Come on, live dangerously,' he urged, with a pleading look in his eyes.

'It would be just my luck for us to bump into Graham on the way,' she said, 'or for my mother to come back, and catch us.'

'Your mother's usually back late when she's out with her pals. You told me that yourself. And Graham never comes near this end of town.'

'He'll be coming to bring Simon down to Margaret's...'

'We'll take a taxi. He won't see us.'

'The taxi man will, though. I'm pretty well known round here and I don't want them blabbing about me taking men back to an empty house!'

'I'm not men! We'll walk it, then, and if we bump into Graham I'm Anthony's shipmate, that's all, just walking you back to your mother's...'

'What liars you men are!'

'Come on,' he coaxed.

Her resistance collapsed. They slid out of the pub before the song was finished, and walked back to Boulevard, Lynn's pulse quickening as they drew near to the house.

'She's left the kitchen light on. I hope she's not in,' she murmured.

'We'll soon find out.'

The door was locked. She inserted her key, but it wouldn't turn. It had been locked from the inside, and the key left in the lock.

'Hold on!' Nina called.

A minute later the door opened to reveal an effeminate-looking chap of about her mother's age, and her mother just beyond him, reaching into the kitchen cabinet.

'I've had to come home,' Nina said. 'Toothache! It's killing me!' She sat down at the kitchen table and took the cap off a tiny brown bottle, releasing the aroma of clove oil. She held the dropper steady and carefully squeezed some onto a tooth. 'Does my face look swollen?'

'No, not that I can see,' Lynn said.

117

'It feels it. I shouldn't be surprised if I've got an abscess under that, the gyp it's giving me. I'll have to go to the dentist's tomorrow.' She screwed the lid back on the bottle, and then sat back, gazing at them suspiciously. 'Anyway, what are you doing here?'

'Alec's lost his wallet somewhere. We're just checking he didn't leave it here,' Lynn said, looking inquiringly at the stranger.

'This is Piers. Piers Marson. He's a friend of a friend. He ran me home in his car.'

'Oh,' Lynn said.

'I'll be off then, Nina. Better get back to Marion,' Piers said, holding out his hand to Lynn.

His palm was damp, and his handshake as weak and flabby as a dead fish, making her feel like rubbing the sensation of it off onto her mini skirt. He gave Alec a similar perfunctory handshake and left, leaving them to search for Alec's wallet, which was nowhere to be found. Lynn made a show of taking some of her own money from the sideboard and then they followed Piers out of the door. He was just starting his car when they emerged.

Alec groaned. 'I wouldn't wish it on your mother, but if she had to have toothache, why couldn't she have picked another night?'

Lynn shook her head, as frustrated as he was at having their passion thwarted. 'Sod's law, I suppose.'

'I can't say I think much to that feller,' Alec said, watching him drive away. 'You don't think there's anything going on between him and your mother, do you?'

118

Lynn shook her head. 'Not a chance. She's not the sort to play around, and she wouldn't give him a second look even if she were. He's not man enough.'

'Well, there he goes, then, back to Marion. And talking about fibbers, you're a pretty nimble fibber yourself,' Alec said.

'Not as nimble at fibbing as at dancing,' she hinted. 'If we go to the West End Club you can mingle with the skippers again.'

Alec groaned. 'I'd rather mingle with you! You don't know what you do to me, Lynn.'

'I've been married long enough to have a good idea, but dancing's as near as we'll get to each other, this trip,' she said, and when passion died down she was glad that her mother and the friend of a friend had been there to save her from herself. Taking a risk like that would have been pretty stupid. It would have landed her in the ante-natal booking clinic on the patients' side of the counter more likely than not, and probably before her divorce came through.

Chapter 17

Just as Lynn was about to set off to collect Simon from Margaret's, the telephone rang.

'Simon slept at our house last night,' Connie said. 'We were only too pleased to have him.'

Connie went on to inform her that Graham had gone to work, Gordon had gone to the bank, and she couldn't leave the shop. Could Lynn pick Simon up?

Lynn thought for a moment of telling her to go next door and ask Alec to bring him down with him, but then decided she didn't want Connie to know anything about Alec. She gave a curt yes, and walked the two and a half miles up to Bricknall Avenue to collect him, fuming at Graham for being too mean to pay for a taxi to take him to Margaret's. There was certainly no chance of him lashing any of his money about – on them, at least. She arrived at the shop determined to collect her son and be gone, but the door was locked and a sign up: Closed for Lunch. A lunch hour would have given Connie enough time to bring Simon down to Boulevard had she wanted to, but she was no more inclined to exert herself for Lynn's benefit than Graham was. Lynn went round to the private entrance and upstairs to the living quarters, to find Simon halfway through a hot dinner of shepherd's pie – not liked at home, but eaten at Grandma Bradbury's all right.

'I thought I'd give him a bit of dinner, before he goes. He loves hot dinners, don't you, Simon?' Connie said, with an arch smile thrown in his direction.

'He gets plenty of them at home,' Lynn said.

'He loves your house on Marlborough Avenue, as well,' Connie challenged.

'He loves the swing, that's all, and I'm getting him one for my mother's garden. It's a shame, Connie, but Marlborough Avenue is over and done with for us. I wouldn't live in that house again for all the tea in China,' Lynn said, not relishing the dispute in front of Simon, but determined to make her position clear, once and for all.

Connie changed tack. 'The words of the marriage service are beautiful, I always think – *till death us do part*. People should stick to their marriage vows. I always have.'

'So have I!'

'But you're going for a divorce!' Connie protested. 'That's not sticking to your vows, is it?'

'Having other women in your wife's bed isn't sticking to your vows, either, Connie. And it's too much for some wives to stomach!'

'Graham's sorry about that; really sorry. He wishes he'd never laid eyes on her.'

'Come on, Simon, hurry up and finish your dinner if you want it, or leave it and let's be going,' Lynn said, abruptly.

Simon didn't budge. 'I'm finishing my dinner so I can have some pudding,' he said.

'Hurry up, then,' Lynn sat down on one of Connie's tapestry-covered cottage chairs to wait for him, watching her spoon rice pudding into a bowl. Poor, stupid fool with her nose to the grindstone all her life, standing in the shop all day while Gordon gadded off with his women! Polishing her floors and dusting her light fittings when the shop shut, and never looking up to see what was going on around her.

'Graham never wanted it to come to this. All this upsetment, it's making him ill. He's not eating,' Connie said.

'It's a pity he didn't take after you, then, instead of–' Lynn began, and stopped. It had been on the

121

tip of her tongue to enlighten her mother-in-law about the way Gordon had stuck to his marriage vows, but the code got the better of her and she bit her comments back. Let Connie live in her fool's paradise if she wanted to. Lynn couldn't blame her; she had been just such a fool herself, once. She would never have believed that Graham had betrayed her if she hadn't had the evidence thrust mercilessly under her nose.

Holding a spoon full of raspberry jam poised over the rice pudding, Connie looked up, directly into Lynn's eyes. 'I know what you're thinking,' she said, softly, 'but those women never meant anything. Gordon's still mine, and he always will be. And who wants a man nobody else wants?'

That bolt from the blue left Lynn speechless. With a smile of quiet triumph Connie removed Simon's dinner plate and put the pudding in front of him. 'He loves my rice pudding, don't you, Simon?'

Simon looked up at Connie with a smile that would have charmed the birds from the trees. 'It's lovely, Grandma,' he said, and it was with a shock that Lynn watched her young son consciously exercising his masculine charisma on his grandmother, and his grandmother playing up to it.

She frowned. He'd better not turn out like his grandfather, that's all, she thought – or his father, come to that. She wanted none of their tomcat tendencies in her son.

Recovering her self-possession, she said: 'I don't want a man nobody else wants, Connie. I want a man who wants nobody else but me.'

'You don't understand men, then.'

'I understand the sort of men who are loyal to their wives and families, and they're the only sort I want to understand. You can keep the rest,' Lynn said, and forbore from adding: *including Graham.*

'You could have knocked me down with a feather,' she told Brenda, when they were sitting in the Criterion that evening waiting for Alec. 'Dozy Connie's not that dozy after all! She's known what he's been up to for years, and she's put up with it.'

'No wonder he'll always be hers then, silly mare,' Brenda laughed, her blue eyes dancing. 'Why would he leave her? Where else would he find somebody daft enough to slave in the shop all day and then go home and slave in the house while he's off out chasing other women?'

'Aye, ironing his shirts so she can send him out looking like the cut-price Playboy of the Western World! My thoughts exactly,' Lynn said bitterly, thinking more of herself in that role than of Connie.

'Play*boy*? Cut price grandad, more like. She should press a few of his wrinkles out while she's got the iron handy,' Brenda said, with a chuckle. 'You've got to hand it to him, though, he's got it well organised, has Gordon!' Her voice held a touch of admiration.

'Not half. "Who wants a man nobody else wants?"' Lynn quoted. 'Can you beat that? I don't understand men, she says. I reckon she thinks I ought to be flattered that her son's bit-on-the-side came charging here from Leeds to move into my house.'

'Maybe it's her that doesn't understand marriage,' Brenda said, looking meaningfully up at Anthony as he placed a glass of Advocaat and lemonade beside her, complete with a cherry on a cocktail stick. 'It's a two-way street, as far as I'm concerned, so don't you get any funny ideas, Anthony.'

'Give us a chance, we're not even married yet,' he grinned, with a wink at Lynn as he set the rest of the drinks down. 'I hope Alec's not going to be long, or his beer will be flat.'

'She doesn't understand decency or loyalty, either. I was too slow. I ought to have told her there can't be many grandmothers who'd make the trollop who wrecked their grandson's home welcome in their house, half an hour after they've found out about her! That shows how much she cares about *Graham's* marriage vows!'

Alec walked in, and the conversation soon turned to morning suits and wedding protocol.

'I'm not looking forward to giving the best man's speech,' Alec said. 'I'd rather be the bridegroom. I wish it were us, walking down the aisle in three weeks' time.'

'I couldn't walk down the aisle, even if I were free,' Lynn said, the thought just dawning on her. 'I'd be a divorcee. If I ever get married again, it will have to be in a Registry Office. I've had it for the white frock business. You'd better get yourself a virgin bride if you want to trip down the aisle, Alec, and do it properly.'

Alec's eyebrows twitched fleetingly upwards

and a smile spread over his face. 'I'd rather do it improperly, with you,' he said. 'In fact, that would suit me down to the ground. Just us, the registrar and two witnesses.'

'Unless death had you parted,' Brenda said. 'You could have a church wedding then.'

'That's an idea,' Anthony said, swiping his index finger across his neck, cut-throat fashion.

'A bit over the top, though,' Alec laughed, 'even to get a church wedding. No, we'll wait for the divorce and then book the Registry Office.'

He seemed absolutely sincere. Such keenness, Lynn thought, with sudden misgivings. Just like Graham, at the start of their courtship ... *this is what I want, and I want it now!* He'd swept her along with him – and look how it had ended. And here was Alec, a year younger than her and as green as grass, galloping them down the path towards matrimony fast enough to break their necks. He could have no idea what marriage and bringing up a child was all about – and somebody else's child, at that. When the reality of that hit him, he'd run a mile.

'How long do you reckon it'll take?' Brenda asked.

Lynn shrugged. 'I dunno. You have to wait six weeks after the decree nisi before you can apply for the decree absolute.'

'We know that, but how long's the decree nisi going to take?' Alec insisted.

'I don't know. I suppose it depends how long it takes to get it into court. They're waiting on Graham sending some forms back.'

'You might be waiting forever, if he's decided

he doesn't want to go through with it,' Brenda said.

'Better see your solicitors and make them gee him up a bit, Lynn,' Alec urged.

'What's the rush? It's not a matter of life and death, is it? And a nice long wait will give you plenty of time to think about what you might be letting yourself in for.'

Like a four-year-old who's aiming to get us both back with his father in the old house, she thought, and a woman who doesn't know what she wants, except that she doesn't want to pour years of hope and energy into another failed marriage. Her priority was to get that midwifery qualification and then a decently paying job, to give her enough independence to go it alone if she had to. That was the only thing that was clear in Lynn's mind.

'I don't need time to think,' Alec said quietly. 'I knew what I wanted the first time we met.'

Lynn felt a stab of guilt. They would be sailing at midnight, and here she was, spoiling his last hours on shore. She couldn't send him back to sea doubting and disappointed, it might prey on his mind the whole trip. She put her hand on his and gave it a squeeze. 'I'll ring the solicitor's tomorrow,' she promised.

Chapter 18

Lynn rang as soon as she got home after an early shift the following day.

'It's the acknowledgement of service that's holding things up,' she told her mother as she replaced the receiver. 'Graham should have sent it back to the court within a month at the outside. They were sent at the end of May, and it's the middle of July. He says we'll have to ask the court to send a bailiff round to serve him with another copy of the divorce papers – or we can get a process server to do it,' Lynn said.

'So what does that tell you? That Graham doesn't want a divorce, obviously! He'd have sent it like a shot, if he had. He wants you and Simon back.'

'Hmm, well, it's not only what he wants now, is it?' Lynn said. 'There's what I want to consider, as well.'

'There's what our Simon wants, as well. What about him?' her mother asked. 'Does he get any consideration?'

'Our Simon's just a child, and he'll be all right. I'll look after him.'

'I'm looking after him as well, in case you've forgotten. And boys need a father, and if you get divorced it won't be long before Graham gets entangled with another woman, and when that happens he won't be round here three times a week to take his lad for his tea, I can tell you that. And if he gets any more bairns he might lose interest in our Simon altogether.'

'He'll manage without him, then. He's got my dad, and our Anthony.'

'A grandfather's not a dad, and our Anthony will soon have bairns of his own, by the look of things. Anyway, fishermen aren't much cop as fathers, they're never there. They're not much better as fathers than they are as husbands.'

'I love my dad! He was a great dad!' Lynn exclaimed, her colour rising and eyes smouldering as she sprang to her father's defence. 'He still is, and I'm just glad he's not here to hear you talking about him being no use as a husband!'

'I'm not saying he was *no* use; I'm saying he'd have been *more* use if he'd been here. And our Simon loves his dad – he talks about him nonstop when you're at work.'

'He can see his dad as much as he wants. I've never stopped him seeing his dad.'

'He won't see him; that's what I'm trying to tell you. And seeing his dad's not the same as living with him, is it? How would you have liked it, if me and your dad had got divorced?'

'I wouldn't have liked it, obviously.'

'Well, spare a thought for Simon, then. "I want to go and live with my daddy, in the house with the swing in the garden." He never leaves that theme alone.'

'Well, I'm afraid he's had the house with the swing in the garden,' Lynn retorted.

'I know what's wrong with you,' her mother burst out. 'Alec McCauley. You'd better get yourself on the pill if that's the case.'

'I'm not going on the bloody pill! I've got no reason to go on the pill,' Lynn said, almost stung into adding: and stop sticking your nose into my life, will you? She checked herself just in time. There was something so touchy and excitable about her mother lately that Lynn wouldn't have put it past her to turn round and tell her to look after Simon herself. That would spell the ruin of her hopes of getting on the Midwives' Register, and that wasn't the end of it. She would need her mother for a long time to come if she wanted to work.

'I think you should hold off on this divorce for a bit,' her mother said. 'Think about our Simon.'

'You mean I should put up with Graham and his other women for Simon's sake.'

'He's only had one other woman since he married you, and he wasn't long getting shot of her – and seeing as she lives in Leeds, he's not likely to be seeing any more of her, is he? Just think very carefully before you throw everything away, that's all.'

'What makes you think he got shot of her? What makes you think it wasn't her that got shot of him?'

'Because that's the way it's always been with Graham, from what I've heard. It was always him that finished it.'

'Well, it's going to be me that finishes it this time. And if you're talking about the house, I've already thrown it away. It's gone. I wouldn't live there again for a king's ransom.'

Her mother shook her head. 'A beautiful house

like that! And his wages! He's got a brilliant job and he's just had another rise – you could be set up for life. You'll never be able to get a house of your own on what you can earn ... certainly not like the one you had with Graham. Our Simon loved that garden.'

Lynn was suddenly sick of the subject, and had no intention of discussing it any further. 'I think I'll go down to our Margaret's, and have an hour with her,' she said.

'Well, you'll have to take our Simon with you, then. I'm going out.'

Lynn took Simon with her, complete with his pyjamas. He could get bathed with Margaret's four, and when she got back to her mother's all she would have to do is put him to bed.

Margaret was sitting on a dining chair on the pavement outside her tiny 'sham four' braiding a trawl net, with two lengths of twine held fast under the sash window. She favoured her mother in looks, with fair hair and blue eyes, and a figure kept trim by constant activity. Lynn watched her for a while, thinking how rough and sore the work had made her fingers. She had often felt guilty when with Margaret, being so much better off with the bigger, better house and the more successful husband. It had all seemed so unfair.

'I had to get away from my mother for a bit. She's driving me mad!' she exclaimed, as soon as Simon had run off to play street games with his cousins. One sweeping glance inside the open door showed her the state of the house – hearth not swept, Jim's best suit still hanging on one of the door-frames, his shoes still unpolished, and a pile of his unwashed shirts, socks and underwear decorating the top of the twin-tub washing machine, just visible through the kitchen door.

'He sailed this morning, then,' she said.

'Before six, and my stomach's still churning. I used to envy you, being married to somebody who's not a fisherman. You never had any worries he might not come back.'

Until Graham's affair had brought her right back to her mother's house and her roots, Lynn had almost forgotten the bag of nerves Margaret used to be every time Jim sailed. 'It's the middle of July! I don't know what you're worried about; there's twenty-three hours of daylight up there now. The twilight greets the dawn; it never gets dark!' she soothed, and added with a touch of irony: 'and the temperature's all the way up to freezing! Just think of it! And there's one thing to be said for being married to a fisherman, you'll never get phone calls from some bloody woman he met while he was away, will you? You'll never have that.'

'I wouldn't anyway, with Jim; he's not the type,' Margaret said, getting up and stretching her shoulders. 'I'll just have a little break, and make some tea.'

It was beginning to grate on Lynn's nerves, the way some women insisted that their men were 'home birds', or 'not the type'. Not the type who had much appeal for other women, more often than not, she thought, following her sister into the tiny kitchen – or maybe not the type who are stupid enough or brazen enough to get found out.

131

'The divorce job's stopped until Graham sends the acknowledgement of service back, so my mother's telling me he doesn't want a divorce,' she said.

Margaret turned to face her. 'I bet he doesn't. It's probably hit him like a ton of bricks, the thought of losing you and Simon, and the house and everything. But what about you, Lynn? Do you want a divorce, really? Wouldn't you be better off patching it up? You had everything, with Graham.'

'I ought to think about Simon and everything I'm going to lose, you mean.'

'Well, what's wrong with that?'

'You sound like my mother.'

Margaret switched the kettle on. 'She can get on your nerves, I know, but a lot of the things she says are true. If it were me, I'd give him another chance – if he's really sorry, I mean. Everybody deserves a second chance.'

'Depends what they've done.'

'I know, but...'

'But Graham doesn't want a divorce, and I ought to think about Simon, and with Graham I had everything,' Lynn recited. 'Yeah, I had everything. Everything but what you've got with Jim: a man I can trust. Graham's destroyed that. And not only that, I've met someone I really like. He's a friend of our Anthony's.'

'Alec, do you mean? But you said you'd never marry a fisherman.'

'I know I did. I didn't say I was going to marry him, I said I liked him.'

Four laughing, shrieking boys went galloping

132

up the staircase with Simon following after them, then charged just as quickly down again, and out into the street. Margaret went to the door. 'Don't go far! You've got half an hour, and then it's bath and bed!' she called, and turning to Lynn asked: 'So what sort of liking is it, then, if it stops you going back to Graham?'

Lynn shrugged, and Margaret looked uneasy.

'What does our Simon think to this Alec?'

'He thinks he's all right.'

'He's a year younger than you, or so our Anthony says.'

'That's not much, is it? It's not as if I'm old enough to be his grandmother.'

'And he's not our Simon's dad.'

'You don't say!'

Margaret bit her lip and turned away to put milk in the tea cups. 'There's no need to be sarcastic, Lynn. Do what you like. It's got nothing to do with me. Take a chair outside, and you can sit beside me while I get on with the braiding. The net man will be round with his lorry early doors tomorrow, and I want to have it finished.'

Lynn took a chair and sat outside watching Simon, who was engaged in a game of hide-and-seek with his cousins and a few other children.

There was a stiffness between the two sisters for the following few minutes and a deathly silence on the topic of the divorce for the rest of the evening, but by the time she went home Lynn was wavering, almost convinced she should go back to Graham. Simon needed a father, and preferably his own, as Margaret had made clear.

But if she ever did go back to Graham, she'd

have to make him so sorry he ever laid eyes on Mandy that there would be no more Mandies. Genuinely, *deeply* sorry, she thought, striding along with Simon trotting beside her with a coat over his pyjamas. He wasn't going to get away with passing this complete betrayal off as if it were a minor slip – and if he really meant what he said about wanting her and Simon back, he'd agree to her terms. If not, to Hell with him.

Chapter 19

Her mother was dolled up and ready to go out when Lynn got back home. 'Graham's been,' she said. 'He says you've really upset his mother.'

'Oh, dear,' said Lynn.

'Sarky. Anyway, he's told me to ask you to lay off her. None of it's her doing, is it?'

'She threw the welcome mat down for his floozie, though, didn't she? Anyway, enjoy your night out.'

'Don't worry, I will. Your dad's back on the morning tide.'

Lynn's mood lifted. 'Good. With a bit of luck he might get home in time for the wedding after the next trip, then.'

'Oh, and Graham left something for you. It's on the sideboard.'

Lynn read the tag: *To My Darling Wife, from your Loving Husband, Graham.*

'Enough to make you retch,' she murmured.

134

Her mother was halfway out of the door. 'What did you say?'

'I said I reckon I'll go to Fleetwood, and get to know Alec McCauley a lot better. I want to know what I'll be missing.'

'I've already told you what you'll be missing – wasting the best years of your life sitting in the house on your own,' her mother said, and was gone.

'I don't notice you sitting in the house much,' Lynn called after her, too late to be heard.

After early shifts on their separate wards Lynn and Janet boarded the bus for the journey into Hull, and took a seat together.

'Graham wants me back,' Lynn said. 'He never thought it would come to this, he says. He's devastated. He can't live without me. He says.'

Janet leaned back in her seat, the better to look at her. 'Can't live without you?' she mocked. 'Can't pay the mortgage without you, you mean. Maybe he was hoping Mandy would take up where you left off. He probably thought she'd chip in – and she didn't. I reckon that's when it all went sour, when they gave the sex a rest and got down to the nitty gritty, like who pays for what. That's when that sort of romance usually comes to a grinding halt.'

Lynn chuckled at the cynicism.

Janet failed to see the joke. 'You've got no help from his family, either, have you? Seeing their track record, it's not likely they'll be doing much to keep him on the straight and narrow, is it?'

'Just the opposite, as we've seen,' Lynn said. 'I

135

don't think the sanctity of marriage is a big deal with Mum and Dad Brad.'

'It would be a big deal if it were their Graham being made a fool of. Anyway, I've said enough already.'

'Say on. I want to know what you think.'

'Right, then. What I think is, the way he's working on Simon and your mother – it's disgusting. So when did he realise he couldn't live without you? As soon as he found out how much maintenance he'd have to pay?'

'Maybe,' Lynn grimaced. There were certainly no blinkers on Janet, she thought.

'Thank God I'll never have to face what you're facing,' Janet said. 'Dave might not be anybody's idea of a heart throb, but at least I know I can trust him. He's never looked at another woman since the day we started courting.'

Bump. Lynn's faith in Janet as an infallible guide to men and their motives took a rapid nose-dive and crashed to earth.

The photographer was already behind his tripod and ready for action when Lynn and her mother arrived at St John's Church. Anthony and Alec were standing by the church door in brilliant early August sunshine, wearing light-grey morning suits, grey silk cravats, white carnations and big smiles for the camera. Alec caught her eye and winked. She returned the wink, and the smile.

Brenda's friends and family were arriving in droves, the adults mostly in couples, the women in light suits or summer hats and dresses.

Margaret arrived with her four boys, and Lynn

136

thought that considering her limited means she had turned them out very creditably.

'I wish they'd given my dad and Jim a chance to get some time off. I think we're the only women here without a man,' Margaret said.

'Huh! Nothing new for me to be on my own,' Nina said, with a toss of her head.

'Our dad's in this morning. He'll just make it, I think,' Lynn said, twirling the white carnation she'd brought for him. 'And Anthony's had a stroke of luck. He'll get a couple of weeks off because the owners are keeping the ship in dock for a survey, so Brenda's dad's paying for them to fly off to the Adriatic on a proper honeymoon.'

'Jammy so and sos!' Margaret exclaimed enviously. 'All me and Jim got was a couple of nights in a caravan at Withernsea, and he sailed the day after that.'

'Well, I got as far as Cornwall,' Lynn said.

A woman in a light-green suit appeared, and took their minds off holidays, honeymoon or otherwise.

Margaret was outraged. 'Look at that! Green! Who in their right mind wears green at a wedding – and a fisherman's wedding at that!'

'Like a bad fairy at a christening,' Nina sniffed. 'Somebody on their side, obviously.'

A flower- and ribbon-bedecked wedding car glided majestically into view.

'She's here! She's here!' one of Brenda's young relatives squealed, and others took up the cry.

'She's here!'

Alec quietly took hold of Anthony's elbow and steered him inside the church. Most of the re-

137

maining guests followed. The car stopped and Brenda's chief bridesmaid got out, daintily lifting the skirt of her long pale blue empire line dress with one hand and hanging on to her bouquet of white roses with the other. A coronet of matching roses adorned her strawberry blonde curls. Two little bridesmaids carrying posies followed, and then Brenda's father in charcoal grey, complete with white carnation.

The photographer rushed towards the wedding car. 'Hold on, hold on,' he called. 'Bride stay in the car for a bit!'

Brenda gave them all a wave, and settled back into her seat.

'I want the bride in the car first, then I'll take the bridesmaids outside the church door, then the bride walking up to the church on her father's arm,' the photographer ordered.

'She's a good-looking lass, anyway,' Margaret said when Brenda got out. 'And so's she,' she added, nodding towards the chief bridesmaid, whose blue eyes and milk and roses complexion were very like the bride's.

'Orla, Brenda's cousin,' Lynn said, briefly.

Orla ushered the two little girls forward and stood behind them for the photographer.

'Pageboy as well,' the photographer ordered. Orla came over to collect him, all smiles.

'She's as nice as she looks,' Margaret whispered.

Simon took her hand and went willingly. He allowed the photographer to pose him and stared self-importantly into the camera with his chin proudly up, revelling in the attention.

Lynn almost burst with maternal pride. When the photographer had finished she leaned down to give Simon his final instructions. 'You come in after Brenda and her dad. Behave yourself, and do as Orla tells you.'

The organist struck up with the Wedding March. Lynn gave Simon a hasty peck on the cheek and hurried after the other stragglers into a church beautifully decorated with posies at the end of every pew and a magnificent flower arrangement by the altar, no expense spared. Lynn only hoped that Simon's behaviour would match his angelic face.

Her father slid quietly into the pew beside her just in time to see his son slip the ring on the bride's finger. Lynn handed him his carnation.

The photographer was lying in wait for them as they emerged into the sunshine, and brought everyone to a halt to take photographs of the groom kissing the bride at the church door. The chief bridesmaid and Alec were next, she linking his arm and gazing up at him, he looking down at her and smiling – not a welcome sight, in Lynn's eyes. With his wife now on his arm, Brenda's father looked as if a ton weight had been lifted from his shoulders. The happy couple and everyone near them were soon covered in confetti, and people shuffled about, laughing and slapping each other on the back and chatting while the photographer tried to herd the two families together for a joint photograph.

'He seems a nice enough lad,' Lynn heard when she dashed into the ladies' room just outside the reception hall, 'but we were hoping for somebody a lot better than a fisherman for her.'

'She's always been headstrong, our Brenda. Orla, now...'

In the mirror above the hand basins Lynn recognised Brenda's mother and one of her aunts. Who the hell were they, she thought, to talk about somebody 'better' than her brother, as hard-working and decent a lad as ever walked? And not only 'better', but 'a lot better'!

'Better in what way?' she challenged as she met their eyes in the glass.

They obviously recognised her. Both women averted their eyes and hurried for the door, with hands still wet. Lynn could almost feel the heat from their glowing cheeks as they walked past her.

Although wounded for Anthony, she let them go, rather than spoil the reception by saying any more. Why bother about them? They were nothing but a pair of bloody upstarts – just like Graham's parents.

'Somebody a lot better than a fisherman!' she fumed, after the door had closed on them.

But wasn't that the very thing she'd been aiming at herself, when she'd married Graham? Hadn't that been one of his major attractions – that he was a cut above the fishermen? She stared into the mirror at her own heated cheeks and bright, angry eyes and wondered at her own hypocrisy.

Well, that was all in the past. That was then, and this was now, and everything was different. It's amazing how love changes people, she thought.

When Lynn walked back into the reception room Orla was sitting next to Alec at the top table, smiling up at him with her long, milky white throat extended and that look on her face that all men recognise; the look that tells him more clearly than words: *I'm game – what about you?* There was another one from that superior family who was not too superior to think a fisherman might be good enough for her, Lynn thought, with a shock. She felt a surge of anger and dislike towards this seventeen-year-old who was so confident of her charms. How dare she? Brenda must have told her that she and Alec were a couple, but Orla was evidently acting on the 'all's fair in love and war' principle. Alec was a free man, and she, Lynn, was a married woman, not free yet even to wear his engagement ring – so what was to stop Orla?

Nothing was stopping her! She was eyeball to eyeball with him, all friendliness and vivacity, with her pouty lips parted in a half-smile. Her mere nearness to Alec was an affront to Lynn. Anger gave way to jealousy and fear, and watching them during the meal Lynn saw that if she didn't make sure of him soon she might lose him to this young predator.

She couldn't let it happen. Alec was the man she wanted and he was the man she was damned well going to have. She would see the competition off, even if the competition was a radiant redhead a full eight years younger than she was. Brenda's aunt would never have cause to complain that *she'd* hoped for somebody better than a fisherman for her daughter – not if Lynn had anything to do with it. At that thought her heart contracted in painful sympathy for Graham, and the grief he would feel when it finally sunk in that he'd lost them.

Brenda's mother tinkled on her glass for silence and Alec stood up. Like most mates, he made an impressive figure of a man, sturdy and well-proportioned with a direct, open countenance and humour in his eyes – a man who looked like a man, and the sort most people would be glad to know. He looked across at Lynn and laughed, took a nervous sip of wine and began.

'Unaccustomed as I am to public speaking, I'm not as nervous as you might think, after six pints of lager...' he began, in his Lancashire twang.

Orla squealed as if it were the funniest thing she'd ever heard, and the room erupted into laughter.

'...and you'll all be glad to know you won't be sitting through a long speech, because in about three minutes I'll be making a dash for the gents'...'

This prompted more peals of merriment from Orla, followed by a gale of laughter from everyone else, but Orla managed to out-laugh them all.

Alec began a mock-serious protest against the routine slur of 'drunken fishermen' from non-fishing folk, and followed it up with a couple of pithy tales of the bridegroom's youthful errors while 'under the influence', which made a mockery of the protest and tended to justify the slur. This was greeted with more laughter; even the waitresses were laughing. Orla laughed herself to tears and began dabbing her eyes carefully on her table napkin, evidently mindful of her mascara.

Lynn watched her annoying and obvious performance through narrowed eyes. That girl certainly knew how to massage a man's ego, and the trouble was that men could never see through it.

'I can see why you like him, Lynn,' Margaret said. 'Anybody would.'

Lynn nodded, glad to see Margaret enjoying herself. She hadn't seen Margaret laugh so much since they were children. Now Alec was looking into Orla's eyes, his own eyes dancing as he laughed at her laughter. After a minute or two he managed to pull himself together enough to pay the customary compliments to the bride, bridesmaids and both sets of parents, and to thank them all for coming. Brenda looked on, smiling demurely while he told her guests how much he was looking forward to seeing them all at the christening and they could 'set their stop-watches'. His ordeal was over too soon for his audience if not for him, but rather than make the anticipated dash for the exit, Alec sat down to listen to the rest of the speeches and drink the toasts. Then Anthony and Brenda stood up and left the table, and everyone else began to follow suit. Alec started to walk over to Lynn, with Orla not far behind.

'Ooh, wait! I nearly forgot!' Brenda called, and went back to collect her bouquet. 'Get ready to catch, girls!'

All the young women in the room turned towards her. Brenda turned her back on them all, and hurled her bouquet over her shoulder. Orla caught it, and tilting her chin gave Alec a come-hither smile, keeping him in conversation so long that Lynn wondered if he would ever manage to tear himself away from her. The bride and groom did a quick tour of their guests to say goodbye, while Simon, his cousins and the little brides-maids started chasing each other in a mad game of tig, until one of the girls fell over a chair and went howling to her mother, pointing to Simon as the cause of the accident.

'Say you're sorry,' Lynn demanded.

'I'm not!' Simon defied her, and began haring after the other girls, who were shrieking as they tried to evade him. Lynn chased after him and grabbed hold of him, but he wrenched himself free, and ran after one of the bridesmaids, laugh-ing triumphantly. Alec intercepted him and put a stop to the game by lifting him onto his shoulders and following the newlyweds out with the rest of the guests, to watch them drive off in a car well decorated with 'newly married' placards, and an old boot tied to the back bumper. Lynn joined them, thoroughly ashamed of her son. His beha-viour was worse than all Margaret's boys put together.

Orla fluttered her eyelashes at Alec. 'A honey-moon in the Adriatic!' she sighed, as the happy couple drove away.

'I hope they make the most of it, our Anthony especially,' Nina said. 'By the time the ship puts to sea again, summer will be over in the Arctic. They'll soon be back to about four hours of daylight, and fishing in sub-zero temperatures.'

'And that's September,' one of Anthony's ship-

144

mates added. 'Come December the only way to tell the difference between night and day around Bear Island will be to look at the clock on the bulkhead. There'll be perpetual darkness and force ten gales, or freezing fog, and the ship icing up...'

'Brrr.' Alec gave a mock shiver, and turned to carry Simon back inside.

'There's something for you to look forward to,' Lynn called after him.

'I can hardly wait!'

Once inside, he carried Simon a few yards away from the rest of them, put him on a chair and sat down beside him, cutting off his escape. Simon looked towards Lynn, as if signalling her to come to the rescue, but she left him there. A couple of minutes later he and Alec seemed to be deep in conversation. Orla soon drifted in their direction, accompanied by a couple of the young brides-maids. Eventually Simon jumped off his chair and went to play with them ... and Orla took his place.

Lynn began to relax. It was her son that Alec was interested in wooing, and by extension, Lynn herself – not Orla.

'Any progress with the divorce yet, Lynn?' he asked her later.

'No. I've been meaning to phone the solicitor, see if he can get things moving, but with all the wedding arrangements, and work, and studying, and one thing and another... Anyway, why worry about it now? There'll be plenty of time when you've gone back to sea.'

'What about coming to Fleetwood with me, then?'

'Sorry, I can't get the time off.'

'Have you even asked?'

'Of course I've asked! It's just that we're a bit short-staffed at the moment,' she said, guilt at her own failure to make a timely request for the days off forcing her into a half-truth, and making her snappy.

'Oh, well, I'll go on my own this time, then. Spend a few days with my mother, and bring the bike back,' he said, with disappointment written all over his face.

It was Lynn's turn to be disappointed. She had been looking forward to seeing a lot more of Alec while the ship was in dock, but she could hardly object to his going to see his mother, especially as she'd been invited to go with him.

Alec was not the only man interested in wooing Simon, Lynn thought, when Graham came to collect him a couple of days later.

'I've got a couple of people interested in the house,' he said. 'It looks as if we might not lose anything on it. So where do you want to live next?'

'You keep the house, if you want it, Graham. We won't be living anywhere next. We're getting divorced, remember?'

'No, I've got a terrible memory for things like that.'

'Go upstairs and get your shoes and your trunks, Simon,' Lynn said, determined to get Graham out of the way. 'Your dad's going to teach you to swim, aren't you, Graham?' If Graham was going to be using Simon as the pretext to intrude on her life at every end and turn, then he could damned well do a bit more with him than just dumping him at his grandmother's. He could do something that would benefit Simon, and that he would enjoy.

Simon looked eagerly up at his father.

'I hadn't planned on it, but...' Graham said, confronted by Lynn's challenging stare. 'Go and fetch your trunks, son.' Simon dashed off, pretty smartly.

'Good lad,' Lynn nodded.

'I am, aren't I?' Graham grinned.

She couldn't help smiling. 'Have you sent that acknowledgement of service back yet?'

'I can't remember getting anything to acknowledge.'

'We'll have to send the bailiff round with another one, then. It's pointless playing these games, Graham. All it'll do is add to the costs – and you'll end up paying 'em.'

'Come on, Lynn, give me another chance. I won't let you down. We had a lot of good times together.'

'And you had a lot of good times with Mandy. No, I'm not letting myself in for any more of that, Graham. I wouldn't trust you as far as I could spit.'

'It'll never happen again. Mandy's gone, and she won't be coming back. I want our family back to the way it used to be. I felt it more than ever when your Anthony got married. I should have been at that wedding, by rights.'

She laughed in his face. 'You're joking! I've heard of people having punch-ups at weddings, but if you'd shown up at that one there'd have been a massacre!'

After they'd gone, Lynn ruminated for a while about Graham's conveniently bad memory. He'd had those divorce papers for weeks; he was just making things as awkward as he could. So, if sending a bailiff round was the only way to progress matters, that's the way it would have to be.

She cleared everything off the dining-room table and set her books out, and then determinedly cleared Graham and everything else out of her mind and sat down to do some serious studying for her exam. It was more important than ever now. She loved Alec but she was set on making herself absolutely independent, and since she'd chosen to earn her own living she would do it in a job that she enjoyed. She couldn't afford to fail, and until she got that qualification everything else would have to take a back seat. She felt fairly confident. After all, she'd put enough work into it.

Chapter 20

Lynn went to see Anthony and Brenda in their little two-up and two-down on Gordon Street as soon as they were back from the Adriatic. The question burning in her mind had to wait while Brenda proudly filled the kettle, pointing out the half-tiling her father had done in the kitchen, and the new electric boiler he'd installed over the kitchen sink while they were away on honeymoon. The living room had been completely redecorated by Brenda's mother, and the pair of long gold brocade curtains hanging at the window had been made by the same woman who had made the bridesmaid's dresses.

'We brought you some fags back,' Anthony said, handing her a package. 'They're only a bob for twenty over there.'

After admiring everything there was to admire and hearing all that they were bursting to tell her about the wonders of the sunny Adriatic, with its golden beaches and warm sea, Lynn broached the subject most on her mind.

'Have you heard anything from Alec?'

'Not yet. Why?'

'Because I haven't seen hide nor hair of him since the day after the wedding.'

Anthony looked dumbfounded. 'Well, I haven't seen him since we got back, either. He's probably still at his mother's. With the ship being in dock, he probably decided to spend a bit of extra time there. He's been catching up with a few of his old shipmates in Fleetwood, maybe.'

'Maybe he has, but why would that stop him phoning me?'

'Maybe his mother hasn't got a phone.'

'There are such things as public telephones, Anthony. But supposing the nearest one is miles from his mother's, why hasn't he written? I've looked for a letter or a postcard from him every day, but it's been over two weeks, and I've had none.'

'Didn't you write to him?'

'No. I didn't get his mother's address. It never crossed my mind to get it, because I thought he'd

149

have phoned me. I just hope he hasn't had an accident on the motorbike.'

'I shouldn't think so.' Anthony seemed at a loss for anything else to say.

Lynn turned to Brenda. 'Did Orla go with him to Fleetwood?'

'No, she didn't,' Brenda said, her cheeks growing pink.

Lynn raised her eyebrows, stunned to have her worst fears so convincingly confirmed.

'She didn't go with him,' Brenda insisted, 'but she's seen him since he came back to Hull.'

'Since he came back to Hull!' Lynn echoed.

'She bumped into him when she went to the dock offices, to see about a job there. He told her he'd be sailing on the *Sprite*, on the twenty-fifth. He'd just signed on.'

Anthony looked as surprised as Lynn. 'That's tomorrow. Why hasn't he been to see our Lynn, then?'

'How do I know?' Brenda shrugged. 'Maybe he doesn't want to be seen out with her on his own before she gets her divorce. Maybe he thought he'd better not disturb her while she's studying for her exams. I don't know.'

'We hadn't seen each other for nearly a fortnight – and he thought he'd better not disturb me?' Lynn exclaimed. 'Wasn't he talking about us getting married not so long ago ... or was that just my imagination?'

'Well, I don't know,' Brenda repeated.

'When exactly was it that Orla bumped into him?'

'Yesterday, I think. Or maybe the day before. I

can't remember, exactly.'

'Hmm,' Lynn said, starting to open one of the packs of cigarettes she'd just been given.

Anthony pushed an opened packet towards her. 'Here, have one of mine.'

She took one and he gave her a light. Brenda disappeared into the kitchen, leaving them alone.

'You'll be sailing yourself in a day or two, I suppose?' she said.

'I've signed up as mate on the *Nimrod*,' he said, obviously over the moon. 'We're sailing after the bank holiday.'

Lynn smiled, glad for him. 'Congratulations! Pity they didn't give you a better ship, though.'

'Oh, well, that's the way they do it. You start on the bottom rung, in the worst ships. If I get a good trip in, I might get a better ship next time.'

He'd be lucky to get a good trip in on that old thing, Lynn thought. Men on the old ships were handicapped from the minute they sailed.

'Have you told my mam?'

'Not yet. I haven't had time.'

'After the bank holiday,' she repeated. 'This must be the longest holiday you've had since you left school.'

'It is.'

They smoked in thoughtful silence after that, while Brenda kept up her clatter in the kitchen, and later upstairs. Lynn left shortly afterwards, with a suspicion that her sister-in-law knew rather more about Alec's defection than she was letting on.

Chapter 21

Graham looked as if he'd swallowed something that disagreed with him when he brought Simon back from his mother's a couple of days later. 'We've had the bailiff round – at my mother's!' he said. 'Thanks a lot, Lynn.'

'You've been served, then,' she said.

'I certainly have. Not served right, though.'

'I'd say you are.'

'I wouldn't. I'm a reformed character now.'

'Really? For how long?'

'For ever. Come out for a drink with me to-night. We've got to talk things over.'

'I'll look after Simon,' Nina volunteered, looking pointedly at Lynn.

'No thanks,' Lynn said, shortly. '*I* haven't got to do anything.'

'You really mean to throw everything we had away then? Lose everything?' Graham asked.

At last, it had sunk in. This was exactly what she had foreseen, and in foreseeing it she had felt an unbearable grief for Graham. His face was haggard; he looked devastated – but Lynn had come a long way since the day she'd stood with Janet in that house in Marlborough Avenue, grieving for his grief. She'd loved and lost another man, had her trust betrayed a second time – and now she felt vindictive. Let him suffer ... why not? He'd made her suffer, and now it was her turn to put

152

the boot in. 'Why do you think I sent the bailiff round, Graham?' she demanded.

He looked at her as if she'd kneed him. Simon turned an angry little face towards her. 'Stop being nasty to my dad!' he shouted, and went to cling on to Graham's legs.

'I can't believe it! Everything we've worked for. What for? She's gone! There's no earthly reason, now,' he almost wept.

'That's a matter of opinion – but we'll keep this discussion for another day,' she said, conscious of Simon's burning eyes on her.

'And I'm in line for another promotion!'

Nina's ears pricked up at that. 'Another promotion?' she said. 'They must think a lot of you, Graham.'

Graham acknowledged the compliment. 'They do. I only wish everybody did,' he said, looking towards Lynn.

'Well, congratulations. You won't have to quibble about the maintenance settlement, then,' Lynn said.

'That's something else we've got to talk about,' Graham said. 'We've got to come to an agreement about that, instead of letting solicitors rack their fees up at our expense.'

The money! She saw Brian Farley's twinkling eyes and sly smile in her mind's eye, and burst into laughter. 'They're not going to be racking their fees up for me, Graham. My divorce will cost me thirty bob, no matter what,' she crowed.

'And it will probably cost me fifty times as much; money that would be better spent on us, as a family. We are a family, Lynn, and I'm fed up

153

with being a part-time father.'

'You see him as much now as when you lived with us.'

'I don't. How can I? And it's not the same. I'm not there when he gets up in a morning, or when he goes to bed. We only ever share a meal at my mother's. He's not in my home, and I want that back. There's the whole question of who looks after Simon to be discussed.'

Lynn stared at him, open mouthed. 'Of who looks after Simon? There's never been any question about who looks after Simon. I look after him.'

Simon scowled at her.

'Hold on a minute,' Nina said. 'When it comes to looking after Simon, I do more than anybody.'

'But that's the same as me looking after him,' Lynn said. 'I'm the one who's responsible.'

'It'll be the same as you looking after him when you are looking after him, and I'm out at work! That's when *you'll* be the one who's responsible,' Nina said.

Lynn looked at her, aghast. 'But you've never had to work! My dad never wanted you to work.'

'Well, I've got news for you; it's not only what your dad wants – and it's not only what *you* want, either. It's time I got some consideration.'

Simon put his hands over his ears. 'Stop arguing,' he shouted.

'You two,' Nina said, 'had better go for a walk, and settle your differences somewhere else, instead of upsetting this bairn.'

Flushed with anger, Lynn grabbed her jacket and went, closely followed by Graham.

'Job done, Graham,' she said, storming on ahead of him. 'You've achieved what you set out to achieve! You've caused a lot of trouble, but you needn't imagine any court would grant a father custody of a four-year-old rather than a mother, because they wouldn't!'

'Why has it got to be either, or? Simon needs two parents; why can't he have both? We had a good life together, Lynn.'

'We had a great life together – that's the reason you started getting your leg over with Mandy. You thought you had me safely fastened in that house with Simon, helpless to do anything about it. Well I'm not helpless. I'm not your mother, Graham, I'm nothing like her, and I won't be sitting on the nest while you're out with your barmaids and' – a new thought struck her – '...maybe your best friend's wife!'

Graham was outraged. 'I'd never do that to Kev!'

'You did it to me, though! So now I'll earn my own keep and paddle my own canoe. You men are all the same, a set of cheating bastards.'

'You've changed, Lynn, and not for the better. You've turned hard.'

She laughed at that, and then assumed an expression of puzzlement. 'I wonder why?'

'There's still Simon. Something's got to be sorted out about him, and if you're busy paddling your own canoe, who's going to be looking after him? It sounds as if your mother's getting fed up with it.'

'She's not fed up with it at all, she loves Simon. She's just trying to push me back to you.'

'Somebody with some sense, then. I love him as well, and I want to be a proper father to him.'

'A bit late in the day, if you ask me.'

'I've always done my best for Simon!'

'The best thing you could have done for Simon would have been to be a decent husband to his mother! Then she wouldn't have had to leave!'

'You didn't have to leave! It would have all blown over.'

'You're not listening, Graham! Get this: I'm nothing like your mother. I object to you having other women in my bed. I even object to you having other women out of it. The solicitor jargon says: "the petitioner finds it intolerable..." – and it's spot on! I do find it intolerable.'

'I wish I could turn the clock back, but I can't! Lynn, listen to me, Lynn, don't throw everything away because of one stupid mistake!'

'It wasn't stupid, Graham,' Lynn said, trying to stop her lip quivering, 'it was evil!'

He looked astounded. 'Evil! That's going a bit far, though.'

'Hard for you to see, that, isn't it? Seeing how adultery runs in your family.'

'Adultery runs in my family! How do you make that out?' he demanded, with a laugh. 'Adultery's not a hereditary disease, Lynn.'

'What is it, then?'

'It's a big, stupid mistake, and it's not worth all the upheaval it causes. I've done with it. I want my family back.'

She looked him in the eye. 'I wouldn't trust you as far as I could throw you, Graham. It'll take you a long time to get that back, if you ever do.'

She turned her back on him and walked briskly away, wondering why she'd said that. Did she mean to go back to him, after all? She couldn't go back to him; Alec was the man she loved. But Alec had stayed out of touch with her for two solid weeks, and then returned to Hull and seen Orla, and then sailed away on the *Sprite* without as much as a word to her – the woman he supposedly intended to marry. Truthfully, half the punishment she'd just dished out to Graham had been caused by her anger at Alec, and her bitter disappointment in him.

Graham ran to catch her up. 'Simon starts school in September; I'd have liked us to be back together before then,' he said.

'Not a chance. You must be out of your tiny mind.'

'So where's he going to start?'

'St George's.'

'With a lot of little hooligans from Hessle Road! What's he going to learn from them, apart from a lot of cheek, and bad language?'

Lynn reared back as if she'd been stung. 'You're talking to a hooligan from Hessle Road! And my nephews go to school in Hessle Road in case you've forgotten, you arrogant little–'

'Ah, but you've pulled yourself out of it – and you want better for Simon, surely.'

'I want better for Simon, all right. I want better for him than having to listen to a lot of bloody condescending crap from people like you and your mother – the ten-bob aristocracy! If only you knew how ridiculous you are!'

'There's no need to be abusive.'

157

'You're the one that's being abusive, looking down your nose at people. And if "pulling yourself out of it", as you call it, entails looking down on your own family, then we'll be a sight better off getting right back in it – me and Simon both!'

'I'm sorry – that wasn't what I meant. I don't want to fall out with you, Lynn. We've got to start talking. And we've got to keep talking, whether we get back together or not. We've got our Simon to think about. We've got to come to some agreement, unless you want him to be brought up on a battlefield.'

He was right, of course. There could be no clean break. Having Simon meant that she would never be free of Graham intruding in her life. There could never be an end to it, and for Simon's sake, she would have to make the best of it, and be civilised about it. She took a deep breath. 'No, I don't want him brought up on a battlefield, Graham.'

'Well, don't take a bite out of me every time you see me.'

'Don't insult my relations, then.'

'I didn't. Even so, you've got to admit there are better schools than the ones around Hessle Road.'

'Don't start.'

'No fear,' he said. 'I know better, now.'

She left him at the gate.

Simon was ready for bed when she went inside, and very off-hand with her. Nina was having one of her rare nights in, so Lynn walked up to Janet's to get the latest episode with Graham off her chest. She still felt too raw about Alec to mention him, but left Janet's house feeling calmer, and went to bed half an hour after she got home.

Simon was still awake. He watched her, stony faced, while she pulled on her pyjama bottoms before taking off her skirt, and put on the pyjama top before wriggling out of her bra and pulling it through the sleeve – all done in less than a minute.

'I want to go and live with my dad in the big house,' he said, when she hopped into bed beside him.

Icy fingers of fear clutched at her heart. 'Not you as well! Do you really want to go and leave me, Simon? Really?'

He nodded. His lip trembled, and then he threw his arms round her and burst into tears.

Chapter 22

'I went to the housing department the other day, to see if I could get a council house near my mother,' Lynn told Janet when they were eating lunch in the staff dining room a day or two later. 'There's no chance.'

'I didn't think there would be. You might get something with a private landlord, though, if you're that desperate.'

'Desperate is right – I've had a look round a few, and you'd have to be, to take any of the ones I could afford. There's none I'd want to live in, and I'd hate to have to take Simon to any of them. He's a connoisseur of houses. He's got very high standards.'

'I don't blame him. Be quite a come-down, wouldn't it, after the house with the swing in the garden,' Janet said. 'Even a kid must feel a move like that. But needs must, when the devil drives, and he might have to get used to it. Is it that bad at your mother's?'

'We get on each other's nerves at times, but it's not that it's bad, exactly – it's more that I'm a grown woman with my own child, and I feel as if I ought to have a place of my own.'

'Hmm, maybe,' Janet said. 'But if it's not that bad, you'll be better off staying at your mother's, where you're both comfortable. At least he's got his grandmother on tap. You don't have to drag him out of bed at the crack of dawn and rush him off to some childminder before you come to work, or pick him up and drag him back home when it's hours past his bedtime, like some of the lasses do. Or rush about shopping, and washing, and getting meals ready.'

'I miss doing my own shopping and cooking and washing, strange as it might seem.'

'I know what you mean; so would I, but then there's the never-ending stream of bills coming through the letterbox, don't forget – and only one salary, and a pupil midwife's at that. I reckon you're better off where you are until Simon's a few years older. You might be jumping out of the frying pan into the fire, if you move.'

'I know, forever skint for the privilege of living in some depressing grot-hole in a terrible area.

I've thought about it, and I reckon you're right. She will keep on dishing her advice out, though. It's annoying.'

'Take no notice, then,' Janet shrugged. 'Just say *aye* and *no* in all the right places, and let it roll off you, like water off a duck's back. It's better than bleeding money out to some Rachman landlord for one of his pig-sties.'

'I reckon you're right, at that,' Lynn repeated.

'He's completely buggered your life up, hasn't he, that little swine,' Janet frowned.

Graham called on the sunny Sunday morning before August Bank Holiday, to take Simon to West Park.

'It's the last chance he'll get to go in the paddling pool,' he said. 'They'll be emptying it before the kids go back to school, getting every-thing ready for winter. Why don't you come with us? Get away from those books for a bit.'

'This is something new,' Lynn said. 'I've never known you to be so clued up about paddling pools before.'

Simon grabbed her hand, and looked eagerly up at her. 'Pleeease! Please, please, pleeease, come to the paddling pool,' he begged.

She looked down at his hopeful little face, wavered, and gave in. Simon was overjoyed. It seemed a small sacrifice, to see him so happy.

'But you needn't think I'll be making a habit of it,' she told Graham.

'I don't.'

Simon held both their hands on the walk up to the park, in ecstasies when they ran and swung

161

him in between them.

'How's the newlyweds doing?'

'All right.'

'He must be back at sea by now.'

'He's not. He's got a mate's job. He sails on Wednesday.'

'Just married, and a promotion. He'll be on decent money, then.'

'It all depends how much fish they can catch. If they don't catch enough, he could land in debt.'

'Ah. Good luck to him, then. Might not be long before he's a skipper.'

The park was packed with people out with their families. The pool was full of young children with the August sun beating down on their pale skins, and glittering on the water. Simon stripped down to his trunks and was in the pool in a minute.

He beckoned to Graham. 'Come on in, Dad!'

Graham took off his shoes and rolled his trousers up, and joined Simon and the handful of other parents paddling round beside their young children. Just as he'd done last summer, in the pre-Mandy days, Lynn remembered. She walked beside them for a while, and then spotted Brenda and Orla, sitting on one of the benches. Well, well, she thought and strolled over to them.

'We wondered when you'd notice us,' Brenda said. 'I didn't expect to see you out with Graham.'

'I'm not out with Graham. I'm just tagging along because Simon wanted me to.'

'He'll like that, being out with you both. We're just waiting for Anthony to pick us up, then we'll get the girls out of the pool and drop them off. We're going to do a bit of shopping together while

162

he's at home.

'Speak of the devil!' Lynn said, as she saw Anthony coming towards them – accompanied by Alec. 'I thought Alec was supposed to have sailed on the *Sprite*!' she exclaimed.

'Oh, yes,' Brenda said. 'There was some sort of trouble with it, I didn't quite catch the details.'

Simon had done a lap round the pool, followed by Graham. He stopped when he saw Brenda and Orla and shouted to them, all smiles and eyes sparkling.

'I'm paddling with my dad! I'm starting school soon! My dad's bought me some new shoes!'

'New shoes!' Orla laughed. 'That's lovely, Simon. I love new shoes! I'm going to get some today.'

But now Simon had spotted Anthony and Alec and shouted the same news to them.

'That's great, Simon!' Alec called back.

'Yeah, wonderful,' Anthony said, sardonically.

Graham wisely stayed in the pool, and Simon paddled away with him.

Orla smiled up at Alec and got to her feet. 'Come and help me round the girls up,' she invited.

Alec looked towards Lynn and when she met his eyes he held her gaze, looking as uncomfortable as any man could.

'You're off into town, then?' she said.

He nodded. 'Maybe for an hour or two.'

He didn't ask her to join them, nor did he ask about the divorce. Lynn chose to cling on to her tattered pride rather than tell him something that apparently no longer concerned him.

163

Orla left them no time for further conversation. 'Come on, Alec, come and help me get them,' she urged. 'They've been in there two hours already.'

Alec did as he was told. Anthony was very quiet as he watched them go.

'Shortest trip I've ever heard of,' Lynn said. 'It can't be a week since he was supposed to have sailed.'

Anthony gave her the sort of look people reserve for the bereaved. 'A bit of trouble with the crew, from what I've heard.'

'Really!'

'Simon looks as if he's enjoying himself,' Brenda said, brightly. 'Which school will he be going to?'

Alec and Orla came back with the little girls while they were discussing the merits and de-merits of various infant schools, and Brenda and Orla began to towel them dry and dress them. The caressing glances and the little smiles she kept throwing in his direction made Orla's interest in Alec obvious to everybody. Alec himself seemed only too aware of them, but kept stealing glances at Lynn, looking as comfortable as an insect on a pin.

'He's a great little chap,' he said, nodding towards Simon, still happy in the pool with Graham.

Anthony was evidently itching to get away. 'Right, we'll be off, then,' he said, as soon as the girls had their shoes on.

'No taxi?' Lynn asked.

'No need, we're turning into landlubbers. We've been ashore so long we've got time to bus it everywhere.'

Alec turned as they walked away. Their eyes met and he waved a goodbye. Lynn returned his wave, thinking she'd never seen a man look so despondent – probably the result of bumping into your old love just as you're getting on with the new, she imagined. They were probably going to drop the girls off, and then they'd be out as a foursome for a meal at the King Edward, or Hammonds or somewhere else, and tomorrow, Bank Holiday Monday, they'd be having a day out – while she was at work, she thought, bitterly.

The bench that Orla and Brenda had vacated was claimed by two other women. Lynn sank down beside them, feeling as if she'd been kicked in the stomach. She would never have believed it of Alec, never in a million years. And what had been the point of all that tripe that Brenda had told her, about him sailing on the *Sprite*? If he wanted to finish with her and take up with Orla, why couldn't he have told her, straight out?

Simon had climbed out of the pool, and was running towards her, followed by Graham. Could he have an ice cream, please?

'This is how families ought to be – together!' Graham said, as they followed him to the ice-cream van. 'Mandy was never the woman for me; not enough personality. I realised that the day you came home and tossed all her clothes out of the window. That's my Lynn, I thought. What a woman!'

'Huh! And you were hiding in the bloody bathroom with her,' Lynn snorted. 'I remember it well.'

'And you nearly kicked the door in. I wouldn't have dared come out!' he laughed. 'You're magnificent when you're angry.'

Lynn's laugh was rather hollow. 'Get lost, Graham,' she said.

'And then you went out and stamped on her watch.'

'Did she ever send you the bill for that?' Lynn asked. 'I told her to.'

'Yeah, you did, but I've never heard a thing from her since she went back to hubby.' He turned to look at her, suddenly serious. 'It's over, Lynn. It's over for good. I want my family back.'

For the rest of the day Lynn was everything that was wonderful, beautiful, witty, and amusing, by Graham's account. She was constantly reminded of all the good times they'd had together, until his relentless flattery and boundless charm began to wear down her resistance. By the time he dropped them off at her mother's Lynn was beginning to think that her feelings for Graham might not be quite dead, after all.

'Boys need fathers, Lynn,' he said, his eyes gazing soulfully into hers through the open car window. 'They do better with two parents. They don't need to be ping-ponging between the two. I made a terrible mistake, I admit, but there's no need to turn it into a tragedy.'

Lynn had no intention of getting into that discussion. 'Thanks for the lift, Graham,' she said. 'Come on, Simon.'

'Bye, son,' Graham said, as they walked to the door.

A mournful quality in his voice sent Simon

dashing back to give him a farewell kiss. 'Bye, Dad!'

'Come on, Simon. He's not going to Australia,' she snapped, irritated by the way Graham was manipulating him.

'Think about what I've said,' Graham called after her, as they went inside.

She closed the door in turmoil, but a minute later Graham, and everything he had said slid out of her mind. It was filled with Alec, and the expression on his face as he'd turned and waved goodbye to her. She'd never thought him the sort of man who says things he doesn't mean, the kind to make empty promises just to get a woman into bed. In spite of three weeks' total neglect she could still hardly believe it, but the fact had to be faced – she wasn't the great judge of character she'd imagined herself to be. She'd got Graham all wrong, and probably Alec as well. But if their love-affair was over, Alec was going to have to face her and spell it out, even if she had to go and hunt him down in his lodgings. He wasn't going to get away with slinking off as if all those declarations of love and promises of marriage had never been made. He was going to have to face her, and explain himself.

'Bank Holiday Monday tomorrow – I thought you'd be going out,' Lynn remarked, when she came downstairs after putting Simon to bed, and saw Nina sitting on the settee watching television.

'Not tonight,' Nina said. 'I fancy a night in.'

Lynn sank into an armchair.

'Aren't you going to get your books out?'

167

'Not in the mood.'

'What's up with you? You look as if your dog just died.'

'I'm just a bit tired, that's all.'

They sat quietly together watching television, and at around ten o'clock Nina got up and made two mugs of cocoa. They sat sipping it like two old women – Lynn staring into her cup and musing about Alec.

'Penny for your thoughts,' her mother said.

'They're not worth it,' she replied, and after a pause asked: 'Do you think it's possible to love two men? At the same time, I mean.'

'I'm certain it is. People can have a dozen kids and love 'em all, so what's the difference?'

'What's the difference? Between the love you feel for a man and the love you feel for a child? Massive, I'd say.'

'Well, it's not the *same*, obviously,' Nina conceded, 'but I reckon you can love two. Men seem to manage it, so why not us? Graham, for example. I reckon he still loved you even when he was carrying on with that Mandy.'

Lynn gave a grim little laugh. 'She was just a "bit-on-the-side", to use his own words. Nothing serious. Never meant anything, he said.'

'She probably didn't, or not much, anyway. He wouldn't have put himself out to run to Leeds, and she'd soon have got fed up of traipsing here. If you'd never found out it would have died a death, and no harm done. What the eye doesn't see, the heart doesn't grieve over.'

'Reminds me of that toast my dad says they raise on the ships. "To wives and sweethearts..."'

168

Nina raised her mug of cocoa and gave the traditional rejoinder: '"May they never meet!" Too right. It causes some shit when they do, as we've seen.'

Chapter 23

Lynn went to confront Alec in his digs after her shift the following day. The landlady showed her into a drawing room smelling of polish and with a bright fire burning in the grate, where Alec sat at a dining table covered with a plush cloth, looking at maps and charts. He looked up, startled to see her there. The landlady shut the door and left them together.

Lynn pulled out a chair and sat down opposite him, looking him straight in the eye. 'Remember me? Or have you had an attack of amnesia, these past few weeks?'

He held her gaze. 'I'm never likely to forget you, Lynn.'

'But you shot off to Fleetwood on your own, and you never once rang me or even dropped me a postcard for three weeks, and then the first I hear of you coming back to Hull is from Brenda, giving me some cock-and-bull story about you sailing on the *Sprite* – and a week later I see you out with Orla. Thanks a lot, Alec.'

'I wasn't out with Orla at all, and I was on the *Sprite*.'

'A trip generally takes three weeks.'

169

'It does unless one of the crew puts an axe through the hydraulics that control the steering gear. I'd heard it was an unlucky ship before we sailed, but I didn't realise how bad it really was. We didn't get past Scarborough because the ship wouldn't answer the wheel, and to make matters worse we had no radar. We'd already called in at Grimsby to get that repaired, and it had gone again. So we were sitting in thick fog with no steering and no radar. The skipper had to ask another ship for a tow back to Hull; there was nothing else he could do. There's going to be a court case about it.'

'Speaking of court cases, have you forgotten my divorce? You seem to have lost interest in it. If you were going to finish it, you might have had the decency to tell me.'

His posture changed. Instead of sitting up straight and tall on his chair he slumped against it. 'I didn't know what I was going to do until I'd been in Fleetwood for a few days, and I thought you'd lost interest in the divorce yourself, the last couple of times I asked you about it. You're still hankering after Graham, Lynn. You're not really free.'

'I soon will be.'

He grimaced and shook his head. 'I don't think we were ever destined to be more than friends.'

'I'm not hankering after Graham,' she insisted. 'I know what's wrong with you, though. It's Simon. You've had a little think, and you've thought better of taking on the ready-made family.'

'It's not the ready-made family at all! Not the way you mean, anyway. I've got no objection to

170

Simon, but I know how he'll feel about me, because of the way I felt about my stepfather. All I ever wanted Jack to do was get lost, so my mam and dad could get back together. He probably wasn't a bad feller looking back on it, but he could have been the best man ever born, and I still wouldn't have wanted him near my mother. I wanted my dad. My own dad – and Simon's the same.'

'You got over it, and so would he.'

He leaned back in his chair to look at her. 'Oh, Lynn – you've no idea! Kids don't get over it, they put up with it – because they're powerless to do anything else. I remember yelling when we were leaving our house for the last time: "I'm staying here!" But my dad was at sea, and I couldn't stay there on my own so they had to drag me out, and I bore a grudge for years. Still do, truth be known. And that day I gave Simon a lift to his grandmother's in the taxi – it took me right back to all that because he talked about his dad non-stop. "My mum and dad argue about me," he said, "but they're going to stop arguing and get back together, my dad says." And I knew he was warning me off, just by the look in his eyes. It's amazing what kids sense, and I thought: what am I doing? But I shoved it to the back of my mind. Then at the wedding – I mention his dad, and his face lights up! His eyes shine when he talks about him: *my dad!* I got a good idea what my stepfather must have felt like, then. Jack was never bad to me; I never had any reason to dislike him other than the fact he wrecked my family – and then he wanted me to call him Dad! It would have choked

171

me – and the more he tried to be a substitute father, the more I resented him. I went to sea when I was fifteen, and I was glad to get out of the house. I don't want Simon to feel like that about me.'

'You saw the way Graham treated Simon in York. Call that a father?'

'I saw him at the park as well, larking about with him in the paddling pool with you walking along beside them, and you looked happy together. Graham's the one that Simon wants, and Lynn, I honestly don't think you know which way to jump. Well, I went to Fleetwood on my own, and I stayed with my mother and stepfather, and I remembered just the way it used to be. So I decided to stay right out of the way for long enough to see what would happen – and what happened was that when I came back you were together in the park, playing happy families. So that was that.'

'We weren't playing happy families at all. I went to the park with them because Simon pestered me to go, that's all.'

'You all looked happy enough together, anyway. It's a serious thing to break a family up, Lynn. I don't want to be the one to do it. I don't know how I could ever have thought of it.'

'The family's already broken up, and he's the one that did it, not you or me.'

'And now he's trying to put it all back together, and I shouldn't get in the way of that, and I think it's what you want as well, deep down. So I'm getting out of the way.'

'That's just excuses. You're the one I want, and you know it.'

172

'But you're torn. You haven't got him out of your system, even if you think you have, so I'm bowing out. Don't make it harder than it is, Lynn.'

He was just making excuses, she thought, trying to put the blame on her, when in reality he was the one desperate to finish it, and clear the way for the Chief Bridesmaid. 'It's Orla, then,' she said.

Alec looked wretched. He shrugged and spread his hands, palms upwards as if to say: I can't help it!

It was Orla, without a doubt. Lynn stood up. 'Bye, then, Alec.'

She loved him, but she wouldn't humiliate herself by begging. Clutching on to the rags of her self-esteem she turned and left, and managed to keep her head up and her back straight until she was out of the door and away down to Janet's to lick her wounds – desperate for a fag and a friend.

'Your Anthony's shipmate! You're a dark horse, aren't you? I never realised you had designs on him. I knew you'd been out with him a time or two, but I'd no idea you were that keen.'

Lynn put her cigarette to her lips with trembling fingers. 'If only I'd got the time off to go to his mother's with him, it would never have happened!' she said.

'And I suspected you were still pining for Graham!'

'That's what Alec thought – or so he says.'

'Did he? What did he say, exactly?'

173

'He said I'm still hankering after Graham, and Simon wants to be with his dad, and he hated his stepfather for busting his family up. He says he doesn't want Simon to feel the same way about him, and that was his excuse for finishing it.'

'It's a pity he didn't think about all that before he mentioned marriage.'

'Yeah, isn't it? But that's the excuse, I reckon – not the real reason. Brenda's chief bridesmaid's the real reason. She was practically throwing herself at him at the wedding, and they've been seeing each other since.'

'What will you do now?'

'What can I do? You can't *make* people stick with you if they don't want. Graham doesn't want Mandy because he never really wanted her in the first place, I don't want Graham because of Alec, and now Alec doesn't want me because of Orla. It's laughable, isn't it?'

But Janet wasn't laughing. 'You could always go back to Graham and make Simon happy, I suppose – if he's the reformed character he's cracking on he is, which I seriously doubt. But at least you'd have your own home.'

'I'd get a place of my own and have done with men altogether if only I had the money. They're more trouble than they're worth,' Lynn said, viciously stubbing out her cigarette.

Janet was all sympathy. 'You haven't had much luck with them, at any rate – makes me feel lucky to be settled with dull old Dave,' she said. 'Ring your mother and tell her she's babysitting tonight. Have some tea with us. We've got the exams looming up; we could get the books out later, and

174

do some revision. Take your mind off your troubles.'

Lynn shook her head. Her mind wouldn't be so easily taken off Alec. 'Thanks, but I can't. I couldn't eat a thing, and I'd better be getting back. She's going out tonight.'

She passed her old home on the walk back to Boulevard, and felt no qualm about losing it, no pull at the heartstrings, but a sudden thought of standing in Fleetwood with Alec, looking up across Morecambe Bay, brought such a lump to her throat she felt as if she'd swallowed a brick. It would have been nice to see what Fleetwood was really like, what his mother was like, and his stepfather. Now she would never know, and the thought cut her. For her, three days every three weeks with Alec would have been worth an eternity with any other man – and that was little enough to ask. How could Simon have stood in the way of that?

No! It was no good dwelling on it. Alec had given her the brush-off, and it was nothing to do with her not going to Fleetwood. It hadn't much to do with Simon, either, for all his talk about not breaking families up. There had been no change in Alec until Orla had appeared on the scene.

Chapter 24

Graham called for Simon about a month later, in a jubilant mood. 'I've got a great deal on the house,' he grinned. 'More than we paid for it, a cash buyer, and they want to be in, as soon as possible. Oh, and congratulations on passing your exam, by the way.'

'Gee, thanks, Graham.'

'We'll be able to cover our costs *and* pay the building society – without being out of pocket! We can start again, somewhere else.'

'*We* can start again?' Lynn laughed. 'I've only just got my decree nisi, Graham.'

'You won't be much out of pocket with it, then, seeing it only cost you thirty bob,' Graham grinned. 'Come on, let bygones be bygones, and start again. You don't want to live at your mother's for the rest of your life, any more than I want to live at mine, and you'll never get anywhere decent on your own.' He smiled down at Simon, and ruffled his hair. 'I've seen a house on Snuff Mill Lane with two apple trees and a pear tree in the garden – better than the one on Marlborough Avenue. The owners are emigrating to Australia, so they're so desperate for a quick sale they're practically giving it away. I bet if I wait until the last minute and then say I can't come up with the price I might get them to knock it down another couple of hundred quid.'

'I wouldn't put it past you, either,' she said.

'All's fair in love and house-buying,' he said, and seeing her expression he averted his gaze and corrected himself: 'Well, not in love, maybe. But it's a boy's paradise! You'll love it, Simon, and we can soon put your swing up there.' He looked up again, at Lynn. 'He can go to school in Cottingham.'

Simon began jumping round the kitchen in a state of high excitement.

Lynn gave Graham a sour look. 'You've been busy, haven't you? He's doing all right in St George's, for your information, and he needs to be somewhere handy for my mother.'

'He'll do better living with both parents, anyway,' Graham insisted.

'So you say.'

'So you'll say, when you see the house. Come and have a look at it.'

Simon tugged at her hand. 'Come on, come on! Let's go and look at the house. Ple-e-ase!' he begged.

'It's too far away to bring you to your Nanna's when I've got to go to work.'

Graham's expression brightened even further. 'Well, now you've got a staff midwife's job you'll be able to afford a car! I'll teach you to drive.'

Lynn saw the gleam of hope in Simon's eyes and thought: why not? She couldn't have the man she wanted, so why not make him happy? Why play around any longer? For months before Anthony's wedding she had been torn between holding on to Alec and going back to Graham for Simon's sake. Now, looking at his eager little face

177

she had to concede that Alec might have been right; maybe he never would have got over a break up between her and his dad. And as soon as all hope of being with Alec had gone, she had known, deep down, that she would go back to Graham in the end.

'Well, you've got rid of the house; you can get rid of that bed, as well, while you're at it. I'm never sleeping on that again,' she said.

'That's all right, as long as you don't mind having secondhand. The vendors are leaving all their carpets, and they'll be leaving all the furniture they can't sell. We might keep some of that, and we could just about furnish the house with what Auntie Ivy left. It's still sitting in storage because nobody wants it. It's not modern, but it's really solid stuff. She had some quite good antiques.'

'All right, it'll do until we can afford our own choice. And another thing: there's got to be honesty – about everything, and I mean absolutely everything ... including money, Graham. You know how much I earn, but you've been earning a lot more than you ever admitted to me. I want to see your payslips from now on.'

'Anything,' Graham said. 'Anything you like.'

'All right then. We'll go and see the house,' she said. The torture of indecision was over. Alec had made it simple for her.

'Mandy was nothing,' Graham murmured, nuzzling her ear as they lay in bed together on the first night after the move to Snuff Mill Lane. 'You're The One, Lynn, the only one that ever mattered. You're my Numero Uno.'

178

'I know that, Graham,' Lynn purred. 'Mandy was just a moment of madness. You've already told me.'

'It's true!' he protested. 'I knew the day you came home and tossed all her clothes out of the window. That's my girl, I thought, and I told her to go home!'

Liar! Instead of sending her home, he'd taken her to his mother's! Lynn gave a sardonic little snort. 'Shut up, Graham,' she whispered, wanting no distraction from the sensations beginning to overpower her, least of all the distraction of Graham's outrageous lies. She shut her eyes, and as their new bed began a gentle, rhythmic bounce Alec McCauley loomed into her mind. She smiled at the delicious thought of him, of being naked with him, skin to skin, doing this with him instead of Graham – because although Graham was good in bed, Alec would have been better. With him she wouldn't have been Numero Uno – she would have been his One and Only. There would have been trust as well as lust – she knew it in her bones. She'd had that feeling off him when he first took her hand, a confidence along with the thrill of his touch. If Graham only knew he was a mere substitute for a better player, she thought, what would it do to his ego? She would never in her life make love with Alec but the thought was delicious, and her smile broadened at her fantasy – at her own deep and secret treachery.

Graham did shut up, concentrating on her pleasure as well as his own. He was giving one of his best performances and Lynn began to move with him, giving herself up to the pleasure, chasing the elusive climax until it caught her.

'I've never had it as good anywhere as I get it right here at home,' Graham said, his voice thick and throaty.

Lynn relaxed, gave a great sigh of satisfaction and breathed: 'Oh h h ... Alec!'

Graham stopped in mid thrust. 'Oh, Alec?' he echoed. 'Who the chuff's Alec?'

'Have you forgotten?' she asked, innocently. 'That friend of our Anthony's. He just popped into my head; I don't know why.'

Graham gave a couple more feeble thrusts, but both the rhythm and the enthusiasm were gone.

'He picks a good time to pop into your head, then,' he protested, moving to sit on the edge of the bed with his back to her. 'That's ruined it for me, now.'

Lynn languidly stroked his shoulder. 'Sorry, love,' she lied.

'Popped into your head! That's just ruined it for me,' he repeated. He turned towards her with a resentful, suspicious look, and a warning. 'Well, he'd better not be popping into anything else, that's all.'

'Sorry, love,' Lynn repeated, but it was as much as she could do to stop herself laughing out loud. Let him chew on that for a while. She turned on her side to switch off the lamp and hide the gleam in her eyes.

'Alec,' Graham repeated slowly. 'I remember him now – that fisherman I saw you with in York, the one who brought Simon to my mother's that time. I wouldn't be surprised if you've been hav-

180

ing it off with him, cracking on to the solicitors that you were Snow White, while all the time you were worse than me! And sly, with it.'

He wanted her to start protesting her innocence so he could start an argument, Lynn thought – but he wasn't going to get the satisfaction. 'No, not worse than you and Mandy, even if I had,' she said. 'But I'll tell you what, Graham – let's suppose I *was* having an affair with him. You can forgive me for that just like I'm forgiving you for Mandy. Then we're all square, aren't we? Even stevens.'

Graham thought for a moment, then lay back in bed, pulling the covers up to his neck. 'You haven't,' he decided.

Lynn smiled into the darkness. The idea that anyone might 'transfer her affections' to an Alec after having had the privilege of knowing Graham was too alien a concept for Graham to consider. It was evidently more than his king-sized ego could entertain.

She gave a sigh of satisfaction. She'd had her little revenge, and it had been sweet ... but better say no more about Alec, she decided, as sleep overtook her. Giving way to nasty, punishing impulses like that might be quite enjoyable, but long term it could only do harm, and she would do no more of it. No, she'd chosen to stay married to Graham, and she would make it for better rather than for worse – for all their sakes.

Chapter 25

'I don't like this kitchen half as much as the one you had on Marlborough Avenue, with all them lovely orange units and that built-in oven,' Lynn's mother said, when she and her father arrived on Bonfire Night. 'This one can't hold a candle to it. It looks pre-war.'

'That's what Connie said,' Lynn replied. 'The garden's all right, though – not that you'll see a lot of it, in the dark. Our Margaret and the lads are already out there – and Jim, for a wonder. They're just lighting the bonfire.'

'Aye, this doesn't happen often, does it? Both of us ashore at the same time,' her father said.

Lynn led them out into the garden where Margaret's husband Jim was just putting a match to a couple of firelighters under the kindling. As the flames roared skyward Simon and his four young cousins jumped and chased around, whooping and shouting with excitement, eyes wide with delight and faces wreathed in smiles.

With Connie a couple of paces behind him, Gordon sidled up to Lynn's father and being more than a head shorter, stared up at him, man to man.

'I'm sorry our Graham let your lass down like he did, Tom. I'm glad they've sorted it out,' he said.

Tom gave him a nod and a smile, and shook the

hand which Gordon solemnly offered.

'He's come to his senses now, all right,' Gordon assured him. 'He soon realised what a lovely family he'd risked losing – and we nearly lost a lovely daughter-in-law.'

Connie didn't rush to endorse that observation, Lynn noticed.

Instead, Nina hurried to fill the awkward silence with an indignant: 'Mandy's what possessed him, obviously! A trollop like that, who'll chase a man from Leeds and put it on a plate for him! What can you expect?'

Connie gave her an approving look. 'There's too many easy women about, that's the trouble,' she said. 'They're everywhere.'

Everywhere including the flat above the fruit shop, Lynn thought, her eyebrows twitching upwards for an instant at the thought of Mandy's sojourn there. That was one easy woman Connie hadn't minded welcoming at any rate – but thanks to Nina they all felt themselves on safer ground now and only too happy to be able to throw all the blame for the marital malfunction on the party not present to defend herself.

Gordon nodded sanctimonious agreement. Tom Carr's face gave nothing away.

'Well, she's back where she belongs now, so she's best forgotten,' Margaret said.

'Let's hope she stops where she belongs, then!' said Nina.

'I'm sure she will. There's nothing for her in Hull, now our Graham's come to his senses,' Gordon said, looking towards Graham, who was sorting fireworks with Jim and five young boys at the far side of the bonfire.

Another lull in the conversation ensued, while they idly watched the busy little group, with the almost leafless fruit trees at the back of them, all illuminated by the flames.

'What a shame our Anthony's not here! He used to be ashore at the same time as his dad, but he had to change ships when he got a mate's job. He's doing great, though! Not twenty-four yet and he's on his third trip,' Nina crowed, with never a thought for Margaret, who might well feel her husband slighted by the comparison, since Jim was pushing forty and had only made third hand.

Lynn looked at her mother, willing her to stop, but Nina was oblivious. 'He'll be home in another three days. They'll probably be giving him a better ship next trip...'

Margaret herself interrupted the flow. 'Brenda could have come, though.'

'She's gone to Orla's,' Lynn said, and at the mention of Orla, her thoughts flew to Alec. If he wasn't at sea, he would be there as well. Her stomach gave a painful little wrench.

'She could have come; she was invited, but they're a clannish lot, that family. Stick together like glue,' Nina said.

'Graham!' Gordon called, beckoning to him. 'Over here a minute.'

Graham answered the summons.

'Shake hands with your father-in-law,' Gordon ordered.

Lynn watched a mildly sheepish Graham hold out his hand. 'All right, Tom?' he said.

184

'Aye, I'm all right, Graham.' Tom grasped Graham's hand and shook it. He didn't let go, but held on, determinedly fixing his son-in-law's gaze and leaning slightly towards him. 'And I want you to listen to me, because I'm only going to say this once. *If you pull that stunt on our Lynn again – I'll kill you.*'

Graham nodded, and said nothing. The rest of them watched in total silence as Tom slowly released his hand and Graham slunk back to Jim and the fireworks with his shoulders hunched up to his ears, looking like a kicked dog.

Gordon stared up at Tom, speechless with astonishment. Connie looked as though she might faint. Nina and Margaret exchanged embarrassed glances and Tom smiled pleasantly and implacably at them all.

Lynn broke the trance. 'I think I'll just go and check on the spuds,' she said, and escaped into the house. The idea of the party had been to bury the hatchet – and instead of that her father had sharpened it, and made it obvious he meant to keep it handy. *The best laid plans of mice and men,* she thought, but couldn't help a chuckle at the look on Gordon's face. She opened the oven door and found the potatoes nearly as raw as they'd been ten minutes ago, when she'd put them in to bake, not too surprisingly. Thank goodness Anthony was still at sea. Her party would have been ruined altogether if he had landed.

Five minutes later they were all chatting together again, all intent on smoothing things over, and all behaving as if nothing untoward had been said. Connie and Gordon were very affable, but

185

Lynn had the feeling that they were not quite as fond of her as they had been, and all were quietly aware of a forced quality in the friendliness and a certain coolness under the surface smiles. Like the bobbins that hold the trawl net up though thrust fathoms down into the sea, Graham came bobbing back up to the surface when they sat down to eat and the beer began to flow, and played the genial host for all he was worth. Connie developed a headache during the meal, so Gordon took her home shortly after they had eaten.

The rest of the party resumed the firework display, interrupted when Jim burned his hand lighting one of the fireworks.

'Run it under the cold tap, Dad!' his eldest said, and the cry was taken up by the rest of them. Jim went into the kitchen with them hot on his heels, all full of advice and sympathy.

'You ought to go to the hospital with that,' Graham told him. 'It might go septic.'

'Nah. I'm sailing in morning. I'll get some salt water on it. It'll be all right,' he said, and they all trooped out into the garden again and sat on a bench under the kitchen window, to watch Tom set the rest of the fireworks off. Graham sat drinking his beer, watching thoughtfully as Tom gently tapped Catherine wheels to one of the trees and set them alight, to the cheers of his grandchildren.

'That was the best party ever!' Simon cried, when the last banger had been let off, and the visitors came in to ring for a taxi.

'Can we sleep here, with Simon, Auntie Lynn?'

one of his cousins asked.

Lynn saw something approaching horror on Graham's face. 'We haven't enough beds!' he said.

'We can sleep on the floor, like when we sleep at Bill's,' said the eldest, called after his father and known as 'young Jim'.

'That's in the summer holidays, when it's warm,' said Margaret. 'It's too cold now, and you've got to be up for school in the morning.'

'So has Simon, and he's in the same class as me,' five-year-old Joe frowned.

'Well, Simon can come and sleep at our house, if he likes,' said Jim.

'Save you dropping him off at our house tomorrow morning, Graham,' Nina said.

Simon seemed all for going, but shrank back, shaking his head when the taxi came, and stood holding Graham's hand until it disappeared down the lane. Graham laughed, and gave his son's shoulders an approving squeeze. 'He knows where his bread's buttered,' he said.

Simon looked eagerly up at him. 'Can we play Snap, Dad?'

'No, it's ten o'clock already, and you've got to be up for school tomorrow,' Lynn said, shooing him up the stairs. She wondered whether Graham would have anything to say about her father now that they were alone, but he seemed to have forgotten the episode, and was eager for bed, as amorous as ever she had known him.

Liar and cheat he may have been, but he was a good lover – you couldn't take that away from him, she thought, as Graham gave her yet another proof of his proficiency between the sheets.

Afterwards, she drowsily wondered how Mandy was faring. Her doting husband couldn't have been good enough in that department to keep her happy, Lynn imagined. Then her mind turned to Alec. She was glad they had never made love. It would only have made the parting harder, and Simon was so happy and settled that in spite of her pangs of regret Lynn knew it was all for the best.

It had been worth the sacrifice. Things were better as they were. Relaxed to the core, she drifted off to sleep.

Chapter 26

Nina dropped her bombshell the following day. 'I've been offered a job. I've got no responsibilities of my own, so I'm taking it. I don't want to leave you in the lurch, so I'm giving you a month to work your notice.'

Lynn looked at her mother goggle-eyed for a moment. 'Leave me in the lurch! How is it not leaving me in the lurch? How am I going to manage, without working?'

'You've got a husband – let him keep you! He's kept telling me how much he wants to be a good husband and father these past few months, so I'm giving him his chance. And think about this: if you're not working he won't have as much money to splash about on other women, and you'll have more time and energy to keep tabs on him.'

'I don't want to keep tabs on him! If I'd thought he needed tabs keeping on him, I wouldn't have gone back to him! I've only just got my midwifery certificate, and I want to use it. I want to work!'

'Yes! So do I – I want to work,' Nina said, and started doing the thing Lynn hated above all – wagging her finger.

'I've helped you get your qualifications, and now it's my turn. I'm going to get out among other people for a change, instead of being stuck in the house all the time. I don't hold with mothers working anyway. I never worked when you were little, and now I've done my stint at looking after bairns. So clip his wings a bit. Make him face his responsibilities. Other men have to.'

Lynn was aghast. 'We've just taken a massive mortgage on, Mother! How are we going to pay that, if I'm not working?'

Nina looked her determinedly in the eye. 'Graham's on a damned good screw, and I know that, because he told me himself. If you can't manage on that, it's a bad job for you.'

'People have got more to keep up these days. We've got bigger outgoings. It's not only the mortgage, the rates are higher, living round there. And we've got to run a car...'

'It's a company car, so they pay most of the upkeep on that.'

'I don't see how we can pay for everything!' Lynn protested. 'We'll end up falling into arrears, and then we'll lose the house.'

'No, you won't. His mother and father won't let you. That shop of theirs is a little gold mine, and I'd be surprised if old Auntie Ivy hadn't left Con-

189

nie a bit in her will. They're not going to stand by and see their spoiled boy lose anything. Anyway, I'm starting work in a month, and that's flat.'

When Graham got home the glad tidings had the same effect on him as they'd had on Lynn a few hours earlier. He hung his coat slowly on the peg. 'She picks a good time to tell you that – when we've just taken on a massive mortgage!'

'She reckons we can afford it, on the salary you're earning. She reckons it's my responsibility to look after Simon, and it's your responsibility to maintain us.'

'She's out of the ark. Nobody can live a decent life on one salary these days. I'd an idea, though. I'd an idea she was getting fed up of looking after him.'

'She's fed up of being stuck in the house, she says, especially since he started school. She'll look after him until I've worked my notice, and then she's starting work. In a hotel.'

Lynn smelled the steak beginning to burn, and fled towards the kitchen.

Graham followed. 'Doing what?' he demanded.

'Chambermaid,' Lynn said, rapidly turning the steaks.

'Chambermaid! Making beds, and cleaning! What's she want to go cleaning for? What's your dad say about it?'

'He's not too happy. In fact, he's not happy at all.'

'Neither am I.'

'Do you think I am? Just as I'm on a decent salary as well.'

190

'*And* superannuated – and bang goes your car, as well! Giving all that up, just for her to have a bloody cleaning job – it's crazy!'

'I know. I offered to give her as much as the job would pay for looking after Simon, but she wouldn't have it. She says she wants a job outside the house.'

'Well, if she's not looking after him any more, he's coming out of St George's, I can tell you that. He's going to school in Cottingham, where he'll have some nice children for friends instead of a set of cheeky brats.'

Lynn's eyes narrowed and her mouth set in a tight line at the insult to the youngsters of Hessle Road. 'Just be careful,' she warned, grabbing a tea towel to pull hot plates out of the oven. 'Shout Simon down and get him up to the table, if you want to do something useful.'

Graham was soon back in the kitchen, with a new idea. 'What's your Margaret doing? Can't she look after him?'

'No. She got a job at Birds Eye as soon as the youngest started school, and the bairns go to Jim's mother's until she gets back – unless they're larking about the streets with all the other cheeky brats round there. I wouldn't have thought you'd want our Simon mixing with them after school – they've even more opportunity for mischief once they're let loose.'

'Shows how desperate I am, doesn't it? No offence to your family, Lynn.'

'Really? Anyway, we'd better make a list of all our outgoings, and have a look at your payslips after tea, and see how we're going to manage. At

191

least we won't be paying as much tax if I'm unemployed.'

'Unemployed!' Graham groaned.

She slid fillet steak and mushrooms onto the plates, piled on some chips and handed a plate to Graham.

'Enjoy it,' she said. 'It might be beans on toast before long – if not bread and dripping.'

Chapter 27

The debate about which staff midwives were going to cover Christmas, who was going to work on Boxing Day, and who would have the New Year off did not concern Lynn. She would be at home for the whole holiday. That fact only really sank in after her last day at work, when she went to hand in her uniform, feeling as she'd always imagined a fish must feel when the gutting-knife is doing its work. She would have worked a dozen Christmases rather than have to leave, and make it up to Simon in the time left after her shift. After all, when her dad was at sea their Christmases had always been delayed until he got back – that was when they'd had their present opening and Christmas festivities, and it had done them no harm at all.

All that poring over books, all that hard work, not to mention the fact that she loved the job ... it was enough to make you weep – and how long would it be before she could get back to it, she wondered? Probably not until Simon was old enough to bring himself home from school; unless she could find something that fitted in with school hours. If there was a job like that any-where, she would find it. Her last couple of pay cheques would take them to mid-January and after that she would do some serious economis-ing. If they were careful, they could just manage on Graham's salary, and since the time off had been forced on her, she would enjoy Christmas and Boxing Day with a clear conscience, and start a job search as soon as the holiday was over.

'We're invited to the firm's Christmas Eve dinner and dance,' Graham said. 'It's a formal, long-frock do, and it goes on until about two o'clock. You'll have get something decent to wear, and arrange a babysitter.'

'I'll ask your mother,' Lynn said. 'My mother's warned me she won't be babysitting at Christmas, and Margaret can only have him if he sleeps at her house.'

But Connie's terms were the same. She would babysit only if Simon slept at their place. These dos go on till all hours, she said, and she was too old to sit up that late.

Lynn hesitated. She'd wanted Simon to wake up in his own home on Christmas morning, to see the stocking hanging at the foot of his own bed. She'd looked forward to being with him at the crack of dawn when he went downstairs, to discover just a few crumbs in place of Father Christmas's mince pie, his milk drunk, and the reindeer's carrot gone – all exchanged for the

193

presents he would find under the tree.

Now she had a choice between disappointing Simon and disappointing Graham, and disappointing Graham would have far worse repercussions. Maybe Simon wouldn't mind waking up at Connie's too much – there would certainly be plenty of presents for him there. With her happy visions of Christmas morning with her young son vanishing before her eyes, she reluctantly accepted Connie's offer, and disappointed herself.

She came home a couple of days before Christmas Eve after spending precious pounds on a stunning long red dress. Holding it against herself she gazed at her reflection in the mirror in the hallway, noting the glow it gave to her complexion, and the way it seemed to make her dark eyes brighter. She was just imagining the impact she might make at the dinner-dance when Connie rang. She was sorry, but she couldn't babysit after all. Gordon was taking her out to some do with other grocers.

Lynn gave the dress a last, lingering look, folded it carefully and put it back in the bag, feeling suddenly gleeful. She might have cut quite a dash at that dinner dance. It would have been nice to meet some of Graham's colleagues, and there might even have been someone there who could have offered her a job. But now Simon would be where he belonged on Christmas morning, and that was the important thing. She walked with a spring in her step to collect him and catch a bus into town. If they got a move on, they'd get to Hammonds before closing time and get a refund on that frock. There were better things to spend the money on, anyway.

How could he avoid going to the company's Christmas Eve party, Graham demanded, that evening. The company had gone to a lot of trouble and laid a lot of money out for this do, and after all the effort they'd made it would look bad if he didn't go and socialise. It would look bad as it was with his wife not going – they might think she couldn't be bothered! He wanted to make a good impression, Graham stressed, and the way he looked at her gave Lynn the feeling that failing to get a babysitter was tantamount to sabotaging his career.

So on Christmas Eve Graham was still out, partying with everybody at Four Winds Pharmaceuticals while Lynn was sitting at home trimming the outer leaves off tomorrow's Brussels sprouts with only the television and the crackling of the fire for company. When midnight struck she tossed the last trimmed sprout into the pan and stood up to stretch herself, then took them into the kitchen, wondering what she'd missed at the dinner and dance. It would have been nice to go and meet some of the people Graham worked with. It was pretty dreary, sitting alone on Christmas Eve, when everyone else was out enjoying themselves – except most fishermen's wives, of course. Jim might be at home now, but Margaret had been without her husband Christmas after Christmas in the past. So had her mother, but her mother's days of sitting in the house with her children were long gone. You could guarantee that Nina would be out with her friends. Lynn suddenly remembered Piers, and the locked door and the toothache. Funny, but they'd never heard any more about the toothache, after that night.

A car pulled up outside. Graham! Lynn dashed to the window and pulled aside the curtain, but it wasn't Graham. Graham would probably stick the party out to the bitter finish, till dawn, if it went on that long.

She ate most of the mince pie Simon had carefully left for Father Christmas, broke most of the carrot off and put a bite mark on the stub and went to bed. Simon would probably be up at five o'clock wanting to open his presents, and Lynn didn't intend to miss an instant of that. They were going to have the best Christmas ever.

Chapter 28

True to form, it was still pitch black when Simon padded into the bedroom. Graham was snoring loudly, dead to the world.

She elbowed him in the ribs. 'Merry Christmas, Graham!'

An excited Simon jumped onto the bed and sat astride him. 'Wakey, wakey, Dad! He's been!' he shouted, pushing one of Graham's eyelids open with his thumb.

'Ho ho ho!' Graham groaned.

'Come and see the presents!'

With eyes still closed, Graham gave him a half-drunken smile. 'Bring 'em up here, and open 'em on the bed!'

Simon ran downstairs and brought up as many parcels as he could carry, putting an end to any further rest for either of his parents.

The day passed off as well as Lynn had hoped. Connie and Gordon arrived for Christmas dinner, which was cooked to perfection. In spite of his late night Graham was the spirit of Christmas personified, the incarnation of goodwill, the ideal family man. He dozed off in an armchair after dinner while Lynn and Connie washed up and Gordon kept Simon amused – and quiet – and didn't wake until after dark, when a car door slammed outside. A minute later the doorbell rang. Nina had arrived, dressed in a new and very trendy trouser suit, the first they'd seen of her in almost two weeks. She radiated happiness, which Lynn couldn't help feeling was rather bad form after she'd left them in the lurch.

Simon gave her an enthusiastic welcome. 'Have you got some presents for me, Nanna?'

'Don't be so rude, Simon,' Lynn said.

Nina produced a large bag and held it in the air. 'Da Daah!' she exclaimed, and walked into the sitting room, followed eagerly by Simon, who proceeded to tear off the wrapping paper.

Graham gave Nina an impassive stare. 'How's the job going?'

'Great. Tom's not very happy, though. He'd rather have me sitting at home twiddling my thumbs, but he can't do anything about it.'

'He's back at sea, I suppose,' Graham said, and Lynn gave him full marks for his forbearance in saying no more about Nina's job, or what it was costing them.

Nina nodded. 'Jim's at home, though, for a wonder!' she said. 'First time I've known it, I think.'

'Nice for Margaret and the bairns,' Lynn said.

'Not to mention Jim,' Nina laughed.

Lynn's hopes of a babysitter on New Year's Eve were soon dashed. Nina was going to some friends to play Canasta directly after her visit to them, and she was going out with them on Boxing Day. They were all going out on New Year's Eve, as well. In fact they might have a couple of days away and go to a hotel somewhere. She talked at length about the various places under consideration and the merits and demerits of the hotels. Now her children had all flown the nest, she had to make a bit of a life for herself, she said.

The rest of them sat listening – having no option, since it was impossible to get a word in edgeways. At eight o'clock the taxi man drove up and tooted on his horn, seeming impatient to whisk her away to her card party. Nina gave Simon a smacking kiss, said her hurried goodbyes to everybody else and then almost ran out of the house. There was a deathly quiet after she'd gone, until they heard a fire engine scorching along the road, siren blaring.

'Nina's tongue's on fire,' Graham commented, dryly.

They all burst into laughter. Connie and Gordon had another mince pie and a cup of coffee and left after Simon's bedtime.

At two minutes to midnight on New Year's Eve, Lynn sat alone downstairs in her living room watching the television, hoping that nobody would ring before Graham did. The second hand crept slowly round until Big Ben struck twelve. She immediately turned the sound off, and listened hard, until the tugs and trawlers in St Andrew's Fish Dock began blasting their hooters to greet the New Year. The New Year erupted noiselessly on the television with people dancing, laughing, and silently cheering. The phone rang just as a tartan-clad Andy Stewart and his White Heather Club started a soundless 'Auld Lang Syne'.

Graham! Lynn eagerly lifted the receiver.

'Happy New Year, Darling!'

'Happy New Year!' she replied, ridiculously grateful to him for tearing himself away from everybody at the company to ring her, his wife. She put the phone down after a two-minute conversation and it rang again – Margaret and Jim this time, giving her their good wishes down the wire. They both sounded very merry, and she could hear her nephews in the background, still up, at this hour! She hung up after five minutes' chat, and the room seemed emptier than ever.

Hearing Margaret's brood prompted her to go upstairs and look at Simon, who had gone to bed at the proper time as all good boys should. On her way back downstairs the thought struck her how tidy this house was, compared to the last. Here, everything had been unpacked and put neatly away within a couple of weeks, instead of hanging around in boxes for months – but that's the difference, she thought, between women who are gainfully employed in jobs that occupy their minds as

199

well as their time and energy, and those who stay at home, filling their time and their thoughts with housework, until a stray crumb or a smear on the paintwork becomes a major concern. She picked the phone up on her return downstairs to ring her mother, but there was no reply. None at Anthony's or Janet's, either. Not so easy to ring her dad, and how good it would have been to hear his voice. But he would be in the Arctic, hundreds of miles away – and so, probably, would Alec. She gave an involuntary shiver. The weather would be dire up there just now – not that it would affect her dad, but it was a different story for a mate. Alec would be freezing on deck or freezing in the fish room most of the time. He would be getting a baptism of ice.

She sat down and stared despondently at the gentlemen in their kilts and the ladies with tartan sashes over their white dresses all smiling as they twirled round each other in square dances, interspersed with Andy singing songs of Scotland. She watched for a while and then turned the television and the lights off and sat in darkness and silence, staring into the fire. Fishermen's wives sit alone night after night like this, she thought, and then wondered, how are adulterers' wives any better off?

Heavens! Why on earth had that word popped into her head? Adultery was a thing of the past with Graham; he had become the devoted family man. There wasn't even a whiff of any other woman. No suspicion of it. Mandy was gone. Graham was out with his bosses, looking after his career, and considering his recent performances in bed, the likelihood that he was sharing himself with anybody else was practically nil. No man could have that much energy.

At half past twelve she heard a car door slam. He was home! He'd come home early, to spend the New Year with her!

She felt a gust of wintry air. A voice like a pantomime policeman called: ''Ello, 'ello, 'ello!' and Anthony walked into the living room rubbing his hands, followed by Brenda pulling her fur collar round her pink cheeks, the first visit they'd made to Lynn in her new home.

'Ooh, it's a bit parky out there,' Brenda shivered, and lowered her voice to say: 'We've come to bury the hatchet, and all that. It's Anthony's New Year Resolution!'

'I thought you were still at sea!' Lynn said, astonished to see them.

'We docked on the thirtieth. That was our Christmas Day, eh, Brenda? And here we are, it's New Year's Day.'

'Take your coats off and sit down! I'll get you a glass of something.'

'He thought he'd keep it quiet, and come and surprise you,' Brenda said. She slipped off her coat, her eyes widening as she scanned the room, well furnished with Auntie Ivy's gleaming antiques. 'Mmm! Very nice! Well, maybe some day, eh, Anthony?'

Anthony nodded. 'Where's the lord of the manor, then?'

Lynn was already at the sideboard, pouring drinks. 'Out, partying with the big cheeses at the company.'

'And left you in on your own, on New Year's Eve!'

'Well, he did ring and wish me a happy New Year when Big Ben started chiming.'

'He should have taken you out, never mind ringing,' Anthony said. 'Couldn't his mother have had Simon?'

'They've gone out.'

'Well, why didn't you drop him off at Margaret's?'

'Because Jim's still at home.'

'That wouldn't have made any difference. They wouldn't have minded.'

'He should have stopped in with you, if you couldn't get a babysitter,' Brenda said, lips pursed.

Lynn handed Anthony a tumbler of whisky. 'The manager asked him to a party at his own house, and he didn't like to refuse. He's up the bloke's arse, and he says he means to stay there.'

Anthony burst into laughter, and gave a broad sweep of his arm. 'Well, you're not doing too bad on it, are you? I'd get up our gaffer's arse if I could, get a few good trips as skipper and get some money together.'

'You've hardly been mate two minutes!' Lynn said. 'Anyway, you're probably earning as much as Graham now you're on a better ship.'

'Not far off, maybe – some of the time – but my money's a lot more dicey than his, and I work a damned sight harder for it, as well. Still, we'll have our own house before long, eh, Brenda? Maybe not as fancy as this, though.'

'You never know,' Brenda said, with a shrug and a smile. 'We went to your mother's, Lynn, but she's not in.'

'She's never in these days. I tried ringing her earlier.'

'There's something got into her lately,' Anthony said, suddenly suspicious. 'She's not running round with Scrobs, is she? Me dad'll kill her, if she is.'

'Scrobs?' Brenda said.

'Fishermen, from Iceland and Denmark, places like that,' Lynn grinned. 'There are some good-looking lads among 'em, but I don't think my mother's the type, somehow. Give her some credit, Anthony.'

Brenda chuckled, and sipped her Babycham. 'Mm, Scrobs! Yeah, I remember now – they look after some of the fishermen's wives while their husbands are at sea, don't they?'

That got Anthony roused. 'They'd better not try looking after mine!'

'Don't worry, I'll be too busy,' Brenda chuckled.

'Busy with what?' Lynn asked.

Brenda and Anthony looked at each other and laughed.

'You're having a baby!'

'How did you guess?'

'Come on, I'm a midwife. I can tell just by looking at you. I knew as soon as you walked in, only I didn't want to be the first to say anything.' Lynn said it with a straight face, and almost had Brenda convinced.

They had a long discussion about pregnancy, and labour, and caring for newborn babies. Lynn managed to restrain herself throughout, but just as her visitors were walking out of the door, she could resist no longer. 'How are Orla and Alec?' she asked

'Orla's fine, but we haven't laid eyes on Alec since that day we saw you in the park,' Brenda said.

'What – at the end of August?'

'Well, we haven't been there since, have we?'

'He's moved his digs,' Anthony said. 'We don't even know where he's living now.'

'Oh,' said Lynn, much taken aback. 'Doesn't Orla know?'

'She's seen nothing of him either, as far as I know,' Brenda said.

Well, had she or hadn't she seen anything of him, Lynn wondered? The house seemed deathly quiet after they'd gone, the silence broken only by the crackling of the fire and the ticking of the clock.

Chapter 29

Simon started school in Cottingham after the Christmas holidays. The weather had been icy since the day the schools reopened; there was no sign of a let-up and before the week was out Lynn was very glad that Graham had insisted on the move. She walked Simon there on a frosty Thursday morning, hurrying along through ice-packed snow and slush until she slipped and crashed down onto the pavement.

'Are you all right, Mum?'

204

She looked up, and saw Simon's little face looking anxiously down. *I've broken my back,* was her first thought. Winded, she gasped: 'Yeah, I'm all right, son,' and attempted to get up.

A couple of passers-by helped her to her feet and she hobbled away with Simon, stepping very gingerly. It might be a broken neck, next time.

She called at the paper shop on her way home for a copy of the *Nursing Times,* to look at the job vacancies.

'Terrible weather,' the newsagent commented, 'and there's no sign of it ending, either, according to the weather man.' He stretched out a hand protected by a fingerless glove.

Lynn dropped her money into it. 'As if we need him to tell us that,' she said.

If it's as bad as this on land, what must it be like round Iceland, and Bear Island, and the White Sea? she thought, as she carefully picked her way home. Once back, she put the kettle on, and sat perusing her magazine at the kitchen table. There was a pearl of a job in Maternity Out-Patients. It might have been made for her, but she knew nobody nearby who could look after Simon before and after school. She would have applied for that job like a shot had she lived near Hessle Road where favours were given and returned as easily as people breathe, and all mucked in together, and somebody always knew somebody who could help out even if they couldn't do it themselves. Simon could have gone, if not to his grandmother or his aunt, then to one of Jim's aunts, or a great aunt, or a cousin, or a second-cousin-once-removed, or one of the in-laws of those aunts or cousins, or to a friend, or a friend of a friend who would have lived no more than a crowded street or two away – a ten or fifteen-minute walk at the most – and she would have known them, or known somebody who did. The vast, interlocking network of support would have made the job possible – but she had bettered herself. She had dragged herself free of all that, and now lived in splendid isolation in a beautiful house with a large garden, well beyond the reach of their helping hands.

What was worse was the fact that Lynn's lack of income had been quickly followed by an unwelcome attitude shift in Graham. She suddenly felt that her value to him was greatly diminished. Nothing had been explicitly said, but she understood quite clearly that her loss of earning power had reduced her worth, both as a wife and as a human being. He'd begun acting more and more as if he were the lord and master of all he surveyed, and she his serf. Although he couldn't – or wouldn't – tell her from one day to the next whether he would be home early or late, he wanted his tea on the table as soon as he walked in. He felt quite entitled to make carping little criticisms about pettifogging little matters, and to lay his opinions down as fact and law, which he'd never done while she was working. Lynn rarely asserted herself lately, too conscious of being a non-contributor to the household expenses, and not wishing to hear another reminder of the fact.

She threw the magazine aside and washed the breakfast pots, resigned to having to rely on him for every penny for a while. After all that working and studying she was no better off than women like Brenda, who stopped work as soon as they married. But Brenda was more comfortably situated, since Anthony wanted her to stay at home. Lynn would never have chosen the stay-at-home life. She'd had some ambition. She'd wanted to be out, among interesting people, doing interesting work, preferably earning a decent salary while she was at it – money she could call her own. Dependency was loathsome to her – and she hadn't yet had a month of it!

'What was the point, Mother, of seeing me through my exams if I had to pack up work as soon as I'd passed them?' she asked the empty air. But maybe, after years at home looking at the same four walls, the point for her mother was a grab at some independence for herself, and if not interesting work, then at least the companionship of a more varied set of people; and if not a decent salary, then at least a modest little wage packet she could call her own. And how could she be blamed for that?

Lynn stared through the kitchen window onto the stark winter garden. The sky was white, and there was a flurry of fine snow. The central heating was on just high enough to keep the pipes from freezing, and the house was cold. She shivered, tempted to turn it up. Then she thought of the bill, and went upstairs to find an extra jumper. She made the beds and tidied everything upstairs, then went down again to peel vegetables and do more housework until it was time to go for Simon – the highlight of her day.

Chapter 30

On Friday morning Lynn opened the door to her father. She knew immediately that there was something wrong.

'Is your mam here?' he demanded, without his usual cheerful, good-natured smile.

'No. I hardly ever see her since she started work.'

'Do you know where she is?'

'At work, I'd have thought, if she's not at home. Come in; I'll make us a cup of tea.'

He followed her into the kitchen, where she stood by the sink, filling the kettle. 'I've phoned work; she's not there. And I've been to our Margaret's and Brenda's. She's nowhere to be found. She's left me.'

'Left you?' Lynn gasped.

He nodded. 'Yeah. She left a note.'

Lynn turned off the tap and left the kettle on the worktop. 'Tell you what, Dad, never mind the tea. Try something stronger,' she said, and led him into the sitting room.

He slumped into the armchair opposite her, his shoulders hunched and his head pulled downwards so that she saw the slight thinning of the hair on his crown, the first time she'd really noticed it. Poor old Dad.

'It's freezing in here,' he said.

'I'll turn the heating up,' she said, and poured

him a glass of whisky, conscious of playing the role Janet had played a few eventful months ago.

'I thought it was funny before we sailed. She never made the song and dance she usually makes whenever I have to work a Christmas holiday. She took it so bloody well, I thought: *maybe our Nina's mellowing in her old age.* I said as much, and she just laughed. "Oh, aye! A cosy night in beside the fire with my slippers and my knitting! That's really my idea of heaven, now I'm knocking on," she says. I knew she was being sarky, but I'd no idea she intended doing a bunkoff. I never guessed she had that in store! I can't understand it. I've given her everything – everything! Except I could never give her enough. That was always your mother: *gimme, get me, buy me.*'

Lynn said nothing, but handed him the tumbler.

'Well, first you – now it's my turn. Cheers! A Happy New Year, one and all!' He raised his glass and took a drink. 'That's a good drop of whisky.'

'Courtesy of Graham's boss.'

'Hmm. Well, that's the one good thing we can say about Graham – he's not work-shy,' her father said, and taking a folded sheet torn from a spiral-bound notepad out of his pocket, he handed it to her. She felt his eyes on her, alert for her reaction.

'*...I've spent too much time on my own for too many years, and life's too short to go on like that. Now I've met somebody else, and I'm leaving you, Tom. I hope you can forgive me. Nina*', Lynn read, unconsciously wiping her right hand on her skirt. She could almost smell the cloves and feel that limp, moist handshake.

'You don't look surprised, Lynn. You look as if you knew,' her father said.

'I didn't. It's just that one or two things I hardly noticed at the time have just dropped into place,' she said.

'What things?'

Lynn hesitated for a moment, but what was there to hide? *I've met somebody else* – her mother had actually put it in writing. The damage was already done. 'I went back home with Alec once, and there was a bloke there with her. She said he'd given her a lift home because she had toothache. He was a friend of a friend, she said.'

'Where does he live, this friend of a friend? Do you know that? Is it somebody she's met at work?'

Lynn shook her head. 'I don't know any more than what I've just told you,' she said. And if she had known any more, she would have kept it to herself, because the look on his face told her that if her father got hold of Piers Marson there would be a murder done.

'Didn't she introduce you? Didn't she tell you his name?'

'If she did, I've forgotten. And like I said, he might not be the one she's run off with.'

'What else, then? What else did you hardly notice?'

'The toothache. She never mentioned it again, after that night.'

Her father looked devastated.

Lynn tried to comfort him. 'I'll give it a month,' she said, 'and then she'll be back.'

'Let her stop where she is. I'm not sure I'd want her back, after this,' he said. 'She's taken the bloody bank book as well; she don't miss a trick, our Nina. "Gimme, gimme, gimme ... I want, I want, I want" – that's been your mother ever since I've known her, but she's in for a rude awakening, and so's the bloke she's run off with. Let him have a dollop of Nina and what she wants now.'

'Stay with us, if you don't want to stop in the house on your own.'

'No thanks. No offence to you, Lynn, but we never made very easy company, me and Graham, and I don't suppose what I said at your bonfire party will have improved matters, 'cause I meant it, and I still mean it.'

Lynn gave him a wry smile. 'I think he knows that.'

Her father nodded. 'Don't tell him about your mother, either,' he said. 'They'll be over the moon when they find out about that, his team.'

'I won't, but they're bound to realise, sooner or later,' she said.

'Let it be later then. Come on, let's go out.'

She got her coat and they walked through icy streets to a pub in the village centre. Her father held the door for her and she went in, glad to get inside.

'Not many braving it today,' the landlord greeted them. 'It's like the Arctic.'

Lynn's father gave him a dour look. 'Ever been to the Arctic in January?' he asked.

'No.'

'Didn't think so,' her father said, and gave their order.

'Like the Arctic,' he repeated as they sat down. 'People have got no bloody idea what a freezing, howling wilderness the Arctic is, in winter. I decided I'd sweat it out in the engine room, and I've never regretted it. It's enough for me to walk from there to the bridge, this time of year. God help the deckies, standing out in it for eighteen hours at a stretch – and more, when the fishing's good. I wish to God our Anthony had never gone to sea.'

They sat together in a corner.

'What's it like, in the Arctic, Dad, really?' she asked.

'I've just told you.'

'A freezing, howling wilderness. That doesn't tell me a lot.'

'What else is there? Men are fishing in temperatures you'd wonder how anyone can survive. The spit freezes in their throats. It freezes their voices – they can't shout. It takes a tot of rum for them to be able to speak. Put your hand on anything, and it sticks to it. You can't take it off without tearing your skin off. If you're inside the Arctic Circle in the middle of winter, there's no sun to rise, and none to set. You only know what time it is by looking at the clock on the bulkhead. You've got perpetual darkness. I do six-hour watches, but the deckies hardly get any sleep when they're gutting fish and hauling nets. Because they're usually dead on their feet and their hands and arms are frozen, there's accidents with gutting knives and machinery. Talk about fishermen and their vast amounts of money ... if you consider the hours they work and the conditions they work in you realise they're the worst-paid people in the world. No, they're not overpaid, fishermen.'

212

'What else?'

'Storms, blizzards, constant wind, seas that wash over the decks, black frost that ices the ship up, and ice, cracking and creaking and groaning all the time. You see the Aurora sometimes, the Northern Lights. They're something spectacular, they light the whole sky up. Icebergs as big as a block of flats, and ice isn't white, it's blue. In summer, you might see some of the animals ... Arctic foxes, you hear 'em more than see 'em. Seals, Polar bears, caribou. Birds, Arctic tern, mollies, ptarmigan. The cleanest, clearest seas you'll ever see – but you'd rather be at home.'

They sat talking until closing time. Her father left his sandwich almost untouched and went with her to collect Simon. They all walked back to the house together, and Lynn rang for a taxi.

Her father hugged Simon before he left. 'Look after him, Lynn. They're the best years of your life – when your bairns are little. I missed too much of you three growing up.'

'I've just had a thought,' he said, as they stood at the door. 'I wonder if Alec can remember that bloke's name? I'll be off down to our Anthony's, see if Brenda knows where I can find him.'

'She doesn't. He's moved out of his digs and they've heard nothing from him since the end of August. They told me that on New Year's Eve.'

With his last hope gone, he seemed to deflate like a burst balloon. He got into the taxi looking as if he'd aged ten years and she felt heart-sore to see him, and to think of him going back to an empty house.

Watching him go, Lynn wondered how she

213

could have ignored all the clues her mother had been giving out. But her head had been too full of her own troubles, and she'd never imagined her mother being anything other than what she'd always been – *there*, at home where she belonged, keeping house for them all. Her dad had never had to fend for himself, so how on earth would he manage if she never came back ... and how well would they get on together if she did come back, after this? He'd always worshipped the ground she walked on, but now she'd done something that was hard for any man to stomach, and it had knocked him for six. Vain, selfish Nina had *met somebody else,* so the love and devotion – not to mention the worldly goods – her husband had lavished on her for the best part of his life counted for nothing.

How could she treat him like that? How could she break their home up? Not only her father's home, but theirs as well – hers and Margaret's and Anthony's. It had been theirs to go back to at Christmas and Easter and birthdays and week-ends, and whenever they wanted to, and find everything just the same. But Nina had gone out and destroyed all that, and now nothing would ever be the same again. She had deliberately trampled it all into the muck, as if none of them counted for anything.

Lynn was suddenly overwhelmed by anger. The intensity of her feeling took her by surprise, and frightened her. It gave such power to her limbs that if Piers Marson had been there, she would have killed him herself, on the spot. She would never make him welcome; him, or whoever else her mother's partner in crime was – not ever. She would detest the slimy creature to her dying day. They would never step over her threshold – either of them. And that she should feel like this ... at her age! A grown woman with a home of her own!

She remembered Alec at their last meeting, and the way he'd looked at her when he said: 'Oh, Lynn – you've no idea! Kids don't get over it, they put up with it – *because they're powerless to do anything else!*'

She had an idea now, all right. Thank God they hadn't done it to Simon. She grabbed hold of him, lifted him up and held him tight, kissing his neck. 'I love you, Simon!'

He laughed and pulled away from her, his eyes dancing. 'Can I have a milkshake, then? Can we watch the telly, now Grandad's gone?'

Chapter 31

'There's no let up, is there?' Graham said, glancing through the kitchen window at the blizzard outside. 'The car heater's never been off lately, and the lights and wipers are getting some stick as well. Where's that bottle of distilled water? Where's that Vaseline? I'd better clean the terminals and top the battery up before it dies on me. I don't want to be stranded anywhere in this weather.'

Lynn stooped and groped in the cupboard under the sink to retrieve them. 'Where are you going, anyway?'

'Work. Where do you think? Mr Senior's scheduled a meeting. He wants us all there.'

'What – on a Saturday morning?'

'Well, he's the boss, he can have meetings when he wants. You don't think they're paying me this brilliant salary for nothing in return, do you? If they want me somewhere, I'll have to go.'

'Yes, but you're supposed to get weekends off, and I wanted you to look after Simon while I go into Hull.'

'What for?'

'My dad's ashore. I want to go and have a couple of hours with him.'

'Well, what's wrong with taking Simon? If they're going on a spending spree, they can kit him out, as well. You as well, if they like. I've no objection.'

'You know Simon hates trailing round shops. What time are you going to be back?'

'How do I know? A few of us might go down to the golf club for a spot of lunch.'

'You don't play golf.'

'You don't have to play golf to eat a meal, Lynn – and if you think I'll be rushing back to sit on my own with Simon while you swan off into Hull for hours, think again.'

'What about taking me out for a meal at the golf club, then? I haven't been out for ages. I had to sit on my own with Simon all Christmas and all New Year as well.'

'I can't help it. I wanted to take you out, and I would have, if we'd been able to get a babysitter. It wouldn't have hurt your mother to have had him so that you could have got to the works' do, at least.'

'It wouldn't have hurt yours, either.'

'She had the chance to go out with my dad. You can't blame her for taking it.'

'Huh! Maybe not! She doesn't often get chances like that, does she? She's usually right at the back of the queue.'

'What's that supposed to mean?'

Lynn sensed the danger, but she couldn't restrain herself. 'It means he's usually busy with other people's wives, by all accounts.' So there, she thought.

Graham thrust his face threateningly near to hers. 'Just leave my parents out of it, will you? They've done nothing to you. You're doing all right, dossing about at home all day. You've got nothing to complain about.'

'So you're not going to be in for your dinner?'

'No. I'm not going to be in for lunch. That'll save you something on the housekeeping money.'

'You can't save money on stuff you've already bought and held over because somebody hasn't come in for other meals. It goes off. So are you going to be in for tea?'

Graham put on his sheepskin coat and snatched up the distilled water and the Vaseline. Lynn repeated her question.

'Maybe, maybe not. More likely not, if I'm going to get a plateful of something that's been held over from other meals,' he said.

'Oh. At least I know where I stand, then,' she said.

'My dad? He called in yesterday, before he went

home,' Margaret said, and it was obvious from the expression on her face that Margaret hadn't a clue what had happened.

Lynn turned to her four noisy nephews, all clamouring for her attention. 'What did Father Christmas bring you?'

The answers came thick and fast. Cowboy hats, cowboy guns, jumpers, coats, gloves, socks, games, boxes of sweets – and a train set they all had to share.

'Go and show Simon then and let me and your mam have a cup of tea in peace for five minutes,' she said.

The boys bounded upstairs, with Simon following. As soon as they were out of earshot Lynn announced: 'She's hopped it. My mam. She's left him!'

'What?'

'He got home yesterday, and she was gone. She left a note, telling him she's buggered off with somebody else. She's done a bunkoff, Margaret. He came all the way up to Cottingham yesterday, to ask me if I knew anything. I thought he might have come here looking for Alec McCauley.'

Margaret turned pale. 'What for? Is it him she's gone off with?'

'No! But my dad thinks Alec might know who it is. I'm really worried about him, Margaret. Can I leave Simon with you for a bit? I just want to nip home, and make sure he's all right.'

'Why does he think Alec McCauley knows?'

'I'll tell you another time. Can I leave him?'

'Well, I don't think he'll be sitting in the house, if my mam's not there,' Margaret said. 'He's not likely to find much out there, is he? Where would you go, if you wanted to find a mate?'

'Rayners,' said Lynn, 'or Dee Street.'

Margaret nodded.

Lynn found herself repeating her father's words: 'You don't look all that surprised, Margaret.'

'Funny, i'n't it? I'm not, really. I wouldn't go as far as to say I've seen it coming, but I just had a feeling. She's been different, somehow, just lately. Anyway, try Rayners first, then the other pubs. I'll come with you.'

They left the boys with one of Jim's sisters who lived within spitting distance, and walked the short distance to Rayners pub, a handsome building on a corner, properly styled the Star and Garter, according to the sign swinging high above and the gold lettering on the large windows. They went in by the Hessle Road entrance, into a choking fog of tobacco smoke, thick enough to make their eyes water. The place was packed and noisy as usual, with 'Your Cheatin' Heart' wailing out of the juke box. The L-shaped bar, over twenty foot long on both sides, was lined with every conceivable cog in the wheel of the biggest deep-sea fishing industry in the world. Trawlermen and engineers and their sundry hangers-on rubbed shoulders with ship's runners, bobbers, fish skinners, filleters and various allied trades, their fishy fragrances mingling with the stench of stale cigarette smoke – which reeked from them, the furnishings, and the very walls. Lynn's eyes searched the room, taking in the two magnificent crystal chandeliers, sadly dulled by a film of nicotine, the polished tables, the padded stools and the upholstered benches which stretched the length of the walls beneath the windows. She spotted her dad in the distance, sitting near a window looking out onto West Dock Avenue with his arm around one of the few women in the place – none of them with much of a reputation to spoil. They made towards him.

'Did you get to know anything, then?' Lynn said.

He was evidently the worse for drink and far from pleased to see her. 'What about?'

'Alec McCauley.'

He returned his gaze to the street. 'Not so far. You'd have been better off sticking with him. He's a better bloke than the one you're tied to.'

'Simon loves his dad,' she said, as if excusing herself for going back to Graham.

'Humph.'

She followed his line of vision to a steady stream of men going into the owner's offices and coming out again, some jaunty and others less so, the mood depending on the amount of the settling, no doubt.

'Did you go and see Brenda?'

'No.'

'I suppose you were here till closing time yesterday, as well.'

'No. I had a stroll up to Dee Street.'

'Come home with me, Dad,' Margaret pleaded. 'I'll get you some dinner.'

'You've got enough to do looking after your own family.'

'You are my family,' Margaret said, and her eyes filled with tears.

He saw it, and his expression softened.

Lynn turned to the woman. 'Give us five minutes, will you?'

The woman looked at their father, waiting for his reaction.

He jerked his head towards the door. She strolled away and put a coin in the juke box.

'You should never have come here,' he said, before she was out of earshot.

'We were worried about you.'

'You can cut that out. I don't want any wetnurses. I'll look after my own business in my own way,' he said, and the sudden glint in his eye forestalled any warnings about women like the one standing by the juke box, and all the rest of the well-meant advice Lynn had intended to give him.

'Come for your tea, then,' Margaret coaxed.

He gave them a curt: 'Cheerio, lasses,' and beckoned his new friend.

'Come for your tea, Dad,' Margaret pleaded.

He raised a hand, and dismissed them with a wave.

'Bugger him, then, if that's his attitude,' Lynn said, when they got outside. 'I've galloped all the way down here in this bloody awful weather, and that's what you get.'

'You can't blame him. He's had a shock.'

'He's had a skinful as well, or he wouldn't have had somebody like her draped round his neck, with her hands in his bloody pockets. She looks a treat, don't she? Made for the job. He might get more than he bargains for off that one.'

'I reckon he's past caring,' Margaret said. 'I

might go and sleep at his house with the lads, if he won't come to mine. He'll have to have his meals.'

'I'd come myself, but I'd have to bring Simon, and if he came he'd soon be blabbing about my mother not being there to "Graham's team", as my dad calls 'em – and he doesn't want to give 'em the satisfaction. Neither do I, come to that. Come on, let's get back. I'm dying for a cup of tea and a ciggie,' Lynn said, feeling annoyed at having to dump everything on Margaret, as usual.

'I'd have thought the stink in Rayners would be enough to put anybody off smoking for life,' Margaret said.

Lynn ignored that. 'It's a bit breezy in Scotland,' she commented as they passed a newspaper hoarding proclaiming that twenty people had been killed by falling masonry because of a 'killer hurricane' there.

'Pity it's not blowing through Rayners,' Margaret said. 'It would take a killer hurricane to get rid of the smoke in there.'

Chapter 32

They got off the bus in Cottingham, and walked home feeling pretty jaded, with Simon dragging his feet all the way. Graham's car was in the driveway and the door was unlocked. Lynn pushed it open, and an eager, jolly, fat little puppy came bounding down the hallway towards them and

222

jumped up at Simon. He laughed, and tried to grab hold of it, all signs of weariness and bad temper gone. The puppy was too quick for him, and dashed away again, to Graham.

'What's this?' Lynn demanded, although it was perfectly obvious.

'What's it look like? It's a puppy. A King Charles spaniel, to be exact.'

'Whose is it?'

'It's ours.'

Lynn shook her head. 'It's not ours. I've got to be careful of every penny, Graham. I could barely scrape the bus fare together to go and see my dad. You're on at Simon not to scuff his shoes or spoil his clothes, and last Sunday when he wouldn't eat his dinner you threatened to take the cost of it out of his money box because we couldn't afford to waste food – so don't come home with any puppies for us to feed!'

'I thought you might have come home with a few parcels, if you've been to see your dad,' Graham said. 'Didn't you take him shopping?'

'I wasn't in the mood.'

'You missed a golden opportunity to save on the housekeeping, there, then,' he said.

'I did, didn't I? But it's up to you to help me save on the housekeeping. You'll have to take that dog back where you found it.'

'I can't. I got her from one of the bosses' wives – she breeds them. I got her cheap.'

'I want to keep her,' Simon said. 'I want to call her Lassie.'

Lynn was focused on Graham. 'How cheap?'

'Cheap enough.'

223

'It can't possibly be cheap enough when we can barely feed ourselves, Graham. What do you think they cost to feed? And what if it needs a vet?'

'Well you'd better pull your finger out and find a job, then.'

'All right, I'll take a job cleaning. There's a postcard in the newsagent's – a woman just round the corner on Hull Road wants somebody a couple of mornings a week. She's all right. Her son's in the same class as Simon.'

'You won't take a job cleaning, and especially not round here! I'm not having anybody saying that my wife does their charring.'

'Well, you find me a decent job that lets me get to school in time for Simon, and I'll take it. I've looked, and there's nothing. And if I get a job, we can't have a dog. You can't get animals and then leave them on their own all day, so take it back, and get your money back.'

'I want to keep it!' Simon protested, gazing into the puppy's eager brown eyes. 'I like it.'

'We are keeping her. Never mind what your mother says.'

'Good,' Simon laughed, and poked his tongue out at Lynn.

She saw that she'd lost the argument. 'Is it house trained?'

'Not quite. And she's a she.'

'Well, you'll be cleaning her crap up, then, until she is,' she said. 'Has she got a name?'

'What shall we call her, Simon?'

'Lassie!'

'Right, Lassie it is, then. When's your dad sailing?'

'Monday – and you'll be looking after the dog on your own tomorrow. I'll be going to see him.'

'You can't. My mother's invited us to dinner, remember? And if we get there late, the Yorkshire puddings will be ruined, and that'll put her out for the week.'

So, we'll let your mother's Yorkshire puddings take precedence over my father's ruined life, Lynn thought – but she couldn't say it, since her father didn't want 'Graham's team' crowing about his domestic disaster. Nor could she ask Graham to take her to Boulevard in the car. Going by bus after lunch was hardly worth the effort, for the little time it would leave her to spend with him, and there was no guarantee he'd be in when she got there. There was no guarantee she wouldn't get another 'Cheerio, lass!' even if he was.

She left Simon and Graham with the dog, and went into the hallway, to phone him. There was no answer, and if he'd been there he would certainly have answered, in case it was her mother. He might have gone to Margaret's, but it was more likely he was still in some pub or other, drinking himself into oblivion – and there was nothing she could do about it.

She would have to leave it to Margaret, as usual. At least she only lived round the corner, and with all Jim's relatives nearby there was always somebody who would watch the lads for her while she went.

Lynn's thoughts drifted back to her parents later that night, after she and Graham had made friends again in bed. She hoped her father hadn't taken that awful woman home – her mother would have a fit if she found out he'd had somebody like that in the house. But her mother was nobody to criticise anybody, now. What business was it of hers who he had in the house now she'd deserted him? And where on earth was she, with that Piers? Talk about gods with feet of clay! Lynn would never have believed it of either of them, forty-eight hours ago. It just goes to show, she thought, you never really know anybody, not even your own mother and father.

And fancy her dad telling her she should have stuck to Alec! He would never have said anything like that if he hadn't been half Brahms and Liszt. Why hadn't she said: *I went back to Graham because I love him*? Probably because that hadn't been the first thought to jump into her mind. She ought to have told him straight out that she would have stuck with Alec, if Alec hadn't given her the brush-off.

But that cut too deep even to think about. That ugly wound had to be kept hidden from everybody – from herself most of all. Yeah, I've buried that, she thought. I've buried it.

'I've had just about enough of that dog,' she complained a few days later, on finding another smelly little pile in the kitchen.

'I'll do it! I'll clean it up,' Simon volunteered, with the puppy prancing and capering around him.

'No, you won't. Don't you go near it! Your dad's the one who should be clearing this up,' she said, delving in the cupboard under the sink for the thick rubber gloves and the toilet roll, and the bucket, cloth and bleach kept for the purpose.

But Graham, naturally, was never there to deal with these stomach-turning little accidents. Typically, he walked in when the job was done and everything had been sanitised.

He arrived home five minutes later, early for once, and no tea ready. He handed her the *Hull Mail*. 'There's a trawler gone missing,' he said, and went to hang up his coat, with the puppy jumping and barking round his feet.

Lynn's heart leaped into her mouth. Anthony, her dad, Jim ... Alec! It might be any of them.

'Not heard of for days. Search begins for Sprite*',* the headline ran. She quickly scanned the column: *'...sailed on 10 January ... last seen off the Lofoten Islands on January 13 ... a full-scale air and sea search has begun...'*

Her dad was all right, anyway. He'd sailed on the fourteenth, only ten days ago. And Anthony was all right, he'd sailed just after the New Year, on the *Silver Fox*. But when had Jim sailed? She couldn't remember. And what about Alec? Nobody seemed to have seen hide nor hair of him for ages. The *Sprite*, the *Sprite*, she thought, with creeping dread. Wasn't that the ship that Alec had sailed on months ago? That ship that someone had deliberately damaged, rather than sail in her? The Lofoten Islands were an eighteen-hundred-mile round trip, as far as she could remember – surely it would take four days to get there, maybe five. Jim was probably all right, but she couldn't be sure, and she couldn't ring and find out, because Margaret had no telephone.

227

She went to phone Brenda, who had not only seen the paper but had heard dark rumours about the silent trawler. The word was that the sparks had refused to sail on her, so she'd left the dock with no radio operator. 'Don't worry about Anthony, he's all right. He's on the *Silver Fox*.' Brenda hesitated for a moment, and then said: 'The *Sprite*'s the one that Alec was on about, that had to be towed back to Hull, because the spare hand took an axe to the steering gear.'

'Do you know whether he was on it this trip?' Lynn asked, careful not to mention his name, in case Graham was listening.

'We've heard nothing from Alec for ages,' Brenda said.

Lynn resisted the temptation to ask whether Orla knew anything about him, and concentrated on Jim. But Brenda had no idea which ship Jim was on, and she couldn't go to Margaret's and find out because she'd sprained her ankle falling on the ice, and was finding it painful to walk. 'Ring your mother,' she said, 'and ask her to go.'

No help there, then, Lynn thought, as she put the phone down. 'You'll have to take me to our Margaret's after tea,' she told Graham. 'I've got an awful feeling Jim might have been on that ship.'

'I can't. I'm going out.'

'What, again? You can drop me off before you go, then. I'll take Simon with me.'

'Simon's at school tomorrow, and what about Lassie? You can't leave her in the house on her own.'

A week of scrubbing carpets and floors and

rescuing chewed footwear convinced Lynn that he was right. She could not leave Lassie alone in the house. 'Ring your mother, then,' she said, 'and ask her to have Simon and Lassie. She can take Simon to school tomorrow, if I have to stay over.'

'I don't want to go to Grandma's,' Simon said. 'I want to come to Auntie Margaret's, and play with the lads.'

'Why should you have to stay over?' Graham frowned. 'Why should you go, in the first place? What can you do about it, even if Jim is on that ship?'

'I can give our Margaret a bit of help and comfort, because if anything's happened to Jim, she'll be absolutely devastated. She'll need me.'

'Here, hand me that paper; let me have a look.' She handed it over.

He quickly skimmed the article, then read aloud: *'A director of the firm said: "The trawler's silence is most likely owing to a radio failure. There is no immediate cause for concern."* So there you are – it's a bit too soon to start panicking. What's for tea? I'm starving.'

'They don't start a full-scale air and sea search for nothing, Graham.'

'No, but you needn't go charging off before you know anything's wrong. And it's not as if you're her only relative. What's wrong with your mother going? She's on the spot. And what about all Jim's sisters? He's got dozens of them, as far as I can make out. Half of Hessle Road's related to him. Let them deal with it. Go on, ring your mother now and tell her to call at Margaret's, and

229

let you know what's going on.'

Never do anything yourself – tell somebody else to do it, and report back to you. How typically Graham, Lynn thought. No wonder this master of the art of delegation was a rising star in the company. He was evidently destined for great things. She walked into the hallway and went through the charade of ringing a house that she knew was empty. Graham followed. She held the receiver to his ear.

'Well, there's nobody there, is there?' he said. 'She'll have seen the paper and gone straight to Margaret's. There's no need for you to go at all.'

Lynn went into the kitchen without another word and silently got on with the evening meal, her mind full of those school friends who had been orphaned after the sinking of the *Jacinta* and *Diego*, lost off Iceland's North Cape with not a single survivor: forty men and boys claimed by the sea and lost to mothers, fathers, wives and children – everyone who loved them. She thought about Margaret and Jim's four lads and tears filled her eyes. Thank God neither Anthony nor her father was on that ship. Thank God that Brenda had refused that awful wedding dress – and how could she, a trawlerman's daughter, ever have thought it a good idea to give her such a thing?

But Jim and Alec – what about them? She hoped and prayed that neither of them were on the *Sprite*. She hoped that Graham and the owners were right, and it was just a radio failure. She hoped to God that the *Sprite* was sitting on top of a teeming 'fish shop' and that the silence was deliberate. If they were on to a good thing skippers sometimes cut communications altogether, rather than let rivals horn in on their happy hunting ground.

How long must it have been, she wondered, since that awful year when the *Jacinta* and *Diego* went down and half the kids she knew were suddenly fatherless? It was the year before she'd moved up to the high school so she must have been about eleven, which made it...

Thirteen years, almost to the day.

Chapter 33

'He's *been* on her, but he wasn't on her this trip,' Margaret said, the following evening after the boys were in bed. The two sisters were sitting in Margaret's tiny living room with a bright fire blazing in the hearth, and the thick red curtains drawn against the icy night. 'He said he'd never sail in her again if he could help it; she's an awful old boat. She could never bring a decent catch home, because the winch hadn't the power to pull the net in. And she was always flooding. They did more baling out than fishing. A sea not much bigger than a ripple on a mill-pond and she'd suddenly drop to starboard and nearly turn over. The lads called her the submarine, Jim said.'

Lynn stared into the fire, thinking of the only one not accounted for – Alec. And how stupid of her to worry herself sick about him, months after their little love affair was dead in the water. She

231

was a respectable married woman again, so what business had she to be worrying about Alec McCauley? And the whole point of crossing trawlermen off her list of potential husbands had been to avoid this sort of torment. 'And no radio contact for nearly two weeks, now,' she said, half to herself.

'That's hardly surprising. They had a problem with transmitting when Jim was on her, not enough voltage, or something. Same problem as with the winch, I suppose – not enough power. The skipper told the owners, but I don't think they did a lot about it, because the radio operator refused to sail in her this trip, if what I've heard is right.'

'Well, that says it all, don't it?'

Margaret grimaced in wry agreement. 'Nobody had any confidence in her – apart from which you might as well have stopped at home for the money you made. They always had trouble getting crews for the *Sprite*.'

A horrid little shiver coursed down Lynn's spine like a mild electric shock. She hunched her shoulders and shuddered. 'Pity the men in her now,' she said.

'Scraped up from men's hostels, or anywhere the ship's runners can find them probably, men who've no idea what they're letting themselves in for – and that desperate they'd take anything. A regular Christmas cracker crew, I reckon, and skippered by a youngster climbing his way up, or a bloke who's had a few bad trips, on his way down the ranking. I don't think anybody who really had a choice would go. It's not that long ago that some maniac took an axe to the steering column. That was after they'd had to call into Grimsby for radar repairs – about five minutes after she'd sailed out of Hull, from what I heard.'

'That was at the end of August. Alec McCauley was aboard,' Lynn said. 'But maybe that axe-man wasn't such a maniac after all, Margaret. At least they all got back alive.'

'They did, and she must have been out of action for a while after that. I'm so relieved Jim didn't sail in her,' said Margaret.

'And me. I was just thinking about the *Jacinta* and *Diego*, and all those kids we knew...'

'I know. Thanks for coming, Lynn,' Margaret said, softly. 'Jim's all right, but it means a lot to know somebody cares enough to make sure – from my own family, not Jim's, I mean.'

Lynn's eyes widened. 'Of course we care! I'd have come yesterday if it hadn't been for Graham. "Let your mother go! She's nearest!" he said. I didn't want to tell him she's hopped it, so I had to stay at home.'

'I suppose he'll have to know sometime.'

'Not from me, he won't. Have you heard anything from her?'

Margaret shook her head. 'I wonder where she is? And how she is?'

'She'll be all right, knowing my mother,' Lynn said. 'She'd ditch him and come home if she wasn't. Did my dad come for his tea on Sunday?'

'No. I went there and helped him get all his gear ready to go back to sea. I think he was glad to see the back of home; it's awful without her. How've you been getting on with Graham?'

'We hardly ever see each other. He's never in,' Lynn shrugged. She hesitated, then with her eyes on Margaret's swelling waistline, asked: 'Are you expecting again, Margaret?'

Margaret nodded. 'The doctor reckons I'm five months, but I'm nowhere near.'

'Five months looks about right to me, and they're not often wrong.'

'Well, he's wrong this time.'

'You'll need a bigger house.'

'Not straight away. A baby doesn't take much room,' Margaret said. 'Anyway, Graham must be in now, because you're here.'

'Aye, on a Monday night. There's not much doing anywhere on a Monday night, is there? He's started spending a lot of time at the golf club, doing some strenuous social climbing. We can barely make ends meet with the mortgage, but I wouldn't be surprised if he joins soon, and then he'll have to have all the gear – the clubs, the hat, the shoes, the whole wardrobe. I can see it coming. Oh, we're really going up in the world, now, you know.'

'He never does things by halves, does he, Graham?' Margaret said. 'Does he still see much of that Kevin Walsh he was so friendly with?'

'Not since we moved,' Lynn said.

'I'm glad. I never liked him. I always thought he was a bad influence on Graham.'

'Ha! Ha! Ha!' Lynn burst into laughter, genuinely amused. 'I think Kevin Walsh arrived a lot too late in the day to be a bad influence on Graham. The damage had already been done. His dad had that job sewn up before he ever met

Kevin Walsh. But he's left his old friends behind now he's forging ahead in the company. He's very popular, apparently. I've left my old friends behind as well now I've left work and moved house, but not by choice. I really miss Janet, now she's not just round the corner. It's such a trek to each other's houses these days. She's not keen on coming to see me because she can't stand Graham, and I don't often get to hers because of Simon, and not knowing when she's working.'

'You could phone her.'

'I do, sometimes, but it's not the same. And having to make arrangements is not the same as just popping in whenever you feel like it, and taking a chance on her being in, is it?'

'No, it's not,' said Margaret, who had visitors 'popping in' all day long. 'Our Anthony's back tomorrow, God willing. He said he'd pop in with some fish.'

Chapter 34

An icy draught and a flurry of snowflakes blew in with Graham. He slammed the front door and looked up at Lynn, who was halfway down the staircase with Simon, bathed and in his pyjamas.

'It sounds as if the owners have given up on the *Sprite* now the life raft's been found,' he said, 'but they're putting it out that they're assuming nothing and they're going on with the search. Pretty hopeless, though, I should think.'

At the sound of his voice, Lassie started barking, and scratching at the closed living-room
door.

Lynn's heart sank at the thought of those
fishermen and their families. She walked slowly
down the stairs, with Simon beside her. 'The life
raft's been found? I've seen nothing in the paper.'

'That's because there's been nothing. It'll be in
the next edition, I expect.'

'How come you know, then?'

'I get to know a lot of things, these days. I'm
getting well in with the cognoscenti,' Graham
said. 'One of our bosses plays golf with some of
the owners and directors. Lucky your relations
weren't on it. Quite a good chap, Jim, I've always
thought.'

'Hmm, that's a big word, though – cognoscenti,'
Lynn said, ushering Simon into the living room to
comb his hair and let it dry before the fire.

'Yeah, I got it from the company. It goes with
the big salary,' Graham said, following them with
the dog dancing excitedly around his legs. He sat
in the armchair by the fire, and caressed her,
rubbing her ears while she kept jumping up and
trying to lick his face. He gave the latest bulletin
on the progress of the company and, seeming in
an exceptionally jovial mood he finally asked:
'What's your news, then, Lynn?'

'Our Anthony's home,' she said, retrieving the
comb from the sideboard drawer. 'He's just rung
me to say the weather up there's the worst any of
them have ever experienced in their lives – and
after they'd battled their way back to Hull with a
boatload of fish they had to unload it themselves

236

because the bloody bobbers have gone on strike. And they buggered the winches before they went by taking umpteen of the fuses out of the fuse box, so by the time they'd got that working and the fish landed they'd wasted half of their first day ashore and nearly missed the market.' She sat down and beckoned Simon towards her.

'Oh, bad luck – but lucky for him he got back at all, by the sound of it. Well, what other news have you got?'

'What other news am I going to have, stuck in the house all day?'

He gave her a penetrating look. 'I thought you might have an interesting bit of family news, for example.'

'I've just told you the family news.'

'Not quite. Hasn't your mother done a bunk? Isn't that family news? That's if it's true. I might have been misinformed.'

With Graham's eyes still fixed on her, Lynn pulled Simon towards her and sat quietly combing his hair, saying nothing.

'I'll take it that she has, then,' Graham said, after a long silence. 'Why didn't you tell me?'

'I didn't think you'd be interested.'

He burst into laughter. 'Oh, that's priceless, that is. After the way your old man put me in fear of my life, you didn't think I'd be interested to know his wife's shoved off?'

'Is that a gem you got from the cognoscenti?'

'No, the fruit shop, as a matter of fact.'

'Come on, Simon,' Lynn said, 'It's your bed-time.'

Graham's unwavering stare came to rest on

Simon. 'Stay where you are, Simon,' he countered. 'I'm not a believer in shielding kids from life's realities.'

'Well, I am. Come on, Simon,' Lynn insisted, but before she could get him out of the way, Graham brought the reality in question home to him in one sentence:

'Your Nanna's run off with another man, Simon, and left your grandad all on his own! What do you think to that?'

Simon was quiet for a while, digesting the news, then: 'Is he from Leeds?' he asked.

Graham looked quite thrown for a moment. 'I don't know!' he said, 'but I suppose your grandad's very upset about it, so we'll have to be really, really nice to him when we see him again, won't we?'

'Yeah,' Simon nodded.

'Good boy,' Graham smiled, rubbing his hands: 'What's for tea, Lynn?'

'Why ask me? I should have thought the cognoscenti would have already told you.'

'What is it, then?'

'Egg and chips, *à la* mushy peas and ketchup. We've already had ours, seeing you didn't let me know what time you'd be in.'

'Wonderful!' he laughed. 'What a marvellous start to the weekend! But not a meal I'd want to serve to anybody whose opinion I cared about.'

Graham was very much in the mood that night. After a particularly lengthy and vigorous love-making session he lay back with his hands clasped behind his head, gazing dreamily at the shadows

238

on the opposite wall. 'I always knew your mother had a bit of a spark in her,' he said, eventually. 'She's the sort of woman that needs something extra.'

Lynn had been on the point of sleep, but was roused to wakefulness by that remark. 'Extra to what?' she asked.

'Extra to what she gets from your dad, by the look of it. He must have been keeping her a bit short. A lot short, probably, seeing he's at sea for three weeks at a stretch. I shouldn't think that would be enough to keep your mother happy. I imagine she takes a bit of keeping up with, in the bedroom department.'

'Mind your own business, Graham. It's got nothing to do with you,' Lynn snapped, repelled by his lurid imaginings about her parents' private lives.

Graham slid under the covers. 'I bet she is, though,' he persisted. 'I bet she's quite a goer, your mother. I thought she had a fancy for me, not so long ago.'

'Huh!' Lynn snorted. 'You think there isn't a woman born who hasn't got a fancy for you.'

Graham yawned, and turned over. 'Well, there aren't many, you've got to admit. I don't know of any, personally.'

'There's Janet.'

'In the words of the immortal Bard, the lady doth protest too much,' he said.

'To conceal her burning passion for you, I expect.'

'Yeah. That's it.'

Had anyone else said it she would have thought

239

they were jesting, but this was Graham. Egolatry, she thought. If it were a medical condition, that would be the name of it.

Chapter 35

'You'll never believe it, Lynn,' Margaret said, a few days later, 'you'll just never believe it...'

It was a rare thing for Margaret to use the telephone, so as soon as she'd heard her sister's voice Lynn had known she must be ringing about something earth-shattering.

'What?'

'...the letter the owners have sent to one of Jim's sister's friends. Her husband was on the *Sprite...*'

'Telling her he's safe and well, I hope,' Lynn said.

'No! They've admitted there's no chance of that, because they're *deeply upset about the terrible loss of life, caused by this inexplicable tragedy to a well-ordered sh-ship and wish to send you our sincere sympathy...* And she's got three bairns!'

'Unexplained tragedy? To a *well-ordered ship?* That bloody leaky old death trap that threatened to sink every time there was a swell, and they're calling it a *well-ordered ship?*'

'It's aw-awful,' Margaret said, and dissolved into sobs.

'Well, what else can you expect? I doubt if their sincere sympathy will stretch to coughing any money up. They're telling her from the outset: *don't think of trying to pin the blame on us. We're not having it!* Because if the families could manage to pin the blame on them and make it stick, they might have to dig into their deep pockets, and that *would* make them "deeply upset" – like nothing else could! Genuinely, deeply, upset!'

Margaret's reply was lost in crying.

'Margaret, Margaret – ring me back when you're a bit calmer,' Lynn said. 'On second thoughts, don't. Go home and make yourself a nice hot cuppa. I'm coming down there as soon as I've done Graham's tea.'

Graham was in late, as usual.

'I'm going down to our Margaret's after tea,' Lynn announced.

'You can't. I'm going out. A couple of the chaps from work are teaching me to play bridge.'

Lynn shrugged. 'All right, I'll take our Simon with me.'

'You can't. He's got school tomorrow, and it's nearly bedtime now.'

'I'll take him with me, and we'll sleep at my dad's. I've still got a key.'

'What about school?'

'He can miss it for once. It won't hurt him.'

'No, he can't. I'm not having it. School's important, and tomorrow Simon goes to school.'

'Ring your mother and ask her to babysit, then.'

'I'd like something to eat. It's been a long day, and I'm hungry.'

'All right,' Lynn said, and disappeared into the kitchen like the obedient, well-tamed little wife she felt herself in danger of morphing into.

241

Margaret put her boys to bed and leaving Jim's twelve-year-old niece sitting in the house with them she walked with Lynn and Simon along Hessle Road in the direction of Boulevard. The pubs were just turning out, and the frost-rimed road was full of people walking briskly along in little groups, occasionally stopping for a moment to chat with others. A party of clean-shaven, smartly dressed young deckhands were approaching from the opposite direction, a bit less unsteady on their feet and a lot more subdued than was usual in young fishermen after a night on the beer.

'Hey, Margaret,' the tallest of them called, 'you know that life raft from the *Sprite*? It was found over a fortnight ago – on the thirteenth! And an Icelandic trawler picked up a Mayday on the twelfth, only a couple of days after they left Hull. No wonder it was *the silent trawler!* They were probably all dead on the thirteenth...'

'But the gaffers were cracking on they were trying to contact her up to a day or two ago!' Margaret said.

'Humph! There's a lot of things that don't really add up,' another said, with a significant raising of his eyebrows.

'No. You wonder what's going on. It sounds like the union's trying to get to the bottom of things, though. There's even an MP going round asking questions.'

'There's a lot of questions about this job, and he wants answers. He's taking it to the House of Commons.'

'And now it looks like there's another one gone missing. Another one they've had no radio contact with for days. Different owners, though.'

'What, another ship? Which one?' Lynn could hear the tension in Margaret's voice.

'The *Prospero*.'

'Oh, them poor lads!' she exclaimed – but Jim was not on the *Prospero*, and to Lynn, her sister's relief was almost palpable.

'Who's the nipper?' a curly-haired young deckie asked.

'Simon, my nephew. Lynn's son.'

'Well, Simon, never let anybody get you on a trawler – never ever! Not even in the middle of summer. You'd be better off going to Hell for a pastime than going to sea for a pleasure trip.'

The tallest fisherman jerked his thumb in the direction of Boulevard. 'There's a woman up there collecting signatures.'

'What for?' Lynn asked.

'A petition.'

'What for?'

'Safety. Safety on trawlers.'

'She's demanding all sorts of changes.'

'Says she's taking it to London an' all. She'll bash on the Prime Minister's door, if she's got to. Maybe bash him, as well, to listen to her talk.'

'We'll sign,' Margaret said.

'We will. It can't hurt, can it?'

'Might even do a bit of good. She seems determined enough,' the curly-haired lad said. 'Ta-ra, then!'

'Ta-ra, then.'

'Ta-ra!'

243

'See ya!'

The sisters walked on with Simon between them. As they neared the Halfway public house a big, handsome woman with a headscarf over her bouffant hairdo stepped forward, barring the way. She was dressed in a thick coat and heavy boots, and the vapour of her breath hung on the cold air.

'Is that the petition?' Lynn asked, nodding towards the clipboard she was holding.

'You've heard about it then?'

'Yeah. We'll sign.'

Margaret took the board and signed. 'My husband's at sea now – not due back until the tenth of February,' she said. 'And my brother sailed for Bear Island yesterday.'

The woman gave a grim nod. 'And my son's fishing off Iceland. Something's got to be done, love, and it's up to us women. The men can't do it; they're never at home long enough.'

Lynn thought of Alec, and said nothing. She took the board from Margaret and read the heading: 'Petition for Fishermen's Safety'. She signed, and gave it back. 'They're saying the *Prospero's* missing now.'

'There's been no radio contact for days, so – not much hope,' the woman said.

'Give me a handful of them forms,' Margaret said. 'I'll get plenty of signatures. I'll take 'em into Birds Eye.'

'Give me some, as well. I'll get as many as I can,' said Lynn.

A few steps further along the road Margaret burst out with an anguished: 'Oh, poor lads! Oh, but thank God it's not Jim! Does that sound awful?'

'Does it sound awful to want your husband alive, when you've got four young sons and you're expecting another baby?' Lynn exclaimed. 'What do you think?'

Chapter 36

Their father's house was freezing when Lynn opened the back door and the three of them stepped into the kitchen. Simon peered into the darkness and shivered.

'Where's my Nanna?'

Lynn groped for the light switch. 'She's gone away. Your dad told you,' she said. 'Brr-rr! I think it's colder in here than it is outside.'

'I don't like it here without my Nanna. I want to go home.'

'I don't like it here without your Nanna either, but it's too late for us to go home now. Don't worry, it'll be warm in bed. I'll put the electric blanket on.'

Margaret filled the kettle while Lynn went into the hallway to turn the heating on, and then with Simon hard on her heels she ran upstairs. She flicked on the bedroom light and as she walked across the carpet to close the curtains felt a squelching under her feet. A drop of water fell with a splash in front of her. On looking up she saw that the ceiling was bulging.

'Oh, for crying out loud!' she groaned. She knew next to nothing about electricity, but had a feeling it might not mix very well with water, so she turned the light off. 'What the heck did your grandad turn the heating off for? He ought to have left it on low; he might have known the pipes would freeze. He's an engineer, for pity's sake!' She ran back down to the kitchen, to ferret under the sink to find a bucket and a screwdriver.

'What's up?'

'Burst pipe! There's water pissing all over the bedroom carpet. Take these upstairs, while I get the stepladder. There'll be no chance of getting a plumber at this time of night, even if we had the money to pay one.'

Lynn dragged the stepladder up the stairs and then by the light from the landing she clambered up with the screwdriver and bucket to make a hole in the plaster and let the water run out, then climbed back down the steps while trying to keep the bucket under the stream.

'Where's the stop tap?'

'Under the stairs.'

Lynn pushed the steps out of the way and set the bucket under the dripping water. Then downstairs again, followed by Simon, to get under the stairs and grope for the brass stop tap. It took all her strength to turn it off.

She called upstairs: 'Put the plug in the bath and turn the taps on, will you?' and then went into the kitchen to fill the sink bowl and every other receptacle she could find, before letting the rest of the water run down the sink. Simon watched her, tired and bewildered.

Margaret came rattling back down the stairs with the stepladder. 'I've turned the heating off again now the hot water tank's empty, so you can't sleep here tonight – you'll freeze. You'll have to come back to my house.'

'No, we'll be as snug as bugs in a rug when we get in bed, and we've got enough water for about a million cups of tea. We'll have the first one now, shall we?' she said, brightly, and thought: oh, Mother, Mother, Mother, why did you leave us?

There was a hammering at the door, and a familiar shape outlined beyond the glass.

'It's Graham,' Margaret said.

Simon's face lit up and he ran to the door. 'Dad!' he shouted.

Chapter 37

The ice was thick on the rails and on the wire ropes, thicker on the upperworks and likely to get worse, everywhere. Buried in layers of woollens and covered by wet weather gear the men on deck were working like fury in the northern twilight – with axes, lump hammers, anything they could get hold of to crack it off.

Alec had just risked life and limb to get the ice off the radar scanner when the skipper yelled from the bridge at the top of his lungs to make himself heard above the howling wind.

'Greener!'

The men below dropped everything and hung

on for dear life to anything they could grab as a wall of green water edged with a crest of white rose up as high as the foremast and smashed down on them, swilling across the deck, propelling everything before it and sweeping the feet from under them – a killer wave. Then it was gone, mercifully with nobody washed overboard.

'The next sea, and we've had it,' the bosun yelled. 'Another sea like that, and we've had our chips.'

Sea water froze on their faces, forming icicles on noses, beards and eyebrows as they made their way to the galley to get some tea. The warmth of the galley fire caused blue and swollen hands and fingers to hurt intensely.

'It's the worst bloody place he could have picked, the west side of Iceland,' a young deckhand said. 'My dad reckons there's nowhere as bad as this for gales, even in summer. It can be fine weather, then a wind springs up out of nowhere and brings the frost with it. You haul the nets in, and the fish are covered in ice.'

'Aye, and in two seconds flat the sodding ship's covered in ice and you can't even get to the land for safety,' said another. 'You end up having to ride it out, and hope for the best. Why the hell he came here...'

''Cause he thinks the fish are here, and only three days steaming and you can get your gear down – that's why,' one of the less excitable souls ventured. 'Go nor' nor' east, and it's five or six days. And you get bad weather anywhere.'

'Not as bad as here. The west side of Iceland's where angels fear to tread, my dad says.'

'Did you feel her?' one of the older deckhands demanded. 'Nearly on her beam end, she was. There's a bloody hurricane blowing up her arse, and he wants to put the bastard gear over the side again. This in't the first time I've done this trip – I've done it many a time, and in bloody bad weather, but this skipper's a bastard lunatic. He'll lose her and us with her if he don't stow the trawl and turn her head to wind.'

The rest of the crew relieved their feelings in worse obscenities.

Alec drank the hot tea and let them get it all off their chests. Then he made his brief contribution: 'We *will* lose her if we don't knock that ice off, so finish your tea and save your breath for chopping.'

He herded them back on deck and was the first to take a swing at the ice. He had to keep them at it. If fatalism took a hold, they would just stand around and wait for the worst. Abandoning hope was not an option.

So why had he abandoned hope with Lynn, he wondered? Why had he let a bloody kid stand in his way? No, maybe not a *bloody* kid. Simon was a good kid and he loved his dad – but he would have had to get used to it, just like he'd had to get used to it, like many another kid had had to do, and if he'd stuck to his purpose, he might have swept her off her feet.

Might have. But he hadn't been a hundred per cent sure until the last minute that she wasn't just using him to bring her husband to heel. He'd worried about it constantly, every time he'd left her to go back to sea, and he'd seen many another fishermen fret himself to death about what his girlfriend might be doing while he was away. He'd seen what it did to them. If he hadn't finished it with Lynn, he'd have spent all his time at sea worrying about what she was up to while his back was turned. He'd never have been able to keep his mind on the job and that would have been no use either to him or to these men. Oh, sod it all, anyway. It was too late to worry about it.

'The next sea, and we've had it. Another sea like that, and we've had our lot,' the bosun repeated.

Sheer adrenaline made Alec laugh. 'Our chips *and* our lot, Jackie!' he shouted, 'Save your breath for chopping!'

The next sea, and there might be a lot of widows and orphans, Alec thought, and if I'd married Lynn she'd have been among them. Maybe things are better as they are. All this hard work is useless. This pearl of a ship, she'll let us all down in the end – just like a woman.

He pushed the thought away. He couldn't allow himself to think like that, not with other men relying on him. He did a gruelling, dangerous job, and although he couldn't expect to be liked, he knew he was respected for it. He was a tough professional and where he led, they would follow – beyond the limits of their endurance at times. As long as he kept chopping, so would they. The rhythm and the effort of swinging the axe gradually dispelled the fear. It added to the music of the eddying wind, the pounding of the waves, and the ear-splitting noise of massive slabs of ice crashing onto the deck and into the sea as they battled to stay afloat.

If they ever got out of this – no, *when* they got out of this, they still had to make a trip – or suffer the consequences. What they'd caught so far wouldn't pay the ship's fuel bill. Try going back in debt and telling the owners you couldn't catch enough fish because the weather was bad! That would be the end of you. They'd tell you not to bother catching any more, and take their pick from the queue of men waiting to take your place. As far as the owners were concerned, there were no excuses. For them, there was one consideration and one alone – money.

'It'll end up in a Board of Trade inquiry, this,' one of the deckhands said.

'And what good'll that do us?' the frozen, fifteen-year-old galley boy asked.

Nobody answered him.

Chapter 38

On the first Friday in February Lynn saw the headline on the board outside the newsagent's: '*Sprite* Given Up – Official' and underneath 'Time Runs Out for *Prospero*'.

The number of men who are lost at sea, and the only paper to show any concern about it is the *Hull Mail*, she thought, stepping into the shop to buy a copy. 'Fishermen might as well not exist, for all the notice the national papers take of them,' she remarked to the man behind the counter.

He nodded towards a pile of national papers. 'Well, they've taken some notice today,' he said. 'This is the day they were both supposed to have been back in Hull.'

'I know.'

'How are you getting on with your petition?'

'All right. Quite a few pages of signatures,' Lynn said, handing over her money.

'Looks as if the government's getting involved now. The Prime Minister's told two senior politicians to arrange a meeting with the fishermen's wives and some of the Hull MPs – and the union.'

'Amazing, seeing hardly any fishermen bother to join a union. I don't think I know of one,' Lynn said, and left the shop to catch the bus, and go straight down to Margaret's.

'There was somebody to do with the Board of Trade spouting off in Parliament a day or two ago,' Margaret said, when Lynn gave her the paper. '"We shall certainly have an investigation the moment that, unhappily, we are forced to assume the vessel is lost", he said. You know the way they talk.'

'Aye, as if they gave a fiddler's fart,' Lynn said, standing as near to the fire as she could, chilled to the bone after walking from Hull's bus station.

'Well, you don't know that they don't.'

'Do me a favour,' Lynn said. 'They're cut from the same cloth as the owners, aren't they? They make the right noises, that's all.'

Margaret laughed. 'You're an absolute cynic, Lynn.'

'I blame it on living with Graham,' Lynn said. 'Did you get many signatures?'

Lynn handed her petition papers over. 'Quite a few. There weren't many refused.'

'The union's organised a meeting in one of the church halls, for all the fishermen's wives. I'll hand 'em in there,' Margaret said, putting the papers carefully into the top drawer of a white-painted chest built into one of the alcoves next to the chimney breast. 'Come with us. There's going to be MPs and people from the telly, by all accounts.'

'I'd love to, but I can't. Graham's invited a couple of the big cheeses at the company round, with their wives. We're having a *dinner party*, if you please. I've borrowed a book from the library that tells you how to go about having a dinner party, seeing I've never even been to one. It doesn't look too difficult. I've done most of the preparation already, but I'll be up to my neck in housework and cooking when I get back – and I don't think it's only my house and my cooking that's going to be under inspection. I'll be under the magnifying glass myself, by the sound of it.'

'Rather you than me, then. What are you feeding 'em on?'

'I suggested a traditional pea and pie supper they could have in a bowl and eat with a spoon,' Lynn said, with a grin, 'and Graham flipped his lid, so I'm doing Beef Wellington – which is only a glorified pie, I suppose, but he's expecting me to give 'em a lot more than peas to go with it.'

Margaret raised her eyebrows. 'Beef Welling-ton? It's more than glorified pie – it's undercut

253

steak, isn't it?'

Lynn nodded. 'We never go out, I have to account for every penny I spend, he pretends we can't afford anything because of the mortgage, but he can afford to buy a dog from one of the bosses' wives, and he can afford to join a golf club. He calls that "making good contacts". It's "provision for the future", he says. Then he asks people who are a lot better off than us round and feeds 'em on fillet steak. And he's got the wine to go with it.'

'Sounds lovely. If I weren't going to the meeting I'd come, and bring the lads.'

'Don't!' Lynn grimaced. 'It would take him a year to get over that. He's only just got over the foul mood he was in about me coming down here with Simon the other day – after he'd slapped his veto on it.'

'I could see he wasn't very happy.'

'To say the least, but it was worth it, and at least we got my dad's leaky pipes mended. His house would have been ruined otherwise. At least he'll have heating and running water when he gets back.'

'And the plumber to pay,' said Margaret. 'I wonder if he really has stopped my mother's allowance?'

'I doubt it. I reckon he's hoping she'll be back, in spite of everything he says. Have you heard anything from her?'

'No, and I'm getting a bit worried.'

'So am I.'

They heard a short rap on the door, and before Margaret had time to answer, Nina herself walked in.

'Well! Speak of the devil!' Lynn said.

Margaret stared at her, speechless with surprise.

'Well? Aren't you pleased to see me?' she demanded.

Margaret put all her disapproval into a look.

'Oh, well, if I'm going to get the silent treatment I might as well go home,' Nina said.

'Where's home, these days?' asked Lynn.

'It's where it's always been.'

'What about Piers, then – or whoever you shoved off with?'

'I've left him, obviously.'

'What for?'

'I don't know,' said Nina, sounding more irritated than defensive. 'Maybe I've been a trawlerman's wife too long. I couldn't do with him under my feet all the time, sticking his neb into everything. Have you seen your dad?'

''Course we have. He'd nowhere else to go, had he?' Margaret said.

'How did he take it?'

Lynn gave a sardonic little laugh. 'I don't think it's made him any fonder!'

'There are two missing trawlers,' Margaret said, 'but don't worry, nobody belonging to us on either of them.'

'I know all about the two missing trawlers, thank you very much, and I already know there was nobody belonging to us aboard, 'cause I know what ships they're on.'

'Why did you do it, Mother?' Lynn asked.

'Because I thought it was what I wanted, out

255

every night, living the high life. I thought he was what I wanted, and he was, for a bit. He was fun. He used to take me to these places your dad never took me to, like the Continental Restaurant on Princes Dock in the Old Town. He knew how to carry himself and he always knew what wine to order with the food.'

'Oh, yeah, I've heard of it. It's one of these night-raking sort of places that are open when everywhere else is shut, where folk go to live the high life. Preferably with somebody else's wife,' Margaret jibed.

'Cheeky madam!' Nina said. 'It's a cosy little quayside restaurant, that's all. You make it sound like a den of iniquity.'

'I wouldn't know,' Margaret said.

'No, you wouldn't, because you've never been. Anyway, it was fun for a while, and then it got boring, so I'm back. So seriously, how did your dad take it?' In spite of her levity, Nina looked worried.

'Seriously?' Margaret said. 'He took it bad. You made a big mistake, leaving him that note. I think you'll have your work cut out, bringing him round after that.'

Chapter 39

Simon and Lassie had been banished to Graham's mother's, and the house was as warm as if fuel bills had never been invented when their guests arrived. Graham led them into a living room gleaming with polish and complete with an impressive flower arrangement, to dispense pre-dinner drinks while Lynn ran upstairs with a mountain of coats, scarves and hats.

'Beautiful wife, you have, Graham! Quite a looker,' she heard Mr Senior saying as she went up, followed by Graham's muffled reply, then the shriller tones of one of the women: 'And how's that little bitch I gave you, Graham?'

Gave him? On the way back down Lynn smelled burning and dashed into the kitchen to check on the dinner. This is why people who do this sort of thing regularly have servants, she thought, fearing for the Beef Wellington.

But the pastry was only singed a bit. She would have that part herself and nobody would be any the wiser. The halibut was nearly cooked. She rescued the Beef Wellington, gave the roast potatoes a good shake and went to join the guests for a few minutes, transforming herself from anxiety-ridden chef to calm and unflustered hostess in the few steps it took to reach the living room.

Tallish, distinguished looking and still slim despite his advancing years, Mr Senior greeted her, looking directly into her eyes. 'Ah, here's Lynn. Lovely house you have, Lynn. Graham tells me he got it for a very fair price.'

'Graham certainly knows how to get the best of a bargain,' she acknowledged, 'and with the stuff the sellers left behind when they embarked to Australia, and what his Auntie Ivy left behind when she embarked to the next world, we've got the place pretty well furnished. She couldn't have timed it better, really, his Auntie Ivy. Oh, yes, he's dead lucky, is Graham.'

Mr Senior smiled. 'Seriously, though,' he said, 'it's a very important attribute, luck. Napoleon certainly thought so. When he was selecting men for important positions, he always chose the lucky ones.'

'He'd certainly have picked Graham, then,' she said.

Mr Senior gave her a thoughtful look. 'You may have realised that we think highly of him, in the company.'

'There's one person here who thinks even more highly of him than you do, Mr Senior,' she quipped – thinking of Graham himself.

He mistook her. 'Naturally, you appreciate him. A wife knows her husband's true worth better than anybody.'

Lynn gave a solemn nod. 'Never a truer word was spoken, Mr Senior. Excuse me, I'd better go and check the dinner. It's the cook's night off.'

Graham led the guests into the dining room, to a table laid with the late Auntie Ivy's gold-rimmed dinner service and Waterford crystal. A minute or two later Lynn wheeled in the fish course on

Auntie Ivy's mahogany tea trolley.

Graham filled their glasses with white wine, while Mrs Orme, the dark-haired, thirtyish, dog-breeding wife of Mr Senior's deputy cast surreptitious glances in his direction – but not so surreptitious that they escaped Lynn's notice.

The sight of the fish prompted a few words about fishermen and the missing trawlers, and some speculation about what might have happened to them.

'That's what all their wives and families want to know,' Lynn said, 'and they want to know why the distress signal from the *Sprite* two days after she sailed wasn't reported, and why nobody reported that the life raft had been found, and why the radio operator refused to sail in her...'

'It *was* reported that the life raft had been found!' Mrs Orme said.

'Nearly a fortnight afterwards,' said Lynn.

'The weather in the fishing grounds has been exceptionally bad, this year. The worst in living memory, I think. It's only to be expected that there would be some losses. Deep-sea fishing's always been a risky game,' said Mr Orme, whose dark hair and saturnine features gave him the look of an undertaker. The dark-rimmed glasses he wore added to the impression.

His comments failed to answer the points she'd made, Lynn noted. 'Aren't there such things as unnecessary risks?' she inquired, with a tight little smile.

'There are calculated risks,' Mr Senior said, 'and the men themselves make the calculation when they sign on. We should allow them to know their own business. This fish is beautifully cooked, Lynn.'

Lynn thanked him for the compliment, and kept her caustic rejoinder to herself. After all, these people played golf with trawler owners and directors, the Gods of Creation as far as Hessle Road was concerned. Graham had probably had his bridge lessons from them. And she knew nothing about the *Sprite* from her own experience. All her information was second-hand, but stacked together it seemed to indicate that the *Sprite* was very far from sprightly – a ship that the owners might be glad to see the back of, in fact. She quietly took away the remains of the fish course and wheeled in the Beef Wellington, with all its trimmings and accompaniments. Her worries about the dinner had been groundless. It was on the table at last, and had turned out surprisingly well. Enormously relieved, Lynn sat down, poured herself a large glass of red wine, and began to relax.

The conversation turned to the Seniors' twenty-five-year-old only daughter, and her engagement to a man who was 'utterly hopeless'.

'He's already had three jobs. He won't settle to anything,' Mr Senior said. 'He takes a job, and he isn't in it five minutes before he starts arguing with his employers, telling them how things ought to be done in their own firm, and then one thing leads to another until he walks out!'

'Probably a Communist,' Mr Orme commented.

Mrs Senior was blonde, still very good-looking and obviously much younger than her husband. 'He's done it three times,' she said. 'He's never been sacked, he just ups and leaves – and before he's got another job to go to! Gerald's used his influence to get him a couple of positions, but it's getting difficult to find anything else for him. He's good at golf though, and tennis, and badminton, and skiing, and squash, and everything Lucy likes doing – but he seems to have very little interest in anything to do with work. I think our daughter's expecting Gerald to find him a well-paid job in the company, preferably with no work attached.'

'I draw the line at that,' Mr Senior frowned. 'I've helped him as much as you can help somebody like him, but I draw the line at having him meddling in the running of Four Winds Pharmaceuticals.'

'Get him a start on an arctic trawler – they'll take anyone on at this time of year, or so I'm told. He might take to the life. At least you'd have three weeks rest between landings – and possibly much longer, if you could whistle up a wind,' Mr Orme suggested, with a smile like the plate on a coffin lid.

Mr Senior gave a barking laugh, soon joined by everyone but Lynn. 'Now there's an idea,' he said. 'I wouldn't object to any boat he was on disappearing without trace!'

'It might be too late for that if the fishermen's wives have anything to do with it,' said Lynn.

'Ooh! You must be talking about the petition they've started,' Mrs Senior said, with a flicker of genuine interest in her eyes. 'I've heard about that.'

Lynn nodded. 'They're having a meeting in Hessle Road tonight, in one of the church halls.

261

They've got MPs and people from the General Workers' Union and the press and all sorts of people going. I'd have gone myself, if I'd been free. I wish I'd thought to bring the petition; you could have signed it. Never mind,' she said, suddenly inspired, 'I've got some paper, I can soon write the heading and do the columns.'

'Lynn's father's a chief engineer,' Graham cut in, careful to remind the guests that his father-in-law was at least half-educated, more than a mere deckhand, and even if running with sweat and grease most of the time, was certainly not involved in menial, hand- and mind-numbing jobs like gutting fish for eighteen hours at a stretch.

The smile had disappeared from Mr Senior's face. 'I'm afraid I don't approve of women meddling in men's business,' he said. 'If the trawlermen have any complaints, they should speak up for themselves.'

His wife looked as if she might have disagreed had she dared, but if there'd ever been a spark of opposition there it had long since been stamped out, Lynn decided. After a few short months of total dependency she could easily see how that could happen.

It had not yet happened to her, however. 'Well, the trouble with that is they're never ashore long enough,' she said, 'and if they did it individually, they'd be sent on walkabout. So the wives are doing it. Other countries try to keep their fishermen safe. They have laws about safety standards aboard ships, so why not us?'

'You can't make it safe,' Graham said, with a weather eye on Mr Senior. 'It's a sheer impossibility. Businesses never get anywhere if people worry too much about safety.'

'So if they send all the trawlers to sea with dodgy radar and without radio operators or the sort of elementary safety gear other countries have *by law*, they'll make more profit, I suppose,' Lynn rasped. 'But is that all that counts? Don't men's lives count for *anything*?'

'You can't achieve anything without risk, and the men are well aware what the risks are when they sign on. Without risk, we'd have no fish, we'd have no coal, nothing would be built!' Graham said, undeterred.

He was rewarded by a smile and an encouraging nod from Mr Senior, and sat triumphantly back to bask in the sunshine of his boss's total approval.

Lynn disliked him then. He risks nothing, she thought. He spends his life nice and safe and comfortable in his office and his car, and on the golf course and in the club house, risking nothing – and in his safe and comfortable dining room he prates about the impossibility of achieving anything without risk.

'Well, I think: good for the wives!' Mrs Senior muttered, *sotto voce*.

'Speaking of nothing being built, it's been a disaster for the building trade, all this safety legislation,' Mr Orme frowned. 'My brother-in-law's in the Federation of Building Trades Employers, and he says the contractors reported nigh on fifty thousand accidents on their sites last year. Men take time off for the most trivial injuries nowadays. If it needs a strip of Elastoplast it needs a week or two off work, as well. The mind boggles at the amount of time wasted in administration over petty little accidents – and he says the amount of lost production is absolutely staggering.'

Lynn was silent. It was evident to her that these people had not the slightest concern for the fate of men like her father, her brother, her brother-in-law – and Alec. Graham filled everyone's glass but hers, and pointedly said: 'Hadn't you better check on the pudding, my love?'

'Excuse me.' Lynn gave them a polite smile and disappeared into the kitchen, soon followed by Graham. 'I think you'd better lay off the wine now, Lynn.'

She gave him a mildly sarcastic smile. 'What for? I'm just beginning to enjoy myself.'

'Because with you, the more the booze goes in, the more Hessle Road comes out.'

'What's wrong with Hessle Road?'

'Oh, nothing at all, except it's of no interest to these people, and they're the ones we need to be cultivating. So let's leave Hessle Road where it belongs, just now.'

'Cultivating? Greasing round their backsides, you mean. Cultivating's what you do to plants.'

'It's what you do with people, as well, if you want to get anywhere in life, so just leave the fish docks and what's happening in Hessle Road alone, all right?' He fixed her with a warning stare and returned to their guests – doubtless to 'cultivate' them for all he was worth.

Lynn determinedly extracted a clean sheet of foolscap paper from her folder of midwifery

264

notes and headed it 'Petition for Fishermen's Safety'. Underneath she ruled the three columns she'd seen on the original petition and headed them Name, Address, and Occupation. Then she whipped the cream, carefully turned out the apple charlotte and returned to her guests, to dole out pudding and hear talk of bad weather conditions and how none of it could be helped, while she could think of nothing but the men lying at the bottom of the Arctic ocean and the harrowed faces of their friends and relatives on Hessle Road. But that was of no interest to their guests, according to Graham.

Mr Senior wanted to catch the news, so when the hour arrived they switched on the television set – and saw a little group of fishermen's wives on the docks doing their utmost to stop trawlers going to sea without radio operators. Lynn's breath quickened and her pulse rate rose at the sight of them being manhandled by police, and she gave a superstitious little shudder at the sight of women on the dock as the ships were sailing and the thought of the bad luck that might bring. One of the ships did sail without a radio operator, and the women were held back, shouting and screaming while the ship went through the lock gates. Another should have sailed, but the crew refused, calling down to the women and demanding that union officials check that the lifejackets carried were up to par. Graham, the Ormes and Mr Senior watched with almost palpable disapproval.

'You can guess what that big woman's language must be like by the way they've cut the sound,'

Mrs Orme sneered.

Lynn felt the heat rise to her face. She went to fetch her paper, her limbs near to trembling. 'That big woman' had a presence about her, a sort of majesty despite her tussles with the police, and if she and the others could stand on the freezing dock in the early hours of the morning and take that sort of treatment, then Lynn had to do something as well. She should have been on that dock among those screaming, shouting women, instead of here, listening to these people, who knew little and cared less about what the fishermen had to put up with.

As the guests left, she quietly asked them to sign the petition. Mr Senior and the Ormes flatly refused. Women should not be encouraged to take matters in their own hands in this way, and besides, they had friends and acquaintances who stood to be ruined by the expense that some of these quite unnecessary safety measures might entail. It was a thousand pities but the problem lay with the exceptionally bad weather, and not the trawler companies.

'Not even if they deliberately send men to the Arctic in a notoriously unstable boat like the *Sprite* – in *January*?' she challenged.

Mr Senior stiffened. 'The men themselves have the final choice,' he said. Mrs Orme's large dark eyes gazed sadly into Graham's, conveying an ocean of understanding and sympathy.

Mrs Senior was the last out. She glanced at her husband, took the pen and signed, and handed the petition back to Lynn with a tiny complicit smile. There's hope for you yet, Lynn thought –

at least you're human.

Graham rounded on her when they were all gone and the door was closed behind them. 'Oh, God! My God! Why did you have to do that? And what you said to him! Are you out of your mind? You just don't know when to give it a rest, do you? And after everything I said!' He snatched the petition from Lynn's hands and tore it to shreds, then scattered the pieces on the carpet and stormed off upstairs.

Lynn swept them up, and cleared the table. There were no leftovers. Not a thing, and she had cooked what she'd imagined was far too much food in anticipation of sharing the leftovers with Simon. They would have made a nice change from chips and egg and beans on toast. With her mind continually distracted by thoughts of those protesting women on the dock and the reaction of Graham's bosses, she washed pots and cleaned and tidied everything up to give her lord and master time to get over the worst of his tantrum, and then went upstairs to join him.

She was amazed to see that his face was blotchy and swollen. He looked so wounded she felt terrible, even worse than before. 'I'm sorry,' she said. 'I really am. I never realised it would upset you so much.'

He turned his reddened, watery eyes on her. 'My mother was right! She warned me: "You can take her out of Hessle Road – but you'll never be able to take Hessle Road out of her. Never in a million years. You mark my words, Graham!"'

Chapter 40

On the Monday morning, after a weekend spent in sackcloth and ashes doing penance for giving her unwanted opinions to the company bigwigs, Lynn took Simon to school and went down to Margaret's, burning to know what had happened at the meeting.

'We've had a terrible upsetment,' Margaret greeted her. 'The *Prospero* should have come home on Friday, and instead the man from the Fisherman's Mission came round and told one of Jim's cousins that there's no hope at all for her husband. Then the reporter from the *Hull Mail* called to see her, and she got up to delve in the sideboard to get the photo of her husband for him – and she just went to pieces. He had to run out to get one of the neighbours. She's not fit to look after the bairns, she's in such a state. Jim's sisters have had to share 'em out between 'em.'

'The man from the *Hull Mail* would have done better to leave her alone,' Lynn said.

'No, she wanted him to go. She wanted them to put his picture in the paper, with all the others. They all do, all the wives – you know that from last time. It's like paying your respects.'

'I suppose. You didn't go to the meeting they were having, then – with the union people, and everybody,' Lynn surmised.

'Oh, yeah, I went, all right. I thought: it's more

268

important than ever, now.'

'What was it like?'

'One of these musty old church halls, all peeling green paint and bare light bulbs – and cold! But we had a real good meeting. Hundreds of people turned up; you could hardly move for prams. I left Jim's mother sitting in the house with my bairns, but I suppose some folk can't get baby-sitters. But why people have to bring their dogs to things like that, I'll never know...'

'Yes, but what happened?' Lynn asked impatiently.

'Well there were some union men and politicians spouting off, and some little shit-stirrer from the University wanting to start a Communist revolution – he wasn't very popular – and then us wives. We were brilliant!'

'We? Who's "we"?'

'I mean the woman who started the petition most of all; she's marvellous, Lynn. If anybody can get the changes we need, she'll do it, through sheer force of personality. Everybody's got faith in her. But I got up as well – little me! And I told them everything Jim had told me, and then another lass got up – she'd thought of loads of ways of making the trawlers safer, and then one of the skippers' wives, and to cut a long story short, the Prime Minister wants some of us to go to the House of Commons tomorrow, to talk to some of the ministers – and I'm one of the ones going! But only if I can get somebody to look after the bairns.'

'Can't Jim's mother do it?'

'She's too old. She's all right to sit with them

269

when they're already in bed, but she's too old to manage four of them, chasing around, giving her lip. And Jim's sisters are–'

'Looking after the bairns whose mother's in hospital. Well, they're out of the running, then,' Lynn said. 'What about my mother?'

'I thought about asking her, but my dad's home today, and he'll still be at home when we go. I thought they'd better be left alone for a bit.' Margaret hesitated, looking at Lynn with pleading in her eyes. 'I really want to go, Lynn, and it'll only be for one night. It matters more than ever, now. And Jim's still at sea...'

Lynn understood. What they both left unsaid was: these things come in threes...

'Well, I'll do it, then. I'll have them. No problem,' she said. After all, Margaret had done so much for her over the years there was no way she could have refused. She didn't want to refuse; but her heart sank at the thought of telling Graham.

Her father would be home by now, and Lynn had just time to make a quick visit to her parents before going for the bus back to Cottingham. Her mother answered the door sporting bruises on her face.

'What's happened to you?' Lynn asked, following her into the living room. Nina nodded towards Lynn's father, sitting grim-faced in his armchair.

'She's had a thump, and she might get a few more before she's finished,' he said, obviously in no mood to make any apologies.

Lynn stayed for two very awkward minutes, trying to keep her eyes off the bruises and trying to dispel the heavy silence by making a few remarks about the wives' campaign, which did nothing to appease her father. 'You women should keep your bloody noses out of men's affairs,' he told her.

Her mother said almost nothing. Lynn left then, upset and shocked to the core. That bruising on her mother's face! It was the first time she'd ever seen such a thing in her own family, and her father's attitude to the safety campaign was no different to Graham's bosses'. This was more typical of the rougher end of 'Road, 'Road as seen through the eyes of people like Connie and Gordon, and an aspect of Hessle Road that Lynn herself wouldn't have cared to defend. Margaret had been much wiser in deciding to stay away from her parents for a while.

Poor Mother, she thought, certain that Nina had been infatuated not so much with Piers as with having a life of her own and being the centre of somebody's attention. After years of having no identity other than as someone's wife, or someone's mother, it must have been hard to resist.

The phone was ringing when she got back home after picking Simon up from school.

'I've been trying to ring you for ages,' Janet said, 'ever since we heard about the *Sprite* and the *Prospero*, but you're never in. I hope your dad and your brother are all right.'

The mere sound of her voice gave Lynn's spirits a lift. 'Well, neither of them are at the bottom of the sea, thank God, but I've had a bloody awful day, Janet.'

'Any chance of you getting out, tonight? We

could go to a pub and have a natter.'

'None. Our Margaret's on the train to London tomorrow, to talk to some Cabinet Ministers. I'll have to get Graham to take me to pick her lads up after tea. I'm looking after them until she gets back.'

'What!'

'Yeah – she's one of the headscarf revolutionaries,' Lynn said, and burst into laughter at hearing herself repeat that nonsensical title that the papers had given to a group of ordinary housewives. 'Can you imagine anybody less like a revolutionary than our Margaret? Just 'cause they're asking for a few basic safety measures.'

'While wearing headscarves,' Janet laughed.

They 'nattered' through the whole of the children's programme, and Lynn replaced the receiver feeling much better.

She gave Graham the glad tidings about Margaret's visit to London soon as he walked in. 'Having the boys while she goes is the least I can do, and I'm doing it,' she said. 'And before you suggest anybody else has them – there is nobody.

'Everybody that could have helped is dealing with their own problems, so I'm their auntie, and they're coming here.' So stuff you, Graham, she thought.

'Pity your mother's otherwise engaged,' he grumbled.

'That's one way to describe it,' Lynn said.

'She picks a good time to clear off, I must say. Well, I suggest you go and stay at Margaret's and look after them there, and make sure they get to school on time. Simon can stop at my mother's

272

until you get back. He can go to school from there.'

I suggest, he'd said – meaning: do it! He'll be in the boardroom before long, Lynn thought. 'All right,' she agreed. 'That's not a bad idea, Graham.'

Chapter 41

Alec stood on the bridge of the *Grimsby Chieftain* and prayed. He prayed harder than he'd ever prayed since he was a seven-year-old child, knowing himself powerless, completely at the mercy of something he could not control. With the gale had come an intense chill, and ice that built up on every part of the ship faster than they could crack it off, making the trawler unstable as it rose and fell and pitched and tossed in waves whipped up to mountains by the howling wind.

They had fished on and on, long after the time they should have abandoned it, hoping the weather would improve. Instead it got worse – and worse. The man in the middle, the meat in the sandwich, torn between loyalty to the skipper and loyalty to the men, Alec had told the skipper it was too dangerous to carry on fishing and had been jeered at for his pains, told he should get a job on shore; he was too easily scared to make a skipper. But although he would never have admitted it the skipper himself was scared, doubly scared, and probably more terrified of getting on the wrong side of the gaffers by failing to make a trip than he was of going down with the ship, and taking every man on board down with him. Three times Alec had protested, and had three times been overruled. Then as the gale rose to force eight the skipper lost his nerve. At last he realised they might not live to catch any fish, let alone spend any money. It would be useless to attempt fishing for at least another twenty-four hours or more in any case, so he'd ordered the trawl stowed below, and had gone to his cabin to snatch a short sleep, leaving the men to dig solid snow off the deck and wait for daylight before attempting the upper works again.

'A short sleep and another few swigs at his bottle,' the third hand commented, when he'd gone. 'You could get pissed just standing next to him.'

Alec had been well aware of the alcohol fumes on the skipper's breath, but made no comment other than a noncommittal: 'Mmm.'

A leaden dawn broke in the Icelandic sky, and a voice Alec recognised came crackling over the radio – of the skipper of the *Miranda*, whom he'd once sailed under in Hull. The *Miranda* was about a mile away, and in a worse condition than the *Chieftain*. She was listing to starboard with thick ice covering her fo'c's'le, upper deck, rails, rigging – and radar. So the radar was out of action, and the mate and the bosun were out in the blizzard trying to crack ice off the scanner. As soon as they got that working they were making for Isafjord on the north-west coast of Iceland, to get in the lee of the wind.

'If we get there before you, we'll save you a space at the hitching rail, Fred,' Alec promised him, and started sailing north nose to wind, the only way to prevent her capsizing. With the wheelhouse constantly battered by heavy spray, peering ahead into the blizzard with his heart in his mouth he struggled to keep her afloat until they reached the fjord and the shelter of the mountains rising on either side of the inlet. The wind speed gauge moved steadily up the dial until it showed a hundred and twenty miles an hour, over gale force eleven. Judging by other voices coming over the radio the weather was the worst in living memory, and seemed set to get worse still – and around four hours of daylight was your lot up here, in February. The only good news was that the *Chieftain's* radar was working.

A warning from Wick coastal station that hurricane force winds were on the way came over the radio, followed by another message from the skipper of the *Miranda*. The *Miranda* still had no radar, but her skipper could just see the lights of the *Chieftain*, and intended following her to Isafjord.

They ploughed through miles of the roughest seas Alec had ever experienced and reached Isafjord to find that at least twenty other ships had beaten them to it. Visibility was practically nil, but the radar indicated that the inlet was already packed to capacity. There was no safe anchorage, and even ships at anchor were violently battered by the storm. Hour after gruelling hour, snow, wind and spray combined to coat the ships with thick ice that the crews desperately chopped and heaved overboard in the attempt to stay afloat and alive, praying for the only thing that could help them – the end of the storm.

Then a giant wave hit the *Miranda*. A plea came over the radio: 'We are heeling over. Taking water, help us... Going over to starboard ... can't get her back... Love to our wives and families...'

The *Miranda* was gone from the radar screen and there was nothing that the crew of the *Chieftain* could do to help her. The blizzard was so thick they could see neither coast nor mountains, nor any other ship. The mast was one huge, heavy, pillar of ice, which was also building up on the radar scanner. If that went, the ship would be completely blind.

Chapter 42

Lynn got to Margaret's house bright and early the following morning, and hardly recognised her sister. Margaret was beautifully made up, with hair done – and without her headscarf. The smart two-piece suit she wore was covered by a borrowed fur coat for protection against the freezing cold.

'Are you nervous?' Lynn asked.

'No. Well – just a bit. The taxi'll be here in ten minutes; we've time for a cup of tea. I've left the lads in bed.'

Ten minutes later there was a knock on the door. Lynn jumped up to answer it and there stood not the taxi man, but the man whose visits were dreaded by every fisherman's family in Hessle Road.

'Are you Mrs Stacey?' he asked. 'Jim Stacey's wife?'

'No, she's inside. You'd better come in,' Lynn said, and stood aside for the man who brought tears in his wake – the man from the Fishermen's Mission.

Margaret froze at the sight of him. Lynn sat beside her while he told her that the *Miranda* was lost with all hands. The news had come to Hull via Lloyd's agent in Reykjavik, among other sources. There was no mistake, and no hope.

'I knew it, I knew it, I knew it,' Margaret kept repeating, holding on to her sides.

'Is there anybody who can stay with her?' the man from the Mission asked Lynn.

'Me. I'm her sister.'

Lynn heard Margaret's lads getting up just as he was leaving, and the taxi was pulling up.

'Oh, I can't go. Tell him I can't go, Lynn,' Margaret cried.

Lynn went out to the driver. 'Go to Hull train station and tell the fishermen's wives bound for London that Margaret's just had some bad news. She can't go with them. They'll understand.'

'The *Miranda*?' he asked.

Lynn nodded.

'It's all over the docks,' he said, and drove off.

Margaret was sitting with a hand protectively on her abdomen in the way common to all pregnant women, and Lynn wondered what her colour might be under all that carefully applied

277

make-up. 'He had a feeling,' she said. 'He never said anything, but I think that's why he stayed at home so long this Christmas. He had a feeling.'

A horrible eerie sensation overpowered Lynn. A feeling of doom, she thought – his own doom. It was uncanny how that happened to some fishermen.

She shuddered. 'Go back to bed, Margaret,' she said. 'I'll see to the lads.'

Margaret shook her head.

Pointless arguing with her. Lynn switched the kettle on again and put bread in the toaster for the boys, who were already clattering down the stairs.

'Has somebody been?' asked young Jim, his father's namesake.

'Yeah, the taxi man, but your mam can't go to London today. She's not very well.'

They stood looking at her, four beautiful boys, each about a head taller than the next youngest like steps and stairs, their faces serious, their eyes full of concern. 'What's the matter, Mam?'

'What's the matter, Mam?'

Five-year-old Joe took her hand, and gazed into her eyes. 'What's the matter?'

Margaret managed a smile for them. 'I'm not very well,' she repeated.

'But you were going to Parliament!' said young Jim.

Lynn coaxed them away. 'Come and get your breakfast, and I'll take you to school,' she said. 'Your mam will be all right if she can just have a rest.'

After they'd eaten Lynn sorted coats and gloves

278

and set out with four quiet, bewildered young-sters, not at all sure that she was doing the right thing. Perhaps they should have been kept off school, perhaps they should have been told about their father's ship, but she couldn't bear to do it. And at least if they were at school they would be looked after for the day, freeing her to concen-trate on their mother. At least they'd get some dinner, and by the time they came home she and Margaret would have decided on the best way to break the awful news.

She saw them into school, and on the way back she thought of Margaret gasping and holding on to her sides – almost as if she had started in labour. But that was impossible. She wasn't even six months pregnant, and all her other children had been overdue.

Margaret was out of her chair when Lynn walked back in the house. 'I'm having contrac-tions,' she said, with the certainty of a woman who knows what she's talking about.

Lynn was still unconvinced. 'I don't think you are,' she said, 'but you've had a terrible shock. I think you should go and lie down for a bit, and they'll probably pass off. Go upstairs and get into bed. I'll make you some tea, and a bit of toast, if you can eat it.'

Margaret got to the fourth tread on the stair-case, and stopped in her tracks, holding onto her sides. 'Oohh!'

'Oohh!' Lynn had turned at the sound and repeated it, on seeing bright red blood running from Margaret and onto the stairs. 'Oh, Mar-garet! Wait!' she said, thoroughly alarmed. 'Have you got any pads?'

Margaret shook her head. Lynn quickly laid the newspaper and a couple of towels on the settee. 'Lie there, with your feet up – and don't move till I get back. I'm phoning the ambulance.'

Margaret did as she was told, too frightened to do anything else.

Lynn tore down the street to the nearest neighbour with a telephone, and rang the Obstetric Flying Squad, then raced back again thanking God for her midwifery training. She found Margaret almost collapsed and the towels covered in blood. The neighbour had followed, carrying more towels. Lynn washed the make-up off Margaret's face the better to see her true colour, and put fresh towels under her. Twenty agonising minutes later the ambulance arrived.

Five minutes after that, Margaret was lying on a stretcher in the ambulance with her pains coming every two minutes, and the doctor busy putting up a drip to counter the effect of the bleeding. Then they set off for the hospital, with Lynn holding Margaret's hand and feeling her knuckles crushed to a pulp when the pains were at their worst. Before they arrived at the hospital, Margaret had expelled two tiny, red, blood-streaked babies, neither bigger than the doctor's hand, and both dead. Margaret looked bloodless. Even her lips were white.

Lynn was more frightened than she'd ever been in her life. It looked as if her four nephews might lose their mother as well as their father, and who would care for them then? She would want to give them a home, but she had no money, and she would get absolutely no support from Graham. She knew that for a certainty.

Lynn's father answered the telephone. 'Our Margaret's in hospital,' she told him. 'She's had a miscarriage.'

'Does she know about Jim? It's all over the docks – the *Miranda's* gone down.'

'Yeah. I think it was getting the news about Jim that caused the miscarriage. The doctors say it's just a coincidence, but I'm not so sure.'

'Doctors don't know everything.'

'No, and neither do midwives,' Lynn said. 'She told me she was having contractions, and I didn't believe her. Is my mother there?'

A moment or two later, Lynn's mother was on the line. 'We went down to see her as soon as we heard. We wondered where she was,' Nina said.

'She was supposed to have been going to London, and instead of that she had the man from the Mission, telling her Jim's ship was lost – and then she had a bad haemorrhage and lost twins, a boy and a girl. I really thought she was going to bleed to death. God, what a nightmare.'

'Where are you phoning from?'

'Hedon Road Maternity.'

'I'll come straightaway.'

'There's no point. They've taken her to theatre to do a scrape, to stop the bleeding. I'm coming back now, to pick the lads up from school. I'll ring Connie before I set off and tell her to hang on to Simon, and tell Graham where I am, then I'll look after our Margaret's lads so you can both go and see her in the hospital tonight.'

281

But the boys were nowhere to be seen when Lynn went to collect them. They had been allowed to go home when the school heard about the fate of the *Miranda*. Lynn found them with one of Jim's sisters further down the street, with pinched, anxious expressions on their faces. The news about their father's ship had been devastating, and then they'd arrived home and found their mother gone. The youngest two had panicked and dissolved into tears both at the news of their father and the disappearance of their mother. The elder two had desperately tried to keep a stiff upper lip and comfort them – which had been more heart-breaking to see than the tears, Jim's sister said.

'Your mum's in hospital,' Lynn reassured them. 'She'll be there a few days, but they'll make her better, and we'll make sure you're all right until she comes home.'

'He was a good man, our Jim,' she said. 'A good brother and a good dad.'

'I know,' Lynn said. She stayed for half an hour, drinking tea and giving genuinely felt sympathy, then took the boys to her parents on Boulevard.

After her parents had gone to the hospital she rang Graham, and found him at his mother's house. 'You'll have heard about Margaret, I suppose,' she said.

'Yes. I hope she'll be all right. Where are you now?'

'Boulevard. My dad's gone to see her. My mother's gone with him. I've got the lads with me. There's nobody else.'

Lynn had been in two minds whether to mention her mother or not, but it barely seemed to register. 'That's all right,' he told her. 'We'll stay at my mother's. She can take Simon to school tomorrow.'

He said all the right things, but there was something distant in his voice, as if he were making the correct responses by rote – as if it were a mere polite exchange between strangers. She decided to drop the bombshell.

'Well, she won't want to look after Simon for a week or more, and I don't want to be away from him for that long either, so if nobody can help me with Margaret's lads, I might have to bring them to stay with us, in Cottingham,' she said, keeping her voice low so that they wouldn't hear.

That certainly woke Graham up, and there was nothing distant about his response to it. 'No, I can't say I favour that option,' he protested. 'It would be awful.'

'Why would it be awful? It wasn't awful on Bonfire Night.'

'Only because their father was there, keeping them under control.'

'Well they haven't got a father now, and I might have to bring them,' she insisted, 'so *you'll* have to keep them under control.'

There was a long silence. 'Well, if there's no alternative, I suppose you'll have to,' he said, grudgingly, 'but they're nothing to do with *me*. I'll be staying at my mother's.'

283

Chapter 43

Her parents called in on their way back from the hospital, both uneasy about Margaret.

'You should have put the lads to bed at our house,' her mother said. 'You could have gone home then.'

'I'll be all right. I'll borrow one of Margaret's nighties and sleep in her bed tonight,' Lynn said, and thinking of getting home, added: 'I suppose you're still working, are you, Mam?'

''Course I am. I haven't packed the *job* up.'

Just the man, then, Lynn thought, so not available to look after four boys. It was obvious from her father's expression and the way his brown eyes caught hers that the same thought was in his mind.

'I might have to take the lads to stay with us in Cottingham, then, and keep them there until our Margaret's a bit better,' she said, 'or bring Simon down here. He might miss a bit of school, but...' she shrugged.

'It'll be a long time before our Margaret's better, going by the look of her,' her father said, thoughtfully. 'I'll miss a trip. I'll stay here with 'em. I'll make sure they get to school in the morning, and I'll be here for 'em at night.'

Lynn's mother's eyes widened. 'What, *sleep* here?' she said.

'Aye, sleep here. I'll go and sign off tomorrow,

and sleep here until our Margaret's fit to look after 'em herself. Best thing all round.'

You're an engineer, Dad, not a nursemaid, Lynn thought, struck by the way he was excluding her mother from his arrangements. 'I'll make us some tea,' she said, and got up to put the kettle on, not daring to look at her mother's face.

'That's crazy,' her mother said. 'They can come and sleep at our house.'

'It's not crazy. They're going to sleep here, and I'm staying with 'em. Lynn's going home tomorrow. That's what's going to happen, Nina,' he said.

It was certain the boys would be calmer sleeping in their own beds, among their own familiar things, Lynn thought, after her parents had gone. She sorted their clothes out for the wash while watching the progress of the headscarf revolutionaries on the news. They had done full credit to themselves and their city in London. They had achieved all they had set out to achieve. Those amazing women had accomplished more for their men in less than a month than either union or Members of Parliament had managed in years. All their demands had been met, and the owners were going to be made to put the proposed safety measures into immediate effect – whether they liked it or not. There would be radio operators on all the trawlers, proper safety checks, and a mother ship near the fleet with hospital facilities. It was breathtaking, a magnificent achievement, a tremendous victory – and despite Lynn's unbounded admiration for them all, it left her feeling quite sick at heart, because it had all come too late for Jim, and because Margaret should have had a share in that triumph.

She consoled herself with the thought that Anthony would benefit, and so would her father, despite his chauvinistic objection to women 'meddling in men's business'.

And Alec, if he was still alive. The sudden fear that he might not be rippled through her insides like a river of ice.

In the calm after the storm Alec was laughing, flooded by a feeling of pure exhilaration. To have come so close to death and to have escaped, to be alive and feel that life pulsing through every fibre was better than any other feeling he had ever known. Better than the big dipper at Blackpool, better than eight pints of lager, better than sex, better than anything he had ever experienced or could ever imagine. He'd passed the test. He felt invincible.

Jackie felt it, and was laughing too. It had been a close shave; they'd come within a whisker of sinking – and escaped. Two trawlers had sunk and another had run aground, but the *Chieftain* had got away with it! She had nearly gone over, but after a heroic struggle she had righted herself and come away unscathed, with all her crew.

The nervous little sparks, still white round the gills, was radioing the company to let them know they still had a ship. The skipper, almost sober, had just gone down to the chart room to try and make his mind up where the 'fish shop' was – those elusive, teeming shoals of profitable fish like cod and haddock. Soon they would be on course, on a two days' steam to Bear Island, Alec guessed. Now all they had to do was make a trip – and hope it would be a good one.

Simon rushed out of school and into Lynn's arms, smiling all over his face. 'I'm glad you're back, Mum.'

'I'm glad I'm back, as well,' she said. 'I thought I was going to have to bring your Auntie Margaret's lads with me, but your grandad's decided he's going to miss a trip and stay in their house and look after them till she's better.'

Simon's face fell. 'You should have brought them. I like playing with them. We could have made a snowman. We could have gone sledging.'

'Well, maybe we can do that this weekend.'

Back home, she left Simon watching the telly and went into the kitchen to ferret about in the fridge for three pork chops that she hoped would still be fit to eat. She sniffed at them suspiciously. They passed the smell test, but only just. She put them to soak in a bath of vinegar and water and started peeling potatoes and chopping cabbage. By the time Graham got home she had vacuum cleaned, dusted and set the table. He followed her into the kitchen, with Simon hard on his heels.

'Did you say your mother was back, Lynn, or did I dream it?' he asked.

'Well, you didn't dream it,' she said, sliding the sanitised chops under the grill. 'I was surprised you didn't comment on it straightaway.'

'I've got my mind on other things, just at the moment. There's a lot going on at work. So how did your dad react? Did he welcome her with open arms?'

287

'Not exactly,' Lynn said, lighting the gas under pans of vegetables.

'I'll bet. He didn't offer to kill her, I hope.'

'No, I don't think it's as bad as that,' Lynn said.

'I wonder why she came back? Maybe her new man didn't live up to expectations.'

'Or maybe she missed us all.'

'Maybe. A stroke of luck for us, anyway, her coming back. At least she's here to look after her grandchildren. I thought I was going to have to go into exile for a week or two.'

'You wouldn't have *had* to go into exile, Graham, you'd have *chosen* to go ... and have your mother running round after you – just about chewing your food and wiping your backside – instead of giving me a hand with four young lads who've just lost their dad. They've got a lot on their minds as well – like a father they'll never see again and a mother at death's door in hospital.'

'There's no need to be coarse. I've got a demanding job, Lynn. I work bloody hard, and I'm shattered when I get home,' he protested.

'Yeah, for an hour or two, but you're never too shattered to go out again, and stay out half the night.'

He was quiet for a moment, giving Simon the chance to jump in with: 'I *want* Auntie Margaret's lads to come and sleep here.'

Graham ignored that. 'How is Margaret, by the way? Without exaggerating, if you can manage it.'

'Without exaggerating she had to have two blood transfusions, and she's not right yet. She's still very poorly.'

'She'll recover all right. Women do from these

pregnancy things.'

These pregnancy things. And there we've got the opinion of the expert, Lynn thought. 'How's Kevin, by the way?' she said, reminded of Kev by her own comment about Graham staying out half the night.

He looked genuinely surprised. 'Kev? I haven't seen him for weeks. I ought to ring him, I suppose.'

'Don't bother for me. I wouldn't care if I never saw him again.'

'I won't, then. I've got too much to do, anyway.'

'If Auntie Margaret's lads aren't coming here, I want to go to their house and stop with my grandad,' said Simon.

'Stop with your Nanna, you mean,' Graham said.

Simon looked uncertainly at Lynn.

'He means his grandad,' she said. 'He's missed a trip so he can look after the lads. My mam's still got the job.'

'They'll have them at Boulevard, then, surely.'

'No, we all thought they'd be better off staying in their own home. We thought the less disruption the better.'

'Your mother's there as well, then, I suppose.'

'I suppose,' Lynn said, evasively.

He looked her carefully in the face for a moment or two. 'She's not, is she?' he concluded. 'She's at Boulevard, and he's at Margaret's. Not just separate bedrooms, but separate houses. That's interesting. Whose idea was it, his or hers?'

'How do I know? Ask the cognoscenti at the golf club. They'll know more about it than I do,' she said, and quickly moving on from the subject of her parents' sleeping arrangements, added: 'We'll ask your grandad if you can sleep at Auntie Margaret's this weekend, Simon. Then your dad can take me out, for a change.'

'Certainly. I'll take you anywhere you want to go.'

'Why not the golf club?' she said. 'That seems to be the best place for getting to know what's going on.'

'Sorry. I meant anywhere but the golf club.'

'Why *not* the golf club, then?'

'Because the subject of trawler owners and fishermen might come up, and some of the members' opinions might not tally with yours. Jim's death got us quite a bit of sympathy, so I've managed to smooth things over at the company. I don't want you upsetting the applecart again,' he said.

'Well, it's not been in vain then, has it, Jim's death?'

'No need to be sarcastic. You know that wasn't what I meant.'

'If we're not going to the golf club, we'll go to the Continental Restaurant on Princes Dock. I've heard it's very good,' Lynn said. She wanted to see this place her mother raved about for herself.

'It's too expensive,' he said. 'What about the *Duke of Cumberland* instead, and a bag of chips on the way home? We can walk it there.'

Chapter 44

One night out and a week later Lynn had just arrived home from taking Simon to school when the doorbell rang. She was stunned to see Piers Marson standing on her doorstep, looking as if he hadn't slept for a week.

'I've tried to stay away, but I couldn't. I had to come. I've got to see her; it's killing me!' he said, holding out a sealed envelope. 'Will you give your mother a letter?'

Lynn gave a short laugh, and shook her head. 'Absolutely no chance!'

'Please. I've got to talk to her. She's broken my heart.' He said it so piteously that she couldn't help feeling a twinge of sympathy.

'You broke my dad's heart between you; I know that. He's not the same man.'

'I'm sorry. It was never our intention to hurt anybody, but Nina wasn't happy in her marriage, and neither was I in mine. I fell head over heels in love with her.'

'You're married, then! Well, what about your wife's broken heart?' Lynn snapped.

'My wife and I have lived separate lives for years.'

'So you say. Well, you're living a separate life from my mother now, so let's keep it that way. She can't have been any happier with you than she was in her marriage.'

'We were happy, deliriously happy for a time, but she missed you and Simon and her other grandchildren, that's all. And then there was the missing trawler, she was anxious about that. That's why she left me. You're the only reasons she went back to him – her children and grand-children.'

'She got fed up with you, Piers, that's all there is to it. You had a middle-aged fling with each other, and now the party's over. Accept it, and leave her alone. She's happy with her husband.'

He looked devastated. 'I don't believe it. I don't believe she's capable of it, and I won't believe it until she tells me herself. I've got to talk to her.'

'It's time you went. You should never have come here, and you'd better not go anywhere near my mother. Leave her alone, unless you want to bring a lot of trouble on her. You've caused us enough grief already – all of us.'

'He hasn't harmed her, has he?'

'You stand a good chance of him harming you, if you push it any further,' she threatened, and shut the door.

Where had they been living, she wondered? She ought to have found that out before closing the door. Maybe she should tell her father he'd called, or warn her mother.

Maybe she should do neither. Maybe it would be far better to let sleeping dogs lie, and hope Piers Marson dropped out of their lives.

'It was awful,' Margaret said. 'My dad had just brought me back from the hospital and we were in their house sitting eating a dinner she'd cooked when he knocked on the door. She answered it, and my dad shouted to know who it was. She tried to make him go away, and he wouldn't, and as soon as my dad realised what was happening he was out there, punching him round the head, and she was dancing around them, screaming, "Don't hit him! Don't hit him!" Oh, it was just awful, and the more she screamed the harder he punched him, until his nose was pouring blood, and he could barely stand up. Then he turned to her and he said, "You tell him to sling his hook. You don't want him."

'Well, I don't know what she would have said if he'd given her the chance, but she hesitated for just a fraction of a second too long for him, and he said, "You make your bloody mind up where you want to be, you – this minute!" Well, she took one look at his face and I don't think she dared stay. I've never seen anybody look as mad – and she was shaking. So she went and got her coat and her bag, and she kissed me on the cheek and she said, "Look after yourself, Margaret," and she went. I've never seen anybody look as furious as my dad did then. He looked ready to kill them both. I don't know what the neighbours must have thought. And she'd only been gone five minutes, when our Anthony turned up. "What's been going on here, then?" he said, "you could cut the atmosphere with a knife," – and I just burst into tears. I thought, if only you'd come five minutes sooner, she might not have gone. I was that upset, I couldn't speak.'

'I bet I know what happened next,' Lynn said, guessing that her father and Anthony would have gone down to Rayners.

'Our Anthony thought I was crying because of Jim and the miscarriage, so my dad told him what had happened. So he brought me home in his taxi, asking me if I knew where she'd gone, and I didn't, so he dropped me off, and he went back to my dad.'

'What a homecoming,' Lynn said. 'But do me a favour, Margaret, and don't say anything in front of the lads. I don't want Simon hearing about it and letting on to Graham. Let him get his news from the bloody golf club.'

'From the *golf club*?'

'Aye. There's not much they don't get to know up there, according to Graham. Probably before it happens, at times,' she said. 'Anyway we'll have to find out where she is, and go and see her.'

'Then my dad will think we're going against him, and I don't want him to, because he's been that good to me and the lads. There aren't many grandads who'll look after four boys on their own for the whole of the half-term holiday, and he's still calling in twice a day, to make sure I'm all right.'

'He didn't have to look after them on his own,' Lynn protested. 'Their Nanna would have helped, if he'd let her.'

'I know she would, but you know the way things were, and he was staying here.'

'He's made it impossible for her.'

'I know he has, but he said – it was just her attitude. She acted as if going off with another bloke was no worse than putting too much sugar in his tea, or spoiling a good shirt in the wash ... a sort

294

of minor mishap. She put him through hell and she thought he should just be glad she was back, and carry on as if nothing had happened. He said he'd idolised her since the day they were married, and she seemed to think that gave her a licence to make him look a fool in front of everybody, and then stroll back home as if there was nothing amiss. She was as cool as a cucumber, he said. He couldn't stomach it.'

'Did you tell him what she said about Piers Marson? About him getting under her feet, and always sticking his neb in?'

'Yeah, that's the only time I heard him laugh,' Margaret said. 'He said, "I could have told him that. After three days she'd had enough, she wanted you out of the way. She wanted you back at sea, earning money." That's why he never took a trip off. He said he'd missed all our young years, but he'd be seeing a lot more of these four, and our Simon.'

'Where is he now?'

'Where do you think?'

'Probably Rayners, with our Anthony.'

Margaret nodded. 'That's my guess. I don't think he'll get drunk, though. He stopped that when he was looking after the lads.'

'Well, she'll be all right where she is, I reckon. The fancy man seems besotted with her.'

'Be nice to know for sure, though, wouldn't it? Just to know.'

Lynn left without breathing a word about Jim, and Margaret gave her no openings. Too raw, Lynn thought. Better leave that subject alone until Margaret brought it up herself.

As soon as she got home and settled Simon in front of the telly Lynn rang the Dorchester, and discovered that her mother was no longer working there. They had no idea where she might be and had no address for her other than the one on Boulevard. She hung up, flummoxed as to where to turn next.

A couple of minutes later Connie rang to say she thought Graham was working himself into the ground, poor lad. 'I'm worried about him. He looked that pale and ill last time he called – haven't you noticed how pale he looks? He could do with a complete rest, before his health breaks down altogether,' she said.

'We could both do with a complete rest, and a change of scene,' Lynn said. 'Is there any chance of you babysitting on Friday or Saturday night? Or Sunday, even? If we could have a night out together it would make a change from all this misery and hard work. It would do us both good,' Lynn said.

'Oh! Oh, I'll see, but ... I can't make any promises. I might be going out with Gordon any of those evenings,' Connie said, 'so I'll let you know.'

Lynn put the receiver down, confident that she would be waiting till the cows come home to be 'let know'. From not being able to get enough of Simon while she and Graham were separated, Connie seemed not to want to look after him at all now they were back together, though she would never have admitted it. She seemed to be-grudge her son and his wife a night out together. It was almost as if she wanted Lynn to endure what she'd had to endure, and Lynn could not believe that Connie had endured her husband's betrayals without a lot of grief, for all the claptrap she talked about 'understanding men'. But sitting alone night after night, wondering what her husband was up to had been good enough for Connie, and Connie now seemed to think it good enough for her daughter-in-law.

Lynn's thoughts drifted to Mrs Orme's large, soulful eyes and her constant glances in Graham's direction at that dinner party. And that look she'd given him before she left – *oh, poor you! what an awful wife you've got!* And Graham hadn't been quite so energetic in the marital bed the past few nights, either. If the Bradburys were running true to form it probably wouldn't be long before they were inviting Spaniel Eyes to tea with them, to add to their collection of their son's conquests.

Lynn was too weighed down by other matters to worry about it. Her head was crammed with more important things – like Margaret, her nephews, her mother, her father – and what might have befallen Alec, that not a soul had heard from him for so long. After the loss of the *Sprite*, she had bought a local paper every day and combed through it for news, grieved to see the names and photographs of the lost crews – many of them from families she knew. She was always relieved not to find Alec's name listed, but trawlers from all the fishing towns were in the Arctic, Fleetwood included, so although no news might be good news it was no absolute guarantee he was safe. His photo could be in one of the Fleetwood papers, for all she knew – or any fishing town

297

from Aberdeen to Lowestoft.

It was time she got Alec out of her head, anyway. She was a respectable married woman again, with a husband who was forging ahead in his career, and Simon was happy. She couldn't drag him away from his dad and out of another beautiful home with a wonderful garden, even if Alec were to knock on her door this minute. And Alec was never going to knock on her door. That idea was nothing more than one of those beautiful fantasies that women tantalise themselves with when their lives have gone sour.

Alec had been nothing but a dream, a mirage of some wonderful oasis she had never quite managed to reach – and never could reach, now. But, as Margaret had said about their mother, it would be nice to know for sure that he was all right. Just to *know*.

Chapter 45

The trip had been a rough one, the conditions extreme, with gales, black frost and heavy icing of the ship. Most of the crew were frostbitten, on lips, hands and feet. Engineers apart, they had spent over eighteen hours a day gutting fish on the open deck, and stacking it in ice in the fish room – a normal working day for them when at the fishing grounds. The catches were so heavy that the cook and galley-boy had been roped in to help when their own work was done. They were all dead on their feet, every ounce of energy expended, and pure fatigue combined with hands and forearms that were blue and numbed by cold had resulted in a fair few slashing injuries from gutting-knives as sharp as razors. But the end was in sight. The fish room was full and they were running out of boards to stack it all. All they wanted now was an order from the skipper to stow the trawl and turn for home.

They could see him, sitting on the bridge, gazing into space, not making a move.

'What the bloody hell's he doing? Is he pissed again? Is he having a nap?' one of the deckies asked.

'Nip up there and see what he wants done, Jackie,' said Alec.

Jackie went and a moment later shouted down to him: 'Just come up here a minute, will you?'

Alec went, and found Jackie gazing at the skipper who was sitting with his eyes wide open. 'Is he dead?' he asked.

'He's doing a bloody good impression, if he's not,' Alec said, and wrapped his fingers round the skipper's wrist. 'I can't feel a pulse.' He pressed his ear to the skipper's back, slightly to the left. 'I can't hear his heart beating.'

'I can't see him breathing, either,' Jackie said. 'What's happened to him?'

'How do I know, you dozy bugger? Maybe had a heart attack, or something.'

'What are we going to do wi' him? When one of the deckies died on a ship I was on a while back we unloaded him at the nearest port and he got sent home in a lead-lined coffin.'

'Well, we've finished the trip, and it's four or five days steaming to get back to Grimsby, so I reckon we'll put him in ice in the fish room, and take him home. He'll get there just as quick as taking him to any port, and a lot cheaper.'

'It's unlucky, to have a corpse on board.'

'If we put into port it'll delay us getting home. Hanging about until the fish is spoiled is what I'd call unlucky.'

'There's that many fish there's hardly room for him in the fish room, and hardly any ice.'

'There's plenty on the ship. We'll hack some of that up and stow him in it on one of the shelves. He'll have to go in the fish room, there's nowhere else for him.' He paused, gazing at the skipper. 'Poor bugger! He was so terrified of not making a trip, I reckon that's what killed him.'

'He nearly killed us; I know that,' said Jackie. 'He must ha' died happy, though – watching us hauling all that fish in.'

'On second thoughts, we'll leave him in his bunk overnight – make sure he really is dead before we put him down there,' Alec said.

He told the sparks to radio the owners, then leaving Jackie and the third hand on the bridge Alec took the skipper's dead weight over his shoulder and carried him down to his cabin. The crew looked on, making no wisecracks, unusually for them.

So – I'm in command now, Alec thought, after laying the lifeless skipper on his bunk. He straightened the body and closed the skipper's eyes and gazed at him for a moment or two, then went to the chart room to begin copying the charts, especially marking the spot where they'd found the 'fish shop'.

The following day he went to check on the body. It felt as cold as clay, no sign of life at all, so he sent Jackie to tell the crew to hack enough ice off the upperworks to cover the skipper, and leave him to lie in state in the fish room. The ship looked like a floating iceberg and was listing a bit, but the danger of her turning turtle was gone. He gave no orders to chop the rest of the ice away. Let the men have a rest. They were sailing south; let the warmer latitudes melt the ice off and then the list of the ship would cure itself. He went to the bridge to relieve the watch, opened the window for a sighting, and quickly shut it again, against the icy sea-spray.

Farewell to the Arctic, to its cold grandeur, its cruel beauty, and its changelessness. It had relented, and it was letting them escape with tons of its treasure. He stood on the bridge with all his senses sharpened, glad to be going home, but acutely aware of the beauty of this awful place, which seemed outside of time. Time meant nothing here. The Arctic breathed eternity, the harmony of nature – and something profound, beyond description. He kept still, barely breathing, the better to feel it. With his senses so alert the throb of the engine seemed to him the very heartbeat of the ocean, of Creation itself. A strange ecstasy took hold of him, until even the ice burns on his hands no longer pained him. He could never have put it into words, he only knew that the vast, empty wastes of the Arctic had infected him with a fever he would never shake off, and he would be drawn back to these cold, inhuman wastes time and time again, in a way that some might call a death-wish.

Chapter 46

'No, I'll get these. I'm working, you're not,' Janet said the following Monday afternoon, handing the barman the price of two halves of lager.

Lynn picked up the glasses and went directly to a table near the roaring coal fire. 'Well, Graham earns a very good salary, you know,' she said.

'How much of this good salary do you see?'

'Not a lot. But that's because we've got a big mortgage, and he's got a big car, and he needs a skiing holiday now and then.'

'What?'

'Yeah,' Lynn said. 'He's in Austria for a week, on the piste.'

'On the piss as well, I suppose.'

'I doubt it. That's not really Graham's style.'

'No, it's not, come to think.'

'He says married couples don't have to take their holidays together, just because their parents did. Things are different, these days. More and more couples are taking separate holidays. It's the latest thing, according to him.' Lynn paused, and took a sip of lager.

'When do you get yours, then?'

'When I've got the money to pay for it, I suppose – maybe sometime after Simon's left home and I'm back at work. I suspect his mother's paid for his. She thought he looked pale the other week. I never saw it; he looked all right to me, but hey presto, this week he's flying away on a winter holiday. There's nothing Graham wants that Graham shouldn't have, to his mother's way of thinking. Three expensive new suits, three pairs of Italian leather shoes and half a dozen new shirts? Needed for his job. Golf club membership? He's got to meet the *right kind* of people. Holidays abroad?'

'He's got to meet the *right kind* of tart, maybe?' Janet suggested.

'Well, for his *health*, you know,' Lynn emphasised. 'But when Simon needs a new pair of shoes, it's my dad we have to go shopping with, and I freeze all day because I daren't put the heating on.'

Janet shook her head. 'Shit,' she said. 'Is he up to his old tricks, do you reckon?'

'I don't know about that, but there's not much I can do about it if he is. I've got no job, no money, no home of my own and nobody to look after Simon, now my mother's baled out. And he likes his school, and he likes the house, and I don't want to rock his little boat again, so I'm stuck with it.'

'I don't envy you.'

'I'm not downhearted,' Lynn said. 'I'm going to make it crack, this week. I haven't got to sit in waiting for his nibs coming home every night, so I'm going to have our Margaret and her lads staying for a day or two. I'll get them out for walks with the dog. Then I'll go visiting people.'

'Hmm, must be nice to be a lady of leisure.'

'It's not. It's lonely and boring, most of the time, and you feel as if you're drifting, instead of getting somewhere. I live for the time Simon gets out of school.'

'Shit!' Janet repeated. 'Well, I'm on an early on Wednesday. Come for your tea, and bring Simon. Dave can drop you both off at home before he goes for a pint.'

'Goes for a pint? You never used to be able to prise him away from the telly.'

'Oh, well, he's made a few pals at the Tap and Spile, and they're on a mission to have a drink in all the oldest pubs in Hull. Not a pub crawl, they pick a different one every week, and stay in it all night.'

'You should go with him.'

'No thanks. If I've been on an early I'm too tired, and if I've been on a late he's already gone. Anyway, I'm not interested in old pubs, and I quite like having the house to myself some nights.'

'I know, but maybe you should make the effort to get out with him.'

'I can see "other women" written all over your face, Lynn. Don't worry about that – it'll never happen. Not with dull old Dave,' Janet said.

Chapter 47

Lynn would have loved to take the whole family to spend a day or two with her in Cottingham, but Margaret wouldn't leave the house, and young Jim wouldn't leave his mother. After the younger three boys had been in her house for a couple of hours, Lynn decided it had been for the best. Margaret was better at home, having a rest from them and the sort of high jinks going on in her living room.

'Ooooh! Ooooh!' Six-year-old George, the most excitable of the brothers, was covered in a tablecloth, slinking round with his hands in the air, pretending to be a ghost and making wailing noises to frighten eight-year-old Geoffrey, the most placid of them.

Geoffrey took cover behind Lynn. 'Stop him, Auntie Lynn! Stop him,' he shrieked.

'Stop it, George,' she demanded, whereupon George was in fits of giggling at his own antics and the highly satisfying reaction they were getting. 'Stop him, Auntie Lynn, stop him,' he mimicked, and ignoring Lynn he continued alternately baiting Geoffrey and then splitting his sides with laughter, so much so that he infected all the boys, and Lynn couldn't help laughing herself, despite being really annoyed with him.

'I'm a ghost, and I'll fart on your head,' George laughed, beside himself with merriment. He went one better: 'I'll pee on your head!'

His threats were accompanied by shrieks of laughter from all the others, including Simon.

George repeated his threats.

'Shut up, George!' Lynn ordered.

Goaded beyond endurance, but laughing in spite of his anger, Geoffrey retaliated. 'I'll piss on yours, then!'

George stopped laughing and pointed an accusing finger at him. 'Ooh, Auntie Lynn! Geoff said a bad word!'

Then they were all in hysterics again, and much as she tried to stop herself Lynn was almost as helpless with laughter as the boys. How familiar it all sounded, and how Hessle Road! But looking after them was harder work than she had anticipated. Better get them outside, to run some of their energy off.

'Come on,' she said. 'We're taking the dog for a walk. Last to get his coat on is a cissy.'

Lynn lifted her coat and the dog lead off the pegs in the hallway, prompting a torrent of excited barking from Lassie, to add to the din. Whatever would the neighbours have thought, if she'd had any, she wondered? Then they were out of the door and away up Snuff Mill Lane.

They should have been exhausted by the time they got back from their cross-country run – climbing trees, playing hide and seek behind hedges and getting their feet wet in ditches. Instead, they were invigorated, and had more energy than ever. Lynn fed them on piles of sandwiches, and then they played Snakes and Ladders.

'Our Simon's posh,' five-year-old Joe observed,

after a few games.

Simon's accent registered a few miles distance from Hessle Road, but it was nowhere near the Home Counties. He looked at Lynn. 'I'm not posh, am I, Mum?'

'*Mum!*' George scoffed. 'He says *mum!*'

'No,' Lynn answered Simon. 'You're not posh.'

'He's posh,' Geoffrey affirmed, very quietly.

'He's *not* posh,' Lynn insisted.

'I'm not!'

'You are.'

'I'm not.'

'Oh, for goodness' sake!' Lynn protested.

'Posh boy, posh boy!' George chanted, quickly joined by Geoffrey, evidently glad somebody else was the target, for once.

'Bathtime!' Lynn announced. 'George and Joe first. Upstairs, you two.'

She gave them Ovaltine afterwards, hoping it would make them sleep. She read them bedtime story after bedtime story, and finally tucked them up and went downstairs to sort out the washing. No sooner had she reached the foot of the stairs than she heard them bouncing on the beds. She shouted a warning. The bouncing stopped and Lynn went through to the kitchen, noting the degree of wear on their clothes; not bad on Geoffrey's, worse on George's, and some of Joe's – youngest and last in line for the cast-offs – were near to rags.

The bouncing started again, accompanied by giggles from all of them, including Simon. Another shouted warning stopped it. Lynn filled her twin tub washing machine and put half the clothes in. More bouncing and giggling called for another trip to the foot of the stairs and another warning.

All was quiet. Lynn returned to the washing, and a gentle creaking started again. A shouted warning from downstairs stopped them for a couple of minutes, and then that gentle rhythmic creaking began again, becoming less gentle by degrees until she had to shout again and threaten them with the wooden spoon across their backsides. The effect was short-lived. After a few quiet moments, their bouncing and their stifled giggles started again and went on until eleven o'clock, doubtless with giddy, tormenting George as the ringleader and inspirer of all the mischief. Lynn couldn't help laughing at him. He might be naughty, but it was good to have a bit of life in the house.

She finished the washing and put the damp clothes on a clothes horse. After setting it around the dying embers of the living-room fire she went to bed, and was asleep as soon as her head touched the pillow.

She was roused a couple of hours later by a terrific screaming and wailing. Feeling as if she'd been dragged from the tomb she followed the noise to the bedroom that Geoffrey and George were sharing. Geoffrey was awake and quiet, George still asleep, wrestling with the bedclothes and howling like a banshee. Simon and Joe arrived and Simon switched the light on.

'He's having a nightmare,' Lynn said, trying to wake George. He fought her off as if his life depended on it.

She took hold of his hands, and squeezed them tight. He awoke, looking dazed.

'Right, back to bed, you lot,' Lynn ordered the others, but George was fearful of being left, so she took him into her bed where he lay awake for ages, not the tormenting little devil of earlier in the day, but a tense and terrified child.

'You'll be all right now, George,' she soothed him. 'You've had a bad dream, that's all.'

'He was in the sea, and he was stretching his arms out and trying to shout, and the sea kept going into his mouth,' George wept, working himself up to hysteria again.

'You're all right, you're safe,' Lynn said, trying to calm him. 'Who was in the sea?'

'My dad!'

'Sh, sh, sh! You'll wake the others. What was he trying to shout, George?'

'"Help me! Help me!" – and he was pulling me down with him under the waves, and the fish were eating us!' he sobbed.

'We eat the fish, George. They don't eat us,' Lynn said. 'It was just a bad dream, that's all. It wasn't real.'

'He's dead,' George said. 'We'll never see him again – except in dreams.'

'There's been a lot of laughter. They've laughed themselves sore and it didn't stop till nearly midnight,' Lynn said, when she took the boys back on Sunday evening. The culprits ran giggling upstairs, to avoid a telling off.

'George had the most awful nightmare, or I wouldn't have brought them back so soon,' Lynn continued, following Margaret into the kitchen. 'He had us all awake – even Simon, and he usually sleeps like a log. I couldn't comfort him. He was so upset I took him into my bed and he cuddled up to me with the bedside light on. He didn't want to be in the dark.'

'He don't like the dark, our George,' young Jim called, from the living room.

'What was he dreaming about?' Margaret asked.

'His dad – drowning, and then he cried himself to sleep.'

'I don't know what brought that on. Maybe something somebody's said at school.'

'I don't know, but in the morning Simon asked him about it and – God love him – he said: "I'm not going to tell you about my dream, Simon, because I don't want it to get into your mind." I was amazed how wise a six-year-old can be, and how good.'

'Oh, aye, he's got his tender side, our Georgie,' Margaret said. 'Don't get upset, Lynn. Drink your tea.'

Lynn held the cup to her lips, inhaling the steam. When she'd recovered enough to speak she said: 'The Memorial Service is on Friday, isn't it? Are you keeping the lads off school?'

'No, we're not going. We've never been to Trinity Church in our lives, so why start now?'

'Well, to remember them; say a few prayers, comfort the living, I expect,' Lynn floundered.

'I don't need a memorial service to remember Jim, and I'm not likely to get any comfort from it,' Margaret said.

310

Since her miscarriage Margaret had never mentioned Jim – not to Lynn, at least. She was well used to being without a husband for weeks at a time, and was coping with day to day living as well as she always had, as if she barely realised what had happened. Maybe she reckoned that going to the Memorial Service would be bad luck, Lynn thought.

'He did exist, you know, Mam,' young Jim called.

'I'm well aware of that. Maybe he exists still,' she answered, calmly.

Lynn looked into her sister's eyes, and the penny dropped. Margaret had not given up on Jim. In spite of everything, she seemed to be hanging on to the belief that he would walk through that door one day, drop his sea bag, and take her upstairs to their sweet, clean, freshly changed bed – as he'd done every three weeks since the day they were married. Then they would carry on as if this catastrophe in their lives had been nothing but a bad dream – as if nothing that had happened to her since that missed trip to London had been real. For Margaret, going to a Memorial Service might mean giving up that hope and abandoning Jim to his watery grave for ever.

But he's never coming back, love, Lynn thought. Never, never, never! She buried her face in her tea cup, the steam adding moisture to tears she wanted to hide.

'I'm going, anyhow, even if nobody else from this family is,' young Jim muttered.

'I'll take you,' Lynn managed to choke the

words out.

'You don't have to go if you don't want to, Auntie Lynn. I'm a big lad now. I can go on my own.'

'You can take me, then,' she said.

Chapter 48

'You're blooming!' Lynn smiled, when a bright-eyed Brenda answered the door the following morning, glossy-haired and glowing. Pregnancy obviously suited her.

'Five months now,' Brenda smiled. 'It's a long time since I saw you. Come in. I thought you'd forgotten where we live.'

'You're never in, more like,' Lynn said, neatly shifting the blame.

'Oh. Well, I go to my mother's most days.'

'I thought as much. Anyway, I got a postcard this morning. I thought it was from Graham – he's skiing in Austria, in case you didn't know. I thought: Oh, I've not been forgotten after all. But it wasn't from Graham, it was from my mam, postmarked Spain, of all places!'

Lynn took the card out of her pocket, and handed it over, with its scrawled message: *I'm all right. Don't worry about me. Hope everything's ok in Cott. Love, Mam.* 'Not a clue as to how long she's going to be in Spain, or where we can find her when she gets back!' Lynn added.

'She sent us one as well, except it says: *Tell our*

Anthony I'm all right. No address on that, either.'

'And have you – told him?'

'Give me a chance. It only came this morning. He's gutted about what she's done to your dad, though,' Brenda said, handing the card back. After a pause, she asked: 'So how come Graham's skiing in Austria? I thought you were skint.'

'We are. I suspect his mother's paid for it.'

'That figures. She should have sent you and Simon as well.'

'Not likely. We don't work hard enough to be tired and pale, and if we were, she wouldn't notice. Have you heard from our Anthony at all?'

'Aye, he says the gales aren't quite as bad up there now, thank goodness. He's home on the twenty-first. I can't wait. I hate being on my own.'

'I know how you feel. What's Orla up to these days? I haven't seen her for ages,' Lynn said, as casually as she could manage.

'She's all right. Getting engaged soon.'

'Who to?'

Brenda laughed, and gave her a knowing look. 'No, not to Alec, Lynn. To a nice lad she met working at the dock offices.'

'I thought she'd have ended up with Alec at one time.'

'I thought you'd end up with Alec, at one time,' Brenda countered. 'Anyway, him and Orla certainly weren't suited. He's sailing out of Grimsby, now. Anthony's heard him on the VHF radio that the skippers and mates use to talk to each other.'

Alec was alive, then! 'Oh! Out of Grimsby!' Lynn said, so taken aback she could think of nothing else to say, but her heart was turning somersaults.

313

'Will you be calling at Margaret's?'

'Yeah,' said Lynn, recovering her composure. 'Have you seen her since...?'

'Since she came out of hospital? I went once, with Anthony, and I saw the way she looked at me and my bump,' Brenda said, looking down at her obviously pregnant shape. 'Terrible – I don't know how I'd describe it, sort of ... *haunted*, I suppose. Anyway, I felt so awful I didn't want to go again looking like this. Too much like rubbing it in.'

'She doesn't talk about any of it,' Lynn said. 'Everything that's happened since she missed that trip to London – it's as if she's washed it all out of her mind.'

'Is she going to the Memorial Service?'

'No. I'm going though, with young Jim, and a lot of Jim's relatives, I expect. Are you?'

'No, it might bring bad luck. Anthony's all right so far, and I want it to stay that way.'

Graham's car was back in the drive the afternoon following the Memorial Service. Sunburned and smiling he heaved his suitcase into the house, dumped it in the hallway, and gave Lynn a kiss on the cheek. Lassie jumped and barked round his feet, excited to the point of delirium. He bent down to rub her ears. 'Did you miss me, girl?'

Simon was just as thrilled to see him. 'Did you bring us anything back, Dad?'

'A lot of washing for your mum,' Graham laughed.

'Have you got anything for me?'

'No. It was a place for grown-ups. There wasn't

314

anything for kids there,' Graham said, ruffling his hair.

'Not even a few sweets, Graham?' Lynn said.

'Sweets are bad for his teeth. And you shouldn't encourage him to be so mercenary, demanding presents the minute he sees people. Is there any hot water? I want a bath.'

'Yeah, there's plenty.'

'Oh, by the way, the company's given a hundred pounds to the fishermen's appeal fund.'

'Very good of them, I'm sure,' Lynn said. 'A scrap metal merchant's given a *thousand* out of his own pocket, and the local paper's given *five hundred*.'

'Huh! Just to outdo everybody else, I suppose, and now they'll be advertising their generosity all over the place,' Graham said, with a shrug. 'Oh, well, I thought you'd be pleased, that's all.'

He took himself off upstairs and started running the bath, leaving his suitcase in the hallway. Half an hour later he was down again, dressed in smart casuals and smelling of aftershave.

'You're not going out, are you?' Lynn protested. 'You've only just got back.'

'Down to the golf club. I want to see if there's anybody from the company there, and find out what's been going on while I've been away. Got to keep my ear to the ground. I think I'll have a round to stretch my legs, as well, after all that travelling.'

He met her eyes, and Lynn felt herself under a minute inspection for a few moments. His gaze travelled from hair that hadn't had a decent cut for months, to a face devoid of make-up and

315

fresh from a sleepless night all the way down to her down-at-heel shoes.

He frowned. 'I never thought I'd have to tell you this, Lynn, but you're letting yourself go. All the fun's gone out of you. You're not very good company, these days.' He glanced round the living room, littered with library books, shoes, Simon's scarf and gloves, and cups and plates used for a TV lunch which she hadn't got around to carrying into the kitchen. 'You've nothing else to do but look after Simon and keep the house up to scratch, and just look at it!'

'Oh, excuse me, but I haven't been having a holiday. I was at a Memorial Service yesterday, with two of Jim's sisters, and my two eldest nephews, who've lost their father. They were all in tears, and Margaret couldn't even face going, so she stayed at home and looked after Simon and the younger two. I don't think it's sunk in with her that he's died, and seeing she'll never have a body to convince her, or a funeral to put an end to it all, I don't think it ever will. I think she'll be in this sort of suspended animation for ever, and it's heartbreaking to see it. So I haven't been having a lot of fun, Graham.'

'Sorry, I suppose not,' he said. 'Well smarten yourself up a bit, and I'll take you out for a couple of hours tomorrow night, if my mother can have Simon.'

'I'd rather not trouble your mother,' Lynn said. 'Better leave her with the opportunity to go out with your dad. She never knows when she might get the chance.'

'Suit yourself,' Graham shrugged.

316

'I'll tell you what, Graham – if you're going out, I'm taking Simon down to Margaret's and we'll sleep at my dad's. We could both do with the company.'

'All right. But don't forget my mother's doing Sunday lunch for us. We've got to be there for two.'

She'd said it herself, but she felt Graham's agreement to her sleeping at her father's like a slap in the face. How times have changed, she thought. A few weeks ago he would have been desperate to get her into bed, especially after a full week's separation. The idea of her sleeping away from home would have been out of the question.

'You'll have to pick us up from Margaret's, then – unless you want her Yorkshire puddings to be ruined,' she said. 'There are hardly any buses on a Sunday, and I don't know the times.'

'I'm sure somebody down there could tell you; there aren't many of them have cars,' he said, and after glancing at her face added: 'All right. I'll pick you up at one.'

He went to the sideboard drawer for a comb and stood admiring his reflection in the mirror over the fireplace and slicking his hair back. 'There's one good thing about it, though – Margaret not having a body to bury, I mean – at least it saved her the expense of a funeral,' he said. 'That would have knocked a hole in her finances – she'd probably have been up to her ears in debt if she'd had all that expense. And with no husband to support her it's a blessing in disguise she hasn't got another two to provide for – and where she'd have put them in that tiny house I don't know. So look on the bright side, I say.'

And there stood Graham, ever the businessman, Lynn thought – a mind like a bloody adding machine. She disappeared into the kitchen and stood leaning with hands either side of the sink, looking down on the viciously pointed vegetable knife in the bowl with visions of grabbing it and sticking it into him – and then watching his blood seep out onto the Australian emigrants' abandoned carpet. How satisfying it would feel! A minute or two later she heard the car pull out of the drive and went back into the living room.

Simon was watching Graham's departure through the window. 'Are you mad, Mum?' he asked.

'I am, a bit.'

He flung himself into an armchair and crossed his arms, his lower lip protruding. 'I am. He never brought me a present. Everybody at school said he'd bring me something back.'

Lynn ruffled his hair. 'Never mind,' she soothed. 'Stick your lip back in. Worse things happen at sea.'

'I know that.'

'I know you know.'

She looked towards Graham's bursting suitcase, still standing in the hallway, still decorated with labels from the Austrian ski resort – waiting for her to unpack it all and do his tons of washing and ironing. Well, there'd be skiing holidays in Hell before she emptied that.

Following her gaze, Simon said, hopefully: 'I wonder if he was kidding? I wonder if there's a present in that suitcase?'

'I doubt it.'

'Can we have a look?' he pleaded.

There was a long pause before she caved in. She opened the case and left Simon to rummage through it, then went upstairs to the bathroom to clear a litter of dirty clothes and a pair of malodorous socks lying under a layer of talcum powder.

She took the dirty clothes down to the washer, to find that Simon had done his rummaging more thoroughly than any customs officer on a trawler, and found nothing but shoes, wash-bag and more dirty laundry.

Chapter 49

'Brenda's invited us to lunch with her and our Anthony on Easter Sunday,' Lynn said, during breakfast on the following Saturday morning. 'My dad's going to be at home as well. It'll be quite a family gathering.'

Graham lifted his eyes from his bacon and eggs. 'Oh, dear. My parents were hoping to be invited here. Can't you get her to put it off until the week after?'

'They're trawlermen, Graham, they won't be here next week, and there's not much chance of them being ashore together again for ages. Anyway, I'll get them to come here, instead, how's that? And then we can invite your parents as well, and our Margaret and her lads, and have a family party. Eight adults and five boys, we might just be able to squash round this dining table.'

Simon's eyes shone at the prospect. 'Oooh, yes!' he said.

'Then Auntie Margaret's lads can sleep here afterwards.'

Graham cast his eyes heavenward. 'Perish the thought!' he said, 'and you can't have forgotten that your dad threatened to kill me?'

'Only once, and then only if you had any more Mandies. You haven't, have you?'

'And risk my life? I wouldn't dare.'

'You're in no danger, then,' she said, 'so why not let bygones be bygones?'

'I'll be very honest with you, Lynn; I've got nothing in common with your Anthony – or your dad, come to that. They can't talk about things that interest me, and I can't talk about things that interest them. They'll be talking about trawling, and I'd be like a fish out of water, literally. It's all too much effort. I'd rather spend my time talking to people who are on the same wave-length, preferably people who can help me on.'

'Like the people at the golf club, I suppose.'

'Well, some of them.'

'Are there many other blokes at your level in the company who've joined the golf club, Graham?'

'No.'

'I suppose they spend their time talking to people in their own families, who might just happen to be in different lines of employment.'

'You might be right. They've probably got no ambition, which is all the better for people who have.'

'So they'd probably rather spend the money on outings with their families than golf club membership, and golf club gear.'

'I dare say they would, but that's not the way to get on in the company. And even then, I spend more time with you than your dad ever spent with your mother. And I know she's hopped it again, by the way,' he said.

She laughed. 'The bloody cognoscenti, again. Was it the cognoscenti at the golf course, or the cognoscenti at the fruit shop?'

'They're everywhere,' he said, with a grin. 'Their eyes and ears are always open, and their tongues never stop wagging, but it would be nice if I occasionally got the news about what's happening in this family before my mother gets it from her customers. Seeing I'm supposed to be a member of it.'

'If you were that keen on being a member of this family, you'd have your bloody dinner with it, on Easter Sunday.'

'Sorry, I'm pleading a prior engagement. Tell them I'll be working hard at the golf club, ingratiating myself with the management of Four Winds Pharmaceuticals, in the interests of this branch of the family.' He looked out of the window for a moment, onto a garden beginning to show signs of life. 'We might get a round of golf in today; it looks as if it's going to be fine. Thank goodness the light nights will soon be here.'

After his Austrian holiday, Graham was out almost every night, leaving Lynn with the dog she'd never wanted as her only and very welcome companion after Simon was in bed. There was no possibility of her going out at night, so she determined that she would do her socialising during the day. She began a routine of walking Lassie to school with them, and then getting a bus straight down to Margaret's, occasionally by way of Brenda's – or to Janet's if she was off work. Even to be on the bus, hearing other people's snatches of conversation was preferable to spending hours in the house on her own, and Lassie seemed to enjoy an outing as much as she did herself. It was good to walk along Hessle Road or along Marlborough Avenue and up Richmond Street, and maybe bump into people she'd known for years.

'I'm rolling in it, today,' Lynn told Janet when she answered the door later that week. 'I can afford to treat you to a coffee on Chants Ave.'

'Come in. I'll treat you to one here, for nothing. You've brought the dog, I see,' Janet said, stooping to pet her. 'Hello, Lassie. Hiya, girl.'

Lynn stepped inside, and took off her coat. 'Do you mind? I don't like leaving her on her own all day. I wish to God I'd never moved. I took *him* back after his dalliance with Mandy, so why couldn't I have taken the house back as well, instead of cutting my nose off to spite my face?'

'It was the way you felt at the time, I suppose – but it was great when you were just round the corner. How's it going, anyway?'

'I'm fed up, Janet. I look at what's happened to our Margaret, and I think I've no right to complain – but I'm fed up of not having any independence, and I'm fed up of spending so much time on my own, and I'm fed up of being hard up.

He's out nearly every night, and I don't say much about it, because he earns the money and he thinks he's got a right to do what he likes with it. And even when he's in it's obvious he doesn't really want to be in with us. He prowls about like a caged animal as often as not, as moody as hell, finding fault with everything, including Simon. Then he'll go out and leave his mood behind, casting a gloom on the whole place.'

'Sounds grim,' Janet said, leading the way through to the kitchen.

'It's getting that way. Everything was hunky dory when we first got back together – he was spending time with Simon, taking us on family outings, treating us, talking about having another baby – but all that's gone by the board now.'

'Dave's going out a lot more these days but when he's in he never prowls,' Janet said. 'He slumps – in front of the telly. I'm glad to see the back of him sometimes. It's nice to have the telly off and have a bit of peace and quiet now and again.'

'I wish I could say the same. I didn't want this little dog when he first brought her home, but I don't know what I'd do without her now. I love her to bits.'

'Don't get like some of those women who treat them like substitute babies, will you? Remember she's a dog,' Janet said, flicking the kettle on and putting a bowl of water down for Lassie.

'I don't think I'll be having another baby. He hasn't mentioned it for ages.'

'Maybe just as well, if he's started hopping off on skiing holidays on his own, and spending all his time away from home.'

323

'You remember that dinner party I told you about a while back, when one of the bosses' wives was ogling him the whole evening?'

'I do,' Janet said, lifting two mugs off the shelf, and throwing a spoonful of instant coffee in each, followed by a splash of milk.

'Well, I was vacuuming the car after he got back from Austria, and I found an earring – a sapphire set in solid gold – hallmarked, not costume jewellery. Not the sort of thing you'd want to lose. I thought it must have been hers, so I found out where she lived, and I posted it to her – with compliments from Lynn.'

'He's up to his old tricks again then.'

'I'm not sure. It came back by return of post. Graham was furious, when he found out I'd sent it. He said he lends the car to other people at the company quite often, and one of their wives must have lost it – except I found it in the back, which is not where wives usually sit when their husbands are driving.'

'No, and wives don't usually do things in the backs of cars that cause them to lose earrings; they generally do that sort of stuff in the comfort of their own homes. Where is it now?'

'He took it.'

'He must know who it belongs to, then. Maybe the boss's wife's not the only one he's grappling with.'

'Hmm.'

'You're not smoking, Lynn. I'd expect you to be puffing like a factory chimney, thinking about this lot.'

'No, I've nearly given up. I started to cut down

after I'd left work, and this week after I'd done the rest of the shopping I had a choice between a packet of fags, or a packet of loo rolls with what I had left. I really wanted the fags, but I absolutely had to have the other. So which would you have picked?'

Lynn grinned, expecting Janet to laugh. She didn't.

'I'd have got the fags and made him wipe his arse on his shirt lap. God, he's a tight little swine, isn't he?' she exclaimed, pouring boiling water into the mugs. She pushed one towards Lynn and led the way into the dining room.

'You don't know the half. He went to Austria for a week, and he never even brought us a present back, either me or Simon,' Lynn said, following Janet into the dining room.

They put their coffee down on the coasters on the polished top, and sat facing each other.

'What are you going to do about it?' Janet asked. 'The fact he's probably got another woman on the go, I mean.'

'What can I do? I've no way of finding out for sure, and I couldn't do much about it if I knew. I'm trapped, Janet. I've no home or money of my own. He can come and go as he pleases, and if he wants other women I reckon he'll have 'em, the only difference being he'll be a bit cautious about letting me find out about it for fear of my dad. He's not brave, our Graham.'

'You could live at your mother's – I mean, your dad's. You'd have the place to yourself the best part of the time.'

'It would mean dragging Simon out of school

325

again, away from his friends and another nice house with a garden with a swing and trees to climb ... not to mention separating him from his dad again. It wouldn't be fair, and what would I live on? If I can't prove adultery I can't get maintenance, and I can't get a decent job. With my mother gone, I've nobody to look after Simon.'

'You could try and find a childminder.'

'I've looked, and there's no one near enough to pick him up from school.'

'You could maybe go for a job on nights.'

'Graham wouldn't look after him if I had to work weekends; he'd be shuffled off to his mother's, and she won't want him. She's got to hold herself ready to go out with Gordon, or so she tells me.'

'It would be too much to ask Margaret to have him, I suppose.'

'I think so, at this stage, and in any case, it's too far away. My dad's helping her out with money, now Jim's gone. The owners paid her his wages up to the minute the ship sank, and that was the end of that. She's keeping the job on at Birds Eye, which she says pays peanuts, and she gets a bit from the National Assistance. He makes up the rest. It would make more sense for her to give her house up and take the lads to live at Boulevard – it would save her the rent, but she doesn't want to do that. I think she's nursing secret hopes of Jim walking through the door one day.'

'Not much chance of that,' Janet said.

'None at all, I'd say, but I wouldn't want to try to convince her. I went to the Memorial Service with her two eldest, because she wouldn't go herself.'

'That must have been a lot of fun.'

'It was really, really sad. All the flags were flying at half mast on the way there, and the church was absolutely full of flowers – bouquets, wreaths, crosses, and anchors, with *my beloved father; my darling husband; my dearest son*, and messages on them fit to break your heart. Young Jim put our wreath beside them. *God Bless Our Jim*, they'd written on it. I couldn't sing any of the hymns, I was that choked. When they started reading the names of all those poor lads you could have heard a pin drop – and the sheer size of places like that seems to magnify the silence, somehow. You could hear people snuffling, and choking sobs back; it was awful. I was glad I'd remembered to bring handkerchiefs because we really needed 'em. I thought: that's it, now. We'll never see any of them again.'

'I saw the flags. I don't think I saw one cheerful face in town that day,' Janet said.

'I think that's why I can't get too worked up about Graham, you know. I'm fed up with the way he's carrying on, but I'm not devastated – or obsessed by it, not like I was the first time round. I think it's just panning down to being a way of life, him being out all the time, probably messing about with other women – like his mother putting up with his father.'

'You can't!' Janet protested. 'You can't let that happen.'

'I can't do much to stop it. Maybe it's just the mood I'm in, but that Memorial Service seemed to put everything into perspective,' Lynn said. 'After that, Graham's carry-on didn't seem to matter all that much.'

327

Chapter 50

Brenda stood by the cooker passing plates to her Easter dinner guests without having to move more than a step in her tiny kitchen. It might have been easier to eat at Boulevard; at least they'd all have been able to get round the table, Lynn thought – but her mother's absence would have been felt even more there than it was here.

Brenda must have read her mind. 'We'll have to get a bigger house. You get more than two people in this kitchen, and it's crowded.'

'You've treated yourself to a bit of a holiday, then, Anthony,' Lynn said, slipping into the chair beside him at the tiny formica-topped table.

'I'll be having another one in a couple of months, if I can wangle it,' Anthony said, with a glance at Brenda's very obvious bump.

'Let's hope the owners decide to have the ship in for an overhaul when the baby's due, and you might get nearly three weeks – like you dropped on with your wedding,' Lynn said.

'That would be good,' he nodded.

Their father took a plate piled high with roast lamb and all the trimmings from Brenda. 'Thanks, love, that looks gorgeous. She's not a bad daughter-in-law, is she?'

'Or a bad cook, either,' Anthony said.

'She's not a bad Auntie, either,' Simon piped up.

'Or a bad sister-in-law,' Lynn laughed, 'Thanks for inviting us, Brenda.'

Brenda smiled, and blushed. 'You're welcome. Did you have a good trip, Tom?'

'We landed a decent enough catch; enough to keep all the coastal towns in fish and chips over the bank holiday. Talking about good catches, you remember Alec McCauley?'

'We were friends for months, 'course we remember him,' Anthony said. 'I've talked to him on the VHF radio a couple of times.'

Did he ask about me? Lynn wondered. 'Pass the salt, will you, Brenda?' she said.

'Did you hear?' their father went on. 'He landed about a hundred and twenty-five tons of fish and a dead skipper, a couple of weeks after the *Miranda* sank. One of the biggest catches Grimsby's ever seen. Caught the market tide, as well. He must have made a packet.'

'And a *dead skipper?*' Lynn repeated.

'Yeah,' Anthony laughed. 'He was on the radio when they were coming back to port, said they'd had about eighty hauls and got the boat full of prime quality fish. He reckons the skipper got so excited watching the last one coming aboard that he had a heart attack.'

'Turned out all right for Alec, anyway,' Brenda said, glancing at Lynn.

'Not as well as it should have done, though,' Anthony said. 'Umpteen kits disappeared, he said. Off on the ghost train.'

Shuffled off before the market, sold for cash, and all in the owner's pockets, Lynn thought. No tax, no records, and nothing to pay the fishermen at the settling for any of that fish that had been 'disappeared'.

'It makes my blood boil, that,' said Brenda. 'Couldn't he have reported them, to the Board of Trade, or somebody?'

Anthony laughed. 'He could. Trouble is, he'd never have got another ship, then.'

'It's not right,' Brenda fumed.

'Get used to it,' their father said. 'The whole fishing industry runs on nods and winks and backhanders – and outright thieving. It's all fiddles and shams and twists from top to bottom.'

'Do you fancy going to the park later, if it's fine?' Lynn said, looking towards Simon.

'No, I want to go now! I want my cousins to come, as well.'

'We'll get a taxi later, and we'll all go,' their father said.

'Not us,' said Anthony. 'Brenda's going to have a rest, and I'll be doing the washing up.'

Later, when they were sitting in the front room with a cup of tea and their father had gone out for a moment, Anthony turned to Lynn. 'A penny for your thoughts,' he said.

She awoke from her reverie, and gave a self-conscious little laugh. 'I was thinking about the one that got away,' she said, 'like many a fisherman.'

'You're talking about Alec.'

She nodded, with a warning glance towards Simon, who was sitting on the carpet, apparently engrossed in a jigsaw.

'Aye, he thinks about you as well.'

'What makes you think that?'

'We've had him on the VHF a few times lately, and he's never failed to mention you. Have you heard anything from my mam?'

'Not a peep. I really miss her, though, and not just for getting Simon looked after, either. She was funny. She was witty. I miss her like hell. She was so ... alive! The house is like a morgue without her,' Lynn said, with a sudden and vivid memory of her mother handing her that bottle of perfume and telling her, 'Spray at your own risk!' That was almost eleven months ago, now.

'I know. That's why I asked your dad to come here for his dinner,' Brenda said. 'I knew he wouldn't go to you because of Graham, and I wanted to be sure he wouldn't be there on his own, although I suppose Margaret would have asked him if I hadn't.'

'No doubt about it,' Lynn said.

Anthony looked uneasy. 'It's bad, what she's done, really bad. But she's still our mam, and I'd like to know where she's got to,' he said.

'There's no way I know of that we can find out,' Lynn said, and looking towards the door said: 'Anyway, change the subject, he'll be back in a minute.'

'All right. What do you think to our Margaret?'

'She seems to be doing all right.'

'It's six weeks since she got to know about Jim and she hasn't shed a tear,' Anthony said. 'I've been to see her a few times, and she never says a word about him. It makes you wonder if she ever really loved him.'

'She told me she doesn't want to grieve,' their

father said, walking back into the room. 'She reckons if you grieve, it means you're letting them go, and she doesn't want to let him go. She loved him all right. I wish your mother had loved me half as much.'

Nothing is ever finished until people are dead, Lynn thought, and not even then, sometimes. She looked at her father, wondering if he'd really intended to let her mother go, or expected that she would, in that moment of anger.

'I'm sure she loved you, Dad,' she said, and found herself hoping that he would forgive and forget, and travel over land and sea to find his wife, and bring her home – weaving the same impossible fantasies of impossible reconciliations that most children weave, when the parents they love are divided.

Chapter 51

On the Saturday before the Spring Bank Holiday Lynn had a letter from her mother. Piers was managing a hotel in Scarborough and if they wanted to go there after the bank holiday they could have a very good room, free of charge. She'd also written to Margaret, to ask her and the lads as well. Lynn put the card in her handbag, intending to go down to Margaret's and see what she thought about it.

She was out in the front garden mowing the lawn that afternoon, when Graham's car screeched to a halt outside the house. He jumped out and slammed the door, and Lynn saw that his upper lip was swollen. Her heart missed a beat. Her father must have done it – nobody else had ever threatened Graham.

Overjoyed to see him, Lassie leaped up and went rushing forward to greet him, jumping up at him, yapping with excitement and furiously wagging her tail. Graham pushed her away, then deliberately swung back his leg and with his full weight behind it he gave her a kick in the belly that sent her yards up the drive. Lynn felt a sharp, sympathetic twinge in her own stomach.

Lassie lay where she'd landed, completely silent and motionless, too shocked even to whimper.

'Lassie! Lassie!' Simon dropped the scooter he'd been riding up and down the drive and ran towards her.

That one deed defined Graham for Lynn. He'd deliberately made that little creature love him, and just as deliberately he had kicked the guts out of her. In spite of his philandering, his conceit and his utter selfishness she'd still had a lingering love for him that he might have revived had he wanted to, but with that one vicious kick, he killed it. Graham had the soul of a torturer, and everything she had ever felt for him was stone, cold, dead.

'What was that for?' she yelled.

'For getting in the way, stupid bitch!' he snarled, his speech slightly distorted by the swelling on lip. He marched into the house and slammed the door.

Lynn went and knelt beside the dog, stroking

and soothing her.

'Is she dead, Mum?' Simon asked. There was a catch in his voice, and tears brimming on his lower lashes. Lassie turned a pair of big, wounded brown eyes up at him, as if grateful for his sympathy but still completely still, not moving even to whimper.

'No, but he's done her some serious damage, by the look of it. You stay with her, for a minute.'

She found Graham in the bathroom, bathing his swollen lip.

'You've probably killed that dog.'

'Your luck's in, then. You never wanted her in the first place.'

'I'd never have done that to her. What's wrong with you?'

He turned towards her and she saw that his lip was cut, as well as very swollen, but after that first panic Lynn realised it couldn't be her father's doing. He wasn't due back for another four or five days.

'How did you get that? Some irate husband?' she asked, quietly.

'The only irate husband's in Leeds. If he is irate. If he even realises that somebody else has had a few slices off his cut loaf.'

'Well, I'm going to ring a taxi now, and take Lassie to the vet, and you're going to pay for her to be put right, Graham.'

'You ring any vets, and you'll be paying for them yourself.'

'Then I'll get the RSPCA to come for her, and they'll have you up in court. Let your cognoscenti chew on that. Let your dog-breeding friend Mrs

Orme chew on it. Wait till she finds out how you treated the little bitch she gave you.'

She went downstairs, lifted the receiver on the telephone, and started to dial directory enquiries. A moment later Graham was beside her, his fingers pressing down on the buttons, cutting her off.

'All right. Ring the vet,' he said. 'I'll take her myself.'

'Yeah,' she nodded. 'They'll be asking some questions I reckon, so better get your lies straight before you get there.'

'I want to come with her,' said Simon, when Graham lifted a whimpering Lassie into the car.

'You're staying at home, with your mother,' Graham snapped. He took Simon by the shoulders, thrusting his face aggressively towards his son's, staring at him, eyeball to eyeball. 'And you don't say a word about any of this, to anybody,' he threatened. 'Not to your friends at school, or anybody else. Do you understand?'

Simon shrank away and nodded, white-faced.

'Answer me, then.'

'Yes,' he whispered.

'And don't you forget it.'

After Graham had lifted Lassie into the car Lynn had sudden misgivings. She issued her own threat.

'Graham! Don't you dare just have her put down. I want her back here when the vet's seen her, or there'll be hell to pay.' She watched him drive away, and then carried on mowing the lawn, adrenaline giving her energy to spare.

Simon came to stand beside her. 'Will she be all

right, Mum?' he asked, his face streaked with tears.

She stopped mowing and looked him in the face. 'I don't know,' she admitted.

'I hate my dad,' he said. 'George says he's a rotten bugger, and he is.'

'George shouldn't be saying words like that, and don't you say it either. Anyway, you don't really mean it.'

'I do,' he said.

Janet rang about an hour after Simon was in bed. 'Is Graham in?' she demanded.

'No, he's out – putting his boyish charm to good use somewhere, I expect. Except he doesn't look quite so charming now. Somebody's given him a smack in the mouth.'

'Has he said anything?'

'What about?'

'Me.'

'You?' Lynn repeated in astonishment. 'No.'

'I haven't got time to talk now, but I'm off the day after the bank holiday. Come down, and I'll make us a bit of lunch,' Janet said, and hung up before Lynn could get another word out. She replaced the receiver, absolutely mystified. Janet had never been one to waste words, but that conversation had been abrupt, even for her.

She was finally dropping off to sleep when Graham switched the bedroom light on. She opened her eyes and glanced at the alarm on the bedside table – past three o'clock.

'Where've you been till this time?' she enquired.

'At my mother's,' he said, peeling off his socks and throwing them in the corner of the bedroom. 'Where else would I go, looking like this?'

'You never told me who gave you that smack in the mouth, by the way.'

'What's that rhyme they say round Hessle Road? *Mind your own business, eat your own fish, don't poke your nose in my little dish.*'

'So what were you doing at your mother's, till three o'clock in the morning?'

Graham's underpants went the way of the socks. 'We got talking, that's all.'

'What about?'

'Stuff you wouldn't be interested in,' he said, pulling his shirt over his head and tossing it after the rest.

'Where's Lassie?'

'Still at the vet's. He's keeping her for a day or two, to observe her, he says.'

Lynn sat up, wide awake. 'What for?'

Graham hung his jacket and trousers in the wardrobe. 'To make a nice fee for himself, what else?' He grimaced. 'There'll be nothing wrong with her, except a couple of bruises. She'd have been perfectly all right at home.'

'Which vet's she gone to? The one on New Village Road? I'll ring him tomorrow, and find out. In fact, I'll go and find out.'

He put the light out, and got into bed beside her. 'It's Sunday tomorrow. He won't be open. He'll ring when she's ready to be collected.'

They turned their backs to each other. Making friends was not on the agenda that night, for either party.

Chapter 52

Lynn took Simon down to Margaret's the following day. After the boys had gone out to play she handed her their mother's letter, and waited until she had read it.

'I'm seeing Janet on Wednesday, but I'm going to Scarborough on Thursday, if I can scrape the money together,' she said. 'Do you fancy coming?'

'I can't. I'm working, and anyway, that's the day my dad's home. He'll have nobody else to do his washing or make him a meal, and he likes to see the lads, so no. Just give her all our love.'

'How's George? Has he had any more nightmares?'

'One or two. He soon gets over them.'

'Do you fancy inviting us to dinner? Graham's decided he's spending the day at the golf club, for a change.'

'Seems to be his home from home,' Margaret said. 'When do you ever get a look in?'

They stood together at the kitchen sink after dinner with Margaret washing the pots, and Lynn drying them and putting them away. A song began gently playing on the radio, called *Sailor*. Margaret stopped her washing up, and listened to the singer declaring undying love for her sailor and pleading with to him to leave the sea and return to the 'harbour of her heart'. Silent tears

338

began to trickle down Margaret's face. At repetition of the words '...*come home safe to me...*' the trickle became a flood, streaming from eyes and nose, down cheeks and chin and into the washing-up water. Lynn dropped the tea towel and led her to a chair, then found her a handkerchief, which was drenched at the first blow. Margaret's tears flowed on and on, silent and terrible, and so copiously that Lynn handed her a threadbare but clean tea towel, and sat with her until she'd cried it out.

'I lost two beautiful babies, the only daughter I'll ever have, but what would I have done – how could I have managed, on my own?' Margaret choked, twisting the towel in her hands and gazing at Lynn with reddened, puffy eyes. 'And I feel so awful for thinking we're better off without them, with him gone.'

Guilt, Lynn thought. 'Oh, Margaret, it wasn't your fault,' she said. 'None of it's your fault.'

'My poor babies, they never had a chance. He took their father, and then He took them. That's what God's done for us.'

Lynn had no answer for her; no solution to offer except the traditional and hopelessly inadequate: 'I'll make you a cup of tea.'

Janet picked up two lunchtime glasses of beer and lime from the bar and handed one to Lynn. 'He's been doing a lot more than sampling a few different ales in a few different pubs,' she said, following Lynn to one of the empty tables. 'He's been sampling one of my friends from work – correction: somebody I thought was a friend.'

'How did you find out?' Lynn asked as they sat down together.

'He got that fussy about the inside of the van being clean – it was just before you said I ought to get out with him more. I started thinking after you'd gone, and I thought: why's he putting himself to all that trouble, just for his mates? It could be a pig sty, and they wouldn't even notice. And he wasn't as frisky as usual, either – in bed, I mean.

'Well, we'd gone to break together, me and this lass, and I started telling her all about it, as you do, when you think you're talking to a friend – and she blushed, absolutely bright red, and she looked as guilty as hell. She'd been to our house a few times, and Dave had run her home in the van. I was stunned, but I didn't say anything. I thought: I know the pubs he goes to – I'll get a taxi round the lot of 'em next time he's out, and I'll walk in and catch 'em together. So the other night he told me he was going to the *Old Grey Mare*, so that's where I started, and I was spoiling for a fight.'

'I've never been in that one,' Lynn said.

'Maybe you should have been. Anyway, Dave and his new friend weren't there, but somebody else was. Maybe I shouldn't be telling you this, but I spotted Graham sitting in the corner in a cosy little twosome with some bint with long blonde hair. I walked through to the ladies', to take particular notice, and when I came out, he was standing at the bar on his own waiting to be served. So I walked up to him and I said: "Does Lynn know you're out with another bird?" "What do you think?" he says. So I said: "I think she doesn't." So he turned round and he says: "You're right. Lynn's my little mushroom. I keep her in the dark and I feed her on shit" – with a sort of "*screw you*" smirk on his face.

'Well, I soon wiped that off. I gave him the back-hander I'd been keeping for Dave, and I split his lip with my engagement ring.' She held her left hand out to display the large solitaire diamond Lynn had often seen before. 'It's quite a big stone,' she added, with grim satisfaction. 'I was politely asked to leave by the management after that, so I did.'

Lynn grinned, in awe and admiration. 'Action Woman! Well, at least it proves I'm not imagining things. It's not Mrs Orme, though. She's dark-haired. So did you find them, Dave and his woman?'

'No, and it's a bloody good job I didn't, the way I was feeling. I was livid. I'd probably have ended up in clink.' There was a gleam in her eye when she added: 'He had to come home in the end, though, and he copped the lot.'

'Poor Dave!'

Janet's face hardened. 'Never mind poor Dave. He'll toe the line, or else. I'm not going to be a martyr to him like you are to Graham.'

'I'm not a martyr, Janet. I knew what he was before I married him, and you weren't the only one who warned me. But I was so full of myself I thought: oh, he won't be like that with *me!* I'm *the one* – the one perfect woman he's been looking for all his life, the one woman in the world who can change him. That's what he told me, and

341

that's what I believed – and it really did look as if I'd succeeded, up until Mandy made her appearance. I still half believed it when I let myself be conned into going back to him.'

'You're not the first to make that sort of mistake, and you won't be the last,' said Janet.

'So now I'm devastated because the penny's finally dropped, and I know he never will change. Why should he? He's found a complete idiot who'll put up with him screwing around.'

'Well, if you'll put up with him screwing around you are a martyr!' Janet repeated. 'What else are you? And now he's kicking your dog, too. You're lucky she's only badly bruised. It might be you next, or Simon.'

Martyr! Lynn felt the accusation like a slap in the face. Everything in her recoiled against the idea. 'If I'm a martyr it's not to Graham,' she protested, 'it's to Simon and the ideal of solid families, and making your marriage work, like all good wives and mothers should. And I've certainly put plenty of effort into that.'

'It needs more than the wife putting some effort into it,' Janet said. 'What about the husband? We haven't seen much effort coming from him.'

'He works hard,' Lynn said. 'I can't take that away from him.'

'He works hard,' Janet repeated, 'and he gets a good salary. So how much of that do you and Simon see? How much of his spare time, even? And is there any sign of it changing? No. Because you'll take as much shit as he doles out for the sake of solid families and doing what you ought to do. And how solid is the family, with somebody like that in it?'

Lynn was silent for a minute. 'He's never going to kick me around, or Simon – I've got no fear of that. He wouldn't dare. My dad really would go for him then. He'd soon know what a good kicking was all about. But I'll have to get a job,' she said. 'I'll have to have some independence or I'll turn into Connie. I can feel it starting to happen. And what's worse is, I'm afraid Simon might turn into another Graham. I really worry about that. I don't want him taken around and about to be shown his father's sordid games, and how to be a deceitful, treacherous little–'

'Don't let it happen, then,' Janet said.

Lynn was silent. Good advice, she thought, but the question was how to stop it happening. That was the bogey.

'You will let it happen,' said Janet. 'He's got you exactly where he wants you.'

'The feeling I've had off him lately is that he doesn't want me at all.'

'He's got his sights on the blonde bit, then,' Janet said. 'Haven't you got any idea who she is?'

'No,' said Lynn.

By the time she left to collect Simon and Lassie from Margaret, Lynn was feeling pretty bruised. Janet had given her a different sort of smack in the mouth to the one she'd given Graham, but she'd only said what Lynn had started to think. She certainly shot from the hip, that woman – but when it came to friends, better a straight talker than a sweet talker any day, Lynn thought.

343

Chapter 53

A very glamorous blonde receptionist sat behind the desk in the Grand Hotel in Scarborough, her face carefully made up, her shoulder-length hair beautifully cut and her nails polished. Simon gripped Lynn's hand and shrank back, suddenly shy of the Nanna he hadn't seen for weeks.

'You're looking well,' Lynn said. 'We were beginning to think you'd dropped off the face of the earth.'

'We had a nice holiday, until Piers was fit to be seen, and then got into hotel work again, that's all.'

'Not a chambermaid any more then?'

'Not if I can help it, but I do a bit of waitressing, if I'm pushed,' her mother said, handing her a room key. 'You've got a room with a nice view. You could have a cup of tea, and then take Simon on one of the cliff lifts, down onto the beach. I'd come with you if I could, but I don't get off until after tea. We can have something to eat then, and have a walk on the seafront or something.'

'Margaret sends her love,' Lynn said, 'and the lads' love. She's working, so they couldn't come.'

Her mother nodded, with a wistful expression on her face. 'How's your dad?'

'All right. He landed this morning, but we were on our way here, so we didn't see him.'

'Well ... can you manage your luggage, then? I

see you haven't brought much.'

'No, we can only stay one night,' Lynn said, and felt a twinge of sympathy at the disappointment on her mother's face.

She looked at Simon, her expression even more wistful. 'Oh, well, we'll get together at tea-time, anyhow.'

After a day of travelling, paddling, sandcastle building and riding up and down the cliff lifts, Simon was weary, and went to sleep soon after their evening meal. Lynn sat in her very plush hotel room with her mother, looking out over South Bay to the castle.

'I used to get fed up of being on my own, especially after you'd all gone,' Nina said, 'but I really wish I'd never started going out with Piers. The novelty soon wears off, and then you've lost everything. I wish I'd never started any of it. I'm sorry I'm not there to help our Margaret with the lads, and Simon – he was like my own child, and he treats me like a stranger now.'

'I suppose a few weeks is a long time at his age,' Lynn said.

'It's a pity Margaret couldn't come, and bring the lads. I miss my own family.'

'You don't have to,' Lynn said. 'We'll talk to my dad. We'll talk him round.'

'You've no chance. He slept in your bedroom all the time he was home, and then he cleared off to Margaret's. He wanted me to grovel, and I wouldn't bloody grovel, so he got nastier and nastier. You'll have heard what happened just before I left. I'm better off where I am now than

345

living like that. I'll be all right. I could do a lot worse. Piers is pretty well off. I keep everything I earn for pin money, and he pays all our expenses. We might be able to get a place of our own, before long.' She laughed. 'He thinks the sun shines out of my rear end.'

'Like my dad used to do.'

'Used to, and never will again. That's gone,' Nina said, 'and I don't want to live with what's left. And I'm going to sue for maintenance, if I can get it.'

'What?'

'Yeah! He condoned what I'd done, and then he more or less chucked me out of my own home and told me to bugger off with Piers,' Nina said, with a face like a sulky child.

'He didn't condone it!' Lynn protested. 'You just told me you slept in separate bedrooms. And he didn't chuck you out. He only told you to make your mind up. You can't do that, Mother.'

'He made me scared to stay; that's the same as chucking me out. You weren't there, so you don't know. And I ought to have told him about your slimy husband coming round with his proposi-tions, as well, before I went.'

'What!' Lynn exclaimed, her eyes widening.

'Aye. I was in two minds whether to tell you or not, it's so sordid. He came while your dad was at Margaret's. Well, I asked him in, and put the kettle on, like you do, like I did for months when he used to call while I was looking after Simon – and he starts by asking where Tom is and I said at Margaret's, and not likely to be back till she's out of hospital. So he stands there giving me this sympathetic look, and then he puts his arm round me and he says, "You know, he doesn't deserve you, Nina. He should look after you a lot better than he does," and all the time his hand's groping round my backside. Because I'd gone off the rails once, I think he thought I'd go with anybody. "Oh, remind me who you are," I said. "Don't I recognise you? Aren't you my daughter's husband?"

'I never told your dad. I wish I had now; because Graham's the one that really deserves punching round the head, preferably till his eyes fall out of the sockets. So now you know what you're up against.'

Lynn was at a loss for words for a moment, unsure whether to believe it. She'd known for some time that Graham had no sense of decency, but this revelation was in a class of its own. Her stomach heaved. 'I feel sick,' she said.

'Well,' Nina said, 'it's God's honest truth.'

Lynn nodded. Disgusting though it was, she believed her mother. 'Slimy's right,' she said. 'He's a slime-ball, isn't he? An absolute ball of slime. I wish I'd never gone back to him, and I probably wouldn't have done if I hadn't had all this "Simon needs a father" crap coming at me from all directions.'

'Well, that was before I knew what a depraved little swine he really is. I wouldn't be saying it now. He's even worse than Janet said he was.'

'She saw him in a pub when he was out with his latest.'

'What?'

'Oh, yeah, he's at it again. Well, he never really

347

stopped, did he? I suspected, but I had no proof, until she told me she'd seen him out with a blonde. So she clouted him. He came home with a fat lip.'

Nina's face lit up, and she laughed. 'Oh, I'd have loved to have seen that. Good for her. I like her even better than I did before, now.' Glancing at Simon she said, 'It's a pity he's asleep. We could have gone for a walk on the promenade.'

'Don't you miss him, Mam – my dad?'

'Yeah, I miss him, but I'm used to missing him. I missed him for the best part of our married life. We hardly knew each other, really,' Nina said. 'If I'm being honest, what I miss most is my own home and having my own family nearby. You're what I miss, my own bairns and grandbairns, but you've all got your own lives, now.'

'What about Piers' wife?'

'What about her?'

'Don't you have any qualms about pinching her husband? Doesn't he miss her?'

'She's a lot older than him – by about sixteen years, I think.'

'What's that got to do with it?'

'If you're silly enough to marry a man young enough to be your bairn, you can expect him to grow up and leave you,' Nina shrugged.

'That's pretty brutal, Mother,' Lynn said.

'It's the way it is,' said Nina.

The death of love – you grieve for that as much as for any other death, Lynn thought, on the train back home the following day. Graham's betrayal would separate them more effectively than death

348

could have done. Jim was gone, but in his heart he never left Margaret, nor ever would have done. He was still hers in that sense, as he had been hers in life. He had died loving Margaret and his boys, and Graham lived not loving Lynn, and not loving Simon all that much, either. Not really loving anybody, she suspected. The kind of worthless, shallow charmer that women ruin their lives for.

Chapter 54

The phone rang shortly after they got home. Graham was out, as usual.

'Hello,' Brenda said. 'You remember that conversation we had in Schofields, about the code that's like the *omertà*, and what you said about people leaving you in the dark?'

'Vaguely,' Lynn said.

Brenda went on with her news, and Lynn's eyes widened as she listened to another straight talker. When Brenda had finished Lynn finally understood how utterly futile it had all been, all that sacrifice on the altar of 'making your marriage work'. She hung up, and turned to Simon.

'Your grandad's at home. I think we'll pack a few things and stay at his house for a day or two.'

'Hurray! I can play with Auntie Margaret's lads,' he said.

While they were waiting to be shown to a table at the Continental Restaurant on Princes Dock in the Old Town, Lynn spotted Graham. He was gazing at a young blonde, with that rapturous expression of total attention that Lynn used to bask in, but that hadn't been directed at her for a long time. The expressions he kept for his wife these days ranged from indifference to contempt. Lynn watched the young woman who glowed under the lamp of Graham's admiration – and felt a curious detachment. No grief, no bitterness, no jealousy, nothing. Graham evidently felt nothing for her, and in return she was happy to feel nothing for him.

At her request, the waiter led her to a table near to them, along with Janet and a heavily pregnant Brenda. Graham's rapturous expression was gone in an instant, and the wide-eyed look of horror that replaced it brought laughter bubbling to Lynn's throat. She managed to suppress it, but couldn't have wiped the smile off her face to save her life.

Janet and Brenda sat down, leaving the chair nearest to Graham for Lynn. She leaned towards him. 'Hello, Graham.'

He seemed too shocked to answer.

'So this is your new mushroom. Aren't you going to introduce us?'

Still no response from Graham. Lynn turned her beaming smile on his companion. 'Never mind. You remind me very much of Mrs Senior – so I guess you must be her daughter. Lucy, isn't it? I suppose you could do my husband a lot of good at the company. Graham loves the company.'

'Shut up, Lynn,' Graham warned.

Lynn went on as if she hadn't heard. 'I say, I like

your earrings,' she said, darting admiring glances at the gold and sapphire studs in Lucy's ears. 'You must be glad to have got the one I found on the rear seat of our car back. I thought it was Mrs Orme's at first, but I've got to admit they look much better on you than they would on her.'

'Poisonous bitch,' Graham muttered.

Lynn turned her ear towards him. 'What? I didn't quite catch that, Graham.'

'I did. He called you a poisonous bitch,' Brenda announced, and attracted a few surprised glances from some of the nearby diners.

'Oh, dear. Graham hasn't a good word for his wife, these days. Probably since he met you, Lucy,' Lynn said.

Lucy's cheeks turned a delicate shade of pink. 'It's not what you think,' she said, 'It's purely platonic. We play tennis.'

'What do I think, Lucy?' Lynn asked, scanning the room. 'Well, I didn't realise there were tennis courts here. We should have brought our racquets.' She turned to Graham. 'Another year gone by, Graham, and we're back to square one, by the look of it.'

He gave her a look of smouldering resentment. 'Nothing of the sort,' he muttered.

'Good luck with him, anyhow, Lucy,' Lynn said, her smile disappearing as she turned to Brenda and Janet, with all expectation of anything even approaching a decent family life with Graham totally annihilated. She no longer loved him. She no longer even liked him, and she had lost all respect for him long ago. This was how her father must feel about her mother, she guessed – except it had come to him a lot sooner.

'It's a shame Anthony sailed this morning, but your dad's still at home.' Brenda looked towards Graham, and left the rest unsaid.

'Not worth it,' Lynn said. 'Absolutely not worth it.'

When the waiter arrived with meals for Graham and Lucy, he found an empty table. He stood with the plates in his hands, looking round for them.

'They've gone, and I don't think they'll be back,' Brenda told him.

He shrugged, and took the plates back to the kitchen.

'I think we'll invite Alec to stay for a few days this summer,' Brenda said, looking at the door Graham and Lucy had left by.

Lynn shook her head. 'Don't bother for me; I'm joining a nunnery. I need a long rest from men.'

'Huh!' Janet scoffed. 'Are you calling that little twerp a *man?*'

Brenda suddenly caught her breath, sat up straight, gripped the edges of the table and held on tight for a minute. 'Ooh. Ooh, dear,' she said.

Lynn and Janet looked at each other and grinned.

'What an eventful evening. I reckon we'll have a little bundle of joy before tomorrow morning,' Lynn said.

Brenda sighed, and relaxed. 'Oh, it's gone.'

'Better have a good feed, then; you'll need something to keep you going,' Janet consoled her. 'They don't call it labour for nothing, and seeing it's your first, you're in for hours of it.'

352

Chapter 55

On Monday evening Graham was back from work just before the children's programmes were finished. He booted the kitchen door open, and stood leaning on the jamb. 'I wondered when you'd condescend to come home!'

'I'm surprised you noticed we were gone,' Lynn snuffled, turning to him with her eyes streaming from the pungency of the onions she was slicing.

'I noticed you were gone all right. I was home early, and I waited up for you till three o'clock – and on Sunday night, as well. And you can turn the waterworks off; they won't do you any good. I could cheerfully kill you for your performance on Saturday night.'

'But you won't – and don't you dare take it out on Lassie, either. And I certainly won't be crying any tears over you this time, Graham,' she said, sniffing back the flow. 'From now on I'll be here Monday to Friday to take Simon to the school you wanted him to go to, and I'll do the house-work and shopping – and we'll be spending our weekends at my dad's. You'll be very pleased to know we won't be getting in your way.'

He burst into laughter. 'Give me enough rope to hang myself, you mean? Well, please yourself where you go at the weekend, Lynn, but don't think I'll be sitting here with Lucy, just waiting for your private *dick* to show up. We're just good friends, and that's all there is to it.'

'Shame. Still, you'll be able to spend every weekend with your just good friend without us cramping your style. Like you've done for weeks, ever since you were on that skiing holiday together.'

It had been a wild guess, but his face told her she was spot on target.

'Oh, yes,' she said, her eyebrows twitching upwards. 'I might never have been invited to the golf club, Graham – but I sometimes get a snippet of information, here and there.'

Simon slid under Graham's arm, and into the kitchen. 'Auntie Brenda's got a baby, Dad!' he said.

'Great! Another addition to the tribe!' said Graham. 'Did she get it in the restaurant?'

Simon looked puzzled. 'No, in the hospital, Mum took her and I stayed with grandad. Why are you crying, Mum?'

'I'm not crying.'

Simon rounded on his father. 'Don't you make my mummy cry!'

Lynn laughed, and sniffed tears back. 'I'm not crying.'

Graham turned puce with anger. 'Don't you talk to me like that! Get to bed! This minute! There'll be no tea for you today,' he snarled, and Lynn really thought that had he dared, he might have kicked Simon. Simon flinched, yet doggedly stood his ground.

'Go upstairs, son. I'll be all right,' she said. 'I'll be up in a minute.'

Simon hesitated, but after a reassuring nod from

Lynn he went, dodging smartly past Graham.

'I've taken it from your father, but I'm not having it from him. Time I kicked him into touch,' Graham said, when he'd gone.

'I wouldn't do any kicking there, if I were you,' Lynn said, quietly.

'Really? I'll do as I like, in my own home, with my own son. Anyway, we've got common interests, me and Lucy – and that's all there is to it. Bear that in mind, because she won't stand for her name being dragged through the mire, and neither will her parents. You'll probably get a solicitor's letter if you try it.'

'Oh, dear,' Lynn said. 'And if I'm sued for slander I suppose you'll have to pay the damages, Graham. Lucy wouldn't do that to you, would she? But even if she did, I don't think she'd win her case, seeing you were on a skiing holiday together – so not much to worry about there, eh?'

A change of subject was Graham's only response to that. 'I'm giving you too much bloody housekeeping money if you can afford to eat at the Continental Restaurant,' he said. 'And if you're clearing off to your dad's every weekend, I'm cutting it by a quarter.'

'I'll have to manage as best I can then, Graham,' she said, apparently defeated.

She didn't mention the 'weekends only' job coming up in the labour suite that she'd heard about while at the hospital with Brenda. Nor did she tax Graham with his visit to her mother, not having the stomach for it – and unwilling to be swamped by a deluge of lies.

Chapter 56

'So how's it feel to have your own ship, you lucky bugger?' Anthony said.

Alec was standing on the bridge with the third hand, talking to him on the VHF radio. He laughed. 'It'd feel a lot better if it weren't a leaky old coal burner built in 'thirty-six. Moves like a snail, nearly capsizes in a breeze, and the fish room's not cooled.'

'What's the crew like?'

'About as good as the ship. Half of them are past it, and the other half still wet behind the ears, but we've managed to make a decent trip,' Alec said. He'd driven the crew hard, not as hard as some young skippers might have done, but hard all the same. He couldn't afford to be soft; he wanted three good trips in straight away or he'd be sidelined, and another young hopeful given a chance. The owners were neither patient nor forgiving. If he succeeded he'd be promoted to a better ship, maybe an oil burner built in the forties. For now, he'd have to manage with what he had, and failure was not an option. He thanked his lucky stars he'd been given the chance in June, and not in January.

'He's at it again, our Lynn's husband – messing about with another one, now,' Anthony was saying, when Alec was almost suffocated by the filthiest stench that had ever assailed his nostrils, a smell nobody could have ignored. 'Brenda was out with her the other night, and they saw him – with his boss's daughter,' Anthony went on. 'She says Lynn's had enough–'

'Ugh!' Alec looked down to where some of the lads were hauling giant cod, and with it a horrible greyish substance that dripped through the net and onto the deck in clumps. 'Ugh!' he repeated, trying to speak without breathing in the stink. 'What the...! The lads have got something in the net, Anthony! Talk about a stink – it's enough to knock you over! I'll talk to you later.'

He looked at his companion, and with one accord they pulled their mufflers up to their noses, attempting to shield themselves from the overwhelming, sickly smell. On the deck every man with a hand to spare was doing the same thing, shielding mouth and nose with mufflers, jumper collars, nose rags, or gloved hands. When Alec got to the deck it was like a skating rink, with men slipping and sliding about in the foul stuff. A couple of deckhands had started shovelling it overboard, as fast as they could.

Then something stirred in the furthest recesses of Alec's mind, a memory of something he'd heard in Fleetwood when he was just a nipper sitting with his dad, listening wide-eyed to sailors' yarns.

'No, no, no! Stop, stop stop!' he yelled. 'It might be worth a bloody fortune!' He ran towards the deckhands, slipping on the foul stuff as he ran, and regaining his balance with arms flailing.

'What the hell is it, Skipper?' one of them asked.

Alec couldn't think of the name of it. 'I'm not a

hundred per cent sure, but if it's what I think it is, we'll be quids in. It might be worth more than the fish – I want it all shovelled into barrels, *all* of it, as fast as you can.'

After most of the horrible, cloying stuff was sealed in barrels, they swilled the residue off the deck and off frocks and boots, then stood on the port rail, gasping in fresh air before going down to the galley for a cup of tea.

Ambergris, Alec remembered. They'd said it was vomited up by the sperm whale, and people actually use the stinking stuff to make expensive perfume. It was worth its weight in gold – or so they'd said.

His mind turned back to the conversation he'd been having with Anthony. So now he was a dad! Alec went back to the bridge and tried to raise him on the VHF, but had no luck. He'd try again later on. It might be worth going back to Hull, to see how the land lay with Lynn. He might go and take a present for Anthony's young 'un. That would give him a good excuse for being there, and nobody would think anything of it – seeing he'd been the best man at their wedding. Yeah, it would be nice to see 'em all again, and maybe take Lynn for a night out on Hessle Road. She might even have got that shitty bastard out of her system, this time around.

Chapter 57

Lynn had often had reason to doubt Graham's word, but she was quite confident that he would fulfil his promise to cut her housekeeping money. He surpassed it. He gave her no money at all.

The shortfall would have to be made up somehow, and much more besides. She needed money now more than ever. She raked through cupboards and wardrobes both in her own home and in her father's, and then put 'for sale' postcards in the post office windows both in Cottingham and on Hessle Road, advertising every item they possessed which was either no longer worn or no longer wanted – except for her wedding dress and all the paraphernalia that went with it. She advertised that in the *Mail* in glowing terms, and sold it for fifty pounds the same day that the advert had appeared. She paid Janet back for the loan of a train fare to Scarborough and a meal at the Continental, and treated herself to a decent hair cut and a natty little two-piece, which she wore for her interview with the Matron of Hedon Road Maternity Hospital a couple of days later. She came out of the interview having got the job, and went directly to the Yorkshire Bank in Hull, to open an account in her own name. The only fly in the ointment was that it would be more than a month before she got paid.

What was it that conniving Connie had said to

her spoiled boy? *You can take her out of Hessle Road – but you'll never get Hessle Road out of her.* Well, since she was considered irredeemably Hessle Road, she would go the whole hog, Lynn thought. She would manage her present predicament in the traditional Hessle Road manner. On Friday afternoon after she'd collected Simon from school she rang a taxi to take them to Boulevard, and got the taxi man to help her with Graham's golf clubs and a large leather suitcase containing his golf shoes, two good suits, two pairs of Italian leather shoes, his gold cufflinks and his second gold watch, a canteen of cutlery that had been Auntie Ivy's and a good deal of her household linen.

'Why are you bringing all that stuff, Mum?' Simon asked, as the taxi man stowed it all in the boot.

'Just borrowing it,' she said.

'You'll be lucky to find a golf course on Boulevard,' the taxi man grinned.

'I shan't need a golf course,' Lynn said. 'You can drop us outside the pawnbroker's.'

'Hell! Folk from Cottingham visiting pop shops? What's the world coming to?'

'It makes you wonder, doesn't it?' Lynn said, and there the conversation ended. She settled herself comfortably in her seat for the journey. When they passed the fruit shop on Bricknall Avenue, Connie's disparaging words came echoing back to her. A top-drawer daughter-in-law like Lucy Senior would certainly be much more to Connie's taste, Lynn thought. She would have rated herself 'middle drawer', but Connie probably ranked her much lower. They might already have had Lucy to tea, in the flat above the shop.

'How long is it since you were at your grandma's?' she asked Simon.

'A long time,' he said with no sign of regret. 'There's nobody to play with, there.'

She left him at the house on Boulevard with Margaret and the boys while she went in the taxi to transact her business with the pawnbroker, and got back to her father's house with enough money to last her for a month in one pocket and a bundle of pawn tickets in the other.

What a hectic week it had been, she thought.

Margaret came to Boulevard with her boys the following day, to let Lynn get to Hedon Road for the late shift at the hospital.

'I'll look after the lads here, I think,' she said. 'In fact, if my mam's not coming back, I might move in, and give my house up. Like you said, it'll save on rent, and seeing as I was cleaning both places, it'll cut the work in half as well. And there'll be more room for the lads, especially now it looks like we'll be having Simon every weekend.'

'I doubt very much she'll be coming back,' said Lynn, 'and if she did, you could get another house, or you could come to live with me in Cottingham. It's nice there, in the countryside. The lads would love it, fields to run in, trees to climb. We could turf Graham out to his lady love's, so he can give me grounds for a divorce.'

'What about my job at Birds Eye? What about getting the lads to school? And can you really see Graham paying the mortgage on a house he'd been turfed out of?' Margaret asked.

361

Lynn gave her a wry smile. 'Not for long,' she said. 'Anyway, I'll have to go, or I'll miss the bus. There's the pawn tickets on the mantelpiece, in case he comes looking for his stuff.'

She went with an easy mind, knowing that Simon was happy to be left with Auntie Margaret and her boys. It felt good to be back in the maternity hospital among good colleagues, especially working on the labour suite. The place felt like her second home.

The pale outline of the moon was set in a still light sky when she got back to Boulevard. In summer, when she was a child they used to play out until it was nearly dark.

'Are the bairns still out?' she asked Margaret.

'No, bathed, in bed, and asleep. How was your first day at work?'

'Busy, but it's great to be back,' Lynn said and went through to the kitchen to put the milk pan on.

Margaret followed her. 'Graham's been,' she said, ominously. 'He called just after you'd gone.'

'I wish I'd been here.'

'You don't. I think he'd have killed you if he'd got hold of you. He was absolutely livid when I gave him the pawn ticket for his golf clubs. He was that mad I thought he'd throw a fit, and Lassie took one look at him and slunk under the table. I told him you'd gone to the pictures, but I don't think he believed me. And he'd no money to redeem them! He won't get them till Monday, now.'

Lynn's face lit up with glee. She burst into laughter. Graham had been soundly punished for

362

his transgressions against her; she had buggered his weekend and cost him several times as much as the housekeeping money he'd refused to give her. Hessle Road had always had its own strategies for making ends meet in hard times, she thought, and they worked as well as ever. The outcome could not have been more satisfying. 'I wonder if he's discovered his suits have gone yet?' she said. 'The pop shops aren't doing as well as they used to, and the one I picked has branched out into gents' outfitting as well. It might be handy for Graham, he'll be able to get another suit, if he doesn't redeem the pledge in time.'

'I really miss my mother,' Lynn said as they sat drinking cocoa later on.

'I suppose you do.'

'Don't you?'

'It was a bit different for me,' Margaret said. 'I was the eldest. I never had a lot done for me. I had to help her with you and our Anthony, so I got used to having to fend for myself, and when I got married we leaned more to Jim's family.'

And here she was again, Lynn thought, taking on other folks' responsibilities, caring for Simon and dealing with his irate father while baby sister swanned off to her interesting, middle-class job. In spite of all that, they got on well together. If Margaret came to live in her dad's house, she might do the same, if push came to shove, Lynn thought. It might not be so bad; the place was big enough. It might be a good move for all concerned. They could look after each other's lads when one of them was at work, or babysit for each other if they wanted a night out. Their father could come home and not be lonely. In fact, it might be quite pleasant to live together in their childhood home.

Chapter 58

On Monday morning, Graham opened the wardrobe door, and discovered that two of his suits were missing. He checked through every item twice, his face dropping all the while. He turned to Lynn, wide-eyed with apprehension.

'Where have you put my good suits?'

Lynn had slept well. She stretched, and yawned, and sat up to rest against the pillows. The sun was streaming through the flowered cotton curtains; it was going to be a lovely day.

'Same place as the golf clubs; in the pop shop. Your gold cufflinks have gone, your second gold watch has gone, a couple of pairs of your shoes, and some of Auntie Ivy's stuff, as well. I had to get a taxi because I'd have looked ridiculous with the golf clubs on the bus and anyway, they're too heavy, and I thought: better not waste the journey seeing as I'm so hard up, so I took as much as we could carry.'

He looked as if he could hardly believe his ears. 'We? Who's the we?'

'Me and the taxi man. He was very obliging.'

'It's – it's...' Graham shook his head, seemed at a loss for words for a moment, then said: 'outrageous! Absolutely outrageous! I've never heard of anything like it in my life before. To steal somebody else's things, and take them to a pawn shop...'

'I didn't steal them, Graham, I just raised some housekeeping money on them that you'll get the benefit of as well as us. That's not stealing.'

'Well, you can bloody well go and get them back. Now.'

'How can I do that? I haven't any money!'

'You've got the money the pawnbroker gave you, for a start!'

'But I need that, for housekeeping; we've got to eat something, Graham. That's why I popped the stuff,' she explained, patiently.

'Why didn't you "pop" your own bloody stuff?'

'Because I've got nothing he'd have given me any money on.'

'You've got that wedding dress.'

'Oh, I sold that outright. I spent that money, ages ago. You've been too busy being platonic friends with Lucy Senior to notice what's going on round here. If you want your stuff back, you'll have to get it yourself, Graham – but don't be too long about it, or it'll be out of pledge. It won't take him two minutes to sell two decent suits and two pairs of nearly new Italian shoes, seeing he's a gents' outfitters as well as a pawnbroker.'

Graham looked horrified. 'I've never been into a pawn shop in my life,' he said.

She flung the covers back and got out of bed. 'Oh, well, there's a first time for everything. I put the pawn tickets on the mantelpiece for you before I came to bed last night. I think Margaret's already given you the one for the golf clubs. You'll find the shop on Hessle Road; you can't miss it. Usual opening hours,' she said, and proceeded to the bathroom.

Connie arrived with all Graham's redeemed property that afternoon, while Simon was at school and Graham, presumably, still at work. She put the golf clubs in the hall, went back to the car to bring the suitcase in, dumped that beside the clubs, and then turned to Lynn with venom in her eyes. The mask of pretended friendship was well and truly off.

'Would you like a cup of tea?' Lynn smiled, with provoking politeness.

'How dare you? How dare you pawn my son's things?' Connie raged. 'I warned him about you before he married you. Why he ever let himself get tangled up with somebody like you, I'll never know, when he could have had his pick of dozens of girls from decent families. We've got some standing in this neighbourhood, and now we're having to run to *pawn shops* – because of *you!* Dragged right down into the gutter – to *your* level!'

'My level – you insulting–' Lynn checked herself, and took a deep breath. 'I dare do a lot of things, Connie – and if you could hear what people say about you, you'd have a better idea how much standing you've got,' she said.

Connie appeared not to have heard. She'd had her rant prepared, and she was in the throes of delivering it. 'Telling him you're going to leave him every weekend! What sort of a wife are you?

366

And what are you up to every weekend on Hessle Road? Drinking and cavorting with fishermen in rough pubs, while your husband has to fend for himself after slaving all week! For you, you worthless trollop! Get to your father's, you lazy, idle, thieving slut! Get there for good, and don't come back. Next time you go, we're having the locks changed and you won't get back in to steal anything else.'

Have the locks changed, so she wouldn't get back in – to her own home? To Simon's home? Lynn suddenly decided that dynamite wouldn't blast her out of this house. All thoughts of going to live on Boulevard were forgotten. Her eyes were like gimlets under the slightly drawn brows, her nostrils slightly dilated, and her mouth set in a tight, straight line.

'I'll get back in, all right, Connie,' she said. 'I'll get in anytime I like. This is my home – and my son's. My name's on the mortgage, just as much as Graham's, and it was *my* father gave us the deposit for the first house we had and he hasn't been paid back yet, so *he* made the biggest contribution here. I've got a better claim to this house than Graham. If he has the locks changed, I'll have no alternative but to get the police to force an entry, just like I had no alternative but to pawn his stuff, because he refused to give me anything for us to live on. That's called *wilful refusal to maintain*, in case you don't already know. You seem to think it's perfectly all right for him to be out and about spending money on Lucy Senior instead of maintaining us, but how do you think a court will see it? Because it'll come to court if he

367

pushes me too far. He'll get his name in the paper, and then all your customers will know what your "standing" in this neighbourhood is, as if they di–'

She felt a stinging blow across her cheek, and then bony fingers gripping her shoulders like a vice, shaking her. With eyes blazing, Connie snarled like an animal and suddenly lurched forward with teeth bared. Lynn recoiled, expecting to be bitten, for a split second.

'Slut!' Connie spat. 'You're nothing but a set of thieves, and whores, and hooligans! You and your slut of a mother, and your ruffian of a father!'

Lynn wrenched herself free. 'Get out. Get out of my house this minute, and don't come back.'

'I haven't finished...'

'You have. Oh, but you have! I'll have you up for assault, if you don't get out this minute. I'll show the whole world who the ruffian is, then your customers will really have something to talk about.'

The look on Lynn's face must have been enough. Connie left the house without another word, and slammed the door behind her. With her heart thumping like a hammer Lynn went to the window to watch Gordon drive her away. She had never had any illusions that she'd been Connie's first choice for a daughter-in-law, but the depth of her antagonism had come as a surprise.

'...thieves, whores and hooligans! ... your slut of a mother! ... your ruffian of a father!' Lynn started to shake with shock and impotent rage as the insults reverberated in her mind.

368

Chapter 59

On Midsummer's Day Lynn took Lassie to pick Simon up from school and called at Brenda's to see her and the baby before going to Boulevard. Anthony was home, and Lynn's heart leaped when she saw Alec there as well. Lassie jumped onto the settee beside him.

'We've asked him to be godfather,' Anthony explained.

'Hello, Simon! How are you, Lynn?' Alec said, with the same broad smile, the same gleam in his blue eyes.

'All right. How are you? I hear you're a skipper now.'

'Yep, not doing too badly. We sold part of one of the catches to perfume-makers, believe it or not.'

'Anthony told me. Ambergris.'

'You were at the wedding,' Simon said.

'I know I was,' he said, stroking Lassie. 'So were you.'

Brenda sat with the baby in her arms, beaming at them all.

'What are you going to call him, Auntie Brenda?' Simon asked.

'I can't tell you before he gets christened,' she said. 'It's really bad luck.'

'Am I coming to the christening?'

''Course you are. Your mum's going to be the

baby's godmother,' Brenda said, looking directly at Lynn.

'Am I?'

'Aye. Alec's the godfather, and you're the godmother, so make sure you get the day off work,' Anthony said. 'We've booked it for the Sunday before the August Bank Holiday. My ship's going to be in for a survey, so I'm having some time off.'

'Bank holiday,' Lynn grimaced. 'I'd better put in for it straight away, then.'

'This time last year we went for a walk on Hessle foreshore,' Alec said. 'I wouldn't mind doing it again.'

'Count me out,' said Brenda. 'I'll be busy with the baby.'

'And me,' said Anthony. 'I'll be spending my time with my wife and son – and my dad docked this morning. He'll be coming round soon.'

'I'll come!' Simon volunteered.

'All right,' Lynn said. 'It'll be a nice walk for Lassie.'

'Can we take Auntie Margaret's lads?' Simon begged. Lynn looked at Alec.

'The more the merrier,' he said.

There were lots of other people out, strolling with pets and children along the foreshore, buying sweets or ice creams, or just sitting looking at the waters of the Humber and enjoying the midsummer sunshine. Lynn let Lassie off the lead and she ran ahead with five boys chasing after her, their feet crunching on the shingle as they ran.

'A year to the day since we were here last,' she remarked, opening the conversation.

There was something else on Alec's mind. 'I was in Isafjord when their father's ship went down,' he said, nodding after the boys. 'I can't say I saw it, because nobody could see anything. It just disappeared off the radar. I didn't know he was on it until Anthony told me. I'd been talking to the skipper on the radio just before it happened. Nobody could have helped them. The storm was so bad we were all fighting our own battles, just to stay afloat.'

She shuddered. 'And yet you still go back,' she said. 'I'll never understand it.'

'Neither will I. I love it just a bit more than I hate it, I suppose,' Alec said. 'And besides, what would I do ashore?'

'You learned that job, you could learn another.'

'That's like saying you learned midwifery, you could learn something else. You wouldn't want to, after learning your trade, because it's the one you really want to do.'

'At least midwifery's safe – for the midwife, at least. Don't you envy other people, with their safe jobs and their steady incomes? They never settle in debt, and they're guaranteed to be home every night.'

And they've never seen the aurora borealis, shimmering across the black winter skies like a curtain of fantastic coloured light. They've never seen a night sky in the Arctic, looking as if someone's thrown a bucket of diamonds up onto a cushion of the blackest velvet. They've never been in a storm, and survived it by the skin of their teeth, or felt the sheer elation that comes from that, Alec thought.

'Their lives are a bit too tame for me,' he said. 'I couldn't stand to be caged in a factory, or a workshop, or even a hospital. Most shore people wash their cars, and mow their lawns, and worry about their tomato plants, and watch the weekly instalments of their telly programmes, and every week's just like the last, and the next will be the same. They've never been afraid in their lives, nor ever expect to be. They're barely half alive!'

She took a deep breath, and let it out in a long sigh. 'Look at Margaret's lads, racing along in front of us. Don't you think they'd rather have a father half alive, than one hundred per cent dead?'

He looked towards the boys and she sensed his sympathy. 'He was just unlucky,' he said, quietly.

'Unlucky? Well, there's no disputing that, is there? He'd have had more luck if he'd had a shore job. So would they.'

He had nothing to say to that. After a moment he asked: 'How are you getting on with Graham?'

'I don't think you'd be taking me for a walk if you thought I was getting on with him,' she said. 'Our Anthony must have told you.'

'But you're still living in the same house,' he said, cautiously.

'And that's all. We're co-existing in the same house. Not very comfortable for either party, but neither willing to make a move,' Lynn said, her face completely expressionless.

'Why not leave him, then, and live in Boulevard, like you did before?'

'It would make a lot more sense, because I could probably work full time then, and get a better salary. But I don't want to drag Simon out of another house that he likes, and I don't want to drag him out of his school and away from the friends he's made there. And it's wonderful for a child where we live, surrounded by woods and fields. It's great for Margaret's lads when they come to stay – and I love it, as well. The only fly in the ointment is Graham, and his bloody mother. And I don't want them to win. Can you understand that?'

'Partly. Everything but the last,' he said. 'What would they be winning, if you leave him?'

'Everything, that's all. They'd have got us out of our home. His mother was even talking about changing the locks, to keep me out! Can you imagine it? She'd love to oust me, and so would he, but they're not going to get the satisfaction. Call it sheer bloody-mindedness, if you like, but he's the one that'll be leaving this time.'

'It's a battle of wills, then. Are you really sure it's worth fighting?'

'You'd think so,' Lynn said, 'if you'd heard some of the things she called me, and my parents. You'll have heard my mother did a bunk, I suppose.'

'With the feller she was with the night we went to the house hoping to–'

'That's the one.'

'Shame we never got that far.'

'Maybe not, from my point of view. It might have turned out badly for me. You jilted me, re-member?'

'It wasn't Orla,' he said, defensively. 'It was never on the cards, me and Orla. I really thought you wanted Graham. Simon certainly did.'

'It was complicated – but anything there ever was between me and Graham is over and done with,' she said. 'Finished. Kaput. And I don't think Simon's as enamoured as he used to be, ever since he saw him kick Lassie in the guts.'

'Oh. Sounds a nice character.'

'You'd have thought so, if you'd seen it. So what about the lasses in Grimsby?'

'They're very nice. I've taken a few of them out.'

'Nobody special?'

'Only you,' he said. 'I haven't had a trip off since last time I saw you. There's no point in having holidays, because there's nobody I'd want to go with.'

'Oh, shame!' she laughed. 'I could do with a holiday.'

'Come and visit me, and I'll show you the delights of Grimsby, then. I'm living with my dad and his wife.'

'So he married a woman from Grimsby.'

'He did. He went over to New Holland to have a drink with an old pal one night and met her in a pub called the Yarborough – and that was it. He moved to Grimsby and married her – that was months before I went. She's a good 'un. You'll like her. Bring Simon. Bring 'em all, if you like.'

'Grimsby! Great holiday destination,' she said.

'Today Grimsby – tomorrow the world! Anyway, Grimsby's not that bad, but we live next door, in Cleethorpes. On Queen Mary Avenue, you know. It's rather select,' he said, adopting a plummy accent and placing a forefinger at the side of his nose to thrust it mockingly upwards.

'It's a pity I'm working weekends,' she said. 'There'll be no chance of me going anywhere until the school holidays.'

'I'm thinking about buying my own house. I've got to do something with the money I'm making, other than keep handing it over to the taxman.'

'Don't buy it in Grimsby,' she said. 'I couldn't live there.'

'Scared of letting Graham have the house?'

'That's part of it. A bigger reason is I couldn't leave Margaret and the lads. They need all the help they can get. And sending Simon to three different schools in just over a year might be too much to expect him to cope with.'

'Come and see Grimsby while you've got the chance, then, before I move to Hull. It's a once in a lifetime opportunity!'

So he was prepared to move back to Hull for her! She threw her arms round him, and gave him a smacking kiss. 'All right, I will,' she said.

Lassie came bounding back towards them, followed by five laughing boys.

'Can we have an ice cream, Mum?' Simon asked.

'Can we have an ice cream, Auntie Lynn?' her four fatherless nephews clamoured.

'I'll get you an ice cream,' Alec said. 'Race you to the van.'

Chapter 60

She went for half an hour's free advice from Mr Farley after Alec had gone back to Grimsby.

'I'm back,' she announced, stepping into his office.

He looked up and smiled. 'And what can I do for you, Mrs Bradbury?' he asked, and in the depths of his bright brown eyes she read the thought: *as if I didn't know!*

'Get me a divorce,' she said.

'Any grounds?'

'The usual – adultery.'

'Of course. Once men start that game, they rarely change.'

'What's changed is, he's a lot wiser now,' Lynn said. 'He's not going to admit to anything.'

'No, it would be too much to expect him to be so accommodating a second time,' Mr Farley agreed.

'And he's desperate to preserve his "lady's" reputation, as well as his own. He'll lie his head off to do it, if he has to. I get the feeling he's keen to marry this one, if he can. She's rolling in it, or her father is.'

'You don't seem very upset.'

'I'm not.'

'A detective, then.'

'I think he could follow him around for a year, and not get any evidence. He never sleeps away from home.'

'In that case, what makes you think he's committing adultery?'

Lynn took a moment to think of the most polite way to express it. 'Certain changes in the matrimonial routine,' she said. 'In the matrimonial bedroom – and blokes like Graham have got to get it from somewhere, haven't they?'

'Perhaps – but it wouldn't do as evidence. There's no dispute as to the custody of the child, I suppose?'

'No, I don't think he's planning on taking Simon to disturb his love-nest that he won't even admit to having. So, is there another way round it?'

'You could try a legal separation and play the waiting game.'

'How long would that take?'

'Years, perhaps, but if he gets tired of waiting – or his lady does – he'll give you the grounds for a divorce.'

'I don't think he will, this time.'

He looked her full in the face and he said: 'How would he react if you were to commit adultery?'

'Divorce me before you can say "decree nisi", I should think.'

Mr Farley's eyebrows twitched upwards for a second and he smiled, as if to say: *well, there you are, then!*

'So I've got to let him play the injured innocent and admit to adultery I've never committed, you mean?'

'Oh, no, that would be dishonest. I couldn't act for you if I thought you might be perpetrating a fraud on the court. And if you were the guilty party you'd lose any claim to maintenance for yourself. If the house is in joint names you'd get your share of the proceeds of the sale, and you'd get maintenance for the child.'

'So I get less than I'm due to, and I get my reputation smirched – and he comes up smelling of roses!' Lynn exclaimed.

'You don't like the idea.'

'I bloody *don't!*' she said, her solicitor's-office politeness falling to the ground.

'Then as far as a divorce on the grounds of adultery goes, we seem to have reached an impasse.'

'Is there any alternative?'

'There are three. Cruelty, desertion and incurable insanity.'

'He's never in, which doesn't amount to desertion, unfortunately – but he's definitely cruel, and probably insane. I'll never manage to prove it, though. So adultery's the only real option. Mine, I mean.'

'Only if you want a *quick* divorce.'

'Hmm,' she said.

Janet was off work, so Lynn called to see her before going home. Dave was in, slumped in front of the television in the living room.

'All right, Dave?' she greeted him, although it was apparent that he wasn't.

'Hay fever,' he snuffled, looking at her through red-rimmed eyes.

'Oh, dear,' she said.

The civilities over, she followed Janet into the

back garden where they sat in the sun, happily breathing in pollen and drinking cold lager. With a face that gave the impression that she was sucking a lemon, Lynn recounted the gist of her visit to the solicitor.

'It's galling,' she said, 'but I might have to cave in. I'd much prefer to be Alec's wife, but better his live-in lover than stay married to Graham.'

'What does it matter? You can marry him anyway, as soon as Graham divorces you,' Janet said, and added: 'That's if you're sure he will marry you. You'd be taking a chance on that, wouldn't you?'

'Well, married or not, if a bloke wants to leave, he'll leave,' Lynn said, 'or make himself so obnoxious he drives you into leaving. So marriage is no protection at all, is it? Not these days.'

'Never was, I suppose. Nicer to be married, though.'

'Much nicer to be married, and nicer still if I could get married without ruining my reputation beforehand – giving people room to call me nasty names behind my back.'

'What do you care what anybody says behind your back? You'll never know. I never let it bother me. Just as long as they don't say it to your face, that's all, and not many people have the guts to do that,' Janet said, and took a gulp of lager.

'You know by the way people start treating you whether anything nasty's being said or not,' Lynn said. 'And I already know exactly what his mother will be saying. I had a taste of her *whores* and her *trollops* when there wasn't a shred of truth in them. She'll be over the moon if I go out and prove her nasty allegations for her – I can't bear to think about it. And then there's matron and the hierarchy at Hedon Road. They're not fond of women with big, fat blots on their characters, are they? Bringing the profession into disrepute, and all that. I'd be lucky to get made up to a sister after that.'

'Do what Brian Farley says, then. Tell him to get his private dick onto it.'

'That's another thing. I might not get legal aid as easily this time round, and where's the money coming from if I don't? My dad's got enough on his plate with helping Margaret and the lads, and my mother says she's sticking a claim in for maintenance from him as well. And Graham's a lot more wary this time round, so it would probably be a sheer waste of money anyway.'

'Hmm,' Janet said. 'Don't you get yourself into some fixes? It's a pity you didn't get rid of him the first time round.'

But they'd covered all that ground before, and Lynn was weary of it. 'Dave's not going out quite so much these days, I suppose?' she said.

Janet's eyes took on a steely glint. 'If I come home off a late shift and he's not in, there's hell to pay and he knows it, so he makes bloody sure he is in,' she said. 'His outings to explore Hull's old hostelries have come to a sad end. That's if he ever did explore 'em. He was probably too busy exploring his fancy piece. I've applied for a job on the district, so I won't have to work with her, but I don't expect I'll get it. They like you to have two years' experience.'

'Poor Dave.'

'Poor Dave my foot. I thought it could never happen to me, but dull old Dave gave me a nasty shock. I've come to the conclusion that there's a lot of self-deception in relationships. People believe what they want to believe, and see what they want to see – until the day the blinkers drop off.'

'If there were no *self*-deception, there couldn't be much deception, I reckon,' Lynn said, with a rueful smile.

'Right. They'd know they weren't likely to get away with it, so they'd think twice. I don't think he'll try it on again in a hurry,' she said, nodding in the direction of the living room.

'Fool me once, shame on you. Fool me twice, shame on me,' Lynn quoted.

'Too right.'

Lynn finished her lager. 'Good luck with the job, anyway,' she said. 'I'll have to go, or I'll be late for Simon.' She stood up, and carried her glass into the kitchen.

Janet followed her. 'I wouldn't worry too much about bringing the profession into disrepute, if I were you,' she said. 'Everybody knows what my ex-friend's been up to, but it doesn't seem to be doing her much harm. People haven't got long memories anyway. Six months after he makes you Mrs McCauley they'll have forgotten all about it and you'll be respectable again.'

'I hope you're right,' Lynn said.

Graham wasn't in for tea, and when Lynn went upstairs the bedroom looked exceptionally tidy. She opened his wardrobe door, and saw it was empty. Was it fear of the pawnbroker, she won-

dered? Or had he gone back to Mammy Bradbury, along with his clothes? Or maybe he and
Lucy had had the courage of their convictions,
and decided to live together and defy the world.
But that wasn't very likely, in view of their
platonic protestations.

She had a delicious little daydream of their going
to the Scarborough Grand and booking themselves in for a dirty weekend while her mother was
away from the reception desk, and then her
mother surprising them in some wonderfully
compromising position – and chuckled to herself.

Oh, if only! She made a mental note to send
Graham's photo to her mother and get her to
circulate it among everyone she knew in the hotel
business with the caption: 'Wanted – evidence
that might lead to a successful petition for
divorce.'

In the weeks that followed there was very little
housekeeping money, and rarely any Graham,
until very late in the evening. Then the cognoscenti put the word out that Graham Bradbury's
wife was back at work at Hedon Road Maternity,
and after that there was no housekeeping money
at all. In view of his attitude Lynn decided there
would be nothing to be gained by complaining, so
she economised on food since he was rarely in for
meals, and managed to eke out her earnings – but
it was not a pleasant way to live, all told. She was
thankful that Simon was exposed to very little of
it; Graham had usually left for work before he got
up for school and was home long after he was
asleep.

At least Graham was paying the mortgage, she thought. Then the letter arrived from the building society, addressed to Mr and Mrs Bradbury. She opened it, and discovered they were in arrears with their payments. She tackled him about it.

'I'd think twice about that, Graham,' she said. 'If they foreclose, you'll never get another mortgage, and what will your platonic friend think to that? And her parents?'

'Get your friend to pay it. The one you and Simon were strolling on Hessle foreshore with.'

She raised a quizzical eyebrow.

'Yes, Simon told me.'

'Platonic friends can't be expected to pay other people's mortgages, Graham,' she reasoned.

He gave her a sarcastic look.

'That's all he is,' she insisted. 'A *platonic* friend. Surely you believe they can exist?'

On Friday afternoons after school Simon was usually desperate to go down to stay with Auntie Margaret and the lads. The time they spent at Boulevard was a time for playing out almost as long as the daylight lasted for Simon, and work provided both company and a refuge for Lynn. Alec kept in touch by the ship-to-shore radio telephone, and she lived for his calls.

Chapter 61

Before the six-week holiday started, Lynn gave Graham fair warning that her sister and nephews would be staying with her in Cottingham during Monday to Friday of the first week of the summer break. Graham took refuge at his mother's, as she had guessed he would. To Lynn, his complete absence was like a weight lifted off her. Margaret's lads had a few days discovering the countryside, roaming free in the woods and fields for a change, climbing trees, making dens, playing at Cowboys and Indians, going for picnics, sometimes with Lynn and Margaret and sometimes by themselves. Simon had company. They quarrelled, made up, ate like gannets and slept like logs – after endless bedtime stories. George seemed to be cured of his nightmares.

Lynn's opportunity for a trip to Grimsby came at the beginning of August, when her father's ship was laid up for major boiler repairs. Alec phoned, and they arranged for her to go to Grimsby for a couple of days when he was next ashore. She decided to let her father have the pleasure of his five boisterous grandsons and a dog and go for a few days alone, rather than take them with her.

The steam ferry from Hull Corporation Pier to Immingham Pier only took twenty minutes, after which she took the train for the short journey into Cleethorpes and soon found Queen Mary Avenue

– a wide, pleasant street of semi-detached houses.

A plump brown-haired woman with blue eyes and a ready smile answered the door and introduced herself as Alec's stepmother. If Lynn hadn't known better she would have taken her for his mother, there was such a resemblance.

'Come in. He'll be in on the six o'clock tide. We'll have a cup of tea, and then we'll go down to meet him off the ship, if you like.'

'Is your husband coming in, as well?'

'Not this time.'

'Well, do you mind if I go on my own, Mrs McCauley?'

'Not a bit! I just thought I'd show you where his ship will come in. And never mind the Mrs McCauley. Call me Rita.'

'Thanks, Rita, but I can't imagine it's much different to Hull. Fish docks are fish docks, aren't they? You can't really mistake them for anything else,' Lynn said. 'Just follow your nose, I should think.'

Rita chuckled. 'Hey, don't cast aspersions on our fish!' she protested. 'Aim for Grimsby Dock Tower. That'll steer you in the right direction. I won't be here when you get back, I'm off to my mother's for a couple of days; I'll be back on Saturday afternoon. Alec's got a key. If you need anything to eat, help yourself. There's plenty in the fridge.'

Cleethorpes was supposedly a separate town to Grimsby, but the two ran into one with not much open countryside between them. With the dock tower and the raucous crying of the gulls for guides Lynn easily found the docks. Grimsby was further towards the mouth of the Humber and nearer to the north sea than Hull, and she was struck by the sound of the tide.

Alec's face was covered in a glad smile as he walked towards her, and Lynn was reminded of the many, many times she'd gone to meet her dad. As soon as she was within his reach he took hold of her and gave her a smacking kiss, squeezing her almost to suffocation. 'You found your way all right, then.'

'Couldn't miss it,' she said, glancing up at the Dock Tower... 'It's a real landmark, isn't it?'

'Yeah, we're always glad to see it when we're coming back to port. It was too much of a land-mark during the war; it helped the Luftwaffe to find their way to Liverpool, so it nearly got de-molished. What do you think to Grimsby, then?'

'Pretty similar to Hull. Same sort of lock gates, same sort of dock, same sort of market, same gulls, same sort of tiny terraced houses behind Freeman Street, all heaving with people. Same sort of fishermen congregating in the same sort of pubs...'

'The Red Lion or the Lincoln instead of Ray-ners and all the rest of them, and Freeman Street instead of Hessle Road,' he said. 'It's a bit differ-ent. Are you hungry?'

'Starving. Are you taking me to the Red Lion?'

'We'll find somewhere better than that. I'll drop my sea bag off and we'll go into Clee some-where.'

'Did you have a good trip?'

'Not bad.'

'Your stepmother won't be at home. She's gone to her mother's for a couple of days.'

His eyes lit up, and the smile stretched from ear to ear. 'I told you she was a good 'un,' he said.

Twilight was deepening into night when the taxi deposited them, well wined and dined, outside the darkened house in Queen Mary Avenue.

Alec opened the door, and switched the light on. 'Would you like a cup of tea, or anything?' he asked, politely.

She picked up the overnight bag she'd left in the living room. 'No thanks, I'm ready for bed,' she said, and gave a mock yawn.

'I'll help you get undressed,' he laughed.

He had a large bedroom with a comfy double bed. She got undressed in the bathroom and slipped on a short, frilly nightie. There was a quiet rap on the bathroom door.

'Come in!'

He came in, half undressed. She was alone with him at last, and it felt even more intoxicating than the wine she'd drunk. She gave him a smile and left him, to slip between the sheets of his double bed and listen to him cleaning his teeth, feeling more nervous than she'd anticipated, and hoping she wasn't making another monumental mistake.

A minute later he strutted into the bedroom almost naked, displaying a broad, hairy chest, flat belly, and strong, capable limbs – altogether a fine figure of a man. He had a gleam in his blue eyes – and his bath towel slung over a massive erection.

She burst into laughter. He gave her a wide grin,

and like a professional striptease artist he flung the bath towel dramatically away and flicked the bedroom light off. She soon felt the warmth of him, and the strength of his arms around her.

'What do you want,' he said, 'a boy, or a girl?'

She could barely speak for laughing. 'A girl! She'll never go to sea.'

'Let's get to it, then.'

'How do you know it'll be a girl?'

'I'm fifty per cent certain, and I'm trusting the rest to luck,' he said.

Chapter 62

There were several people at the christening who'd been at the wedding, including Orla, who would have been chosen for godmother, Lynn suspected, but for the conspiracy between her brother and his wife to nudge her and Alec into each other's arms. It was a rather reticent and demure Orla who smiled at Lynn and Simon. She barely gave Alec a glance, having eyes only for her betrothed. The former bridesmaids were there in pretty summer dresses. Simon and his four cousins were scrubbed and combed to a shine, and behaving themselves as creditably as they had been warned to do. The ten full months between Brenda's marriage and the birth of her baby was enough to satisfy anyone who might have taken Alec's advice to set a stop-watch.

There was nobody wearing green, Lynn noted,

nor were there any bad fairies present; but her mother had turned up dressed to the nines and every inch the unrepentant, erring woman doing the only thing she could do – look everyone in the eye and brazen it out. Piers was absent and their father was at sea, much to everybody's relief. Graham's absence was taken as a matter of course. Margaret and her boys stood protectively on one side of Nina, and Lynn and Simon on the other, until Lynn was called to the designated place for parents and godparents in the front pew.

The service was a long one. After hymns, readings and sermon the vicar led them to the baptismal font at the back of the church. There he made the sign of the cross on the baby's forehead, parents and godparents made the promises he prompted them to make, and then he held the baby over the font, and poured water over his head.

'I baptise thee Thomas Alexander...'

Anthony looked as if he would burst with pride, happier, if possible, than on his wedding day. Brenda looked radiant. Thomas Alexander began to bellow. What a pair of lungs for such a tiny boy, and not yet three months old, Lynn thought. Simon quietly put his fingers in his ears.

'Thank goodness I'm not giving a speech,' Alec whispered. 'Who could compete with lungs like his?'

After the service, they stood chatting with Brenda's parents, who had completely forgiven Anthony for being a fisherman – and seemed almost as eager to clasp him to their bosoms as they were to clasp the lusty, bawling grandson he'd exerted himself to produce for them. The dis-asters of six months ago seemed to have brought a general increase of sympathy and appreciation to fishermen, especially from their own families, Lynn thought – and Anthony was now on a good ship, and likely to become a skipper before much longer. Quite a passable son-in-law, all told.

Alec held Lynn's hand as they filed out of the church, and gave it a squeeze. 'Hope we manage to get the wedding in before the christening,' he murmured.

Lynn looked towards her mother, and laughed. For a daughter who might soon be joining her in notoriety, she made a worthy model.

Chapter 63

The night was still warm when they drove along one-track Snuff Mill Lane under the light of a half-moon. As they approached the house the white, ghostlike form of a barn owl swooped sud-denly and silently across the path of the taxi. The driver drew to a halt, and they saw Graham's car in the drive.

'I won't come in,' Alec said. 'I'll just drop you off, and go back. See you tomorrow?'

Lynn nodded, and got out with Simon. Inside the house, Graham was standing with his back to the living-room fireplace, and Lynn was sur-prised to see Lucy, sitting in an armchair.

'Anyone for tennis?' she asked.

Lucy looked from Graham, to Simon, to Lynn and back again, seeming a little ill at ease. A touch of conscience, maybe?

'Go to bed, Simon,' Graham ordered – all he had to say to a son he hadn't seen for days.

Lynn went upstairs with him and helped him to get ready, evading his questions and preoccupied with one of her own – what the game was downstairs. A re-run of Mandy, maybe – but if Graham thought she was going to go running back to Boulevard again and let herself and Simon be barred from their own home, he had another think coming.

She laid her cards on the table as soon as she got back downstairs. 'You can park Lucy in this house if you like, Graham, and there's not much I can do to stop you. But I'm not leaving, this time,' she said. 'If anybody's leaving, it's going to be you. I'll buy you out.'

'How can you buy me out? You've got nothing. Where are you going to get the money from?'

'From somebody else.'

'Who might that be?'

'Nobody you know.'

He gave her a penetrating look. 'It wouldn't be somebody called Alec McCauley, would it?'

'Might be.'

'Is it?'

'It might be. What do you care, as long as you get your money?'

But she saw that he did care – like a child who has discarded an outgrown toy, and seeing it claimed by somebody else is no longer sure he had quite finished playing with it, after all.

Lucy caught that look on his face too. 'Graham!' she said. Her voice sounded plaintive.

He glanced at her, and turned back to Lynn. 'I'm petitioning for divorce,' he said. 'On the grounds of your adultery. I've had a private detective tracking you.'

Lynn had to laugh at that. 'Have you, Graham? That must have cost you a fair bit, unless you got legal aid. And what did he find out?'

'That you've been having an adulterous relationship, with Alec McCauley.'

'Where? When? Which days? What time?' she demanded.

He couldn't answer, and his silence convinced her that his private detective claim was sheer bluff.

The situation seemed to be weighing heavily on Lucy. In spite of her make-up, she looked drawn round the eyes and was almost squirming in her chair. Why should Graham's top-drawer tennis partner be so uncomfortable, Lynn wondered, and looked at her a little more closely. She was wearing a light cotton dress with a plunging neckline – and was it just Lynn's imagination, or had Lucy gone up a couple of bra sizes since that night in the Continental Restaurant?

Lucy suddenly jumped to her feet and, clamping her hand over her mouth, made a dash for the kitchen. A second later they heard the sound of retching, and then volumes of liquid splashing intermittently onto the kitchen tiles.

Lynn looked at Graham. 'Oh! Oh, dear! Morning sickness, at eleven o'clock at night! It takes some people like that. And I thought it was a bad conscience that was making her so uncomfortable,' she said.

While Graham was taking her home, Lynn cleaned Lucy's stomach contents off the kitchen floor, surprised to find herself feeling very little rancour towards her rival. But then, Lucy was doing her very best to relieve her of a husband she would not be sorry to be rid of. They were working towards the same end. The only thing that rankled was Lucy's evident determination to preserve her own immaculate, middle-class image and make Lynn the scapegoat for the whole break-up.

She was sitting in the chair Lucy had occupied when Graham returned.

'For sheer, lying, stinking hypocrisy you take the biscuit, Graham,' she greeted him. 'You and your platonic friend.'

'You should talk. How long have you been carrying on with your fisherman? Since you cleared off to your mother's, eighteen months ago, I suspect – and I haven't forgotten the night when we first got back together, either.'

'Suspect all you like, I'm protesting my innocence, just like you and Lucy. But you put your petition in, with your nonexistent evidence from your non-existent private detective and then I'll carry on like you did last time. You'll end up having to chase me down with bailiffs to get the acknowledgement of service back, and before *your* petition for divorce on the grounds of *my* adultery gets into court, I'll have my cross-petition ready. Your boss's daughter will be nursing her shameful bundle by the time there's any divorce. How's that?'

'I'd never have believed you could be so bloody spiteful, but you'll never get the satisfaction. She'll have an abortion before she'll let that happen.'

Lynn's jaw dropped. 'Are you telling me she'd do away with her own child, just to save face?'

'It's not a child, yet. And if you ever accuse her of being pregnant, she'll deny it – and I'll back her up.'

Lynn shook her head in disgust, and then echoed her solicitor's words: 'Well, in that case, we seem to have reached an impasse.' She rose to make a dignified exit, but Graham barred her way.

'There'll be no impasse. I've stopped paying the mortgage. You'll be out before much longer, whether you like it or not.'

'And you're going back to Mummy's, are you, to live the single life and wait for me to trip up? Are you sure you've thought this through, Graham? In the first place, you'll trip up a lot sooner than I will. In the second place you'll never get another mortgage if you get foreclosed. That won't impress your boss. In the third place you'll still be married, with a wife and child to maintain – and no grounds for divorce, and that won't impress Lucy. In the fourth place, dynamite wouldn't blast me out of this house after your mother threatened to change the locks on me, and the building society won't manage it, either. Not without taking me to court. Do you really want to give the golf club cognoscenti so much to chew over? Not to mention the ones at the fruit shop.'

'What do you suggest, then?'

'Sign the house over to me. I'll take over the mortgage.'

'You're a woman.'

'You don't say!'

'I mean they won't let you take on the mortgage.'

'I'll have a male guarantor. Maybe two. Maybe three.'

'We're back to Alec McCauley, then. He's going to guarantee your debts – and you're trying to tell me you're not sleeping with him.'

'I'm not trying to tell you anything, except that as soon as this house belongs to me I *will* sleep with him – just to oblige you and Lucy. Then you'll have all the tongues wagging in sympathy with you, and you can divorce your trollopy fishwife without paying her a penny in maintenance and live happily ever after with your fairy princess – with none of the shit sticking to her. How's that for a bargain?'

He was quiet for a while, thinking it over. 'I'm sorry it's come to this,' he said, eventually.

'Oh, give up!'

'No – I'm genuinely sorry. But for a man who wants to get on in life, you make a hopeless wife, Lynn.'

'No doubt you'll fare much better with the boss's daughter,' she said, certain that Graham's unending stream of other women was not about to stop for Lucy or anyone else. So how would the boss's daughter fare with Graham, she wondered? She might turn out to be another Connie – happy to turn a blind eye to it all, even if it included her own mother. That would certainly earn her the approval of her mother-in-law.

Chapter 64

Naturally, Graham got the best of the bargain when, a month later, he sold his interest in the house to Lynn. In order not to impede the divorce with any hint of collusion between the parties, Lynn's father and brother put up money provided by Alec and acted as guarantors for the mortgage, in the certain knowledge that Alec was the ultimate guarantor and that as soon as Lynn was divorced he intended to redeem the mortgage with his own savings, plus a loan from his father.

As soon as the transactions were completed Connie reclaimed all Auntie Ivy's antiques and put them back into storage, probably more to Lynn's satisfaction than to her own. The house was cleared of them before Alec stepped off the ferry.

Lynn's father was ashore on that day, and he went to pick Simon up from school and take him back to Boulevard – to let the guilty pair go alone to the house on Snuff Mill Lane and concentrate on giving Graham and his private detective enough ammunition to start divorce proceedings.

It was with a feeling of victory that Lynn turned the key and opened the door. So much for Connie's threats about changing locks. The house was hers, and Graham had given up all claim on it. She'd won.

She turned to Alec. 'Are you going to carry me

over the threshold?'

He hoisted her into his arms and carried her inside. 'It feels a bit funny, carrying another feller's wife over his threshold and into his house,' he said.

'It's our house now, and I haven't been his wife for months,' she said, 'and seeing they've taken everything that belonged to them there's nothing of theirs in it. The carpets belonged to the folk who went to Australia. But if it bothers you, we'll put it up for sale.'

'Really?'

She nodded. 'Yep. Any time you like, as long as we can live somewhere near, so Simon doesn't have to change schools again.'

There were no neighbours near enough to be scandalised by Alec's staying in the house overnight, but a car stopped outside in the wee small hours of the morning. It drove away again after Alec had been to the door in his pyjamas, on the pretext of bringing in the milk. After a leisurely breakfast they took a taxi down to Boulevard to see Simon and Lynn's father, run ragged by all five grandsons, who soon surrounded Alec.

'We're going to the Saturday matinee, with Grandad and Auntie Margaret!' Simon beamed up at him.

'What to see?'

'A cowboy film!' George exclaimed.

'I like cowboys,' Alec said. 'I've just got to nip down to the dock offices for a minute, to see about a ship. If I'm back in time, I'm coming with you.'

'Great!' Lynn said. 'While you're all enjoying

yourselves, I'll be at work.'

On Sunday evening Lynn took Simon with them in the taxi to see Alec off on the ferry to New Holland. He gave Lynn a squeeze and a peck on the cheek, and ruffled Simon's hair. 'See you in three weeks,' he said, and followed the queue towards the ferry.

'Can we go and see another cowboy?' Simon shouted after him.

Alec turned his head. 'Yeah.'

'With Auntie Margaret's lads?'

'Of course!'

They waved him off, then Lynn turned to Simon. 'School in the morning,' she said, and ushered him into the taxi for the journey back to Snuff Mill Lane and bed. When they passed the fruit shop on Bricknall Avenue she imagined the sort of things Connie would soon be saying: *she's just like her mother* ... et cetera, et cetera, et cetera. And no doubt she was in many ways, Lynn thought – but she was determined to make a better wife for a trawlerman than her mother ever had.

Chapter 65

'I thought I might have been asked to give evidence at that inquiry into the *Sprite* after being on her when that feller took an axe to the steering gear. The radar had failed twice before we even got to Scarborough. She was a terrible ship,' Alec said, thoughtfully, when he returned to Hull in the middle of October to sail as mate on one of Hull's older ships.

'Well, it's all wrapped up now,' Lynn said. 'If they'd taken evidence from everybody that knew something was wrong with the *Sprite*, they'd have been stuck in the City Hall till next Pancake Tuesday. They've moved on to the *Prospero*, now.'

'I'm not complaining,' Alec said. 'I didn't actually want to do it. If I'd had to go, it would have meant missing a trip. I wonder when the report will come out, though? It might make interesting reading.'

'Oh, I'll just have a squint in my crystal ball,' Lynn said. 'Here's how interesting it will be – if they can't pin the blame on the skipper or the crew, they'll find out that nobody was to blame.'

He laughed. 'We'll wait and see. Well, we've got five days to enjoy ourselves before I sail. How do you fancy a cowboy at the Saturday matinee?'

'I don't mind, I'm on holiday this weekend. Simon will love it. He loves to go to Boulevard to get in among Margaret's lads, but the other day he asked me if he could stay at home next time you come. Now I know why. You're nothing but an overgrown kid yourself,' she said.

'Does he realise...' Alec began.

Lynn gave a closed-lip smile, and nodded. 'I don't know how much. He knows his dad's gone back to live with Connie and Gordon, but not the ins and outs of everything.'

'We'll have to be ever so careful, Lynn. Take it slowly. Never try to stop him seeing his own dad,' Alec said.

'Not much chance of you doing that is there, here for three days out of every three weeks. No sooner home than you're gone again. The real question is, does Graham want to see his son? Not showing much sign of it, up to now.'

The wreck report on the three trawlers came out on the first of November. The loss of the *Sprite* had come as no surprise at all to any of the fishermen who had sailed in her, and the cause of it was plain to see. According to them she was slow and unstable, she leaked like a sieve, and had problems with the radar, radio, and the winch. According to the official inquiry her loss was an unfathomable mystery. She'd had a survey, Lloyds had classed her A1 and the owners had managed to get her insured, so as far as the court was concerned, she was A1 and watertight. The Icelander who'd heard the Mayday must have been mistaken, and the ship must have gone down where the life-raft was found. The multifarious problems she'd been notorious for before the survey were not looked into, nor was there much probing into the owners' motives for failing to raise the alarm when their attempts to make radio contact with her had failed.

Lynn and Margaret decided to have Bonfire Night at Boulevard. To have had it at Snuff Mill Lane might have been too painful a reminder to Margaret's lads of the father they had lost. Grandad and Alec were both at sea and since the boys were at school the following day, the party was small and short. Lynn put Simon to bed at Boulevard, and spent the evening with Margaret.

When the boys were settled they sat with the television off, drinking tea and toasting their toes by the coal fire.

'What do you think to the report on the *Sprite?*' Margaret asked.

'What's there to think? The owners sent a notoriously unstable ship to dangerous seas at the worst possible time of year, with an inexperienced skipper and no radio operator. Then they failed to alert anybody for nearly a fortnight after they lost radio contact with her – and they're not to blame for anything! That's the way it is. That's the way it always will be.'

'One of the skippers told the court there was nothing wrong with her,' Margaret said.

'I suppose he wants to make a living. I suppose he'd like command of another ship. If he'd stood up in court and said anything the owners didn't like, do you really think he'd ever have got one?'

'Do you think they actually *wanted* to lose her?' Margaret asked.

'Well, I wouldn't go as far as that, but it's an ill wind that blows nobody any good, isn't it? And my guess is that the wind that sank the *Sprite* probably blew the owners a nice cheque from the insurance for a leaky old tub that was costing them more money than she was earning. Which would you rather have, in their shoes? I'm just glad that Alec sailed in her in August, and not January.'

'It's a pity anybody ever sailed in her at all,' Margaret said. 'I think the reports on the other two are a bit fairer, though. Nobody ever said there was anything wrong with them. And the weather was bad. The worst storms since 1925.

401

All the fishermen were saying so.'

Margaret seemed to take comfort from feeling that the *Miranda* was a good ship, that the owners had raised the alarm straightaway, and that Jim hadn't been callously left to his fate, but talking about the disasters enraged Lynn, especially talking about the *Sprite*. Could she do it? Could she stay the course as a fisherman's wife? She was sure she could do it, because she was going into it with her eyes wide open, with no illusions about it whatsoever. She knew what she was in for, and would not have done it for any man in this wide world other than Alec McCaulay. In another six days he would be home again.

So much waiting and worrying, she thought. So little time together.

The skipper's would-be wife and the third-hand's widow were together on Christmas Eve in the house on Snuff Mill Lane. It contained a few new pieces of furniture, bought from the proceeds of Alec's last trip, and all thoughts of selling it seemed to have fallen into abeyance. Five Christmas stockings stuffed with goodies were hanging from the mantelpiece and the tree was decorated, with parcels placed underneath it, their beautiful wrappings waiting to be ripped off by five eager young boys in the morning.

'I saw three ships come sailing in...' The sweet old carol was playing on the radio. If only, Lynn thought. If only those three ships had come sailing in, her nephews would still have a devoted father, and Margaret a husband who truly loved her. 'And what was in those ships all three...?'

The loves, hopes and support of sixty families, their men and their boys.

She shivered. Alec had been given his first command, of an old ship, by common report not much better than the *Sprite*. After everything he'd said about the *Sprite* he'd sailed on one that was nearly as bad, in the middle of winter, his only justification being: 'Well, you could stay ashore and get knocked down by a bus, couldn't you?' Whatever was wrong with these men, she wondered? He had an old or inexperienced crew – men like him, who would work when nobody else wanted to, either in hopes of getting a better ship next trip, or because they desperately needed a job. But at least she was watertight and they'd sailed with a radio operator. The women's campaign had achieved the miracle of making trawling safer, but no one could prevent hurricanes or black frost, and in such conditions a ship like his might be capsized and gone to the bottom before any mother-ship could rescue it. She went to the window and pulled the curtain back to stare out at the weather, and wonder what it was like in the Arctic. Her Christmas wouldn't start until she saw him again. This was what fate had always had in store for her, she realised. It just showed you how useless it is to try and resist it.

Not for them, though. Not for Simon – or Margaret's lads, if she could help it. She wanted them all to see that there was another life – a better life, away from the fishing industry. For that she had to get them away from Hessle Road as much as she could, away from the docks, and the smell and the spell of the sea.

On that starry, freezing Christmas Eve Alec was at the wheel on the ship he'd nicknamed 'the slow boat to China'. He ordered the mate to shoot the trawl, hoping he'd calculated right and teeming shoals of beautiful fish were below, just waiting to swim into his Christmas stocking. Just hope it stayed calm enough for long enough for them to stuff the fish room with more than enough quality fish to please the gaffers and let them make for home, as fast as the engineers could coax this old tub to move.

The sparks came out of the radio room to put an end to that pleasant prospect. They had hurricane force winds heading their way, according to a report from the Icelandic weather station. They might just have time to haul the net and run nose to wind for shelter, otherwise they'd have to keep 'dodging' and ride it out.

He gave the sparks a grim smile and the adrenaline started to pump. *Prepare for the worst, Alec.* Battling gales and black ice with this crew would be a challenge for anybody – even the master mariner he knew he was fast becoming. Full credit to the women's campaign, they'd improved the odds, but if they were caught in anything over a force eight in this old ship she'd stand a fair chance of sinking, radio operators and motherships regardless.

There was one thing for certain. However bad it was, he would never tell Lynn. The most he would ever say to her would be:

'We've had a bad trip, and I'm glad to be home.'

Acknowledgements

I am indebted to:

John Conolly, songwriter and performer, for permission to use the words of his song 'The Trawling Trade';

The volunteer tour guides of the *'Arctic Corsair'*, Hull's last sidewinder trawler, located behind the Streetlife Museum on the River Hull and maintained by Hull City Council;

The staff of Hull History Centre, Hull Libraries, and Hull Museums;

Dr Alec Gill, for his many books and videos on the subject of Hull's fishing heritage;

Stuart Russell, former journalist, for his book *Dark Winter;*

Austin Mitchell and Anne Tate, for their book, *Fishermen – The Rise and Fall of Deep Water Fishing;*

William Mitford, for *Lovely She Goes;*

Jeremy Tunstall, for *The Fishermen – The sociology of an extreme occupation;*

James Greene, for *Rough Seas – The Life of a Deep-Sea Trawlerman;*

Jim Williams, for *Swinging the Lamp* and a very informative pamphlet about the *'Arctic Corsair';*

Brian Lavery, for *The Headscarf Revolutionaries: Lillian Bilocca and the Hull Triple Trawler Disaster;*

Rupert Creed, for his play 'The Northern Trawl'.

My gratitude also goes to many other less well-known writers on the fishing industry and Hull's fishing community, and to all those people who have shared their experiences on the internet.

This Large Print Book for the partially sighted, who cannot read normal print, is published under the auspices of

THE ULVERSCROFT FOUNDATION